David Fiddimore was born in 1944 in Yorkshire and is married with two children. He worked for five years at the Royal Veterinary College before joining HM Customs and Excise, where his work included postings to the investigation and intelligence divisions. *The Forgotten War* is the third novel in the Charlie Bassett series following *Tuesday's War* and *Charlie's War*.

Also by David Fiddimore

TUESDAY'S WAR

CHARLIE'S WAR

DAVID FIDDIMORE

The Forgotten War

PAN BOOKS

This edition published 2013 by Pan Books
an imprint of Pan Macmillan, a division of Macmillan Publishers Limited
Pan Macmillan, 20 New Wharf Road, London N1 9RR
Basingstoke and Oxford
Associated companies throughout the world
www.panmacmillan.com

ISBN 978-1-4472-4737-1

A CIP catalogue record for this book is available from the British Library.

Typeset by SetSystems Ltd, Saffron Walden, Essex

Printed and bound by CPI Group (UK) Ltd, Croydon, CR0 4YY

For

RUT, STEFAN, RAGNA, SISSI and OLA

. . . the last of the Vikings

I can't let this book go without acknowledging the contribution of others.

The work of my editor and copy editor is crucial to the telling of these tales: I just write the stuff, but they make sure it's readable!

Finally I have to thank the soldier who bore the service number 22602108, and lent it to me for this book – he has been a faithful and supportive brother for sixty years: they don't make them like that any more!

PART ONE

Welcome Home, Charlie

1. Doin' My Time

Someone once told me that policemen are trained to deliver the bad news.

The sergeant in front of me had obviously failed that part of his course. I had been waiting for about five hours to be arrested anyway, so I just wished that he would get on with it. He fingered my fibre name-tag a last time. I noticed that the leather bootlace I wore it on was cracking: I'd need another one. He laid it down on a file cover on which he had recently printed my name in thick blue pencil.

'I have bad news for you, Mr Bassett.'

'OK.'

'Someone should have told you before this.'

'What should they have told me?'

'That you're dead.'

'What?'

'You're dead, son. Deceased. You got the chop. Kaput. Finito. Charles Aidan Bassett, RAF service number 22602108, died of injuries sustained in an air crash at Tempsford in

December 1944. Tempsford's near here.' The cop had a fruity old Bedfordshire accent, and spoke slowly.

'I know where it is. I was stationed there.'

'You are buried in the graveyard at Everton. That's near here too.'

I smiled. I couldn't help myself.

The copper frowned at me. 'Why are you laughing, son?' Men often called me 'son' or 'titch' on account of my size. It teed me off no end.

'Someone I know is buried there. We called him Black Francie. He would have found this funny. Are you telling me that you don't believe me?' I had walked into his police station to tell him that I was AWOL. I was embarrassed to have missed the end of the war by nearly two years. The cop sighed before he replied.

'I'm glad you're so quick on the uptake.'

'So can I go? Just like that.'

'I don't think so, son. I think that I'll have to invite you to sit in a small room with bars on its windows, while I ask myself some questions.'

'What questions, sergeant?'

'I'll start by asking myself just who you really are, and, seeing as you're reluctant to tell me, how I can find that out by myself.'

He looked so depressed at the prospect that I had to make an effort to stop myself from feeling sorry for him.

How the hell had I got into this mess?

Now, I'm going to run this past you quite quickly, and just the once; so pay attention. In 1944 I completed a tour of operations as a wireless operator with a Lancaster squadron at Bawne, west of Cambridge – it sits a cough and a spit from the Bedfordshire border. You may recall that a few years ago I wrote a book about that. In the course of that tour I met, and sort of fell in love with – well, we all did, actually – an ATA pilot named Grace Baker. Grace became pregnant, but I'm not holding my hands, or anything else, up to that. I asked her to marry me because that's what I was like when I was twenty. I know it was a mistake. She had said 'Yes,' but added, 'if you can find me.' Then she ran away. Cow. So I tried anyway.

This is where it all becomes a bit tricky.

My next posting, at Tempsford, was the airfield that the cop had mentioned. It was the airfield used by squadrons that flew clandestine missions in and out of wartime Europe, and my job was to keep their radio operators straight. Sheer boredom put me in one of their old Stirlings, and it served me right when the old bitch buried herself in a local field a couple of minutes after take-off. The old guys in the service always warned me never to volunteer for anything. I should have listened. I woke up days later in a hospital ward in Bedford. That's where my story and the cop's diverged. In the copper's account I emerged from hospital in time for my own burial. Play the slow march, and carry him along. Pity about that.

In my story my escape from the butcher's shop was for the purpose of finding Grace; which didn't work out, of course. It was like this: I had recovered to find myself with the patronage of a clever sod who appeared to be a squadron intelligence officer. The word 'appeared' is a very important one in this context. He pointed out that the squadron no longer wanted a slightly charred radio officer: anyway, they had replaced me already, with one in more or less pristine condition. However, he had put in a word for me, and found me a nice job for the last few weeks of the war: finding Grace. Sorry about the pun, but that was me; tagged onto a culinary intelligence mission, careering across Europe in a big old Humber staff car at the fag end of the war, chasing a girl who had once agreed to marry me.

Love's not always what it's cracked up to be, you know.

My companions had been a frighteningly resourceful driver, Les Finnegan, and his boss Major James England. I never did believe that those were their real names. Their job was to follow the advancing British army, assess the food needed to supply it, and call that back to something like a large stores depot that sent forward the needful. Their job became complicated if they found themselves ahead of the Allied advance, rather than behind it. That's when Jerry shot at them.

Grace had joined up with a commie group – French, and Eyetie doctors and nurses who shared the bizarre notion that medical care should be offered freely to anyone who needed it, regardless of which side they were on – they were always a step ahead of us. Somewhere along her journey she produced a spiffing little baby boy, who she spoiled by giving an Eyetie name. I never caught up with her during the war. The nearest I got was catching up with a makeshift hospital in Bremen, where she left me the boy, and a sarky letter. By that time he was my second boy: I already had a five-year-old German lad, who I had found on a battlefield.

I think that a lot of us were behaving oddly by the end of the war. That's my excuse for what I did next. I left the German boy with a German woman I had just proposed to . . . yeah, I know: you don't have to tell me . . . and carried on blundering across Europe with Les, Maggs, an old lady I had met in Paris, and Grace's kid. It took us more than a year to catch up with Grace, in a small town south-west of Siena.

*

The square was too bloody hot.

Les and I found some shade thrown over the cobbles by the small church, and leaned against the wall. I recognize now what it felt like, although it was new to me then. It felt like the setting for the last gunfight in one of those dreadful spaghetti westerns my son and his wife watch in the Curzon at South End Green.

The sun came off the buffed stones like daggers. Even the swallows were fed up. They sat on shady ledges and gaped with exhaustion. There were olive groves all around the place, but the village baker Ludovico said that the future was in the vine.

A small church stood with its door open. The priest had told me that the door had stayed open since before the war, and all through it. It had been open to anyone who had need of it, he told me. Even for the Jews. Then he spat near his feet, and observed that he couldn't actually remember the last time he had seen one of those. I had also been inside his church a few times in the last few days: most frequently to escape the searing sun, but once, at least, to pray to a God I'd never believed in.

Les pulled off his grubby black beret, and lifted a roll-up from it. I noticed that he had a few grey hairs in his curly thatch that hadn't been there a year ago. He couldn't get rid of the beret, even though the war had been over for more than a year. I wondered if he ever would. The rest of his clothing was still uniform bits and pieces. Most of it had come from dead men in other services – and other races, come to that: his laced Jerry desert boots had lasted the distance for him. He offered me a fag which I took without thinking, because my pipe had gone stale. Like all of Les's fags it burned through as quick as the match that lit it.

There was an old authority administration building inside the humped walls, behind the town square, only there was no council to use it any more. It sat near the stumpy, squat castle keep, by one of the fortified gates. We had left *Kate*, our old Humber, outside the walls a few days ago, parked up in an empty barn at the foot of the hill. Les had jacked it up on bricks, let the tyres down, removed the rotor arm and disconnected the battery. The walk up the hill to an arranged meeting with the baker had taken more than thirty minutes in the company of Maggs and the child. We weren't hiding the car from the war any more, merely from thieves. Europe was full of them. Anyway, this was an Italian place again: I wanted to leave England on the other side of its walls.

You wouldn't have expected Grace to think like that.

She rode the right-hand seat of a jeep that roared in through the fortified gate, one booted foot on the dashboard in front of her. The jeep had been liberated, just like the Italians. Its divisional badges and number had been daubed over in grey, and the bonnet star painted out. You could see hundreds like that. Her driver, without a shirt, had grimy skin the colour of a chestnut cabinet, and wore flying goggles over slicked-back black hair. He looked light and fast and muscular . . . albeit dusty. He wore a pair of fatigue pants stolen from the Americans. She wore old KDs, too, and a khaki vest with quarter sleeves. Her hair was shorter than I remembered: a black brush yellowed by road dust. She reminded me of Lee Miller's style and look, all those months ago. They slid the jeep fancily to a stop in front of the bar. Ludo told us they hit the bar the same day, most weeks, and stayed for a couple of hours. She stood up, stretched indecorously, and looked lazily around the square. That was when she saw me. Me and Les in the shadow of the church. She didn't mess about, of course. It wasn't her style. Les stepped away.

He disappeared. He was good at disappearing. Now you see him; now you don't. When Grace walked up to me my heart lurched. Up close she was small: my size. I always forgot that. Her vest stretched tight over her breasts, which were also still as small as I recalled. There was a sweat mark between them. Nipples like twin Bofors. I wished I couldn't remember. Her face was tight, too. Tight and angry.

'What the fuck are you doing here? *Still* following me?' she asked.

I made one false start, then answered her.

'I came to see you. You once said that if I could find you after the war finished, you'd marry me.' Pause, Charlie. Make it count, even if you don't mean it. 'It's finished: so marry me.' There was a heart-stop for a three-beat. I swear the world stopped moving. It was as if Grace and I were totally alone: as if every other sound and motion had been frozen. Then she laughed. It was a dry, short little sound. She shook her head and looked me in the eyes.

'I lied,' she said. 'Now bugger off.'

She walked over to her driver and didn't look back. I felt immediately that I'd probably never see her again. It wouldn't have mattered so much, except she had given me that *I win* smile before she had spoken. When she reached the jeep she berated the driver, calling him a *corno*, which a nurse in Siena had told me was the local slang for a homo, and *gabinetto*, which I translated as *toilet*. Her voice was deliberately pitched so that the entire square could hear her, and she slapped him viciously on the shoulder raising a sudden pink splash on his tanned skin. No vino-for-Gino today. No Grace, either. Minutes later the only sign of their existence was the dust cloud their jeep had left in the air.

Inside the bar a small lady with a lined, dark brown face served me beer, which she brewed from potato skins and flavoured with vine leaves. She named it *Fausto*, which I took to mean *happy*, or *lucky*. I needed some luck. One of the three free-flowing springs that had led to the siting of the village ran under her floor, in a narrow stone channel put there by the Romans. I guess that she was lucky. She had lifted a row of floor tiles in her brewing room, and sat dozens of the screw-top bottles in the flowing stream. They emerged icy cold. She pulled out four bottles. Two for me, and two for Les. I gave her dollars, and a stolen family ration book that had come Les's way. I wondered what Grace paid for her drinks with these days? Were her family secretly getting money out to her?

Les slouched in half an hour later and sat beside me. He wiped his forearm across his brow to spread the sweat.

'What happened to you?' I asked him.

'I went down to check *Kate*.'

'OK?'

'No problem. There was a farmer's boy guarding it. I think he's been there since we left it. I think that Ludo arranged it.'

I gestured towards the bottles. 'Beer?'

'Thanks, guv'nor.'

'*Charlie*,' I told him firmly. 'This job's over, and so is the fucking war.'

You had to admit that Grace had been explosively superb when we had met face to face for the first time in eighteen months: expecting me to bugger off. It's the sort of phrase that has an unmistakable meaning. So I did. It had left me, Maggs and Les in a small village in Italy without a purpose. Just like the three musketeers: all for one, one for all, and all for bloody nothing. Time to go home, Charlie. Time to face the music.

One last thing. Les had got hold of an old Italian Mannlicher-Carcano rifle that had caught his eye, but we gave that and most of our Italian cash to our host before we left. When he handed over the gun Les told us that he had used one in Spain in the 1930s, and had fond memories of it. Then he said, 'A head shot from a Mannlicher doesn't leave much to the imagination, if you know what I mean . . .'

It was one of those conversations that come back to haunt you years later.

I crossed the Channel in a borrowed Austin Tilley, on a shuttle landing craft that dumped us off at Deal. I sat in the front. Maggs kept the kid quiet in the canvas box behind me. We weren't even asked for our papers. Two days later I settled Maggs and the kid into a guest house in St Neots, gave her some money, a couple of emergency addresses, and turned myself in at the local nick. I made sure she knew how to find Les or the Major if anything went wrong. Les fancied his chances with his old unit, so made for London alone in our old car. When I walked into the police station and told them that I was a bit late for the end of the war, they treated me like an everyday occurrence. You never know: perhaps by then I was.

2. Nobody Knows You When You're Down and Out

I had been locked up in a cell in Paris by the Americans in 1945. The difference between the Paris and Bedfordshire cells was that although the volume of food they offered me in Paris had been greater than that in Bedfordshire, the quality was worse. For some reason that surprised me. I was the only person locked up in the small police station, and the sergeant and his wife must have felt some sort of responsibility for me because they fished me out of the cell to eat with them. My first supper in England was strips of braised liver and kidneys, under a thin crust of pastry. The sergeant's wife was improbably plump – there had been a war on, you know – and still had a dab of flour on her forehead. The sergeant didn't talk shop at table, and when he returned me to the cell I still didn't know what the future held.

The next morning when the sergeant moved me out of the cell and back up to his small tiled interrogation room, he looked shifty. He served me aircrew breakfast – bacon, real eggs and a couple of slices of fried Spam. He produced his notebook, and wrote in it as he asked me questions.

'You said that there were people who could vouch for you. Give me their names again.'

I told him about my dad and my uncle – and the address I last had for them near sunny Glasgow. I told him about the Tempsford Intelligence Officer – David Clifford – who was a bastard who had turned up surprisingly in Germany in 1945 and then nicked a girl I thought I loved – but that's another story. I told him about the Lancaster crew I had flown my tour with – he already had my service number. I told him about racing through the Low Countries to Germany with Les Finnegan and James England. Any one of those people would have told him I wasn't dead, although it did occur to me between the Spam fritters and the tea that maybe I *was*, and that this was purgatory.

Finally I said, 'If you can't find any of those, try the Ralph-Baker lot at Crifton. It was them who had me chasing their daughter Grace all over Europe. It wasn't my fault that when I eventually found her she told me to piss off.'

The sergeant snapped his little black book shut and sprung the black knicker-elastic strip around it. I suspected he liked his number too much to risk approaching the Ralph-Bakers, but it was always worth a try. Then he started to collect up the breakfast things. I would have got up and stretched my legs if he hadn't cuffed one of my ankles to the chair. I was fed up. He looked at me, and said seriously, 'I'll do my best for you, son.'

'You don't believe me, do you?' I said, challenging him.

'I don't believe many people these days. I think that I stopped believing people the day Chamberlain waved that silly piece of paper, said “Peace in our time”, and my eldest boy started sharpening his bayonet. He was in the TA.’

‘Did you get your boy back?’

‘Most of him. Lost his brother, though: DLI. Mother still hasn’t got over it.’

‘Sorry.’

‘No reason why you should be.’ Then he said it again, ‘I’ll do my best for you.’

I started to get concerned. ‘I’m sure you will, sarge, but I don’t quite know what you’re getting at.’

‘Two policemen from London are coming to fetch you away. They’ll be here by dinner time.’

Then he locked me in. *Get used to being locked in, Charlie*, I told myself.

According to my RAF documents I’m five feet four. Although I kid the girls I’m taller than that, they never believe me. The two London coppers were at least a foot taller, and they had dark brown felt trilbies on top of that. Giants. They both wore fawn raincoats that stretched almost to their shoes and were as friendly as timber wolves. They weren’t best pleased when my old sergeant insisted that they sign for me before they took me away to the railway station in a local taxi. They didn’t speak directly to me, either at the police station or in the car.

Something about England had bothered me for a couple of days and on the journey I realized what it was. There were road signs. During the war they had all been taken down to confuse Nazi parachutists. The Nazi parachutists had missed their cues, but we had succeeded in confusing each other and the Americans. We sat outside the station in the car until the train drew in.

They took me onto the platform after the Bedford passengers had embarked, into a compartment at the back with a 'reserved' notice in the window. The first time a train had ever been held for me.

After the train had started moving the bold boyos pulled down the window blinds, put their hats and raincoats on the netting luggage rack, and gave me bit of a doing-over. It wasn't much of a doing-over because it was finished quickly, and I could still speak afterwards. My face was unmarked. I slumped in a corner as far from them as I could get.

'I suppose you're wondering what that was for?' Tweedledee asked me. I nodded. Tweedledum smirked at me: 'Education.'

'We're taking you to an old aircrew interrogation centre in High Holborn, where they'll sort out who you are. Until then we are prepared to be your friends . . .' Tweedledum told me. 'But we want you to believe that if you try to escape, or embarrass us in any other way—'

Tweedledee interrupted: 'We'll beat the living shit out of you. Understood?'

I nodded again. My ribs ached, but I'd live.

'Good. Let's all sit back and enjoy the trip. My missus made us up some sandwiches.'

They took me off the train at a small London station before the main terminus. I was bundled into the back of an old Bedford ambulance whose stretchers had been replaced by two wooden benches that had brackets for handcuffs. Neither Tweedles spoke to me, and when the back door was opened it was onto the courtyard of a high old building. We might have been in London. I could hear heavy traffic from somewhere. There was a small reception room with a big reception officer dressed like a city copper – where did they get all these big guys from? The thing was that neither the Tweedles in their civvies, nor this uniformed copper, looked like coppers. They looked . . . sort of military. The uniform had a book and papers to complete. When I gave him my name and service number he consulted a black-bound loose-leaf booklet, sighed, and told me, 'We'll write you down as *A. N. Other*.' He consulted another black-bound volume: 'Number 4741. Until you tell us who you really are. Then we'll update them. OK?'

I shrugged. All I had to do was wait until somebody came forward to bear witness for me. Then the real trouble could start. Maybe I was better off as A. N. Other 4741. Albert Norman, maybe. I always liked the name Norman: there was something dependable about it.

I had a cell of my own, and a dirty blue-and-white-striped suit they said had come from Germany. There was an enamelled bucket with a lid in the corner, for life's little inconveniences, a bed with a hard flock mattress, a Gideon Bible and a single dingy warehouse wall-light that went off soon after dark. I don't know at what time because they had taken my wristwatch – treasured war booty – but I estimated that they switched the time around to disorientate us. 'Us' were me and a thin German named Gunther Schlicht. We met for an hour each day in the exercise yard – a small enclosed space overlooked by other cells and offices. I never saw or heard any other prisoners. For all we knew we were the only two. Gunther spoke fair English. He seemed shy at first, and accused me of being set to spy on him.

That was exactly what I had thought about him. When we unwound he told me that Schlicht meant 'honest' in German. I told him that Bassett was a kind of dog. *Hund.* He smiled when I told him that. He had a better name than me. I asked him what he was there for – the war had been over for a couple of years.

'I didn't go home when I was supposed to.'

'Why not?'

'I worked on a farm in Somerset. Fell in love with the daughter. Nobody wanted me to go back to Germany when the time arrived, so they hid me. Eventually the police found me . . . it was like being rounded up by the Nazis.'

'Weren't you a Nazi, then? Back home.'

'I had a letter from my brother last month. He lives near Hanover. He says that no one was a Nazi in Germany. Even people who can remember the Nazis are difficult to find these days.'

'Like Chelsea supporters,' I told him.

'I don't understand you.'

'Don't worry – English joke.'

'Ah – comedian. I told you: you must be working for the police.'

Days before we'd agreed that all policemen were comedians, but the trouble was that he was almost right. I'd been interrogated twice by then: no rubber truncheons, but they didn't need them when they woke you in the early hours of the morning and then shouted at you until your head felt like it would burst. The odd thing was that no one seemed interested in me. All they asked me about was my conversations with Gunther. I wondered whether or not to tell him. Best not. Look out for yourself, Charlie, because it looks as if no one else is looking out for you. On one occasion Gunther told me, 'They think I'm a spy. Fuhl! Idiots. What do I spy? How many cabbages it is possible to grow in a field?'

'You'd be surprised: I knew someone in the war who spied like that.'

'This is peacetime, Charlie.'

'Is it? Can't say that I've noticed.'

'Why have they captured you?'

'They didn't: I walked in. I didn't go home when I was supposed to either. They don't believe I'm who I told them I was. I told them I was a deserter. I'm supposed to be dead.'

'So they think you must be a spy.'

'Idiots,' I told him. The conversation had run full circle.

It seems daft now, but I soon lost track of the days so I don't know how long I was there, or when a couple of superior types stopped asking me questions about Gunther. Maybe two or three weeks. One afternoon I was taken back up to the interrogation room to find Tweedledee and Tweedledum sitting there. Each of them had a small suitcase, and the clothes I had walked in with, including my American flying jacket, were neatly folded on a side table. It looked like someone had cleaned them.

'Get changed,' Tweedledee said. 'You're moving.'

'Where to this time?' I asked.

He ignored me, and read from a typed sheet on the table in front of him. He read aloud, 'Prison number 4741. You have been tried by courts martial and found guilty as charged. You will serve a period of imprisonment with labour in a civilian penal establishment. Your transfer to civilian authorities will be effected today. Do you understand that?'

I looked at him with astonishment. 'No. There was no trial. What was I charged with? What did I do?'

Tweedledee didn't answer me directly. He read the paper slowly. Then he turned it over and read something that was pre-printed on its reverse. I could see a blurred round stamp, and an untidy signature. Finally he looked up at me. He had watery blue eyes. He shrugged his shoulders. 'Buggered if I know. It doesn't say. I've never seen one of these before.'

'How much did I get?' I asked him. 'How long?'

'It doesn't say that, either. I told you to get dressed. We've a plane to catch.'

Welcome home, Charlie. At least I didn't have to worry about where my next meal was coming from – unlike about twenty per cent of the population.

I recognized the airfield when we got there: Croydon Airport. I was back where my chase across Europe in 1945 had started. We were admitted through a side gate on Purley Road, and driven away from the main areas of the terminal. Most of the scattered aircraft were converted ex-services jobs, although I noticed a lovely tubby BEA Vickers Viking airliner, which reminded me of the old Wellington bomber that I had done some of my early training on. There was also a huge American job that looked like a pregnant Boeing Superfortress. I wondered if they could get across the pond in that. What was waiting for us was a drab Airspeed Oxford with its engines ticking over. Even its fuselage number had been painted over. It had lost its identity, like me. In happier times Grace had once flown me from Manchester to Twinwood in one of those.

I think that that was the worst moment, because they handcuffed me to the wireless operator's table – my old seat behind the pilot. I could see the back of his head, which rolled with his jaw movement, and the gum that moved around in his mouth. The cops strapped themselves into the seats for VIP passengers about ten feet behind me. Tweedledee pulled his hat over his eyes, leaned back and feigned sleep. Tweedledum stared at me. Every time I turned to look at them, he was staring. He didn't look as if he harboured particularly friendly feelings towards me. Glancing at the back of the pilot's head, I got the feeling that I had seen him before. When he threw back, 'OK, bud?' over his shoulder, I knew I had. It completed the circle of jokes really, because – if he was who I thought he was – he actually *was* supposed to be a dead man.

He made a good take-off over the bumpy grass at the back of the airfield. I could see the terminal laid out beneath me as he banked us back over it. There were maybe twenty aircraft scattered about the terminal building, all in distinctive different liveries. The Tweedles didn't seem to object when the pilot continued to talk to me.

'You see all them crates?' he asked me. 'All private. Half the RAF has started up its own bitty airlines with their demob money.'

'They'll lose it,' I told him. 'The government will muscle in.'

'Happen we will.' Then he said, 'Sit back and enjoy the flight . . . boy. It looks like the last you'll get in some while.' For a moment there I could have sworn he was going to say 'Charlie', rather than 'boy'. I might have been wrong. The weather thickened a bit after Birmingham; I heard Dum and Dee getting a bit restless, and then the sound of one of them throwing up. It gave me a great surge of delight. The pilot spoke to me again, his soft American accent flowing back like honey.

'Don't I know you, son? Ain't we met before?'

In 1944 I had hitched a lift to Ringway with him, and Glenn Miller had been strapped in behind us. If he'd been Glenn Miller's pilot, then he was supposed to be dead – like the band leader. I could have answered truthfully, but my instinct kicked in. I could feel a pair of Tweedle eyes boring into my back.

'No. Sorry, I don't think so.' I answered with a lie. 'I would have remembered you if we'd met.'

'Yeah. That's what I thought.' The pilot made a noise that sounded like a sigh, and then he turned his attention away from me and spoke to a traffic controller a mile or so underneath us. When I turned to look, Tweedledum was no longer staring at me. He had a small notebook on one knee and was writing in it. I'd either just failed or passed a test. I asked the driver what his flight plan was. Neither Tweedle vetoed the answer.

'Charterhall. That's just inside Scotland; we'll refuel there and fly on to Evanton. That's north of Inverness. You know Charterhall?'

'No.'

'Your Richard Hillary killed himself there. Night flying. You heard o' Richard Hillary?'

'No.' I had an urge to look back. I was sure that Dum was scribbling in his little book again. I asked, 'What's at Evanton?'

'Fuck knows. Nothing good as far as you're concerned, if

those 'cuffs are anything to go by. Easy let-down over the sea and the Cromarty Firth. That's good enough for me.'

North of bloody Inverness. A girl I had once known called that area the Forbidden Zone. What the hell was up there that was worth flying me to?

A prison was.

A prison at Inverness. It was small and discreet as prisons go, but a prison nevertheless. Porterfield. The most northerly prison on the British mainland. Bastards.

The most northerly prison on the British mainland was, in a word, cold. They took away the service clothes and the flying jacket I had surrendered in, and gave me a summer-weight battledress blouse and trousers in navy blue and a couple of pairs of black socks, one pair of boots, a few vests and rough shirts, pants with slack elastic and a grey pullover that had seen better days. I figured that the only way to stay warm, unless I was working, was to wear it all at once – I looked as if I was pregnant.

After I had been kitted out and written into the records of the dismal place, I had a one-sided interview with the governor. A short fat prison officer stood alongside me. He had a hefty black wooden truncheon, and an old .38-calibre service pistol on a lanyard. Maybe I was considered to be dangerous. The governor didn't look at me – he looked out of his office window towards a distant sea sparkling in the evening light. He was a skeletal man with thinning black hair and a small square moustache – moustaches like that were creeping back into fashion now that the

Dark One had snuffed it. He sniffed dolefully and then stated, '4741 . . .'

'Yes.' I yawned. Not because I was tired or ignorant, but because I was scared.

'Yes, *sir* . . .' the warder corrected me, but the governor ignored him and ran on.

'. . . 4741, we live in a fair country; a *just* country. I've always believed that that's why we won the war.' He had a gentle voice – and an unrealistic view of the world. I thought we'd won because we'd dropped their own weight in bombs on the German civilian population, and killed half a million of them.

All I said was, 'Sir.'

'. . . And part of that fairness dictates that all prisoners are told precisely how long their sentences will be. You're expected to have a release date to aim for, unless you're in for life – or condemned to death, of course.'

'I haven't been told mine yet, sir.'

'And I can't tell you, because I do not know it. Only once before have I received a military detention order conveying as little information as yours. The name on *that* one was Rudolf Hess. Yours hasn't even a name on it. You're *not* German, by any chance?'

I shook my head emphatically. 'No, but they don't believe I am who I tell them.'

The warder smiled wryly at me, and shook his head.

The governor continued, 'Neither do I, laddie; neither do I. But I'm certain you'll tell us one day. Keep your nose clean, and do what you're told. That will suit *us*. I'll try to get a release date for you.'

'Can I write letters, or see a lawyer?'

'Why?' the Governor asked. 'If you haven't a name then you don't exist. People who don't exist don't have anyone to write to, do they? You can see the padre. Apart from that you can break up stones. It will keep you fit.'

I had arrived after the evening meal that first day. I went to sleep hungry, in a cold cell that stank of disinfectant. It was their way of telling me something.

My passivity might worry you. It worried *me* when I realized it about a week later. The truth is that if you had seen Germany in the last month of the war, like I had, then you'd have seen worse places than prison. Not only did I not know what I had been sentenced for, I didn't know what I had done to be kept in solitary. I even got to look forward to the arrival of my own private prison guard. I wonder what *he'd* done to deserve *me*. Apart from being Welsh.

My food was delivered to my cell. Porridge, tea and a wad each morning. Meat – usually Spam or corned beef – and potatoes for dinner. Tea and wads before lights out. At half past eight each morning, rain or shine, I was taken into a small yard enclosed by high brick walls and invited to break up stones with a small sledgehammer. The same happened in the afternoon. Each morning when I went out to the yard my previous day's work had been cleared away, and fresh stones awaited me. The stone was limestone: not the hardest rock but dusty. Nicknamed Taffy by me, my prison guard (who I learned subsequently was called Officer Hughes) told me later that it was taken away to add to runway beds at refurbished airfields. Another little irony.

After a week my hands were peppered with small cuts from stone chippings, and my stilted conversations with Taffy were punctuated by the noise of rocks being pounded. The muscles in my arms and shoulders came on nicely, though. I didn't get any ideas about the sledgehammer because of the .38 on the lanyard around his neck – I knew instinctively that he'd use it.

I paused from the constant motion. Taffy asked, 'Want a breather?' He gave me a cup of water, while he drank tea from a flask. I could smell the sugar in it from ten feet away.

He asked me, 'So what do I call you? You're in the books as 4741; nothing else. I looked you up. It's very irregular. We've only got two specials; you're one of them.'

I didn't feel particularly special just then but I told him, 'When they were interrogating me they booked me in as A. N. Other 4741. I thought that the A stood for Albert. You can call me Al.'

'But that's not your real name?'

'No – my real name's Charlie.'

'What you here for, Charlie?' He pulled himself a thin fag from a packet of five. Player's Weights. He noticed me looking, but didn't offer me one.

'I walked into a police station two years late for the end of the war. I was in the RAF, and got lost in Germany. Germany and Italy. Germany and Italy and Belgium and Holland and France.'

'What you'd call well travelled?'

'I suppose so. I told them who I was, and gave them my identity disc. That's when the trouble began.'

'What kind of trouble, boy?'

'They said that the man who owned the disc was dead. Ergo, I must be someone else . . .'

'"Ergo". I like that. You must be an educated man.' Patronizing git.

'. . . And because I can't tell them who that someone else is, they've locked me up.'

'You won't mind my saying that that sounds a trifle Irish: thin and somewhat harsh?'

'No. I wondered about it myself, Prison Officer . . .?'

'Hughes. Edward Hughes. You can call me Prison Officer Hughes.'

'OK. Prison Officer Hughes.'

Hughes shook his head at me in disbelief. 'You won't mind my asking, but since you've been shut up for an unlimited period of time, without remission and with hard labour, for what appears to be the not uncommon crime of deserting in time of war, why aren't you kicking up all sorts of hell, and shouting "Unfair, unfair" into the long dark nights?'

'I wondered about that myself.' I was bloody repeating myself. But at least the bastard's question gave me pause. I turned away from him and savagely battered another small boulder into submission. I realized that it had all started with the beating I had been given on the train. After that if someone said jump, I jumped . . . albeit wearily. It was as if my brain had stopped completely. It's what happens if you lose the concept of *future*. Why had I believed that the bloody RAF would sort me out and come galloping to the rescue? I suddenly realized that there was no man in a white hat, just Prison Officer Hughes. He'd have to do. When I swung back he was grinning. He said, 'Good boy. Got to you, didn't I?'

'Yes. I don't care whether you believe me or not, but I *don't* know why I'm being treated like this.'

'Nor do we . . .'

'What can I do about it?'

'Maybe you should see the chaplain. The company would do you good.'

'How do I do that?'

'You ask me. Time you was back at work, anyway.'

I asked him the next day. As I was led along a stone corridor to the sky pilot's office another man left it. I thought I recognized him.

The chaplain had an amazing Adam's apple. It had a life of its own. It roamed from side to side along his collar as he spoke. His voice was a sibilant hiss, and his hands, white and long, looked as soft as a girl's. He too asked me what I was in for. Either no sod knew, or they were trying to trip me up all the time. He rephrased it, and asked me what my sins were. I told him I had too many to list. He shook his head; I was obviously a hopeless case.

'You really should start telling the truth. God can't find you in here unless you do.'

I shrugged. Like I told you: I'd seen Germany. God hadn't helped much *there*, either. I remembered that I had driven across Europe wearing a padre's battledress blouse – second-hand. Maybe this was God's payback. It had had two neat repair patches where the bullets had gone through. This parson wouldn't have understood that; he didn't look like one of your active-service types. I asked him what denomination he served. He smiled apologetically. 'Sorry. I should have made that clear at the start. I'm a Catholic priest; is that a problem?'

'No. I was in a Lancaster in 1944: our engineer was a Catholic too. He was from Newcastle: the one in Northern Ireland. After we'd finished our tour he went off to some priests' school to become a padre. If I told you his name, could you get a message to him?'

'Confidentially?'

'Yes. I always trusted him, you see.'

'I'll see what I can do. What was his name?' So I told him about Fergal.

The chaplain asked me to pray with him. I didn't mind that as long as he stayed on his own side of the room. The fact that someone wanted to pray for me at all, whether he believed me or not, moved me in some obscure way.

When I went back to my cell there was my old pipe, an ounce of Erinmore and a box of matches on my bed. A present for cooperating, I supposed. Grace had given me the pipe. I sat down on the bed and nearly wept. It was a close-run thing. Stupid.

It was a long couple of weeks before I was called up to the governor's office. He looked embarrassed, while Prison Officer Hughes looked rather pleased with himself.

Fergal was there too, standing in the centre of the room. He looked magnificent, only younger . . . and he'd let his hair grow. He also looked bloody angry: like an avenging bloody angel. In all the time we flew together – me as radio operator and him as flight engineer – I had never known him properly angry; not even at the Germans. I had heard shouting just before I entered the room. Now I realized that Fergal had been doing it. He looked back over his shoulder at me, and said, 'Hi, Charlie. Your things are in the car. I've signed all the papers, and you've accepted the War Office's apology for their mistake. OK?'

I nodded.

'Do you need to collect anything else before we leave?'

I shook my head. I didn't trust myself to speak.

The governor looked at me for the first time since I'd entered the room and said testily, 'He'll have to return his prison-issue clothes before he goes.'

Fergal leaned over the man's desk and said quietly, 'We're three floors up, governor. If you just so much as touch him again, I'll throw you out of the fucking window, and apologize to the Good Fella later on.'

The governor kept quiet after that, and didn't even look up from his desk as we left the office. It looked as if I'd never happened.

When they opened the gate for me nobody said anything. There were no signatures. No formalities. I expected a voice to call me back at any minute, but it didn't happen. On the street outside Fergal hugged me, and didn't say a word. I'm not big on being hugged by other men, and Fergal's bigger than me, so it was a bit like being suffocated. There was a big khaki Humber saloon with the word *Kate* painted in careful italics on its scuttle: it was the car I had driven across Europe, and I'd last seen it in France. The regimental and unit flashes had been carelessly crossed through with green paint: it had been demobilized. A familiar smiling figure was behind the wheel. Les turned to shake my hand once I was settled. 'Hello, guv'nor,' he said, 'I wondered where you'd got to. Can't you stay out of trouble for a minute?'

I couldn't reply because there was something the matter with my voice. There was something the matter with my eyes as well, because my cheeks were wet. Les asked, 'How long you been inside?'

'Not quite sure.' I sniffed; then I explained. 'More than a few weeks. I lost count in the middle for a while.'

'Fancy a wet, anyone? The pubs are open.' Les was always good at getting things back on track. He added, 'There's half a dozen papers in the back I got for you. Thought you might want to get up to date.' I opened the *Mirror* to find that someone had cut out the *Jane* cartoon. Always the bloody same. I suddenly realized that I had forgotten what year it was, and had to look at the masthead. How the hell had that happened? 1947.

The barman at the Station Hotel was Czech, obviously one of those who'd managed to stay behind after the war. He told us that he could mix any cocktail we'd care to name. I didn't know any. Les said, 'How about a got-out-of-jail-free cocktail for this unfortunate young man here?' He touched my shoulder. 'Something that will make him very drunk, very quickly.'

The barman put four large whisky tumblers on the bar, and added three fingers of an amber liquid to each. The bottle was unlabelled and greasy but the peaty whisky smell from it was unmistakable. On top of that, from a bottle he produced from under the bar, he poured three fingers of something brown and sticky-looking. Then he put a small iceberg in each. Les said, 'I drank this before: it's somethin' Canadian.'

'Cheers, Charlie,' Fergal said and raised his glass.

I was slowly coming out of the daze in which I'd felt since being put in the slammer. It was like surfacing into the sunlight after a particularly deep dive. I looked at Fergal.

'Have I said thank you yet?'

'We'll take it as read. Thank the barman for pouring us these lovely drinks, and ask for four more.'

I did. Then I realized that the smile that had been on Les's face since we'd driven away had been an *anxious* one, and that it had gone. The old Les grin had come back. We sat at a small round table in a corner where Les could see the door. The barman polished glasses and kept his eye on us.

I asked Les, 'What happened to Maggs and the kids?'

'The Major's got them. He did what he told us. He bought a little pub down on the South Coast, and is adding an eatery and tea shop. I hope that the locals have strong stomachs; his cooking was . . .'

'*Experimental* . . .' I remembered.

'The German kid is in the local school, and the nipper's toddling. They live over the bar with Maggs. She runs the bar for the Major; he'd better keep an eye on her or she'll turn it into a knocking shop.'

That's what Maggs had been doing when I met her. That was after she had woken up in her house in Paris one morning, found a Lancaster full of dead men in her garden, murdered her husband, and had an affair with the German salvage officer who came to take the aircraft scrap away. Her story is better than mine.

I smiled as I thought of her. 'Good old Maggs. How's Carlo?' Grace's kid.

'I told you. He's a late mover; toddling, but he's a wicked way with the ladies already.'

'What about Dieter?'

Dieter was the other kid I'd inherited. We found him when he was five on a battlefield just over the German border. He was sitting holding the hand of his dead elder brother; a little boy soldier all of fourteen years old . . . as old as he was ever going to get. I don't need to tell you there are worse places than prisons.

'The kids in the school gave him a hard time at first; him being a German. They were in Doodlebug Alley down there. Then Maggs told the teachers how you found him, and that seemed to change things. Some of the teachers told some of the parents an' of course it got back to the kids. Things were different after that; he's got a lot of pals. I think that the Major would like you to contribute to their keep when you're mindful. A visit wouldn't be out of order. The boys keep asking where their father is.' The Major had been our boss across Europe, of course. I felt bad about the kids. I felt bad because I didn't want to be tied to someone else's children: it was just something that had crept up on me. Or perhaps I'd just been plain stupid.

'Yeah. I've got a fair bit of money somewhere.'

'. . . And we got those houses in Germany we bought from Tommo. He's rented them out to the Yanks, and is depositing the rents for us.'

'Is that legal?'

'Seems to be. I invested some o' mine with the Major. That's already paying off, too.'

Another glass. Fergal seemed to be getting the hang of it. I felt drunk. I asked Les what had happened to him after I'd handed myself in.

'I went back to the house in Highgate. The unit still has it, although I think they got no use for it now: the Army's going all regular again. My brother Stan is housekeeping it for them – moved in with his wife and kids when he got demobbed. He's got a nice little window-cleaning round on the side, so he's doing OK.'

'I'm pleased.'

'He told me that the Major had got out, too, and where I could find him.'

'So you went to . . . Bosham, wasn't it?'

'Nah; the Major's club in London. He goes all round the country buying up food for his restaurant. He spoke to the Army an' told them I'd returned from the last mission he had sent me on – which was stretching the truth, I thought, because as I recall it was you and me who decided to follow your Grace off to Italy when the armistice was signed . . . the Major was out of it by then; he stopped thinking for a few days, remember?'

'Yes.'

'. . . And he tells them that I'm pretty beat up, and suffering from battle fatigue, and won't be fit to be interviewed for a while, but that he'll keep an eye on me for them. The interview ain't happened yet, but me demob papers came through, and so did my back pay.'

'Jammy bugger.'

'Eventually I went to Maggs to find out what had happened to you. She said that she hadn't heard from you since you walked into a cop shop in Bedford and did the proper thing. You'd disappeared, she said, and she was running short of money. She couldn't go to the cop shop herself, because she only has a French passport, and if they had taken against her the kids would have ended up split up in care. She knew that you wouldn't want that.' He paused for breath, and a gulp at one of the beers that the Czech had conjured up, then finished his bit of the story. 'So I went to the police station, didn't I? Flashed our old pass at the sergeant who told me that you'd been nicked back by the military – he obviously wasn't happy about it, because he'd been asking questions about a list of names and addresses you'd given him. Caused so much of a fuss that his Chief Constable told him to back off or lose his pension. He gave me his stuff, and I followed up on some of it until I met the same sort of threats. So I went back to the Major.'

Fergal interrupted: 'About then I received a letter from your prison chaplain – seems a reasonable chap despite being English. Eventually there was me making daily phone calls to my Member of Parliament, and the War Office, and me bishop . . . and Les and the Major were still stirring things up, and then someone told your dad, and that was that.'

'My *dad*?'

'He went straight down the Legion, and kicked up shit. Did you know that he was big in the Legion?'

'I knew that he was a member. Armistice Day and all that.'

'He's a Grand Wizard, or whatever they calls themselves.

Anyway, your British Legion started rattling the War Office's cage, and the War Office quickly threw in the towel. No contest. It was simple in the end. It's nice to think that soldiers can still be trumped by *old* soldiers, isn't it? Apparently you're now a misunderstood war hero. I got a phone call from me archbishop, I did, telling me to come and extract you discreetly from the pokey – here we are.'

'How did you meet Les?'

Fergal raised his eyes piously towards the ceiling, with a grin. 'God moves in mysterious ways. He was on the end of a telephone number the archbishop gave me. Les and I decided to spring you together.'

'Thank you, Fergal. Thank you, Les.' They both smiled. It was good that they didn't feel they had to say anything. I added, 'I still don't know what I did wrong, apart from going a bit AWOL, that is.'

Les shook his head and said, 'You're a bit of a tit, Charlie: you did it the *proper* way; that's what you did. Bound to end in tears. Didn't you learn a thing from me and the Major?'

'What yer gonna do, then?' Les asked me. 'I can't afford to hang around here for the rest of the year. Stan has offered me a partnership.'

'Cleaning windows?'

'Cleaning windows, chimneys an' a nice little contract, driving gang-mowers for the council parks offices.'

'What are gang-mowers?'

'Six or seven grass-mowers all linked up behind a tractor. That'll do me.'

My response had been all about delaying answering his first question. I was suddenly unused to making decisions for myself. They have a word for that these days: *institutionalized*, only it shouldn't have happened that quickly. After a further delay Les asked, more kindly this time, 'Still hard, is it?'

'As the actress said to the bishop.'

'Just bloody answer my bloody question, Charlie.'

We were sitting on a long railway seat on platform one at Inverness station; less than thirty yards from the hotel and the bar. Watching passengers. We had been at the hotel for three days now. Fergal had slipped away to practise taking confessions in the Big House – he relieved the local priest, who usually ended up in one of the small harbour-side bars. I thought that I could get the hang of being a Catholic. I told Les, 'Yes, Les. It's still hard. I can't seem to make my mind up about anything.'

'Don't be surprised. You've just spent weeks doing nothing unless you were told to. Besides; maybe you were sort of ill at the same time, but didn't know it.'

'How do you mean, ill?'

'When I got back to the big house in Highgate there was no one there, just my brother Stan and his family living in the basement. He gave me the address and telephone number of the Major's club. I phoned, and he was there . . . so I went round to him to report. He said for me to go home, an' wait till I hears from him. To take a rest. Maybe he thought we were dead.'

'Did you? Rest?'

'Yes.'

'. . . And you never heard anything from the Army?'

'No. I told you. What the Yanks would call a home run.'

'Where's home?'

'Belmont in Surrey, out on the edge of the heath. Didn't I ever tell you that?'

'I think you did, once. Where's all this leading, Les?'

'So I went home to Kate and my kids, and my old man and mum, an' most of my brothers . . . and was drunk for three weeks solid. I can't remember any of that. I can remember waking up late one morning; the sun was comin' in through the curtain. For some reason I touched my chin – I couldn't have shaved for days, and there were a couple of fighting scabs. You listening?' I nodded. Les continued. 'Kate looked around the door. She looked tired: sort of pinched. She came back with a big cup of tea, just like we used to do on Sundays before the war. I asked her what happened? She just said, "You were ill for a couple of weeks, but I think that you're all right now." That's all she said: "You were ill for a couple of weeks . . ."'

He had my attention, although I couldn't quite make out what he was getting at. He was obviously uncomfortable talking about it at all, so I wondered why he was trying.

'What do you mean, Les? How were you ill?'

'Off my bloody head. Drunk . . . and raving most of the time. You remember that trench in Germany with all them dead boy soldiers in it?'

'Yes. I try not to.'

'I told my kids about it one afternoon. Scared them half to death. They don't want to talk to me much now; I can see it in their eyes.'

'They'll come back; you'll have to give it some time.'

'That's what I wanted to say to you, Charlie. It happened to the Major at the end, didn't it? He suddenly stopped giving orders. I think that it happened to us as well. I went to see my local doctor that evening, and all he said was, "Exhaustion." Does that sound about right to you?'

My mate Les was a very subtle man. It was what had kept him alive and only marginally damaged over nearly six years of war. So I said reassuringly, 'Yeah. That sounds about right, Les. You all right now?'

'Yeah. Next day we took a picnic down into the bluebell woods at Woodmanstern. I made the kids bows and arrers, and Kate and I started to talk about what we'll do now. Panic over.'

'Panic over,' I told him. I meant for me as well. 'I think I'll go and see the old man in Glasgow now I'm up here, then go south again, find out if I'm still in the RAF and what happened to my back pay. Then I suppose I'd better find a job. Haven't even begun to think about it, Les – but at least I have a starting plan, haven't I?'

'Yeah. Fergal will be pleased. He wants to get back to his parish.'

'He has a *parish*?'

'Yeah. Liverpool. Poor kids and an orphanage.'

Fergal and I took the train south together – as far as Edinburgh. I slept most of the way with the sun on my face. I remember that there was a long set of stone steps from the station to Princes Street. I was out of breath before I reached the top. I needed some exercise, and healthy living. The last thing I asked Fergal was who had paid for the hotel at Inverness, and our bar bill. He told me that it had all been arranged for us, and that it was probably best not to ask too many questions.

'I don't know how to thank you for what you did, Fergal.'

'Then don't. I'm supposed to ask you to go to church on Sundays, but you'd backslide sooner or later and feel guilty about it. That wouldn't do anyone any good. Go to the Armistice Parade whenever you remember, and say a prayer for *Tuesday* and Brookie: they didn't deserve what they did to each other.'

Tuesday had been *Tuesday's Child*. She was the Lancaster we had flown into Germany. Brookie was Brookman, the pilot who'd taken her after us. *Tuesday* hadn't liked Brookman, and things hadn't worked out for them. They'd burned.

Les was practical – that was probably why the Major had chosen him to drive around Europe at the fag end of the war. He'd brought me my cheque book and bank papers: he'd found them in the car I'd left at Highgate before our trip. I went up to the Royal Bank of Scotland building in St Andrew's Square. In a counting-house room so beautiful that I couldn't take my eyes off it, a girl so beautiful that I couldn't take my eyes off her either talked to me about how to get my money. She was slim, and her nose was as straight as the blonde hair that fell below her shoulders. She had a problem when I asked her how much money I had. Her small mouth made an upside-down smile, and she asked me to wait whilst she consulted. She consulted a very tall man in a baggy grey demob suit. He looked about thirty, although his hair was thinning already. He asked me to join him in an interview room.

'Just need to ask you a few questions. Formality.' His voice was clipped. Definitely ex-services. 'Do you have any identity other than your bank book, old boy?' They'd given me back my fibre tag and pay book. I gave them to him. When I think about it, I must have worried them, dressed as I was like a scarecrow in a ragtag of service-issue clothes and an old US flying jacket. All my other possessions were in a small pack at my feet. Grey Suit came to a decision. He stuck out his hand for a shake. 'Allan Fraser,' he said by way of introduction.

He already knew who I was, didn't he?

'What's the problem with my bank account?'

'I don't know if there is one. It isn't our bank, of course, and yours doesn't have a branch in Edinburgh, so I'm allowed to help you if we feel inclined. We have to check, because bods turn up from time to time with bank books they've half-inched from the honoured dead and then try to draw the cash out. They always ask how much they've got first. You understand? You mind sitting here while I call your branch – it may take a few minutes?'

'I've got nothing else to do,' I told him, and shrugged.

He gave me a newspaper named the *Scotsman*. It was very optimistic about Scottish independence. I remembered a copper telling me that a bunch of Scottish Nationalists had tried to make a separate peace with Germany and let the Nazis in through the back door. That seemed a bit rich to me, so maybe Scottish independence would have benefits for the neighbours as well. That's what I was thinking about when Fraser came back in.

He brought a piece of paper with him but kept it under his hand, face down on the small table between us. He asked me a variety of security questions including my mother's maiden name, the same questions I'd been asked when I'd set the account up in a little bank near Bedford. I seemed to pass the test because he smiled at me and told me, 'You're worth more than three thousand pounds. What was it? Pools win?'

'A family property I inherited,' I lied. 'I rented it out to the Yanks.' I didn't feel good about lying to him, because he seemed to be a good-natured straightforward sort of chap, but it was the lie I had set the account up with. I would have felt worse if I had said '*It was black market money from goods we inherited from our gunner when he was killed.*'

'How much do you want?'

'Fifty quid will do for the present. Thanks.' I wrote out a cheque for him. It was my first, but I didn't tell him that. We didn't have bank accounts in my family, just pay packets and cash.

'Could you do with some investment advice? A sum like that could be making you some money, you know.'

'Life's too short.' A girl named Grace had taught me those words.

He shook his head. 'Not any longer, but you can always come back.' Then he gave me a shrewd sort of look which told me that he'd been an officer, and asked, 'Before we go back out there is there anything else the bank can help you with?'

It was my turn to shake my head, and I answered the question he hadn't asked me.

'No, but thanks all the same. I'm all right now; I'll get by. You're right: it's hard to get used to being back home.'

*

I spent two days in a bed-and-breakfast place on Calton Hill, saw the sights, and drank my way along Rose Street with some sailors from an aircraft carrier. I saw the girl from the bank in a Rose Street bar. She sat with her arm through that of a craggy-looking older fellow. She looked in love. They heedered and hodered away about how the world would be saved by the Reds and poetry, once the perfidious English had stopped running it. It wasn't an argument I knew enough about to join, so I moved on to another pub that had an accordionist and a couple of singers. Life was too short.

I smoked my pipe on a bench in Princes Street Gardens, and chatted up a pretty young nanny looking after two children in a huge Tansad pram. That didn't go anywhere, and I found that I didn't care, so I spent three bob on a bus ticket to Glasgow, and wondered if the old man would be pleased to see me. He'd moved to Hamilton to be near his brother's family after we had been bombed out down south. I wondered if he would ever move south again.

My mood lifted once I was on the bus; it was a single-deck Bedford that still smelled new inside. There weren't many passengers, and across the aisle from me a small boy of about six read all of the notices displayed in the passenger area, mouthing the words silently. One was headed *Diphtheria and Tuberculosis Regulations (1947)* and read *Spitting in this vehicle is prohibited*. The kid suddenly looked up at the woman with him, and announced solemnly, 'Hey, mam – you can't spit in here!'

The blush it brought to her cheeks was worthy of a music-hall turn. She didn't look like a spitter to me, but you never can tell.

I had to get another bus to Hamilton. My father had moved out of the red sandstone tenement my mum and little sister had died in and into another one, half a mile away. Part of me understood why, but another part wondered why he'd bothered: they looked identical. I arrived about half past five in the afternoon. Most of the doors on the tiled common stair stood open, and level by level I could smell what his neighbours were having for supper. Mostly cabbage.

Dad's door was open. I walked in and found him sitting in the kitchen, with the remains of a fish supper. He pulled off a new pair of glasses, put down his paper, and said, 'You took your time.'

'What are the licensing hours round here?'

'That's the best thing about Scotland, son . . . there aren't any, not so's you'd notice.' That meant we were pleased to see each other, and that I'd said thank you. The truth was that I found it galling still to be got out of trouble by my dad when I was nearly twenty-three.

There was a three-day-old letter from the War Department (RAF Records Branch) inviting me to go down for an interview at an address in Kingsway in London. They would welcome the opportunity to explain the problem that had occurred with my personal record, it said. Somehow I thought that I already knew the building from the back.

I stayed with Dad for a couple of weeks, and let the bastards wait. What I noticed in that fortnight was that I didn't look out of place. There were large numbers of men still wearing out the bits and pieces of uniform that we had fought across Europe in. It wasn't the fabled Scottish frugality on display; it was just a reluctance to let go of the men we once were. Then the demob suits came out at the weekends.

Dad said that you could see a few flash types now, up around Glasgow Green – but they were mainly gang members. They fought with knives and bicycle chains and bottles most Saturday nights, so succeeded in keeping their own numbers in check. We were in a pub named the Greenmantle one night when one of them walked in and shoved an older fellow off a bar stool. Three guys in khaki tops that had had their badges removed quietly took him out through a back door and came back without him five minutes later. They hadn't even broken a sweat. The barmaid was a pretty twenty-year-old who had a nice smile for me, and didn't seem to be with anyone. Dad said he was living in an area where, if you fancied a girl, you still asked her old man, or an elder brother, if you could take her out. It was good of him to give me the gypsy's warning, so I decided to pass up on that one.

Bloody London. Even in my eighties I still don't know whether I love or hate the damned place. The train was a streamliner with corridor carriages, and took six hours. It was still painted war-time matt, and I slept most of the way. I was getting good at sleeping on trains. My pack was over my head on the luggage net. When I woke up there was a boy standing on the seat trying to get at it. My slap rolled him into the corridor, and he ran off crying. I don't know what I'd expected. The Old Man had come home from Europe in 1919 to find the country wasn't quite the 'home fit for heroes' he'd been promised, either. I couldn't say that I hadn't been warned. I hoped that the kid would take a lesson from being caught stealing. Or there again, maybe the lesson he'd take from it would be to start carrying a knife in case he met people like me again. I wasn't exactly feeling like Captain Sunshine when I left the train, anyway.

There were men in cast-off military-uniform clothes in London as well. What shook me was that many of them were begging. Some of them had their families sitting beside them in the drizzle. Mute. Shivering. You couldn't pay them all off. What the hell had happened to the country in the last few years? I took the Tube to Highgate, and then hoofed it to the big safe house that the Intelligence Corps had run there during the war. I hadn't met Les's brother Stan, but he was expecting me.

They looked like twins, although Stan was the younger by two years. Even their voices were creepily alike. I bet they had had fun with the girls on dark nights. Stan's wife and children were down visiting the family, he told me, in Belmont. They would be back on a late train, and he would drive down to Victoria to meet them. Would I care for a mug of char? Would I. He warmed the pot, and put in three spoonfuls of dark fine tea from a wooden caddy which locked with a key. When I picked it up and looked at it he said, 'Spoils o' victory.' The metal stand he put the teapot on, to spare the table, was made of aluminium, and was in the shape of a swastika inside a geometric sunburst. 'That too.'

'Serves them right. Where were you?'

'Not far behind you and Les. I drove tank transporters – Scammels.'

'Didn't Les do that once?'

'Nah. He drove tank-recovery vehicles. Big Thorneycroft cranes. That was out in the desert.'

'That's right. He told me. I thought I'd see if my car was still here. Les put it up on bricks in a garage out the back whilst we were away.'

'Course it is. Only it's not on bricks. I run it once a month just to turn it over; hope you don't mind.'

'No. I'm pleased.'

'You left a couple of kitbags in it. They were collected by an American who says they were his. That kosher?'

'Yes. David Thomsett. Tommo. They were full of money, did you know that?'

'No, an' maybe it's better I still don't.'

'OK. What's petrol like? Still scarce?'

'Not if you know where to get it. Bloody tax cripples you, though.'

We were in the basement service flat that went with the house. It had its own outside door under the front steps. The overshadowed windows were slick with drizzle. The light was drawing in.

Stan made a decent cup of tea. Self-sufficiency must have run in the family. Sometime after dusk he asked me if I had somewhere to stay. 'It's difficult finding somewhere in town at the moment. Too much bombing, and too little building – an' every building site's on strike every other week.'

'I thought a small hotel, or a B & B . . .'

'You won't get one, an' if you do you'll pay through the nose for the privilege o' sharing your bed with bugs. Why don't you sleep upstairs? There's no one there, an' I'll give you the key. You're almost an old boy, after all. No one would mind.'

So I spent my first night free in London after the war sleeping in the same bed I'd slept in on my last night in England in 1945. Before I'd set off with Les and the Galloping Major for big bad Germany. The ghosts from Germany and Holland crowded around me for a while, but eventually I slept, and the sun was shining when I awoke. O, Brave New World.

3. I Hate a Man Like You

At least they had the taste not to interview me in the same cell. I was met by a tall, thin civil servant. He had thinning greased hair and a manner and accent that sprang from one of the better schools – and Oxford. He sounded like one of the officers from my old squadron. His pale skin clung to his bony face. It was like talking to an animated skull. I hated him immediately.

He had a sticky, wet handshake. 'Hello, old boy, take a pew. I'm Piers Fortingale.'

I got my hand back, and felt like wiping it on my handkerchief. I sat on a plain wooden chair and Fortingale sat behind his desk.

'The War House asked me to apologize for our little mistake, Charlie; can we take that as read?'

'"Little mistake"? You sent me to bloody prison!'

'If you ask my opinion, I'd say that it was largely your own fault. You were a deserter, after all . . . what did you expect, flags and a street party?' It was a sudden waspish snap.

'I wasn't a deserter,' I spat back, 'and I believe you know that. I was finishing a job I was sent out there to do. It was just that the job and the war didn't stop at the same time.' He sighed – a schoolteacher with a tiresome child.

'Yes, and in consideration of that the Secretary of State and all of his little Under Secretaries of State undid your sentence. They were uncommonly merciful because they accepted that you might have misinterpreted your responsibilities.'

'No, they weren't. That's a load of old bollocks. The British Legion or the Bishop of Liverpool rattled their cage so hard that they began to wet themselves. Then they let me go.'

'You don't honestly think that the War Office is afraid of a bunch of old soldiers in the Legion, old boy? Don't kid yourself.'

'I won't. I'm beginning to see how things work. Yes, I *do* think that the War Office doesn't want to take on the Legion at the moment. I don't know why, but I'll find out.'

Pause. Stand-off. Piers made a steeple of his fingers and rested his mouth against it. Then, incredibly, he smiled. Like a camera flashgun. He said, 'Do you know, I really believe that you might? And you could be right. They wouldn't tell me, of course.' He made a production of looking at his wristwatch, which was a thin gold thing that looked incongruous on a wide military strap. 'Care to slip down to the pub for a couple of jars, and lunch?'

It was not quite 11.30 a.m. Welcome to peacetime soldiering, Charlie.

We walked to a pub in a little back street. It called itself the Printer's Devil. On the way there Piers stopped at a news-stand and bought a copy of the *News Chronicle*. He said, 'Thank you, my dear,' when the newspaper seller returned his change. He knew the image that he was creating, but somehow I got the impression that that was maybe all it was: an *image*. Underneath it all, I suspected that Piers was as tough as old boots.

In a small cubicle of age-blackened wood we drank pints of Fuller's beer, and he told me that I was still in the RAF. OK – I wasn't soldiering any longer, so why did I feel so uneasy? Between the first pints he handed me a large brown Ministry envelope. I looked at it suspiciously. 'What's that?'

'Back pay. Nice fat cheque. You can cash it at a bank, or pay it into your own account if you have one.' The way he said it made me suppose that he thought that was unlikely – so maybe the bastard didn't know as much as he thought.

'You don't need envelopes this size for a cheque. What else?'

'Movement order and joining instructions, old boy.'

'Bollocks. I'm demobbed.'

'Not yet, old boy, not yet . . . and, to be frank, we're not demobbing radio ops at the moment. There is a sudden scarcity of members of your trade. You can apply to get out, of course, but that will take weeks and weeks to process. If I was you I'd get used to giving Mother England another six months of your life. Nice safe little place near Cheltenham; you'll love it.'

'Who said?'

'Never you mind; another drink? It's a good pint here, isn't it?'

I still don't know how the government manages to find so many greasy bastards like Piers. I asked, 'And what if I tell you to sod off?'

'Jankers again, old boy. Haven't you seen enough of that recently?' When I didn't reply he asked, 'What do you fancy for lunch? The place is famous for its mutton stew.'

The woman who served the tables was a tall Australian with hair the colour of Chianti. It seemed as if she knew most of the customers by name and that they were there for the banter they enjoyed with her. She had a very fast return of serve. When it came to our turn she said, 'Hiya, Piers,' and then she held out a hand to me and said, 'Hiya. My name's Denys – spelled with a Y – my old man couldn't spell. Wasn't much cop at telling the boys from the girls, either.' She'd said that before. I liked her handshake; just a quick up and down and let go. And she was firm without being grippy.

'I'm Charlie Bassett. I think that Piers owns me.'

'Then you'll be OK, won't you? Piers owns all of us, but he looks after us as well.'

'Den was a WREN, weren't you dear? She didn't want to go home after it was all over. HMG was thinking of insisting – too many waifs and strays in the country at present.'

'What happened?'

Denys was more than capable of speaking for herself. 'About a year ago, when I was serving here, I felt old Piers's hand go up between my legs, and I knew that I was going to be all right.'

'He hasn't done that to me yet.'

'Good job: they're arresting people for it again. Now: what grub do you want?'

I asked for the mutton stew.

'When am I going to meet an adventurous man?' She laughed when she walked away.

'You really french her?' I asked him.

'Saves time, old man. Know where you are immediately. She

held a table knife to my throat, as I recall, and sweetly bade me desist.'

'What did she say?'

'Something like, "Get yer fingers outta there, afore I cut yer effin' tongue out from underneath yer effin' chin." It was an interesting turn of phrase.'

'Then you helped her?'

'Let's just say that we cut a deal, shall we? Just like the deal I'm going to cut with you.'

When Denys came back to the table with two plates of fatty mutton swimming in gravy and sliced potatoes, I asked her if she'd come out with me. She put both plates down without spilling anything; then she straightened up and said, 'Charlie, I'm nearly a foot taller than you. People'd think I was out with my little brother.'

I persisted. 'Will you come out with me?'

She suddenly switched a smile on. She didn't wear lipstick. Didn't need to: her lips were dark, like the hollyhocks when I was a kid.

'Love to,' she told me, and when she walked away from us she was laughing again, her hips swinging out an invitation. It had been a long time: I hoped the invitation was for me.

The deal was that I had another week's leave to 'sort out my affairs' before I reported to my new station, which Piers told me was a small RAF radio station in Cheltenham – west of Oxford along the A40. The RAF wanted another six months out of me until they could train a new generation of radio officers . . . or convince bods they had already demobbed to re-enlist. Oh yeah; I had a new rank. I was a sergeant once more. It was on the replacement fibre discs they gave me. My old Pilot Officer rank had disappeared like snow off a dyke: that's the old usage of the word, mind you.

I stayed at the Highgate safe house, the only occupant apart from Stan and his family downstairs. He had a pretty and friendly wife, a daughter and a couple of boisterous boys . . . I enjoyed the company. Two days later I dated Denys. She'd exaggerated – there were no more than six inches between us.

The address that Denys had given me was in Kensington, and it took me a while to find. It turned out to be a small street of mews garages with flats above them. Most of the outside brick-work had been freshly painted white – it cheered the street up. Denys came down to the small street door to let me in, wearing a dark red bath robe that almost matched her hair and smelling of soap. Her skin had that scrubbed look that you fall in love with; at least, it had had that effect on me before. I followed her up the narrow stairs and out into a large room that combined a kitchen, dining room and sitting room. I liked its economy. She poured me a glass of red wine which matched a half-consumed one of her own, her hair and the robe. She obviously went for matching colours.

'This is a great place,' I said. 'How'd you find it?'

'Through Piers. Cheers.'

'Cheers.'

'His friend Stephen owns it. He's the dentist who lives next door. Only just qualified, I think, but he has loads of friends, and *money* to spend. Stephen gets us dates when we're in the mood and splits the money with us.'

'Money?'

'Men pay good money to dance with a pretty girl. I'm pretty.'

'I noticed.'

'But that's not why you asked me out, is it?' she challenged me.

'No. I liked your lip.' Don't ask me why I like lippy girls – I always have done. Something clicked from earlier in the conversation. 'You said *us*.'

'Yes. My flatmate. She's at work at the moment.'

'What does she do?'

'Anyone ever told you that you ask too many questions, hon? Ask her if you meet her. Pour yourself another glass. I'm going to get dressed.'

She dressed like money on legs – a pattern-printed skirt with a hundred small pleats that swung as she walked, a crisp white blouse, expensive stockings and low-heeled pumps. I think that the choice of the latter, which didn't quite match her outfit, was to spare my feelings. As it was, my line of sight reached the dimple on her chin. That would do for me.

We drank Mother's Ruin in a small backstreet pub she took me to, played shove-halfpenny with a couple of thousand-year-olds who couldn't take their eyes from her cleavage and then took in a Bogart double feature . . . *Casablanca* and *The Big Sleep*. Den insisted on sitting at the centre of the front row, so there were no back-row shenanigans, and I ended up with a crick in my neck from staring upwards. It occurred to me that if I dated girls this tall I would have to get used to the sore neck.

Then she took me home, fed me corned-beef sandwiches, and rolled me into bed. I played hard to get, which slowed down the action for all of about thirty-five seconds. She made me watch her undress; I could touch *her*, she said, but not her clothes.

'These stockings cost too much for me to risk you getting your paws on them, hon.'

I was stupid. I asked, trying to be funny, 'So who do I pay? You or your Stephen?'

She laughed, looked away and shook her head, but it was as if she was laughing to herself. She told me, 'Neither: we never danced, did we?'

It was my fault, but it wasn't the same after that. Me and my big mouth had changed the evening.

Morning. Den looked even better in the half-light and half asleep. She looked like someone with an appetite. Afterwards she lay face down on the bed, whilst I sat on the edge taking simple pleasure from stroking her back. The light from the window leached in under the curtain: it was going to be another wonderful bloody day. Her head was turned away from me. She asked me quietly, 'Does it worry you? My taking gifts from men?'

'Do you sleep with them?'

'Only if I want to.'

'It would worry me, if you were mine. My girlfriend, I mean.'

I felt inadequate enough as it was. The odd thing was that my old girl Grace had been the same; and I had learned to put up with her. But I think that that's something love does to you.

'But I'm not.'

'No.'

'So that's all right, then.' That was a phrase we used a lot in '47 and '48. She rolled over and grinned at me. It was a genuine grin: 'Y'know, Charlie, you'd make a bloody good Australian. You don't really give a toss, do you?'

So why did I feel such a little shit?

Sherlock would have probably called that a one-pipe problem. So I pulled on my shirt, and went out into the kitchen to find my pipe and tobacco – in a pocket of my old flying jacket that was draped over the back of an upright chair. It was one of those pre-war shirts with tails down to your knees – and I was glad of that because I was standing there in nothing else, smoking my pipe and looking out of the window watching the mews come to life, when a woman I thought I recognized walked out of the other bedroom.

We got an eye lock, and her face said, *I know you*. Nothing. No sound. Then she smiled, and looked just as pretty as I remembered. 'Pilot Officer Bassett: you once asked me for a date. I thought that you were a fast worker.'

'You said yes. I thought you were a fast worker too, but I didn't come back for it.' My memory kicked in: 'You're Section Officer Dolly Wayne.'

She sat down at the kitchen table, and crossed her ankles under the chair. I remembered those ankles. Close to the end of the war she had driven me from Highgate to Croydon Airport in an RAF staff car and I spent half the journey watching her calf and thigh muscles tense and untense each time she changed gear. I didn't know what to say next, so she took pity on me.

'I'm glad you made it. I thought that you had a nice face.' I was conscious of my grubby shirt and flapping shirt tails. Dolly was still wearing most of a WAAF's uniform. Everything except the jacket.

'Are you still in the mob?'

'Yes, I stayed on – or rather, they *let* me stay on – nearly everyone else was demobbed. For months afterwards you'd meet people you knew, all looking for jobs.'

'I'm still in too, only I'm a sergeant now. I wanted to leave but they say I have to stay on for a bit.'

'Hard cheese.' Dolly helped herself to a cigarette from a packet that Den had left on the table, waved it at me and said, 'Breakfast.' Senior Service. The smoke she left in the air was very blue in the hard morning light. *Only Senior Service satisfy* – that was the promise on the inside fold of the packet. She closed her eyes the first time she inhaled. Denys shuffled in with the bed sheet wrapped around her. All we could see were her head and her feet. She still looked bloody marvellous.

'What's this, service reunion? Where're my fags?' she asked.

Dolly left after a car horn signalled to her from the road. She scurried back into her room for a uniform jacket and a raincoat, and then didn't seem to know how to say goodbye. I smiled to see that she still carried a gas-mask case . . . they had been doubling for handbags for years.

'Goodbye, then,' she said. 'I'll probably see you later.'

I said, 'Yes. Maybe. It was nice meeting again.'

Then she was gone, leaving just a breath of floral perfume in the air.

Den asked me, 'Were you two something together in the war?'

'No, I only met her once. She drove me somewhere. Nothing happened.'

'Coulda fooled me. It's the first time I've ever seen her embarrassed about a man.'

'Maybe it was the shirt. I look like a bloody Arab in this.'

'Try again, Charlie. Dolly's seen men in their shirt tails before.'

She boiled us a couple of precious eggs and fried old bread in dripping. It was a delicious breakfast, of course, although we didn't say much. She did ask me what I wanted to do when I got out.

'I always wanted to emigrate. To Australia. Do you think they'd have me?'

'I already told you: you *think* like an Aussie, so you must be in with half a chance. What are you any good at?'

'Nothing much. Radio operator.'

'You could always try the Flying Doctor service; you never know.'

'I rather fancied being a sports journalist.'

'What for? Most of the bastards over there can't read.' That put an end to it, really.

I had a proper stand-up wash in the girls' tiny bathroom and was on the street half an hour later. Den had offered me a razor they kept for visitors, but I hadn't needed to shave since my face was singed in that air crash in 1944.

The rest of London was rushing to work. The sun was shining, and they hadn't noticed it. I felt pretty pleased with myself. Den had been the first woman I had been with for at least a year. I wondered if she'd noticed anything and decided I didn't care if she had. I still felt as if I'd behaved like a bit of a shit. I decided that I didn't care about that, either.

4. *Everybody Loves My Baby*

I rode the platform of a tram to Covent Garden, and found a pub open for the market workers. At mid-morning I moved on to Kentish Town, and from there hoofed it back to Highgate in a good frame of mind. I needn't have bothered.

Les was sitting in one of the old Chesterfield chairs in the house's small bar, smoking one of his infernal roll-ups and sipping a Worthington IPA from a bottle. There were four dog-ends in the glass ashtray on the chair arm, and an empty beer bottle alongside him. He had the *Daily Mirror* opened at the strip cartoons page. Jane had lost her knickers again, and her little dog Fritz was taking in the view. I always liked that dog.

'I didn't know that you needed glasses,' I told him. 'When did you start them?'

'Yesterday. All they do is make the print bigger. I could still read it all right when it was smaller. I went to the eye hospital because I woke up from a nap last week and my vision was blurred. First time it 'appened.'

'Probably all that wine we drank in Italy.'

'Could be.'

I could see that he was worried about something else, so I gave him another opening.

'What tobacco do you put in those things, now that we're home again?'

'Ringers. Why?'

'Just asking. Waiting to find out what you really want.'

'Stan says that you haven't been demobbed; that you're going back to the RAF . . .'

'That's right. They want me to hang around for a few months until they've trained a few more radio ops. I was bloody wild at first, but then I thought that it would give me few months to sort myself out.'

'Not still going Down Under, then?' I could sense him getting closer to whatever it was.

'I haven't given up on that altogether yet. I met a girl who says she can get me a passage for ten quid, but I'm not sure I believe her.'

'Maybe she just wants shot of you. What about your kids?'

Bugger!

'Christ, Les. I'd forgotten them.' There was a big gap in the conversation.

'Good job I'm here askin', then, isn't it? You know, a lot of people wouldn't believe you, but I know you better than that. You got the sort of mind that forgets people when you're not with them, don't you?'

'Yes. I didn't think you noticed.'

'Why don't you pour yourself a decent drink, Charlie? We got some serious talking to do.'

I never had an elder brother: if I had I suppose that he might have been like Les. It took a couple of hours, and I was a bit crocked before we finished. Les completed it with a summing-up, like a judge at the Bailey.

'Either you got to be a decent father to those kids, Charlie, or you got to get outta the way an' let someone else do it. An' the Major's making a fair stab at it so far. What's more, he's getting on well with Maggs – I was there in Paris in '44 when they first took a shine to each other, remember. The sea air's doing her wonders – she looks ten years younger.'

'I thought that she was supposed to be with his cousin?' Les's Major England had a German cousin who had been removed to Britain at the end of the war. Maggs had been his mistress in Paris before it was liberated.

'The cousin was married, wasn't he?' Les reminded me. 'The Major *isn't*. Kings over tens.'

'So you think that I should step back, and let Maggs, the Major and the boys play happy families?'

'Unless you got strong feelings about it, yes . . . an' I don't think you have. In fact I don't think you have strong feelings about anything much, have you? Did you ever?'

'Yes, Les. I did.'

'Where'd you leave them?'

'In Grace's pocket. She took them when she left.'

'You're fucking pathetic.' That was the worse thing that Les ever said about anyone. Then he asked, 'So why didn't you go to see her for a last try before we left Siena?'

'I was tired of being pathetic.'

'Thank Christ for that. Maybe there's hope for you yet.'

We agreed that Les would take the Singer, drive down to the

Major's place on the South Coast the next day, and negotiate the details. He'd get the Major to open a drawing account into which I could pay a chunk of the boys' keep. Les asked me if I wanted to go with him . . . *see the kids* was how he put it. I suddenly pictured their faces: Dieter would be seven now . . . and Grace's son Carlo – he'd be nearly three, I supposed. In my mind both boys wore expressions of reproach and regret and, selfishly, I didn't want to face that. I'd promised Dieter a father, and hadn't been one. Anyway: I told Les no, he could make the trip without me. He looked away for a moment, as if he was disappointed. Bad one, Charlie. Les was always the responsible one.

His dark mood lifted after that, and we went over to the Hollybush to get really sauced. The only other reference he made to the children during the evening was oblique. He said, 'If ever you have proper kids of your own, Charlie, you'll 'ave to do better than this.' I couldn't trust myself to reply, so I just lifted my glass to him. It was my turn to look away.

Stan shouted up the internal staircase to tell me that there was a telephone call for me. It was Piers Fortingale. He said that my plans had changed. That didn't surprise me – in my limited experience, planning was never an Armed Services strong point. Apparently they wanted to test my abilities before posting me, so he asked if I could find my way to somewhere in West London without getting lost.

'I'll try . . . where?'

'RAF Eastcote. That's near Ruislip: it used to call itself the Government Code and Cipher School, now it's just a government communications HQ. You can either use the Tube, or get a bus from Archway Road. Even you should be able to find Archway Road without getting lost, it's barely five minutes' walk for you.'

I wondered where this new-found distrust of my navigation skills had come from. Maybe it was how they had squared my service record – I hadn't been AWOL in Europe for a couple of years: merely lost.

'When?'

'Tomorrow. Ten-thirty. Go to the entrance in Lime Grove near the television place. Have you seen television yet?'

'Only in a shop window.'

'My aunt just gave me one for my thirty-fifth birthday, made by Puratone. Useless piece of junk. They'll never catch on.'

'I'll take your word for it. What are these people going to check out?'

'Your radio skills. Morse – that sort of thing.'

'I could do that anywhere.'

'These people are good. Trust me, Charlie.'

Why the hell should I? So much for the rest of my leave.

What seemed odd to me was that there was a television set standing in the reception area of RAF Eastcote. And simple lounge chairs. Maybe I'd walked into a private clinic by mistake. And then there were those guys in brown or blue warehouse coats, flapping around the corridors like dull-coloured birds – it was more like a laboratory complex than an RAF station. The security was old-style RAF, though – a desk run by a gigantic Warrant Officer policeman who took about four minutes to notice me: the sort of thing that happens to you at an unfriendly bar. I paid him back by delaying my salute until he looked. Then I threw him a sloppy one.

'Call that a bloody salute, airman?' he snarled. He examined my pay book as if it was evidence, consulted half a dozen ledgers, and made a couple of telephone calls. It didn't make any difference; I was still expected, and there was nothing he could do about it, but he tried again. 'Where did you learn to salute like that?'

'Over Germany in a Lancaster, WO, whilst you were chatting up the grass widows at Victory Corner.' There were three other-rankers beside the WO behind his imposing desk: they froze. They smiled, but they froze. Before he could come over the desk at me, I was rescued by a small white warehouse coat wearing a pass that read *Dr Junor*, but the WO hadn't quite finished with me. He grinned and said, 'Wotcha, Charlie, you look a fucking sight. Three years ago I would have broken you for being dressed like that.' And he stuck his meaty hand out.

'Hello, Alex. When did they make you an officer?' This was God's week for teaching me that it's a small world after all; I knew the man from my first operational station. He was almost a friend. Shaking his hand had always been like trying to do one-arm press-ups.

'When the rest of you were demobbed. It's not a real promotion. They just messed around with what work was going to be done by which rank, and you followed the job you were doing at the time. When my work moved onto the warrant officer rung, so did I. I didn't complain.'

'Nor would I. I was an officer once, but when I came back they took it away again.'

'When did you come back?'

'About three months ago.'

'A bit late, then?'

'So they tell me. It's a long story.'

Alex laughed loudly. 'As I remember it, most of yours were.'

I didn't qualify for the pass with my name on: Alex kept back my pay book and said I could have it when I left, if I was lucky. Junor had followed the conversation keenly throughout. He was a small man, like me, probably about thirty and as bald as a coot. He had an accent: European.

He gestured for me to follow him. 'You're with me today,' he told me as we walked down one of several parallel corridors, each as long as an aircraft carrier's flight deck. He said, 'Remarkable; I've never seen him smile at anyone.'

'We were on the same station in 1944. Where were you?'

'1944? Peenemunde,' he told me. 'Junor's not my real name.'

I've noticed it for years now – no one seems to use the name they were born with any more. I said, 'I bombed there in '44.'

'Then thank you for not killing me. My room's the next one on our left.'

Junor had a long laboratory with radio sets rigged in tandem and parallel, along a bench that ran along one wall. I recognized the set-up: I had built a smaller version of it for myself when I was flying a bench at Tempsford. Junor made me a cup of Camp coffee, which tasted just like the junk they drank in Germany, sat me at one of the rigs, and took the one alongside me.

When he turned to me his opening gambit, after a smile, was 'Let's just assume that you know your business, Pilot Officer, and that I know *my* business, and get straight on to the difficult material . . .' There was nothing about my decrepit clothing to indicate rank, previous or current, so how much did these bastards know about me? I didn't put him right.

'Bastard' was right. The bastard put me through it. By the end of the day I felt as if my mind, and my hands, had been wrung out and hung up to dry. We stopped near midday to eat in a room that was a mess room for the military and a canteen for the civvies. I was interested to note that the civilian men were outnumbered by young and pretty female counterparts, but I didn't get a peck at any of them because Alex joined me for lunch. Junor left us and sat opposite a very tall, pretty blonde. They laughed a lot, and she stole a couple of surreptitious glances at me. Alex and I brought each other up to date. The only difference was that I believed his stories, whilst he shook his head over mine. Policemen have suspicious minds. I asked him about Eastcote.

'Designed to be a hospital. The government built them all over the place in 1940 – seriously, at least twenty of them. This one was never needed.'

'But it's huge!'

'Standard design: long parallel corridors with opposing wards off each side.'

'I can see that now. Why wasn't it used?'

'Some boffin convinced the government that German bombing was going to create more than two million wounded, so they went on a hospital-building spree. I told you: at least twenty of them. As it was, the casualties were in the high tens of thousands; maybe not even that. This was going to be the new London lunatic asylum for the war-damaged, but they gave it to us instead.' When I looked up, he added, 'Don't say *anything*, Charlie.'

Back in Junor's radio lab I told him, 'That was an exceptionally pretty woman you sat with at dinner time.'

'I thought so too, Charlie. That's why I married her. In the cathedral in Bremen in 1943.'

'I bombed Bremen once, too. I think that the cathedral may have copped it later on.'

'Then thank you for not killing her, also.'

Back in the labs the light was fading when Junor at last let us shut down the rigs. He lit up a cigarette: Woodbines in a dirty green and dirty orange packet. They were ready-made, but almost as small as Les's roll-ups. I filled a pipe. Then I asked him, 'Am I still any good, then?'

'Fishing for compliments, Pilot Officer?' Junor smiled. I didn't answer. He continued, 'Yes. You know that you are still good. But I suppose the real question is, *are you good enough?*' Again he paused, before going on. Then: 'Yes: I shall tell the people at Kingsway that you are good enough.'

Good enough for what? I wondered.

I slept late. Stan woke me. That bloody phone again.

''Ere!' Piers said, trying to sound like Tommy Trinder: it didn't work. 'Who said you could knock off?'

'You. I've got a couple more days.'

'That was when you still had a couple more days, old son; now you haven't. Besides, you're not doing anything.'

'How do you know?' I asked. 'I might have been getting across your Australian bird.'

'Don't think so, old son; she said that you were a mite disappointing.' Cow. 'You can climb back into your pit, though. I just phoned to tell you that you sit your Part Two tomorrow.'

I sighed. 'Where do you want me to go now?'

'Hendon. There's an airfield there. Straight up the A1; you can't miss it.'

'I can if I haven't got a car; I've lent mine to someone else for a couple of days.'

'Damn! Wait one, won't you . . .' There was a clunk as he put the handset down. In the background I could hear *Workers' Playtime* belting out of a radio in his office. Someone was doing 'The music goes round and round'; it was very popular . . . and he must have had the volume racked right up. When Piers picked up the telephone again he said, 'That's fine – I just fixed you a car and a driver; one of mine, in fact. Get in here for ten, OK?'

I agreed – it wasn't like I could really do anything else.

That time I didn't get past the lobby at Kingsway. A copper waved me to a hard seat in a waiting area, after having handed me a small brown envelope. It contained a transport chitty – a small form authorizing me a car and a driver for a period not exceeding twenty-four hours. It was signed by an Air Vice-Marshal. Was that what we paid the bastards for?

I hadn't anticipated Dolly Wayne walking in, but it didn't surprise me that much, either. It was a logical development. We walked down a wide internal stairway that led to a car park, without saying much. She chose a big brown civilianized Austin. It had been polished until it shone.

She told me, 'It'll take me an hour or so, sir. Bank-holiday traffic.'

'Cut the *sir*, please, Dolly. No need. You outrank me anyway. I didn't know that it was a bank holiday. Which one?'

'You're serious, aren't you?' She stopped the car at the foot of the dark ramp which led up into the daylight, turned to watch my face as she spoke, and brushed a lock of hair from her forehead. 'It's Good Friday. What did they do to you over there?'

'It wasn't what happened over there that was the trouble. It was what happened when I got back: the brass flung me into prison. Can I come and sit in the front?'

'Give me ten minutes to get out of the city first. What did you do?'

'I was late for the ball: late getting back for the end of the war.'

'How late?'

'Coupla years.'

'Golly.'

I must have smiled, and Dolly must have glanced at me in her driving mirror because she asked defensively, 'Are you laughing at me?'

'No. I'm pleased. Pleased that someone can still show surprise without swearing about it, that's all.'

'I can eff and blind if you want me to: I'm getting better at that.'

I suppose that I smiled again.

'No, Dolly. "Golly" will do just fine for me. Thank you.'

*

I was watching Dolly's legs again, and wanting to pull her skirt back to check them out. Bad one, Charlie. Was I wrong, or were skirts already a couple of inches shorter than those that women had been wearing in 1945? I asked her, 'So what's the plan? Nobody briefed me.'

'I drive you to Hendon, and hand you over to a Squadron Leader Rees. He has a patch over one eye, only one hand, and a very fierce manner – but don't let that fool you; he's a pussycat, really. Then I cool my heels in a mess somewhere for a few hours, I suppose, and wait for you to finish.'

'What's he going to do to me?'

'I'm not supposed to know, but if you're the same as a few others who have come this way you'll be doing the same sort of thing you did yesterday, but in an aircraft this time . . . see if you still have the knack.'

'They're going to want me to fly again, then?'

'That I *don't* know, Charlie.'

'Then do we get the rest of the day to ourselves?'

'Not quite. I have to take you to Woolwich Arsenal, and after that I can drive you home.'

'Long day for you.'

'That's another thing that I don't know, Charlie.'

I'd missed something somewhere, hadn't I?

'What does the Arsenal want with me?'

'Uniform, Charlie. They'll give you a new issue. You look like a pirate in that get-up.'

'You like pirates?'

'I was always on Captain Hook's side when I was a girl. Peter Pan behaves like a hysterical old virgin.'

'Is that why you have a soft spot for Squadron Leader Rees?'

She smiled and said, 'You're a sly one, Charlie Bassett.'

I asked her, 'Have you noticed how the world seems to have gone to hell in a bucket, now that all of the pirates have gone? I wouldn't be surprised if it wasn't cause and effect.'

I still had my battered old RAF cap. I slouched back in the seat and tipped it over my eyes – as if I was going to sleep.

Squadron Leader Rees had my RAF file in front of him on his desk. It was a lot thicker than the last time I had seen it. He stood up, and offered me a metallic handshake.

'Welcome home, Charlie.' He was the first person to have said that. For the second time in a couple of weeks I nearly blubbed. Stupid. The effect was spoiled by his eye patch, which was pink and had a livid blue eye painted on it. The original, on the other side of his face, was brown.

He wore a set of very clean white coveralls, with his rank boards on epaulettes on the shoulders. I had never seen that before. There was a similar set over the back of an upright chair in front of me: it had no insignia. On his desk were two shanghaied ammo pouches, a soft cloth flying helmet, and a face mask with the usual attachments for ox and a radio pip. 'I suppose that that damned girl has already told you that I'm a pussycat?'

'If she did, then I didn't hear it, sir.'

'Thought so: minx. What point is there in my looking like Captain Kidd when children like her only find it endearing?' He ploughed on: 'Would you mind getting kitted up sharpish? I'll see you out at the kite, old lad.' It was good to hear that the peacetime service spoke the same lingo as its wartime counterpart. He hefted one of the ammo pouches over his shoulder with his crude metal paw, and grinned. 'Coffee and rock buns; in case we get peckish up there.'

The white one-piece was large enough to wear over all of my clothes except my leather flying jacket, which I reluctantly left in the office. It was also padded. That meant that these people flew high, to where the cold things were.

I've got to tell you about the Lancaster bomber that stood on a pan near the office, because I'd seen prettier. For a start it was silver all over, like a big gleaming sea trout fresh from the water. It had a clear rear gun turret – where my mate Pete used to skulk – but no guns. It had no mid-upper turret, and the front turret and bomb aimer's fishbowl had been faired and painted over. Above and between her shoulders, where the mid-upper should have been, was an elongated bulbous pod, with open ends fore and aft. I've saved the best for last. Sticking out from her nose was a gigantic spike about fifteen feet long. It tapered to a point on which was fitted a sphere the size of a football, like the safety button on the end of a fencing foil. She looked like a Lancaster modified for aerial jousting. Rees or his crew must have had a ghoulish sense of humour, because the name painted in black on her unlovely snout was *Golgotha*.

A tall thin erk, also dressed for flying, walked over to her with me. He also offered me a hand to shake, and said, 'Welcome home, sir; we've heard a bit about you.' I was prepared this time, muttered my thanks, but turned my head away. 'I'm Ernie Ells. The kite-keeper.'

'What's that when it's at home, Ernie? And don't call me *sir*, it gives me the willies. I'm a sergeant again, anyway.'

Ells frowned. 'Oh no; I don't think so, sir. You're definitely an officer. The kite-keeper looks after the aircraft. I get flying pay, but I also run the ground crew . . . an' I'm a civvy, so I get a proper pension at the end of this lot.'

'What is she?'

'Mark ten Lancaster, Mr Bassett. Canadian built.' We were nearly at that small square door in the rear fuselage now.

'I can see that, Ernie. I lived in one like this. I mean, what the hell do you do with her?'

'Testing, sir. Research and development. That's a stretched Rolls-Royce jet engine on her back.'

'What about the awful thing sticking out the front?'

'Counterbalance sir. Stops her from dropping her tail.' Ernie said that with an absolutely straight face, but when he saw my alarmed look and faltering step he added, 'Nah. It's the radar rig. We're testing a forward-looking radar for rockets. We also do some big weather flights: we had over thirty-three thou on her clock once, but the skipper said that she was probably only kidding us on.'

'What are we doing today?'

It was his turn to look startled. 'Radios, sir; isn't that why you're with us?'

I had been right about the black sense of humour. The RAF had always had a penchant for painting instructions on airframes, like *Step here*, or *Don't walk*, or *Rescue here*. Some wag had seen fit to use the same stencil to paint a message over *Golgotha*'s crew door. It read *Abandon hope, all ye who enter here*. As I climbed in and dogged the door shut behind me I couldn't help reflecting that one of my last flights in a four-engined bomber had taken precisely three minutes, and had ended in a spectacular crash from which I'd emerged the only survivor. *Great.*

There were some differences inside. Metal poles dropped vertically through the old mid-upper's space to support the jet pod, and some of the bomb-bay panels had been lifted to reveal new tanks, gauges and pipework. I had to wriggle between the poles to get to the radio and nav stations. There would be no getting out of *Golgotha* in a hurry if things got out of hand. The W/Op's station had grown a bit since my last Lancaster trip. There were the rear-facing sets I knew and loved, on a bulkhead over a narrow table, and my forward-facing chair. What was new was another seat behind that, facing aft, and a bank of electronic equipment big enough to run a squadron on behind that.

The chair was occupied by a slim fair-haired boy; he had a shy smile, and freckles, and looked as if he had stepped from the pages of the *Beano*. 'Welcome home, sir . . . and well done.'

What the fuck was going on here? Ever since the provost on the gate had waved us through without looking for an identity, perfect strangers had been treating me as if they knew me. I nodded as if I knew what they were talking about, and slid into my old seat. It was a tight squeeze. I noticed that both seats had lap straps. That was an improvement on wartime conditions – although there had been straps in my old Lanc, *Tuesday's Child*; but we had filched them from a smashed-up Mosquito.

'What's your name?' I asked him.

'Carrington. Percy. Perce,' We were back-to-back. He had drawn makeshift stripes on the sleeves of his white overall with indelible ink. If he wasn't excessively rank-conscious, it could be that he was the joker in the crew. Come to think of it, apart from the odd 'sir', none of the bods I'd met so far looked all that rank-conscious. That suited me.

'Pleased to meet you, Perce.'

'Likewise, sir.'

He had left my radios dead for me. That was a nice touch, unless he had been told to. They came alive under my hands. It was like undressing an old girlfriend: I didn't even have to think about it. I had this self-image of the great cynic to hold on to, but it didn't do any good: when I heard the static buzz, a lump came to my throat. Perce had rotated his chair so that he was looking over my shoulder: that was neat. He had a pad strapped to one knee that had some kind of form on it. He made a note on it as I finished my checks. It felt as if I was doing my training finals all over again, and the stupid thing was that I suddenly cared. I wanted to show the buggers what I could do. Perce nodded.

'Very smart, sir. Very economical. They said that you weren't flashy.'

'Who's "they"?'

'Your original trainers. Didn't you know?'

'No.'

'Probably didn't want to blow you up too much.'

'No, they left that to me, didn't they? We blew up a lot of things all over Germany.'

Perce looked away. He said, 'I was too late for all that. It was all over by the time I reached a squadron.'

'Then go to church on Sunday, and say thank you,' I told him truthfully. 'I can't think of a better war to be too late for.'

He had a soft laugh; like a girl's . . . and it didn't go on. 'You don't mean that, sir.'

I was suddenly irritated by him. I remembered that I had felt like that when I met the new guys coming on the squadron when we were finishing our tour. They seemed clean, untainted, and I hated them for it. Perce coughed, and hid it behind his hand.

'What was it really like, sir?'

'We drank a lot. I remember that. War's very good for drinking.'

'What about the rest?'

'The rest is what I try not to remember. OK?' I said gently.

I hung my earphones around my neck, and banked sharp and low starboard to look forward. Ells was in the navigator's chair but he didn't seem to be doing any navigating. He saw me looking, and nodded. Beyond him I could see the back of someone on the flight engineer's jump seat alongside the pilot. Was that Rees? He was some sort of academic for certain. I could hear the murmur of conversation between pilot and engineer as they pre-flighted her. For a moment they sounded like Grease, my skipper, and Fergal . . . but Grease had gone back to Canada, and Fergal was looking for a different set of wings in his Liverpool church.

I was OK until Rees called to me. *Golgotha* was singing very gently to herself by then; the airframe around us shook almost imperceptibly, like someone in the warm-up stages of an epileptic fit. I always liked that. It was as if the aircraft was actually alive, and talking to you – which was all right as long as she wasn't saying '*I am about to crash and burn*.' Rees clicked back to me. 'OK, Charlie?'

'OK, sir.'

'Call through, please.'

Everyone checked in. Quite like old times. Percy was behind me. He said, 'Powered-up. OK.' When I turned to look at him he mouthed '*Radar*.' It's an easy word to lip-read. I nodded. Ells called over, and waved to me. The engineer called over – but I didn't recognize his voice. Then that left Rees; and that was us. It meant that Rees was flying the bloody thing, of course. That was Rees without an eye: Rees without a hand. I glanced at Ells again. He smiled, and looked unconcerned. I gripped the edge of the small table so that no one could see my hands shaking. That had happened before, too.

Rees saved my blushes. He held *Golgotha* back on the end of the runway, and called me forward. 'Do you want to come up to the office, Charlie? There won't be anything for you to do for a while, and Percy can mind the shop for you.'

As I passed Ells he patted my arm as if I was a good-luck charm, and smiled again. There was something seriously wrong with these people. Once I was standing behind Rees's seat I touched his shoulder to let him know that I was there. I did that out of instinct – it was how I always used to tell Grease. It can't have been that uncommon; Rees didn't even turn his head. He'd had a ring welded to the control-column spade grips – for his fat metal thumb to fit through. That bloody great spar on the aircraft's nose spoiled the view; I could actually see the damned thing bouncing up and down while we waited for clearance from Flying Control. We had to wait for an incoming Halton wearing a curious royal blue and silver civilian livery.

Those people who told you that a Lancaster bomber could be lifted into the air like a sport plane were definitely exaggerating. In truth Lancs were always like ageing long-jumpers with bad knees. They needed a very long run. Rees had her up without a fuss. I liked that. Even the staggered thumps of her undercart pulling into their nacelles behind the inner engines didn't seem as violent as those in my memory.

Golgotha was like Rees: an old smoothie. Like the rest of us he had an old-fashioned cloth helmet, and as soon as he'd pulled us through six thousand feet, switched on the automatic pilot, and dropped his earphones around his neck, he asked me again: 'OK, Charlie?'

'Fine, skipper. Where are we going?'

'Out over Anglesey; off the Bristol Channel. There's a listening station there. You been there before?'

I shook my head.

'First visit for you, then: they say that travel broadens the mind.'

'When do you want me to get down to work?'

'When we get there. I'll tell you. Go and watch Ernie; you'll find it interesting.'

I went back down the step and stood alongside Ells. I had been right the first time. He wasn't navigating: at least, not in any way I'd seen before. There was what looked like another big bank of radios above the old nav table. The most obvious differences from standard receivers were two ally spools, and a thin strip of punched paper rolling from one to the other. It was always noisy down here. I shouted, 'What's that do?'

'Navigate: it tells George where to go.' 'George' was the automatic pilot. *Golgotha* climbed gently to port: she seemed to be looking for a further few hundred feet. I had to hang on to the back of Ells's chair.

Ells shouted, 'We punch the route up on ticker tape while we're at the briefing, still on the ground. Once the skipper passes over an agreed way point at an agreed height, he just flicks on George, and these boxes do the rest.'

'What about the variables? Winds, cloud layers, temperatures and inversions?'

'That's the clever bit. Perce's gizmos are constantly repeating to three remote ground stations, so by triangulating with them we know where we actually are all of the time, as against where we're supposed to be. That means that, as well as the predicted route from the paper strip, small adjustments are being fed into George all the time; that's why her flying is a bit twitchy. Don't worry; you'll get used to it.'

'If the kite has a mind of its own, what do they need us for?'

'To catch her when she drops it.'

Golgotha must have been listening to him: she dropped it immediately. The nose went down, and we lost a couple of hundred feet before Rees hauled it back. The dive threw me to my knees, hanging on to the back of Ells's seat. I gasped, 'What the *hell* was that?'

'Something to do with one of the signals from the ground. We haven't got it fully ironed out yet. Did she scare you?'

'*Everything* about her scares me.'

Golgotha eventually put us into a broad circuit above Filton airfield, and waited for Rees to get his hands back on her. She'd only tried to kill us another two times. Perce said that she was having a particularly benign day: I'm glad that I hadn't met her on a bad one. As Rees set out over the Bristol Channel he ordered me back to my seat and put me to work. Perce looked over my shoulder the whole time, and scored my performance on that pad strapped to his knee. There was a female ground operator at Filton who sounded sweet but browned off, and a keen young RN W/Op in the back of a Yeovilton Firefly that climbed into formation alongside us. He used fourteen words whenever he needed four. He sent fast, clean Morse, though: had I been like that once? I didn't miss a letter. Perce lifted one of my earphones and asked, 'What do you think?'

'Wanker,' I replied gruffly.

Perce nodded and smiled. 'Fleet Air Arm,' he said, as if that explained it. Then he said, 'Full marks so far, sir. You haven't lost your touch, have you?' Patronizing little git.

Rees turned west, and started boring out to sea. A few miles beyond Anglesey, which was greener than I'd imagined, over a sea which was bluer than I'd imagined, he started to fly square searches, as if he was looking for something. I was back up with him by then. There was a spare set of headphones with a jack point behind me. One of the odd things about *Golgotha* was the number of jacks – they seemed to appear every few feet. Rees was searching for a signal, it turned out. I listened with him. Eventually I heard it; or *them*, rather. Two Morse operators hammering away at each other out at the edge of our range. The signal drifted a bit. They weren't all that fast; just good and solid.

A couple of men who weren't willing to sacrifice accuracy for speed. Not that it meant much to me: it was all encrypted stuff. Rees turned briefly to look at me, and put his thumb up. We trailed up and down for a few minutes, eavesdropping on absolute rubbish, and then Rees pointed the plane's lance at land again and let *Golgotha* take over. He asked, 'What did you make of that?'

'Old stuff. Some of the signalling protocol was, well . . . anachronistic, I suppose you'd say, sir. Who *was* that, sir? Who were we listening to?'

'Couple of Jedburghs; maybe even yours. They were either in the South of France, or Germany. You realized they were right on the edge of our range?'

'Who's Jedburgh?'

'Didn't they tell you yet?'

'No, they bloody didn't . . . sir.'

'Then neither shall I.'

I tried him a couple more times during the remainder of the trip, but he wouldn't budge. Thought it was funny, too. Bastard. There was nothing for me to do on the return trip except feel a bit airsick. I had imagined that I had got over that during my early aircrew training in 1943, but there was something about the way *Golgotha* flew herself that disagreed with my stomach. I think that it was all of those niggling little changes of height and direction she made, in response to messages from Perce's magic boxes. All in all I preferred a human being to be doing the flying; even those who weren't much good at it, although my flying career so far had included far too many of *them*. I had a mug of coffee, which was its usual awful self, and sucked one of my rock buns. I reckoned that they were probably issued to airmen for use as weapons if they survived being shot down. We broke from cloud about ten miles west of London, and flew into hard sunlight. That was almost like a metaphor for the times: the war had finished, but some of the things that peace could do were enough to make your eyes water.

As I walked away from the Lancaster I noticed for the first time that on the other side of her nose from her name there was a row of mission credits painted up, also in black. *Golgotha* was an old lady. I counted twelve small bombs and a small aircraft silhouette. Twelve bombing missions and an enemy aircraft claimed. Underneath them was a longer row of smaller symbols. I stood on tiptoe to make them out. They were tiny black crucifixes, shaped like those handed out in Sunday school on Palm Sunday. There must have been more than thirty of them. I suppose they went with her name.

I pointed them out to Ells. 'What are they? The number of church parades she attended?' I asked.

'No, Mr Bassett. Her previous pilot, Mr Whittaker, took a very religious turn after the war. He named her, of course, and every testing flight she made earned her another cross. It was a bit creepy.'

'I'll say. What happened to *him*? Funny farm?'

'Nah. He walked into her propellers one morning, when we were ground running the engines. I still think that it was deliberate. We found his head half a mile away.'

'Good head, was it?'

'As far as heads go, yes, sir, I'd say it was a good head. We buried it with his legs. Most of the rest of him had blown away on the wind. 'S funny – if you thinks about it, there's still loads of him around here somewhere; probably fertilizing the grass.'

'Would he have minded that?'

'I don't know, sir. He was very High Church; *very*. We stopped painting the crosses after that. Enough was enough.'

It was a good Easter story. I wasn't sure that Ells wasn't having me on. I had known a Whittaker once. He'd been shot down over Holland, and had successfully baled out. *That* was what I called a miracle. He was one of the good guys: he couldn't have been the same man.

Perce sidled up. I didn't know that men as tall as that could sidle. He was just as shy on the ground as in the air, but he asked, 'Would you care to join us for a drink before you go back to London, sir? Because we are partly a civvy establishment there's a super mixed bar that opens when flying is over for the day. Everybody's keen to meet you.'

I'd been right first time: there was something the matter with this lot. Maybe they should go to the zoo more often, I thought.

'Can I bring my driver?'

'She'd be welcome too, sir. I'd be proud to sign you in. Just over there.' He indicated a red brick building with a pre-war look about it.

Golgotha's engines powered down one after another, and her great paddles ground to a stop. A small Bedford truck swung out from a hangar: that would be her ground crew coming to put her to bed.

'Go on ahead, then. I'll just speak to my driver and follow you.'

I went back to Rees's office first. I recovered my old jacket, and left him the white coveralls, hoping never to see them again. I had just discovered something: I didn't like flying. I wondered if I ever had.

Dolly was asleep in the back seat of the Austin. At least she was alone. I walked slowly from the car to the bar, with Dolly alongside me. She paced with her hands crossed behind her back. In her tailored uniform, with her cap tipped slightly to one side, she looked quite the thing. I walked slowly because I wanted to talk.

'There's something odd going on here, Dolly; these people are all talking to me as if they know me.'

'Ah. I wondered if that would happen.'

'Wondered what?'

'If you knew about *The Pink Pole*.'

'You mean Pete?' I asked with confusion. 'He was our rear-gunner; of course I know about him. We called him the Pink Pole because he wasn't a Red. Some of the other Poles were Reds.'

Dolly looked at me. No, she didn't smile.

'Charlie, *The Pink Pole* is also the name of a book that came out a few days ago. There was even a story about it in the newspaper – the *Daily Express*, I think. Your friend Pete has written a book, or someone over here has written it for him: I'm not sure which. Ever since *Enemy Coast Ahead* everyone's writing their war story; haven't you noticed? He's published it without permission, and caused a bit of a kerfuffle.'

That made me grin. I liked the idea of Pete still causing kerfuffles, and I liked the words that Dolly used.

'He probably couldn't work out whose permission to ask. He

changed services at least twice, maybe three times . . . and ended up in the Polish army, I think,' I told her. 'Good old Pete. What's he say in his book?'

'Not much that anybody didn't know; but maybe too much about you. Apart from writing about flying with you, there's a story about meeting you in Holland after your tour, where you were on a mission of some sort and won a French medal for bravery. Then you saved the lives of hundreds of German civilians trapped in a cellar, and liberated a hospital. Bremen, he says. Do you *feel* like a hero?' Then she added 'sir', just in case I replied yes.

I stopped. Dolly stopped.

'That's bollocks,' I said. Dolly looked down. She had pretty feet, in fashionable not-quite-WAAF black shoes. Even so, I didn't know what she found so fascinating about them. She didn't say anything, so I explained. 'None of it happened that way. It's complete bollocks.'

'I suspected that. Most of these stories usually are, but I don't think that you will be able to do anything about it now.'

The small serving-bar was an atoll in a pitching sea of bodies, many of whom carried that indefinable niff of aeroplane. As we pushed into the room Dolly had to hold on to my sleeve at the elbow in order not to become separated. I liked that. Rees greeted me: 'Ah; Aircraftman Shaw.' That meant nothing to me. It was probably something amusing in his circle. He pulled us into the crowd, where I came up against Dr Junor with drinks for us in his hands. He greeted me with, 'Well done, Mr Bassett. It is often the way.'

'Cheers. What is?'

'People who talk freely about killing Germans turn out to be those who actually saved some. Well done.' Bollocks.

Party. If anyone ever asks me what the RAF is good at, I will think for a long time, and eventually answer with the word *party*. An hour or so later I was halfway to getting crocked. Dolly Wayne got into the swing of things, and circulated: it was second nature to wartime WAAFs. They were used to roomfuls of women-starved men. Eventually we backed into each other, like strangers. I turned and asked, 'What about the Woolwich Arsenal?'

'They'll probably keep it open for you; enjoy this while you can.'

That night we slept at Hendon. In separate beds. In separate rooms. In separate bloody blocks. The RAF hadn't changed *that* much.

In the morning Rees came to see us away. His one eye looked horribly bloodshot. It was also twenty degrees off centre, and rolled horribly. Who had certified him fit for flying? He asked, 'You got my drift yesterday, when I playfully called you "Shaw"? Mean of me, by the way. Sorry.'

'No, Squadron Leader, I didn't.'

'T. E. Lawrence. Of Arabia fame, and all that. He joined the RAF as Aircraftman Shaw in order to get away from all of the fuss. That was his excuse, anyway. Foreigners gave him medals too, I think.'

'I still don't understand.'

'Trying to tell you to keep your head down, old son; the RAF and the Army don't like odd bods like you . . . never really liked *him* either, you see; shafted him in the end. Bye.'

In the car I asked Dolly, 'Do you know what all that was about?'

'Yes, but I'm not going to tell you. It's one of those things that are better for you to work out for yourself.'

'Has Pete dropped me in the shit?'

'The better I know you, Charlie, the more I believe that you were never out of it. In your whole life, probably.'

When we hit the London suburbs and headed for the Woolwich Arsenal she stopped the car and made me get into the back. She also started calling me 'sir', again. I'd already had the car for longer than the twenty-four hours it had been signed out for. I wondered if Dolly would get into trouble. Maybe she'd spent her life deep in it, too.

I should have credited her with more savvy. She'd phoned Piers before the party really took off. At Woolwich Arsenal I was whisked from one low red-brick building to the next, and re-issued with a uniform which was folded into large cardboard boxes.

It started with more shirts than I'd ever owned at one time in my life. Dolly followed me around with the car. We filled its back seat, and the boot. A thin old man with wings of silver hair and a shiny pate wouldn't issue me with boots or shoes until he had measured my feet about eight different ways. I was embarrassed because I hadn't washed them for a couple of days . . . but he didn't seem to notice. I hadn't realized that the Arsenal covered so much ground: acres and acres of it inside a high periphery wall, just like a dockyard.

'I'm 'onoured to have met you, Mr Bassett,' the old boy said as he finished giving me my clothes. 'The missus will be chuffed when I tell her.'

Somewhere in the background Dolly sniggered, and covered it with a little cough. They let me go after I'd signed for enough uniform to clothe a small squadron. As a sergeant I'd had to make do on less than half of that issue, and even then some had been falling to bits before I signed for it. That was when it hit me. The bastards had promoted me back again. I suppose that I had Pete to thank for that. Bollocks. Double bollocks.

I tried my luck with Dolly on the way home. We were chuntering away about some inconsequential nonsense, the way a man and a woman do when they're sizing each other up, when I put my hand on her knee and carried on talking as if nothing was happening. Bloody childish. She also carried on talking as if nothing was happening, but just as deliberately lifted my paw and dropped it back in my lap. Nothing doing, Charlie. She helped me out with my luggage, but only as far as the tiled Victorian hallway of the Highgate house; the rest was up to me. I opened my mouth to say sorry, when she beat me to the draw with 'Would you like to come to church with me tomorrow?'

'Give thanks for my deliverance?'

'That too; if you like.'

'If you like.'

'You're repeating me.'

'No: I'm replying to you. It means yes, please, and I'm sorry that I put my hand on your knee.'

'Oh. I see. Good . . . and I'm not, by the way – sorry, that is.'

'For what?'

'That you put your hand on my knee. My place at ten-thirty tomorrow. We can walk.'

'Uniform?'

'Definitely. Number ones. We'll have to see if we can scrounge some coupons and get you a few civvies next week. You look a bit like a rubble rat in that lot: I don't want to go out with a man that the police are always stopping.' I realized that there was still a lot to learn . . . about England, and the way that women thought.

'What are "rubble rats"?'

'The people who still live in the shelters, and in the cellars on the bomb sites: they're also squatting in unoccupied houses, and unused Tube stations. The *Sketch* said that there are nearly a hundred thousand of them in London alone.'

'That can't be right; but I've seen the soldiers and their families you see begging on the streets.'

'Yes, those – and deserters and criminals.'

'People like me, you mean?'

'No, Charlie. Not people like you. They'd never come to church on Sunday.'

'Have you ever asked them?'

Dolly bit her lip, as if a thought had suddenly occurred to her, then said, 'No . . .'bye, Charlie,' spun on her heels, and headed down the steps to the car.

She'd won this set whilst I didn't even know what game we were playing. She made a mess with the clutch, and ground the gears. After that I started to feel pleased with myself again.

*

After I lugged the kit up to my room and laid out my number ones for Sunday, I went downstairs, collected Stan and his boy, along with a few bottles of beer and lemonade, and crossed the road to Highgate Woods. We watched the cricket for a couple of hours. One of the teams had a black player who reminded me of my dead friend Francie. This guy must have been nearly seven feet tall, and bowled like a demon. When I thought about Francie I wondered why I always recalled him as my *friend*, when the truth was that I hardly knew him: all I remembered about him now was how the English used to make him laugh, and how he'd made *me* laugh. Behind the house I saw that my car was standing outside the garage doors. Les hadn't left a message. I was probably still in his bad books.

I didn't see the match out. The local Calton Cricket Club was fielding against a Joint Services Eleven when I left. One of the slip fielders had only one arm, and leaped around like a one-armed grasshopper. If he'd have had two he would have been good enough for the MCC. Stan's wife crossed the road to fetch me: a policeman had called, she said. He wanted me to return his telephone call. There was no doubt about it: the telephone was here to stay.

This one was in the lower hall: I dialled the number that Stan's wife had been given, and a big voice answered, 'Station Officer. Hornsey Police Station.'

I asked for the policeman who had left me a message.

'Sergeant Southwell speaking.'

'You asked someone to tell me to call you. My name is Bassett.'

'Pilot Officer Bassett?'

'That's right. Is there a problem?'

'Not for you, sir, no. Do you know a Mr Paul Fortingale?'

'I know a *Piers* Fortingale.'

'Can you wait a moment, sir?' There was a clunk. The sergeant had put the telephone handset down. In the foreground I could hear a rustling of papers, and in the background a mutter of voices. When he came back he said, 'That's right, sir. He says that you would know him by that name. He says you work with him and will vouch for him.'

'What does that mean?'

'I can't release him until someone vouches for his good name: he gave us yours.'

'Bugger him.'

'An apt phrase, sir, under the circumstances. Could you come by the police station for him?' I wasn't that keen; the last time I'd walked into a police station I had walked out again in handcuffs, remember? The problem was that Piers was nominally my boss, I supposed, until I reported to a new station.

'Where is it – this police station?'

Southwell gave me simple directions, slowly, and using small words. Policemen get very good at that.

London is made of brick. I've never understood the Victorian and Edwardian love affair with the humble brick. Maybe they just over-invested in the LBC – that's the old London Brick Company. On the ten-minute drive I passed eight different bombsites. I found myself counting them. On each the bricks had been collected, cleaned and stacked; ready for reuse. The houses had gone, and the people had gone, but the bricks went on for ever. There was a bay in the pavement outside Hornsey's brick police station long enough for two cars. I slotted the Singer in behind a tired-looking Wolsley police car.

Southwell was one of those men who sound like they look; and also sound like their given name. If you'd met him in civvies you'd have taken him for a working farmer. He asked, 'Mr Bassett?'

They must have been having a slow afternoon.

Then he said, 'Sorry to break into your Saturday.'

'That's OK. What's happened to Piers?'

'He was detained on the Heath, sir. Coming out of the bushes with another gentleman.'

A couple of years earlier I would have blushed.

'Is that all? What did he say?'

Southwell looked at his notebook. 'That they were looking for his pocket watch. He said he lost it around there a few days ago, and his companion had offered to help him find it.'

'Are you satisfied with his explanation?'

'Frankly, *no*, sir. They said they didn't even know each other's names. Unfortunately your friend has been cautioned in similar circumstances before, but if you'll vouch for him I'll let him go again this time – being a civil servant has got to count for something – as long as he realizes this is his last caution. Next time he'll be nicked.'

'I understand. I'm also sure that Mr Fortingale will understand. He's not stupid; he wouldn't want to put his career in jeopardy.'

'I'll take your word for it, sir, if you'd just identify him.'

The sergeant took me downstairs to the cells, which gave me a bit of a turn. The heavy scent of disinfecting Lysol in the air was still too familiar to me. The cells had old-fashioned open-barred doors, like animal cages. Piers's face wore a sulky look. He didn't say anything, so I told Southwell that I recognized him.

'Fine, sir . . . just some papers for you, and we'll have him out in a jiffy.'

'What about the other man?'

'A Dr Junor, sir: a foreign gentleman. He has a diplomatic passport; we had to let him proceed.' You should have seen my face.

I had two forms to sign. I didn't like the second one: it made me legally responsible for Piers's good behaviour for thirty days.

Outside, I waited in the car. Piers was another ten minutes. When he came out he was carrying his tie – RAF, of course – belt and shoelaces in one hand. He slid into the passenger seat and said, 'Not a *fucking* word, Charlie. Not *one*.'

'OK. Where to?'

'That's two.'

'You can always walk,' I told him.

'Bugger you.'

'The copper told me that that seems to be the problem.'

I drove him over to the Bull and Bush on the other side of the Heath. He said that some people he knew were usually there. There were several bars; I was relieved that they were all empty. We sat outside and drank warm and watery bitter. The sun was beginning to go down, and it was too early in the year for there not to be a nip in the air – you'll have heard the old Pearl Harbor joke, so I won't repeat it. Piers went for another round. I was oddly relaxed. I felt as if my body was expanding; settling down.

By the time Piers re-emerged with a couple of pints I had got my pipe going. He said, 'What are you looking so goddamned pleased about?'

'Want a truthful answer?'

'Why not?' He lit a fag from a fancy packet; probably American.

'For the first time in years I feel as if I'm more or less in control of my life. I know the RAF still has its hooks into me for a few months, but anyway, that's what it feels like.' I tailed off; a little lamely, I thought.

Piers surprised me because I expected a smart return of serve from him – that was his way – but instead he said, rather wistfully, 'That must be a good feeling.'

'Tell me about Piers and Paul.'

'Mind your own damned business,' Piers snarled at me aggressively.

'I've just got you out of a police cell, Piers. I'm entitled to a few answers.'

It was nice for the boot to be on the other foot for a change. He paused and thought about it. He eventually said, 'Yes; I suppose so. No mystery. My family named me Paul. I thought that Piers was more romantic, so I changed it, but not officially.'

'You know, I didn't think that you were a pansy when I met you. I thought it was all an act.'

'Maybe it is.'

'I don't understand that.'

He sighed. My Latin teacher used to sigh like that whenever I handed a translation to him. Exasperated. 'Look, Charlie. Can't we just say that I may be not quite as discriminating as the next man, and leave it at that?'

'What about Dr Junor?'

'I meet him for a drink now and again. He's an interesting man. Now: I told you – change the subject.'

'To what?'

'Anyone spoken to you about the rubble rats?'

'I've heard the phrase a couple of times. Homeless people.'

'That's a generous description, Charlie. It's an organized unwashed and unscrupulous army of scum – the *untermenschen*. They have occupied great chunks of London. Mr Attlee is frightened that it could bring his government down.'

'Don't be daft.'

'I'm serious. They just move into empty houses or office blocks and camp there.'

'*Are* they organized?'

'They're run by the CP – the Communist Party: our friendly social democrats. They deny it, of course. Their aim is to destabilize the LCC, and then the rest of the country, into voting in a Communist administration that we'd never get rid of. The point of democratic socialism is that it never *is* democratic. Someone mentioned that moving in with them for a few weeks, and feeding us information back could be just up your street . . .'

I made a production of filling and lighting my pipe again. 'Not a bloody chance, Piers.'

'What if I ordered you to?'

'Instead of sending me back to jail? I fell for that line a couple of years ago, and look where it got me. No, I'd ask you to put the orders in writing and get them signed by an Air Vice-Marshal. I don't think you'll do that.' I only stuck the word *vice* in to needle him.

He gave me the little-boy smile. 'No . . . I suppose not.'

I could have also counter-threatened to talk about his romps in the bushes to the *News of the World*. But instinct told me that might be a dangerous thing to do.

So I offered him a compromise. 'Look; I'll go to this radio research unit in Cheltenham that you mentioned, and serve out my six months.'

'Then what?'

'If you let me go, I'll get a proper job, I suppose. When do I report?'

'You got green lights from your examiners, so I suppose you could travel on Tuesday and report on Wednesday. That OK?'

'Fine.'

'You got your car back?'

'Yes. Why?'

'It's nice country up there; you could tour a bit on your days off. Drink cider and sing folk songs. Marry a girl with a moustache, and grow cabbages. You won't like it, you know. It's not like the services up there: they've slipped off the edge of the world – it's *Ultima Thule*. Anyway, sod off now, and leave me to my peers.'

'But there's no one here.'

He looked at me and shook his head as if he was dealing with an idiot. He was. *Pun*.

*

I have to admit that I felt well set up in an officer's number one uniform. I topped it off with my old cap, so I looked quite the battle veteran. Dolly was in her number ones as well, and I remembered her distant floral perfume. The church was the Church of Scotland in Pont Street, and the walk, under glowering skies, took us twenty minutes. Dolly had a powerful marching pace; like a Girl Guide leader. She took my hand and held it as we filed through the door, straight off the street. It was roomier than it looked, and if we were twenty minutes early we needed them if we wanted to get a seat.

By the time the mad minister appeared in the pulpit, apparently by an act of levitation, it was standing room only. The hymns were the old ones. I hummed along with them, the congregation bellowed like buffaloes a-wallowing, and I could hear Dolly's voice rising above it all, like an angel. Dolly whispered that the minister was a visiting itinerant. All I can remember about his Easter sermon was the usual guff about sacrifice, and brotherly love, which he said should be offered to all human beings, except the communists. He obviously wasn't all that keen on an understanding with the godless Reds: they featured in his splutterings several times. While I had been away people seemed to have forgotten that they were once our friends and allies.

I was glad that we weren't in the front pews, because the perspiration flicking from the minister's brow as his head moved fell over them like a gentle shower. The congregation seemed to hang on his words, and I half expected a round of applause for his effort. I looked around: some of the folk, particularly the women, had rapt expressions on their faces, and looked ready to go out to fight the foe. Was I the last man left in England who thought that Europe had had quite enough of that for the time being?

Back at the flat Dolly made me a cup of tea, and I was sipping it when Denys trailed in from her room still wrapped in her bed sheet. She was followed by a tousled man in his shirt tails, the way I had been a few days earlier. The shirt was an odd minty-green colour. He had a friendly smile, curiously hairless bowed legs and a soft voice. He introduced himself as Stephen, the landlord and dentist.

'Any of that tea left?'

I reckoned that Stephen was about twenty-four or twenty-five, and he looked soft. I suppose that he'd had a tough war learning how to be a dentist. I made one-off judgements about people all the time in the 1940s: it's more difficult now.

While Dolly was fussing over his cup of tea he asked her, 'Doing anything tonight, love? I was introduced to a nice Rhoesian ridgeback yesterday. An artillery major, actually. He's looking for a nice bit of sophisticated company.'

'What kind?'

'Pretty girl, theatre and dinner. That sort. I can't ask Den; Ike's back in town, and wants her.'

Everybody deliberately didn't look at me; I was sure of it. Pause. Then Dolly murmured, 'Love to. Tell him to pick me up at seven, if that fits in.'

'Sure it will, love.' Then Stephen could look at me again. 'Why don't we get dressed and all go up for a spot of lunch? There's a nice new pub near Fulham – the Martyred Minnow or something like that. It was built on a site thoughtfully cleared by a doodlebug. There used to be a school there.'

'The New Mitre,' Dolly told him. 'I don't want to be back too late tonight, in case Piers wants me to work. It should be a day off, but with him you never know.'

I privately agreed with her; with Piers you never knew.

'That will be OK,' Stephen said. 'I'll phone him and fix it: he must owe you an hour or two.'

These people were as far up each other's backsides as circuit judges, I thought. My old man wouldn't have liked my thinking that: he was very mysterious about his membership of another brotherhood altogether. Stephen was an odious little shit, and I had already decided to cut it short and get away as quickly as I could. One of my dad's rules was *Whenever you find yourself out of your depth, get back to the shallows as fast as you damned well can.* With these slippery people I was out of my depth. Time to swim for it, Charlie.

PART TWO

Beauty and the Beast

5. *Reckless Blues*

There was a fundamental difference between the country I left behind in 1945 and the one I returned to in 1947 . . . and it's not one of those that you've already thought of. It was the bloody weather. In 1944 and 1945 rain followed me around the country like a homing pigeon streaking for its loft: it never missed. Maybe God had been trying to find out just how wet a human being would have to be kept before he started to shrink. However, after prison, wherever I went the sun seemed to shine.

I took my time meandering the Singer up to Cheltenham with the lid off the car, between a couple of decent beer stops on the way. I thought a couple of pints always improved my driving.

I had been given a number for my new station, to telephone before I arrived. I called it from a public phone box on the other side of Oxford – I didn't know what was on the end of the number. I presumed that it was the guardroom, but it could have been the group captain's mistress for all I knew. Not a bad guess, because it was a woman who answered the telephone. She asked me to hang on, and I had to punch more money into the slot. Then a man's voice spoke. Deep voice; Home Counties.

'Hello, old boy.' RAF. Definitely. 'Wasn't expecting you until Wednesday.'

'I thought I'd better tell you that I was in the area, sir.'

'Good thinking. Fancy a beer later on?'

'Thank you, sir.'

'Stop when you get to the Lamb Inn at Great Rissington: it's not far off your track. Book in for the night; there's nothing ready for you here yet, but I'll join you for a drink if that's OK and give you an early hello. Useful, really.'

Adjutant, I thought. Passed-over flight lieutenant and all-round Mr Fixit. One of the sad old guys.

There was a pre-war AA atlas in one of the Singer's door pockets: lodged there with a packet of johnnies by a previous owner. I'm good with maps and Great Rissington is a long enough name not to be easily overlooked – so I drove into the pub car park in the last of the afternoon sunshine, parked up, tipped my cap over my eyes, and snoozed until opening time. Even without a girl on your arm, or a drink in your hand, life doesn't get much easier than that.

The big man walked in at about seven, just after I had pushed my dinner plate away. A decent slice of gammon, broad beans – probably last year's stored under brine – and floury potatoes. I hadn't tasted gammon since before the war, and blessed the pig that had lost it. I should have said that the big man *rolled* in, because he had a rolling gait like a sailor's. Tall, heavily built, ruddy complexion and stiff brown hair which stood up from his head. Maybe he was forty. He wore a brown tweed jacket, brown trousers and a silk cravat. He looked more like the lord of the manor than the lord of *my* manor, but his voice was unmistakable when he fitted himself into the other chair at my table.

'Mr Bassett. I'm Watson, David Watson: your new boss. Welcome to peacetime Gloucestershire.'

'Charlie, sir, if that's all right with you. What's Gloucestershire *like* in peacetime?'

'Nice pubs, if you like pubs, but you'll find most of the girls are spoken for . . . otherwise it's just bloody dangerous.'

'Why?'

'CFS – Central Flying School. Just around the corner at Little Riss. They drop more aircraft around the county than Jerry ever did. Five last month – seven bods killed, including two passers-by.'

'Will that concern me much, sir?'

'No. Just duck if anything you hear gets too close. Although we park our communications flight up here, that's an old Hudson – so you might be up here now and again.'

He held up two fingers, Churchill fashion, to the landlord behind the bar. The man smiled, drew two pints of cloudy liquid into glass mugs and brought them to our table. Watson signed a paper chit for them, like in a mess, and nodded at the landlord. 'Thanks, George. Quiet tonight?'

'Mr MacDonald was very cross about the last accident, sir. We think that he's ordered everyone CB until they pull their socks up.'

'MacDonald's the principal at the CFS now: he runs the show,' Watson explained to me. 'He's a fine type: DFC.'

The landlord rejoined the conversation. To Watson he said,

'Didn't recognize Mr Bassett as one of yours, sir; he's much too smart. I thought that he was going up to the school.'

Watson looked me up and down briefly. 'See what you mean, George. We'll do something about that later this week – in the mean time toddle off, and forget you ever saw him in uniform. Buy yourself a drink, if you like.'

Watson eyed me, and then took a huge gulp of his beer. I copied him, but it wasn't beer: it was something thicker and sweeter, with a bite that grabbed the back of your palate on the way down. I was instantly in love with it.

'What's this terrific drink, sir?'

'Scrumpy. You'd call it cider. It's made less than ten miles from here; scarcely has time to stop slopping around in its barrel before you're a-drinking of it. I told you you'd like the pubs, but go easy with the cider – it's twice the strength of beer; you can get seriously rat-arsed on it, and ill the next day.'

'OK, sir.'

I had gone from feeling good about my uniform to being worried. I asked him, 'Is there a problem about my clothes? I've always been told to report in . . .'

'No, Charlie. You weren't to know, if nobody told you . . . I suppose that was Fortingale. I don't know why he dislikes us so much. He's such a little rat sometimes. We're really an out-station of RAF Eastcote up here: you've been to Eastcote?'

'Yes, they gave me the once-over. I met a policeman I used to know.'

'Good for you. You'll find that happens time and again. The RAF's about a fifth of the size it was when you were on a squadron, and getting smaller with the day. You'll keep tripping over bods you know. Anyhow – we piggyback on a Ministry of Pensions site at present. It's called Benhall Farm: on the other side of Cheltenham. The civil servants are moving out, and Eastcote's moving in, and because we'll eventually be working alongside other ministries there, the service thinks it better that we don't flash uniforms all over the shop. Fortingale should have told you. We're not supposed to worry the locals.'

'Why would we?'

Watson looked around before he answered, and then lowered his voice. 'Because there could be a couple of thousand of us out there eventually; and not everyone will welcome that with open arms. A soldier is popular when he's fighting or marching . . . not when he's living next door.'

'I'm not a soldier; I'm still in the RAF . . . anyway, the people I met at Eastcote didn't look much like soldiers either: more like boffins.'

'Metaphor, old boy: do try to keep up, and welcome to the Listening Flight, by the way . . .'

'Thanks. It's just that this isn't the RAF I joined, is it?'

'It never was, Charlie, but nobody told us until now. Another mug of this wallop? And then I have to head home, before the supper's burned.'

Watson had given me a new *Bartholomew's Cyclists' Map* for the area, on which Benhall farm was marked. I used it to get over there in the morning. I'd gone back to the ragbag of uniform bits without insignia that I had returned home with, and hoped that it wouldn't turn too many heads. I looked like a bloody refugee. The camp was mainly a series of temporary long brick office blocks surrounded by barbed wire, neatly mown grass, and concrete paths. The guardroom was manned by half a dozen hard-looking MPs, and half a dozen civilians. I was surprised to find that it was one of the latter who appeared to be in charge. I say *appeared*, because with these people you never knew. He was a neat fellow of about thirty, who wore wire-framed specs. He was obviously expecting company, because as I walked in he said, 'Mr Bassett, is it? Welcome to Station, sir,' and held out his hand. He didn't hang on for too long, so that was all right.

'*Station?*'

'That's what we call your part of the set-up, sir. Station . . . but you can't proceed to it until you've completed the formalities.'

'*Formalities?*' I reused his word. He must have thought that he was dealing with a halfwit.

'Sign you in, sir . . . security passes, and all that sort of thing. Then I'll get Ming to show you round the site.'

It took me nearly two hours to read, complete and sign the forms that the bugger produced for me, and I'm no slouch at that sort of thing, I can tell you. The gist of his continuous commentary was that if I ever spoke to anyone about anything after this, the government could fling me back into prison without a trial. He didn't know the half of it. He took my Bartholomew's map away, and locked it in a cupboard with a thousand others. Maybe it was a top-secret cycling tourists' map.

Ming was one of the military policemen. He was a British oriental with the build of a sumo: one of the few corporals I met who must have had his uniform tailored for him. It began to drizzle with rain as he walked me round: he didn't seem to notice. He called the more permanent buildings TGOs – temporary government offices. Put up during the war, he said, but he didn't know what for. Currently it was a teacher-training establishment run by the Ministry of Pensions. Most of the trainee teachers were ex-service types: swords being beaten into ploughshares – the phrase all the politicians were using: they didn't have a clue. I didn't know quite what the RAF had in store for me, but I wasn't feeling like a ploughshare yet.

Ming named off the different buildings for me. The only two that grabbed my attention were *Female Students' Accommodation* and *Civilian Refectory and Bar*. Both off limits. I don't know what the civvies were being fed, but it was bound to be better than what was being offered to the service personnel – it was the way of things.

The RAF buildings were in a wired compound off the main camp, behind a padlocked wired gate. Ming let us in with a key on a chain, and locked the gate behind us. I was damned if I liked being locked into places any more. It was about six times the size of a doubles court. All but one of the small buildings were identical. The others were small creosoted wood huts on raised brick foundations. In the middle of them there was one that looked like a cricket pavilion, veranda and all. It was painted green to extend the metaphor. Watson, smoking a cigarette, came out onto the veranda to greet us, and Ming took his leave. Before he did so he insisted on shaking my hand, saying, 'Welcome to Benhall, Mr Bassett. We're pleased that you're here: things will be OK now.'

'What *things*?' I asked Watson.

'What things, *sir*, if you don't mind, old boy. We still preserve some of the old niceties, even if we *are* at war again.'

He'd made two distinct points. I liked neither of them.

'What things, sir?'

'Your last two predecessors didn't stick around for long. The service police are superstitious old buggers when it comes down to it: they like things to stay the same. Pity is they never do. Do you want to come in, and take a pew?' After I was sitting in the room that appeared to be his office he asked, 'Char all right? Ready for one myself.'

'Fine, sir. Thank you.' I thought that sticking a *sir* on every sentence might be gilding the lily on this station. 'Wing standard, if that's OK.'

'Wing standard' was milk and two sugars. NATO adopted that in the 1950s, but that's NATO all over: always at the back of the queue, and stealing the best lines. Watson rang a small handbell that stood at the end of the desk, and a smart WAAF appeared from a side door like a ferret out of a rabbit hole. She must have been waiting for it. He smiled at her, and she seemed to melt.

'Two teas, please, Daisy. This is Mr Bassett. He's joining us: Hut 7.'

She blushed and said, 'Pleased to meet you, sir. Welcome back.' It was obvious that too many people had read Pete's book already. I smiled. I hoped that I didn't leer. I used to get the two mixed up when I was younger. I wondered if she had a boyfriend. She made a decent cuppa, too.

Watson blew on his tea to cool it; like an Epsom bookie. 'So what do you need to know?' he asked me.

The word *need* was interesting, wasn't it?

'How about what I'm doing here, sir? As far as I can make out, the RAF has confirmed that I'm still in the service, and likely to remain so for a few months until demob, and you've revalidated my radio-operator ticket. Apart from that, I keep walking into perfect strangers who are very pleased to meet me, and no one will tell me what I'm supposed to do. It feels like Tempsford all over again.'

'Bravo, Charlie.' I suppose the words just seemed to fit together. 'You've rumbled us. Why didn't you ask me with whom we are at war, when I mentioned it a few minutes ago?'

'I was trying to ignore it, sir. I was considering coming over all conchie if you're serious.'

'I am, and you won't.' Watson's voice had a sudden bleak edge. It was the first direct order I'd been given since my resurrection; the old RAF was back. That horrible fat personal file, bearing the title *Bassett C* and my number, was on his desk and between his hands. It seemed even bigger than the last time I had seen it. He leafed through it in silence. Eventually he said, 'You even knew some conchies at Tempsford, didn't you? It's all in here.'

'Yes, sir. They were an operational aircrew. When they stole their aircraft and buggered off, someone tried to blame me. Have you any idea what a Short Stirling costs?'

'No. Frightful lot, I expect . . . never worth the money, were they? Ever wonder what happened to that lot?'

'Occasionally. They nearly did for me, after all.'

'They filled the belly up with overflow tanks, and took her all the way to Palestine as a gift to the Jewish resistance. She's still there.'

'As long as no one's blaming me for it any more, sir.'

'No, they're not, Charlie. You've been officially rehabilitated for whatever piece of nonsense you got up to in Europe last year. The Air Lords must have been feeling particularly forgiving this month . . .'

'Either that, sir, or you have a nice round hole, and no round peg except me to bung into it.'

'And your file does say that you're an insubordinate little sod, did you know that?'

I shrugged – it didn't surprise me. 'I prefer *a bit of a joker*,' I told him.

'That too. Maybe you'll cheer us up, and live a bit longer than the last two.'

Ah.

We passed the time until lunch filling out more forms: it was the new way of going to war. He outlined my duties to me as we left the building. He did that quickly, as if he was embarrassed to be telling me what the RAF expected of me.

'Officially we're 12 Flight: but that's only for stores chitties. Actually it's a different number, which adds up to twelve. If things hot up we'll be a squadron one day. I called us the Listening Flight last night. Did you pick up on that up?'

'Yes, sir. I did.'

Sooner or later someone would tell me who we were supposed to be listening to. I suspected that it might have something to do with some silly buggers in London.

'And this morning I said something like "now we are at war

again", and you didn't turn a hair. Who do you suppose that we are at war with?'

I could read the newspapers, couldn't I? And that preacher's sermon at Pont Street had upset me. I replied, 'I guess we're not getting on too well with the Reds any more . . .'

'You guess right, of course, Charlie, and your section's task is to listen to some of their radio traffic: couldn't be simpler . . . as long as you tell no one else about it. If you do you'll end up in the Tower.'

'Is that an *official* caution, sir?'

'No. The official caution is when I say "Let's stop piss-balling about." That was taught me by my old boss, and I've liked it ever since. We call it the Scriven Caution, after him. When I say those words, you write in your notebook *official caution received*, and date and sign it.'

'I haven't got a notebook.'

'Then I should issue you with an official caution for that.' Funny bastard.

'Can we actually hear much Russian traffic from over here?'

'A fair bit. Mainly their German and Polish stuff. Then there's what we get from the weather flights, of course.'

'Weather flights, sir?'

'Yes: weather reconnaissance flights. They get closer to the borders. Occasionally you'll be asked to go up on a weather flight, and sniff around in Ivan's backyard.'

'That wouldn't be what happened to my predecessors, sir? Just asking.'

Watson looked away and slightly upward, with a pained expression on his face that said my question had offended him. He ignored it.

'Open the gate, Charlie. There's a good chap.' He'd issued me with a key to the compound that I was supposed to wear on a chain at my belt at all times. It was on a ring containing keys to the two huts under my care. If I lost the keys, you guessed it: I'd end up in the Tower. This mob's punishment scale was clearly not imaginative.

The food that we ate was as unimaginative as their punishments, and we consumed it in a small brick block behind the guardroom. Watson nodded to the civvies' canteen as we walked past. The rain had stopped, the sun shone and the lawns steamed appreciatively.

'They tote our food over from there. Most of our people can't be bothered, and eat in their huts. We don't eat or drink with the civvies. If you forget that . . .'

'. . . You'll end up in the Tower?'

'Glad you caught on.'

'Crowded, is it, sir? The Tower?'

'They were bloody right about you, Charlie, weren't they?'

They had given me five girls, and two huts. Dead and gone to Heaven, but not enough to send you power-mad. I met them all that afternoon. Each of the huts had two fair-sized radio rooms, a small kitchen and washroom area, and a small office, all off a short corridor. The small office in 7A was mine. The small office in 7B belonged to my number two, an equally small and vivacious WREN Third Officer named Gloria Miller. I met her there. I knew that she was a WREN from the uniform on a hanger on a peg on her office wall. She wore a dark civvy two-piece, greyer than her eyes. The skirt was short, and hugged her hips under a tailored jacket. I noticed the small bumps on her thighs where her suspender clips would have pulled her stockings out of shape. You may not remember it now, but you notice that sort of thing when you're in your twenties. I smiled when we were introduced and that prompted her to ask, 'Is there anything the matter, sir?'

'No; nothing. Just one of those coincidences. I'll tell you another time.'

Watson sloped off, saying, 'Leave you to it, then,' and as he turned to leave he touched his brow, curiously like a salute, and said, 'Afternoon, Mrs Miller' to Gloria. Once he was out of earshot she said to me, 'The Commander's full of old-fashioned courtesy, have you noticed that, sir? We like that in a man.' *We*? Was that 'we' as in *women*, or 'we' as in *Hut 7*?

'I'd rather call you Gloria, Officer . . . and you can call me Charlie, if that's OK with you?'

She gave me a shrewd up-and-down look. I don't think that she was particularly struck by what she saw: it only takes a glance for a woman to be able to value the clothes a man has hanging on him to the nearest ten bob. Remember that everything I wore that morning was borrowed or knocked off. Anyway, eventually she smiled. It was half a smile – she had a small mouth – and it was a long time coming. It nearly knocked me over.

'OK, Charlie. That will be fine, when we're not with the others. All right?'

'Fine.' I'd have to stop picking up on words that others had just used.

'And while we're on the subject of the Commander, you'd better know that he doesn't actually understand a damned thing about what goes on in here, despite what he thinks. If it's guidance we need – technical, operational or moral – we're on our own.'

'Moral?'

'You'll find that sometimes you're called upon to make decisions not covered by King's Regs, sir . . .'

'Charlie . . .'

'Charlie.' She tried to smile again. I was going to enjoy making her smile.

She introduced me to the two operators in 7B. Each had their room and their own radio rig. A fussy civvy, who sat with her hair up in a scarf, disapproved of me before I opened my mouth. It was written all over her face. She must have been thirty, and was wartime-thin: she might have been beautiful once. Her name was Weronka – or Ronka – Karska, another Pole. If Pete showed up again I'd get him to jolly her up. The woman in the other room looked like Jane from the *Daily Mirror* strip, except when she opened her mouth: then she was as Manchester as faggots. She was introduced as a junior WAAF. She'd be OK if she could do her job. When I asked her name she said, 'Jane. Just Jane.' Served me right. *Just Jane* would make a good name for an aircraft.

This lot were going to be bloody hard going.

When I let myself into the other hut and walked past the rooms containing my other operators they kept their backs to me, and didn't turn to look. Ming was in my new office, sweeping items from the desk into a large cardboard box. He froze as he saw me in the doorway, and straightened. 'Sorry, sir.'

'Carry on, Ming. Don't mind me.'

He continued clearing things away. He was collecting my predecessor's personal belongings. I'd seen this ritual too often on the squadron to mistake it for anything else. The card written in ink and pinned to the door read *Fl. Lt. Timperley*. I removed it carefully and handed it to Ming. Wherever Timperley had gone he wouldn't need his things again. I asked Ming, 'What happens to his stuff? When I was on a squadron we used to auction it.'

'Not these days, sir. The CO will vet it, and we'll send what we can back to his family.'

'Do you know what happened to him?'

Ming looked away. 'Sorry, sir, but I couldn't tell you if I did. As it happens, no . . . I don't know. You might be able to ask the CO yourself.'

Somehow I thought that Gloria Miller would be a better bet.

I turned away, and as I did so I jumped at the voice directly behind and below me. It said cheerfully, 'Hello, I'm Elizabeth. One of your operators.'

'Hello, Elizabeth: Charlie Bassett.' I gave her my right hand. Hers was small and brown with a pink palm. She was even smaller than me. She was also the first coloured girl I'd ever been that close to. I don't know what perfume she wore, but I'd guess that it was newly applied. Late-summer flowers, and a wide dark chocolate smile to match.

'Pilot or Flying Officer, Bassett?'

'Pilot Officer, I think. I haven't been to pay parade lately. How did you know?'

'Two-syllable surname, Charlie. Two syllables for a pilot or flying officer, three syllables means flight lieutenant and above. It's the way you English order things.'

'You're not English?'

'Do I look it? I'm from Falmouth; the Hampden estate.'

That meant nothing to me. 'The last time I looked, Falmouth was still in England,' I said.

Elizabeth had a nice laugh. 'Not the one that grows sugar cane: Falmouth, Jamaica – land of my fathers. I'm a civvy now, if you haven't already guessed. We don't do "sir" and "madam" in the Jamaican Civil Service, and if you don't like that you can always fire me.'

'How about if I just said "Pleased to meet you, Elizabeth"?'

She smiled and nodded. I pressed on. 'Can you use that radio?'

A grin again. 'Better than you can – and I'd better get back to it.' Then she was gone. I felt I'd been sideswiped by a brown tornado. Hello, Elizabeth.

Ming turned, and nodded as he let himself out. He locked the hut door behind him. My new job was going to be all about locks and keys, which was a pity because I've never been terribly good with them.

After that, meeting Mrs Boulder was easy. Mrs Boulder, the last member of my team, hadn't come out to meet me; she'd waited at her radio. It was a modified American AR 88 Receiver, connected to an old Chain Home aerial mast above the site. When I asked her about its range she said, 'I don't know, sir. All I know is that it's wide enough for our purposes – although that depends on the signal strength over the other side.'

Mrs Boulder was in her late thirties, and had the most direct stare I'd ever seen. When she answered a question she never lost eye contact and rarely smiled: an interrogator's nightmare. She was another civvy, and could have passed for Gloria Miller's elder sister: same grey eyes, but her hair was a light mousy brown against Miller's fine blonde. When I asked her what she'd like me to call her when we worked together, she delayed her reply for a three-beat, and then said, 'How about "Mrs Boulder", sir?' One of those people who score points: I had an aunt like that. Her headphones were around her neck, and her radio was playing that old sweet song of static.

'Can you get music on that thing?' I asked.

First smile – point to me – and she flicked a toggle. She must have preset the frequencies. It was the Light Programme and Al Bowlly was singing 'Close Your Eyes' with the Ray Noble Orchestra.

The music followed me to my own office. I sensed that Mrs Boulder actively disliked me already. That was a bit of a record, even for me.

Miller came in at about eighteen hundred hours to tell me that they were jacking it in for the day. She was 'Miller' immediately, I'd decided, despite our earlier conversation on the subject; not Mrs Miller, Third Officer Miller, or Gloria. I don't know why, but it suited both of us; probably because there was usually a grin on my face when I said it.

'Got a few minutes, Miller?' I asked.

'Of course.' She went back and closed the office door before she sat down. Once she had done so the room seemed very small. Even with each of us on opposite sides of the desk, she seemed to be very close to me.

'Are you going to tell me how to do my job now, Miller?'

The pause was only a few seconds, but it seemed to go on for ever. Then she said, 'If you like.' She fussed around taking off her jacket and draping it over the back of her chair. When she crossed her legs and leaned back, I could see her knees. They were pretty ordinary knees; so why couldn't I take my eyes off them? She said, 'I don't really smoke, but I fancy a cigarette. Do you have any?'

I shook my head, so she told me, 'The Commander will have told you that our duties are reasonably undemanding.'

'Something like that.'

She smiled. I began to realize that she didn't smile all the time; only when she meant it.

'And I disloyally told you that he knew damn all about it, really?'

'Something like that.' I grinned, which was a mistake.

'I must warn you never to laugh at me, Charlie: it doesn't work with most women, and it *won't* work with me.'

'I'll remember that, Miller . . .' I used her surname again because it gave me pleasure to do so. 'But that means we're going to have a hard time, because I laugh at a lot of people. Defence mechanism.'

She smiled again: she didn't seem to mind. 'The Commander had it more or less right: but it depends on what you mean by *reasonably*, doesn't it?'

'Start with the operators. What do they do?'

'They weren't recruited for their skills as radio operators, but as stenos. That is stenographers . . . their ability to write down accurately what they hear, and then transcribe it to signal pads without making errors. They're all exceptional,' she assured me.

'So they listen to foreign signals, and record them?'

'Exactly; but not necessarily always foreign.' That was interesting.

'Why are we all knocking off tonight? Surely you'll leave someone on a listening watch?'

'They wouldn't know where to listen, would they? We get our instructions from Eastcote – which isn't RAF any more, in case you hadn't already worked that out.'

'What is it?'

'Joint services, I think. They give the orders. You'll see the batting order on the ops board in my office. I get a weekly order. What wavebands to listen in to, when and for how long – never more than four at a time: just what we can handle. There's nothing on the board for tonight.' I didn't interrupt. I nodded, and Miller moved on: 'The girls transcribe the signals, most of which are encrypted, so they usually mean nothing to us. At the end of each shift I collect the transcript flimsies up, put them in the pouch and drop them off at the guardroom on my way home. A dispatch rider collects them during the night and takes them to London. It doesn't always work out like that; sometimes we get urgent band or frequency changes during the day. You can work all night then . . . and then there are big flaps or operations when we're here around the clock.'

'Do you get more people in then?'

She shook her head. Her hair bobbed, coloured by a red

sunset pushing into the office. 'No, we work shifts; you and me too. We lock the station down, and everybody sleeps over. The two huts behind the Commander's office are rigged for accommodation: ten tiny cabins in each.'

'One boys; one girls?'

She nodded.

'Same old RAF,' I said

'Not any more. I told you – it would be best to remember that.'

'OK. What do *you* do?'

'I supervise your operators . . . collect up the flimsies. Do all the day-to-day admin, and listen to their moans: yours, too. Report to you.'

'And what do I do?'

'Make the decisions I won't, and make sure that I do *my* job, countersign the reports I write from time to time, and the requisitions; pitch in when things get difficult . . . and fly, of course.'

I nodded as though I knew all this. 'The CO did tell me that I'd have to fly weather flights occasionally.'

'*Weather flights*?' It was just the way that Miller said it.

'Yes. How do I find out about them?'

'You'll get a signal. Anything more before I go home?'

'Just like that?'

'Just like that.'

Something bothered me. 'Mrs Boulder hates me already, and I don't know what I've done.'

Miller thought. Then she decided to tell me. 'She was going

out with Freddy Timperley: that's all. She'll come round eventually.'

'An American I know has a new phrase for things like that.'

'What is it?'

'Shit happens.'

'Yes, it does, doesn't it?' When she looked up at me her eyes glistened. I was suddenly rather jealous of the late Freddy Timperley. I was back on the slippery slope myself, of course.

'Anything you want to ask me?'

'Yes.' Two discreet dabs with a clean handkerchief from her jacket pocket. 'Why did you smile when the Commander introduced us?' Some women have memories for that sort of thing.

'I knew a girl once, who called herself Gloria . . . in certain circumstances. It was a name that she asked me to give her. A pet name. Do you have a name like that?'

Good try, Charlie. Miller sniffed and informed me, 'I'm nobody's pet, Charlie, and if I have a name like that the only man who knows it is called *Mr* Miller.'

Not so good try, Charlie. Some girls close doors on conversations gently; some slam them right in your face. Best to know where you stand from the start, I suppose.

I spent a second night at the Lamb, and a second evening in its bar, reacquainting myself with its cider.

Ming was the first person I saw after I signed in the next morning. He wasn't in uniform. He wore a huge khaki overall, and was tending the flower beds around the guardroom. I hadn't noticed them before. He was delicately lifting weeds from a mass of deep pink bell-like flowers. This time he saw me. He stood up and said, 'Morning Mr Bassett: I get extra money for tending the garden on my day off.'

'I didn't notice them yesterday.' I indicated the flowers. 'What are they?'

'Love lies bleeding,' he said. 'If you're kind to them they'll last all summer.'

'But then they die?'

'Yes, sir. Then they die.' Can't say I hadn't been warned. 'But then they come again the next year. Better than ever before.' In my head I wrote Ming down as an optimist.

'Can you tell me where people stay around here? I can't live in a pub all the time – my dad wouldn't like it.' I had intended that to be funny but Ming didn't smile.

'You've got digs all fixed up. Didn't you go there last night, sir?'

'No, no one told me. I went back to the Lamb.'

Ming looked away, and spoke from the side of his mouth. 'Useless bleedin' civvy shower, begging your pardon, sir. I fixed you up myself: then they forgot to give you your envelope. I'll fetch it for you.'

It turned out that there was a bank of pigeon-holes on the floor behind the guard desk. That was where things were left for you, but you had to ask. Nobody offered. The envelope was a welcoming pack – a list of do's and don'ts and operational procedures. I had been supposed to read it the day before, initial a copy and return it to the SPs. There were more don'ts than do's by a factor of ten, so I decided to read it again and make the buggers wait.

There was also a fat envelope with a London ministry date stamp that had come in the internal mail – it carried with it a suggestion of Dolly's perfume. A third envelope contained details of my billet. I was to live with a Mrs Abbott, at a farmhouse about three miles away. There was a hand-drawn map of how to get to her – it was exceptionally finely drawn in ink, almost like a fly-leaf illustration from a Victorian book, and was signed at the bottom right corner with a single large flowing M. There was even a sketch of a farmhouse, and a woman in a summer dress at the door. She didn't look old.

The operators were already working as I let myself in. I sensed Mrs Boulder stiffen as I walked past her open door, and Elizabeth waved an arm over her head but didn't turn to look at me. The choice in the small kitchen was char or Camp coffee. The coffee won; flavoured with condensed milk. Miller paced in just as I was opening the envelope from London and tipping its contents onto my desk. A ration book, petrol coupons and clothing coupons: three books of them. No message. Miller said, 'Gosh. You wouldn't have any to spare, I suppose? When did you last buy yourself anything to wear, Charlie?'

A question which needed serious calculation. '1942 or '43, I think. A blue blazer and a pair of grey off-duty trousers. I lost them somewhere.'

'Well, they've certainly sent you more than enough to catch up – if you can afford it,' she told me.

'I probably can; I didn't get much opportunity to spend my pay in the last couple of years. Where do I go?'

'There's a Co-op and two gents' outfitters in Cheltenham, but they're only any good if you're a farmer or a doctor. The

Commander shops there. Oxford's better, and not too far away. You could buy a cap and gown . . . or a fancy suit with a felt collar. Go when you get a day off. Either that, or wait until you get up to Town.'

'Maybe you could help me?'

She saw that one coming, and struck it straight for the boundary. 'Ask one of the single girls, Charlie. They'd enjoy it: I wouldn't – I don't like shopping.'

'Perhaps I could ask Elizabeth. Elizabeth who, by the way?'

'Regina Brown. You could; and you'd end up with a cowboy outfit – she's got a thing going with the Americans at the moment. I'd do it yourself, if I was you.'

Miller didn't leave too much to chance. Her hips swung as she walked out. I thought that we'd drawn that game. Then she stopped and turned back, offering me my fourth brown envelope of the day. I'd forgotten that I was waging a war armed with paper: it was going to be that type of job. She said, 'There was a call before you got in: you're flying tonight. Ciao.'

She blew me a kiss. Game, set and match.

6. I Like to Go Back in the Evening

I went to see Watson. He sent me off to check into my digs and get a few hours' kip. Transport at the guardroom at 1430: working uniform to be carried in a travelling bag. I didn't have a travelling bag.

I'd known a man named Abbott when I was on the squadron; in fact, I was driving his car. Pete bought it from his widow. I had it from Pete, because cars lasted longer than people did in those days. That was the reason I drove warily up the farm track to Mrs Abbott's house. I needn't have worried: she was a different denomination of Abbott. She was a heavy, cheerful woman who smelled of hens. Abbottsville was a chicken farm on a scale I'd only ever read about: thousands of chickens in four big fields around the farmhouse. Mrs Abbott collected the eggs twice a day, and every night used two gentle dogs to herd hens into low houses built on stilts. I guessed that I'd eventually get used to the smell: it hung like mustard gas for hundreds of yards around.

I showed her Ming's drawing, which made her smile; she asked if she could keep it. The figure in it, she said, was her daughter: I'd get to meet Alison when she came home from school. Mrs Abbott wore a mourning ring. You don't see many of those these days: a plain gold wedding ring with a black band set around its centre. She was missing someone: I guess that we all were in 1947.

They let me stick the Singer behind the guardroom. I hadn't expected Miller to meet me there. She handed me a package wrapped in greaseproof paper, tied inexpertly with string. I remembered that Grace could never tie parcels either.

'Bread-and-dripping sandwiches, for later,' she told me with an embarrassed smile. 'I guessed you would forget. You'll get coffee or soup.'

I should have been interested that she knew the form: I was actually interested in the fact that she was embarrassed about handing me food. It was as if she was afraid I would refuse.

'Smashing. Thanks. Pork or beef?' And then, before she could answer, I stuck in: 'I love the brown bits, don't you?'

'Pork. Yes. Our family loved the dripping when I was a kid. Charles hates it; makes him want to throw up, he says.'

'Who's Charles?'

'My husband. I should have told you.' Then Miller opened her mouth to speak again and I knew that the 'Good luck' was coming, so I reached out and gently touched her upper lip with my forefinger,

'Don't say it . . . please. And don't worry; it'll be OK.'

I wasn't sure, but I might have felt just a faint pressure against my finger before I pulled it away. Miller held my gaze and said, 'Fine,' in a small, flat voice. Then she turned on her heel and walked away. She didn't look back.

A small American GMC crew bus pulled in a couple of minutes later. It was wearing RAF blue, and RAF markings. The AC1 driver nipped round and asked me, 'Pilot Officer Bassett?'

I nodded and headed over to him.

'Hop aboard, sir. I'll get you to the CFS in half an hour.'

'Don't worry; I'm in no hurry.'

He didn't believe me, and laughed. What had Watson told me about the CFS at Little Rissington? Something about them dropping kites all over the county, and killing people?

A twin-engined Hudson was waiting outside one of the hangars, alongside a Harvard trainer with a crooked wing. The latter looked as if it had been in a taxiing accident. My misadventures in France had started in a Hudson. This one was painted silver, which looked a bit strange to my war-educated eye. The pilot sported a black beard above his smart uniform jacket. That looked even stranger.

'Joe Humm,' he told me as he offered his hand. 'Don't worry about the face fungus; I get a shaving rash so I have permission to grow.'

'Charlie Bassett. 12 Flight. If I had permission to grow maybe I'd be as big as you.'

He grinned, inclined his head to the hangar and asked, 'Like to nip in there and get changed? Then we can get off.' He must have seen doubt in my eyes: I was wondering how far I'd get in a clapped-out old Hudson. 'Don't worry; I'm only your lift to Waddington. After that you're with the big boys.'

Joe Humm had a navigator, but there wasn't much for him to do and on the flight we found a common interest in jazz. They promised to introduce me to some of the local clubs. Apparently, Nat Gonella and the Georgians sometimes came down from London.

Waddington was locked down – just like a wartime station before a raid. After landing we were met by an SP in a jeep. He insisted on carrying my bag for me. That was embarrassing, because my non-flying clothes were now in a large brown-paper carrier bag that I had borrowed from Mrs Abbott. It still contained one or two downy feathers, and smelled of dead chickens. We were followed away from our flight by another SP jeep. The passenger in that jeep was carrying a rifle at port. When the RAF begins to take itself that seriously it's time to get out the toilet paper. I didn't get my bag back; they drove us directly to a small Nissen hut on the airfield periphery, where I was dropped off. The hut was like a fighter-squadron dispersal of years before. It had a decent brick fireplace, big leather chairs, a table and a couple of map boards on the wall. And six men.

I've always liked bomber men – these were already in their faded flying overalls, and looked like crap. The skipper who walked over wore more mend patches than flying suit. He drawled, 'Hi, I'm Tim, your driver – you are?'

'Charlie. Radios. From—'

He cut me off. 'Doesn't matter where you're from, Charlie, welcome to the party. All we need now is the radar, and we're set.' What he meant was we *don't* want to know where you're from, Charlie. Just about then the young boy I remembered walked in. He said, 'Hello, everybody, I'm Perce.' And to me, 'Hi, sir, long time no see.'

'I'm *Charlie* on this trip, Perce, not *sir* – like I once told you.'

He shrugged, and smiled. That worried me. There was a light of excitement in his eyes that hadn't been there before. He was wired. Here was a kid who had missed his best war, who still wanted to win his spurs.

They gave us padded brown overalls in scarcely better condition than their own, soft leather helmets, gloves and ox masks. Oh, yeah, and a parachute. It was when they handed you the parachute that you began to wonder. Then you began to sweat.

The RAF has this tendency to do things by numbers; did anyone ever tell you that? There were two crews going out, and they'd kept us separate. So now they bussed us together for the briefing, in a classroom hut twice the size of the one we'd been parked in earlier. There were no introductions, and the other crew looked as professional as mine. I couldn't identify their interlopers, if there were any; perhaps they'd worked together before. A ranker swept in with his assistant in tow: we all stood – some things don't change. It wasn't like any briefing I'd been at before: it was conducted by a Wingco, very low-key, and was about as informative as a dead elephant. In retrospect it was as interesting for what we weren't told as for what we were. He began with a secret little smile, stroked his moustache and said, 'Welcome to Waddington, gentlemen. My name is Peterson.'

That's when I realized there were other strangers here.

'Your target for tonight is in the Soviet Bloc.' He was using the old form of words, which was why he smiled. They couldn't be serious, could they? No. He banged on. 'The first thing I'll say is that everything you learn in the course of the next few hours will be *classified*. We're back to the *walls have ears* rules of a few years ago. *Be like dad; keep mum*. Got it?'

We all nodded. I would have had difficulty responding immediately anyway: my mouth had gone dry. That was never a good sign.

'The background to your mission is an assessment by minds better than ours that we will be at war with the Soviet Union and its axis within two years.'

Bang. Just like that.

'If they look like getting the atom bomb, maybe even before that.' Peterson paused for effect. He didn't have to. I was all ears. 'Bomber Command will have a leading role in that conflict, just as we did in the last, and what you do tonight will give us the edge. The navigation of aircraft in the next war will be carried out by radar – not by a man with a hand calculator and dividers. Aircraft will fly from one pre-plotted geographical radar profile to the next – what you are going to do is to come back with those profiles. Over the last few months officers like you have flown routes to strategic targets accross the Soviet Zone, capturing the radar profiles of significant navigation features or way points. You're going to do the same. One aircraft will make the actual penetration of Soviet airspace. The other will fly a diversion mission along the borders to draw up his fighters, which will leave gaps for the lead ship to sneak through.' *Ship*, I thought. Another bugger who'd spent too much time among the Americans. 'Navs and radar, stay behind for separate briefings, please. Radios and guns will be briefed by aircraft captains. Weather brief in about one hour fifteen: take-off in about ninety minutes. That will be all, gentlemen. Good scouting, all. Good afternoon.'

Good scouting, all: that was it. Charlie was off to war again. Only this time with a bunch of Boy Scouts. Where was Baden-Powell when you needed him? I still remember the promise: *On my honour, I promise to do my best, to do my duty to God and the King, to obey the Scout Law, and help others at all times.* We'd all been there. Funny what you remember.

We gathered in two groups, each crew around its own small bus. A lot of shoes were scuffing on the tarmac, and a lot of fags were being smoked. I filled my pipe and leaned on the bus's front wing, trying to work out how to stay alive. Neither our nav nor Perce had reappeared yet. Tim mooched over, looking about as nonchalant as a cat with its tail between a dog's teeth. He started to offer me a fag until he noticed my pipe. 'I'm glad you're with us, Charlie; you're the only one with actual operational experience.' If that was supposed to make me feel good he was mistaken.

'Weren't you out in the last lot?' I asked.

'No, they liked my flying so much they kept me in a conversion unit as an instructor. It was all over before I got to a squadron.' That meant that he could fly properly, anyway.

'What are we going out in?'

'Lincoln B2. Have you seen one?'

'Never heard of them.'

'They called the prototype the Mark 6 Lancaster – just a big Lanc, really – a bit bigger all round. Goes a bit faster, a bit further and a bit higher: you'll like her.'

'Will I?'

'Yes.'

'What do you want me to do?'

'A bloody long listening watch, writing down anything you hear and understand. Anything you recognize . . . and I understood that you were good at the feeling once: that's what I need tonight.'

I don't know where he'd got that from. 'The feeling' was what happened when a radio operator was eavesdropping on an opposition night-fighter controller talking to a night fighter and realized that it was about *him*. Even if you couldn't understand their language, or their codes, sometimes you just knew they were talking about you. That was 'the feeling'. I suspected that it was a function of fear, but I didn't tell him that. 'Listen to the Reds for me tonight, Charlie, and tell me when they're stalking us.'

'What else?'

'There's only one other thing you need to know: anything that you dial into will be relayed automatically as a separate signal to a ground station here in England, where the operator, unlike us, will be proficient in Russian, German or Polish. We'll be like a flying aerial for him. If he thinks that we're about to get into trouble he'll call you up. OK?'

'Is that it? Is that the radio briefing?'

'I can tell you the same thing using longer words, if you like.' At least he was still smiling. 'Any advice for me?'

'Yes. Do we have Monica with us?'

'Yeah. We all have them these days.'

'Monica' wasn't some sweet girl carried to entertain the airmen: Monica was a crude radar beam-detecting device. She detected the buggers that were using *their* radar to track you. Her problem was that she emitted a beam of her own in order to do so. Once Jerry cracked that, he just recalibrated his sets to follow her beam back and look up her skirts. When you switched on Monica in the wild night skies it was like saying 'Come and get me' to a night fighter. Not many folk knew that.

'Switch her off as soon as you can.'

'Why, Charlie?'

'Just trust me, boss: she's bad news. Just switch her off. I've been there before.'

He gave me a long look before saying 'OK' and turning away.

The navs and radar guys were coming from the briefing hut now. There was none of the noisy banter I remembered from the squadron. Each group whispered, like mourners at a funeral. Mind you, I'd already worked that out. If this work was as dubious as the Wingco had suggested, they'd want to brief as few airmen as they could. If they had just briefed two new crews, it was odds-on that they'd lost the previous two. Somewhere out in the cold air over Vodkaland. Bastards.

The first time I saw a Lincoln was in that twilight. She was a beast. She couldn't have been that much larger than a Lanc, but she looked huge, and black and serious. Every time I climbed into a black aircraft I got into trouble. I stepped up into her from my old place: second from the end of the line – the rear gunner was behind me. I remember now that his name was Neil . . . someone called him Nutty Neil. Like the others, he looked a bit on the young side to me. He dogged down the small fuselage door behind us. I checked that he'd done it properly. He wasn't offended. He just nodded and said, 'See you later, Charlie.'

'Sure. For breakfast.'

I'd said something similar to the Pink Pole on his last trip: then our own fools blew him out into the blue with an anti-aircraft shell.

The Lincoln moved around on her legs the way a big aircraft was supposed to, as we found our places and buckled in. I was back-to-back with Perce again. The bastards at Hendon had put me through a dress rehearsal without telling me. If I had shut my eyes and excluded the noises that Perce made, I could have been in *Tuesday's Child* again. I reminded myself that I wasn't; *Tuesday* had burned. It was the wrong time to admit to myself that I missed her. Another thing that I could have done with my eyes closed was fire the radios up. The soft hiss of the static was like the return of a badly missed old friend.

When I was satisfied, I dropped the phones around my neck and looked forward. As in the Lanc, by leaning to one side I could see up into the cockpit. It was another clear sunset, and up there the men were bathed in a pink orange light that dissolved into a faint rainbow before it reached me but painted the nav into a coat of many colours. Their murmured cockpit drill was almost identical to that in my memory. Then they ran up the starboard outer engine twice, because they failed to get a decent mag drop first time round – and my ring twitched. When the Stirling I'd been in had done that we'd left her in bits all around Tempsford.

Perce tapped me on the shoulder. When I turned round he said, 'I'm scared and excited; both at the same time.'

'Don't worry; you'll be OK. I've done dozens like this.' Sometimes I told lies. I realized then that I hadn't been told whether we were the hare or the hound. I suppose it didn't matter; my job would be the same either way. I pulled the headphones up again, and on cue the pilot clicked and came in with, 'Call through, please, radios.'

I responded with 'Charlie, Skipper . . .' and ran the rest of his call-through for him. The voices rang very loud and clear in the headphones. The engine revs rose, and the bird began to tremble. The nav said, 'There's the light; that's a go, Skip,' and she began to rumble forward on Waddington's long runway. It would have been nice if someone had asked me if I actually *wanted* to go back to Germany.

We flew half a dozen big squares around Lincolnshire to let the other aircraft draw well ahead of us. That probably annoyed a few farmers because we did it at about a hundred and fifty feet. Low enough to make the tiles rattle and the church bells sing with resonance. It did occur to me that we could have just stayed on the ground for another twenty minutes and not upset anyone. Tim called me up to the office for the outward flight. Looking back, I saw the last of the sunlight sinking beyond our spindly rudders, somewhere out over the Atlantic. Standing behind the pilot as we pulled out over the Wash I felt as if I'd been there half my life. It was probably where I'd be when we landed . . . assuming a positive outcome. The sea streamed away in front of us, dark grey with whitecaps that winked on and off like fireflies. The Linc smelled new inside, and trembled like a thoroughbred greyhound before the off. Tim was right: I liked her.

We were halfway to Denmark before I went back down to my station. Perce got out a spare map case and spelled out our intentions to me. The other Lincoln was overflying Denmark – without official sanction, of course – to pop up onto the Reds' radar screens somewhere south of Hamburg. Then it was going to play hide-and-seek all the way down the demarcation-zone border, and fart in their faces. The Reds didn't have the same wartime experience that the Germans had at intercepting incoming raids – maybe they'd commit their fighter resources to it and have none left over for us. That was the theory. We were to insert low over the North Sea and climb through an alleged radar gap above Szczecin to our maximum operational height. After that we were to cruise over Rostok, Riga and Tallinn – all Russian fleet ports – mapping ground profiles as we did so, and eventually escape to violate the airspace of neutral Sweden by closing up to a Swedish airliner homeward-bound for Stockholm, and hiding in her radar shadow. I don't want you to get the idea that we were supposed to completely hide from the Ivans. They were supposed to be able to see some of what we were doing but feel impotent to prevent it. It sort of sent them the message that we could be back any time we wanted, with a full load of bombs.

'What if the ground controller down there is *German*?' I

shouted at Perce. 'Some character who spent the last six years learning our ways?'

'Then we'll get company, sir. I expect that that's what happened to the last bods.'

I was glad that he'd worked it out as well.

I had never been more scared. That was something to do with not being in the right of it. I hadn't really doubted that the scrap with Jerry had been necessary, or proportional: there wasn't much I wouldn't have done to help defeat the Krauts. This was different. The Reds hadn't done anything to us yet – except mouth off a bit. I couldn't see that that was a good reason to go flinging bombs at them, or even to threaten it. What I mean is that somewhere in my head a little voice was squeaking out that if one of their fancy jet fighters pumped a dozen cannon shells up our jacksie, then it would only serve us right.

The other Lincoln must have done us proud: the airwaves were as full as the fair on the downs on Derby Day. I got some of the transmissions in bits and pieces: mostly in German, or coded traffic that I instinctively took to be so. Some poor sod could puzzle them out if I made it back. It was stirring up a hornets' nest from the Baltic to the Austrian border: there were aircraft everywhere, either scrambling from their airfields or returning to them empty of gas. You could almost smell the frustration in the air out there.

It got tricky near Kaliningrad, which is what the Russkis call Konigsberg in old East Prussia. There was a short series of exchanges in what I took to be Russian – between what sounded like a couple of pilots, and then between them and the ground.

The hair on the back of my neck stood up. I clicked immediately: 'Skipper, Charlie. They got us.'

Click: 'Charlie – are you sure?'

My old skipper, Grease, would never have asked the question. He would have had *Tuesday* on her side by now and skidding downwards.

'Of course I'm sure!'

'OK, Charlie, don't panic – I've got her.'

Yes, prat, but for how long? Perce jumped in, click: 'I've got them, Skipper: I'll follow them in.'

The foreign voices in my earphones were hoarse now, urgent: hounds off the leash. I said, 'They're close; they're—'

'Shut up, sir, we've *got* 'em . . .' That was Perce.

As he spoke I glanced outside through my small window to the left. A small tubby silver jet aircraft was climbing past us at an impossible attitude; there was a faintly phosphorescent blue glow over the leading edges of its wings and forward fuselage. It couldn't hang in that thin air for ever.

It didn't. Tim rolled our beast gently away from it to starboard; the MiG tried to stay with us in the turn, and couldn't. Its wing broke off: just like that. The thin silver wing, with its red star, fluttered down like a falling leaf. The unbalanced fighter span amazingly along its own axis, following a shallow parabola. I saw the canopy break away – then nothing. They were gone. Perce clicked. He sounded cool; almost laconic.

'This is Perce, Skipper. It broke up. The other one's not even trying.'

Someone's breath was rasping over the intercom. I realized that it was mine. There was another click, and Nutty Neil said,

'Aaw . . . didn't lay a hand on him.' It was a joke we used sometimes.

The top gunner spoke for the first time since the call-over. 'That must be the tenth MiG that's broken up in a climbing turn this year; don't they ever fucking learn?' He sounded worldly-wise, but his breath was rasping too. I was sure that this was also the first time he'd met the Reds; like me. Even so – someone could have bloody told me.

Just short of Tallinn the Reds threw up to our height a curtain of heavy flak that was thick enough to walk on. Probably they were using old German guns. The sirens must be wailing down there, I thought, just like in the war. Maybe people were dashing for the shelters. We blinked first. Tim rolled the Lincoln indecorously to port and headed out to sea. Privately I thought that he had made the right decision; we should get back with the material we already had. It still felt like funk, and Grease wouldn't have done it, no matter what the rest of us told him to do.

Tim let us down slowly towards the ETA with the Swede over the Baltic. I was still scared. If the Reds got a couple of fighters up to us now it could get interesting. As it was we slid in beside the Swedish C47 without further interference.

The Swedish pilot flashed his lights at us in a friendly sort of way, and Tim just slotted under his port wing until the civvy peeled off for Stockholm. That left us illegally overflying Sweden in the dash for home. From the reaction of the airliner I was left in no doubt that any diplomatic protest would be half-hearted. Maybe they thought the Russians were about to declare war on the rest of us as well. I had ten minutes up in the office over the

North Sea. We were down to a hundred and fifty feet again as we went back in. The sea should have been black or dark grey, but it wasn't: it was silver. A huge low moon polished the world the colour of old pewter. The sea swell looked greasy and long.

Coming in over the Wash two Meteor jet fighters dropped down on each of our wing-tips. I saw one of them through my small port, but I was back at work by then. They took us back to Waddington, where we landed at about six in the morning. Just as we were turning in for finals I heard a brief burst of Morse, and a reply. I could swear that they were the hands I had heard out over the Bristol Channel days before. I managed to scribble the exchange onto my spare pad, tore off the page and stuffed it deep inside my uniform. I don't know why I did that. I shut down the radios before the Skipper asked, whilst we waddled around the peri-track to the beast's hard standing. Then I sat exhausted, with my head in my hands, until we came to a stop and the propellers slowed one after the other. All that was left were the mechanical clicks and wheezes as everyone shut down their equipment and began to move around.

I understood something about myself for the first time: fear made me tired. I turned to face Perce. He still looked excited, but there was something else there as well; he wouldn't be so keen to go out a second time. He looked suddenly older. 'Is it always like that, Charlie?' he asked.

'No,' I told him shortly. 'Usually it's worse. That was a milk run. Do you know if you got what you were supposed to?'

'Yes, I mapped the whole route, up to the suburbs of Tallinn. Did you see that flak?'

'No. I had my head down.'

'We could have been killed up there!'

I looked at him as if he was a newborn, and I was a million years old. 'Of course we could: that's the point.'

Perce dropped his gaze before I did. He hadn't really got what it took, and we both knew it. There again, neither had Turnaway Tim – I had started to call him that in my head – so perhaps Perce would fit into the crew just fine. I just wanted to get away from them.

The other Lincoln wasn't back yet, and a load of shifty eyes at the debriefing table told me that it was probably overdue. I gave them my pad with the scraps of foreign signal scribbled on it, and my radio log. They asked me twice to describe how the Mig's wing folded back, and sounded disappointed to learn that the canopy had gone as well, because that meant that the pilot just might have got out. Then they left me alone.

The debrief of the other trades was more detailed. I leaned back in my chair and closed my eyes again. The officer who gave me a mug of coffee stiffened with rum looked familiar; then I remembered that he had conducted the met briefing twelve hours earlier. We talked in low voices for about twenty minutes: he wanted to know how accurate his forecast had been – where he'd got it right, and where he'd got it wrong. He was a really decent one; the only one of the whole damned bunch worth bothering with.

We were given the warning again as we dismissed – and were told that we could record the flight in our personal log books, but as 'CSACZ' – Central and South Allied Control Zone – and 'weather flight'. There you are. Fucking weather flights; it was the first time that the weather had shot back at me.

7. *Down-home Rag*

Someone had been kind. They had realized that it might rain during the night and had thrown a tarpaulin over my open car. Either that or they hadn't expected me back, and were hiding the evidence.

Coming back on the Hudson with Joe Humm I discovered Miller's sandwiches buttoned into my battledress-blouse pocket. I had forgotten about them. The circumstances conspired to make the first bite convince me that they were the best sandwiches I had ever tasted. The SP who drove me out to Humm's aircraft handed me back my small clothes in a new RAF blue canvas holdall with leather straps: he'd stencilled my name and number on it. When I looked inside, even the paper carrier bag was there, neatly folded – it might even have been ironed. I dozed in the seats behind Joe and his nav, and again on the crew bus from Little Riss. I got as far as the guardhouse at Benhall before Ming intercepted me at the door. He had a grin on his face. 'All right for some, sir – that's you finished for the day, I expect.'

I had expected to go on to Hut 7 to be frozen out by Mrs Boulder and sign whatever nonsense Miller shoved my way. I was obviously going to be no good at this job. Ming must have already made a call, because Miller drove up in a rather smart new jeep. She showed a bit of leg when she stepped down, noticed me noticing and didn't scowl.

'How were the sandwiches, sir?'

'Wonderful. The best. Salty.'

'My mother taught me to always roll pork lightly in salt before you roast it: that brings out the flavour.'

'Your mum sounds all right.'

When she asked, 'Was it OK last night?' she spoke almost shyly.

'If I told you, then I'd have to kill you.' It was a line I'd heard before. Then I told her the truth. 'I'm dog-tired. Finished . . . but still smiling.' We both were: she gave me a tired smile in return.

'That's all right. Go home and get a few hours' sleep. The Commander won't expect you in today,' she said.

'Are you sure?'

'Absolutely, sir. Nor Saturday or Sunday. This is our weekend off.'

I drove along the track to the brick farmhouse between two of the fields overrun by hens. Bella Abbott was in one field, moving hens around with her dogs. Their tongues lolled out. She came over to the fence. She smelled of hens.

'If you're hungry, you can boil yourself a couple of eggs,' she told me. 'There's bread, and the butter's in the cold safe.'

'Thanks, Bella. I'm just tired. Bushed. I'll turn in, if that's all right.'

'When you wake up, then. Alison will show you where everything is. I've got to go to Oxford, and I won't be back before evening. She's back from school at about four. I'm glad everything went all right last night.'

'How did you know that?'

She glanced away, and then back at me. 'Well, you're back – aren't you?'

When I awoke I could hear music That wasn't unusual: since my accident I've woken up each morning with different pieces of music in my mind. They stick around for most of the day. What was different this time was that the music was real, coming from a radio downstairs somewhere. Dorothy Squires was singing 'There's Danger Ahead'. She didn't know the half of it. I was lying on my side, facing the door. The first thing I noticed when I opened my eyes were my clothes lying on the floor, where I had stepped out of them. Untidy, Charlie. The second thing that I noticed was that the bedroom door was open. I was sure that I had closed it. The third thing I noticed was the girl leaning against the door jamb. She was probably in her mid-teens; still wearing a rough blue school skirt and a white shirt. Her arms were crossed over her chest, and the hair that hung to her shoulders was a deep golden brown, like newly polished oak. A couple of freckles on either side of a wide smiling mouth. Brown eyes. She said, 'Hello, I'm Alison.'

I yawned. 'Charlie.'

'Hello, Charlie. Have you been out being brave?'

I yawned again.

'No, I've been out being cowardly.'

'Freddy was always out being brave on Thursdays. Do you wear clothes in bed? Freddy always slept with his shirt on, with the rest of his clothes in a bundle on the end of the bed – in case there was an air raid.'

'Freddy sounds like a bit of a nutcase. I don't wear anything in bed. Can't be bothered.'

Her face fell: realization:

'He's not coming back, is he?'

I'd stopped yawning. I felt grubby.

'I don't know, love; probably not. Maybe he's been posted somewhere important.'

Like Heaven. Alison was old enough to recognize when a man was lying to her. She pouted.

'Do you really go to bed without any clothes on?'

This had gone on long enough.

'I'm going to count to ten and then get up. If you're still here you'll find out. One . . .'

She fled, laughing. A diminishing shriek that concluded with a door slamming. She seemed a nice kid. Her mum must be proud of her. I was smiling as I closed the bedroom door.

There was a large handbasin behind a curtain in the corner. In luxuriously hot water I treated myself to a decent stand-up wash. The girl didn't come back, but Bella returned at about seven. She looked tired, but happy. Her cheeks were flushed, and a few thick strands of brown hair escaped from the rough bun she had tucked it into. She had sold eighty dead chickens, and twenty dozen eggs to the three university colleges she usually dealt with, and had been stopped in the street by a butcher looking for another supplier. Success – and money in her purse. She said that it was an excuse to get out the sherry bottle.

I shared their supper in a kitchen lit by two tilley lamps. The electricity in the house hadn't reached there yet. Bacon omelette, chips and HP Sauce. I remembered that my mother made a fine omelette, and the memory silenced me for a while. The tilley lamp hissed on the table and perfumed the air with traces of burnt paraffin. In its light our faces gleamed almost yellow, whilst their hollows and angles were cast into shadow: like one of those Rembrandts that I've seen in the V & A.

Alison didn't say much: her mother explained that she was shy, and needed taking out of herself because she studied too much. The little smile that Alison gave me occasionally made me feel as if I shared a secret with her, which was probably how I was supposed to feel. They let me do the washing-up, and Alison dried the dishes afterwards. Then we sat in what Bella called the small sitting room, played crib, and listened to the radio. Arthur Askey had his own show, told risqué jokes that had us giggling, and sang some of his wartime songs. When he sang 'Kiss Me Goodnight, Sergeant Major' I was transported in my mind back to Bawne, and the men who flew *Tuesday's Child* with me. I still missed the bastards. Bella caught my change of mood, and said that that was a good reason to get out the port bottle. Alison had half a glass, and went to bed at nine: I found a book on Bella's shelves that looked promising, and she and I spent the next hour or so reading on either side of her stove. When I finally stumbled upstairs Germany had retreated back into my imagination, and I slept without dreaming.

*

I followed the music back to the farmhouse kitchen the next morning. Alison was waiting to feed me. Bella was riding herd on the chickens. When she came back for a cuppa I was tucking into fried eggs and fried bread. When I'd finished I said, 'Isn't it about time I started paying you for some of this?'

'That would be good, Charlie, but I'd expect you to be home for supper, or let me know that you weren't going to be here. We don't waste food.'

'Nobody does. Thanks. What should I give you?'

'Five shillings a day all right? You can settle up at the end of the week.'

'Great . . . and thanks for making me feel at home.'

'Thank Ming,' she told me, with a smile. 'He recommended you.'

I gave her a few pounds to be going on with, and my ration book. That was probably worth more to her than the cash. The RAF was paying for my bed, but the board was down to me: I'd see how it went. I was sitting in the small sitting room again when Ming strolled in. 'Ready for another cup of char, sir?'

'No, thanks, Ming. I'm up to here.' I put my finger to my throat. 'And you can call me Charlie when we're off duty. I'd prefer that. And I can't keep on calling you Ming. What are your other names?' All the Orientals in the Charlie Chan films I'd seen seemed to be called *Li*, or *Chang*, or something easy to say but impossible to spell. The chair he neatly fitted himself into creaked with his weight.

'It's Eric, actually . . . but I'm comfortable with Ming, if that's all right with you. Everyone else calls me that.'

'Thanks for getting me in here.'

'That's all right, sir . . . Charlie, I mean. I know Bella quite well. I try to give her a helping hand when I can.'

'Why did you recommend me?'

'I looked at your service record. Policeman's perks.'

'What did it say?'

'Mainly that you are an argumentative bugger – but something that an acting Squadron Leader Brookman wrote impressed me. He wrote that you were a good man.'

I looked away. Poor old Brookie had burned in *Tuesday* the first time he flew her.

'What happened to Mr Abbott?' Ming looked uncomfortable. I'd asked him about his friends, and he didn't want to answer. I liked that. I waved a hand. 'Sorry. I shouldn't have asked. Forget it.'

He met my gaze with a level one of his own. 'Bella would tell you, anyway. There never was a Mr Abbott. She's a *Miss* Abbott.'

'That must have been hard for her. How old was she when Alison came along?'

'Eighteen. Aye; it would have been hard – but her people were all right. They stood by her, even when she told them that she would keep the baby. Farming folk, you see – they're different. They put city folk to shame half of the time.' So Bella was thirty-four – she looked older; maybe forty. Maybe that wasn't so surprising.

'Her mum and dad both died of that flu in 1938,' Ming continued. 'It almost broke her, and she's still mourning them. Rotten luck. She sold off most of the land for a nest egg, and kept enough ground for this idea she had about chickens – she wanted something small enough to do herself, you see.'

'What about you, Ming? Is there a Mrs Ming?'

He gave me that level, guileless gaze again, pausing before he said, 'There's a Miss Abbott. That'll do for me for the time being. What about you?'

'I'm good at making a fool of myself over women, Ming,' I admitted to him. 'There was a special girl when I was on the squadron: she buggered off. Then there was another special girl in Germany, but she buggered off as well – with one of my mates that time. I'll sit back and think before I ask another girl out.'

There was a wide patio of old bricks surrounding the square house. Grass grew between them. You felt that they had been there for five hundred years. I sat in the sun on a kitchen chair, leaned it back against the wall and smoked a pipe. The truth was that I was buggered if I knew what to do with myself.

Alison came out, drying her hands on a dishcloth. She said, 'Why don't you go and buy yourself some clothes? You can't go around in those rags all the time; besides, they need to be dumped in the tub and washed.'

'That bad, huh?'

'That bad,' she agreed, and then she giggled.

'Another woman said that to me two days ago. And another, the week before that. I could drive to Oxford, couldn't I?'

'That would be best. Could I come too, if mum says yes?'

'No.'

She pouted around a wild smile, and said something that sounded like 'Pou . . . ff . . .' as she flicked the tea towel at me.

My chair overbalanced. So did I. I fell into a flower bed. Alison fled, laughing. I heard more laughter, and when I struggled up I saw Ming and Bella in a cloud of dust in a field, waving at me. They were surrounded by hens. I felt good. I had to keep reminding myself: *this is peacetime. Things are different.*

I drove to a men's outfitter in the centre of Oxford; the sun was warm enough for me to keep the hood down all the way. Men in black gowns, looking like Dracula, flapped along Holywell Street. They brought Fergal and his priest's gear to mind. I found a pub there, and swallowed a pint to steady my nerves. Then I went out and bought a load of civvies. That included a couple of Fair Isle pullovers. My last major had worn one of those under his uniform jacket; I'd liked him for that. It felt poncy buying clothes without either my mother or my kid sister to advise me.

At a shoe shop I bought a pair of overpriced brogues and had my feet measured for two bespoke pairs of shoes. They were going to cost me as well, but the shop assistant told me that they'd last my lifetime. All the girls say that. I was less intimidated by the bookshops, and finally chose a small leather-bound copy of John Donne's poetry and a James Hadley Chase – I fancied the girl on its paper cover. The other thing I bought was four more pints of beer in a riverside pub, and I scraped the Singer against a milestone on the way back.

I detoured by way of Benhall because I had nothing else to do. The guys at the front were polite but firm: they weren't keen on my turning up when I wasn't rostered, but they made an exception and let me in. Both my huts were locked, so I didn't bother with them. Only one other hut in the compound had people in it. Duty team, I supposed. I didn't know them, so I didn't bother with them either.

Watson was sitting on his veranda, wearing a white suit. He was smoking a long cheroot, and had what looked suspiciously like a whisky and soda on a small table alongside his chair. He looked like an off-duty District Officer from nineteenth-century Simla. He hailed me with a 'What ho!' as I fetched to.

'What are *you* doing? Practising for a posting to Singapore?'

'What are you doing, *sir*.'

'*Sir.*'

'Better. No: Dutch courage. Chairing the cricket club AGM in an hour or so, and there are some frightful types there. What are you here for, on your time off?'

'I'm not used to time off. I didn't know what to do.'

'Go and buy some decent clobber.'

'I've already done that, sir. Why does everybody make remarks about my clothes?'

'Because you look such a bloody sight. It might have been good enough for racketing around the Continent in, but it's not good enough for sunny Cheltenham.'

'Anyway, I've done it, sir . . . but I'm glad that you're here. I can tell you what I was going to tell you on Monday.'

'Which is?'

'It occurred to me that if we didn't insist on flying weather flights only on Thursdays maybe the Russians wouldn't be able to guess that we're coming, and be waiting to dance. That way maybe we wouldn't be losing our bloody aircraft, and the bloody people in them. Sir.'

'Why should you think that we always fly on Thursdays?'

'Because the teenage girl at my digs told me, sir: maybe the Reds have teenage girls, too . . . or maybe they can even work it out for themselves.'

Watson stood up and sighed. He picked up a panama hat I hadn't noticed, and his glass. 'Why don't you come inside and have a drink, Charlie? Maybe they'll listen to you.'

He connected me to two different staff officers who obviously still worked Saturdays. I used a green telephone that he kept in his desk drawer. I hadn't seen a green telephone before. I hadn't seen a telephone that lived in a desk drawer before, either. There were some strange people around.

Both officers listened politely, said 'Thank you, Pilot Officer Bassett,' and hung up on me. I decided that if people like that had come into the top jobs, then the RAF was too dangerous a service to stay with. Roll on demob.

Watson asked me, 'I don't suppose that you used to play a bit of cricket?'

'Yes, sir, I did. But it's a bit like bombing Germany to me now,' I told him.

'How's that?' He didn't see the joke. 'How's it like bombing Germany?'

I laughed. 'I don't want to do it any more.'

I walked back to the guardroom to collect my car, locking the compound behind me. Maybe I could get the hang of all these locks and keys after all. I had to wait after they lifted the barrier for me, because a man with a dark raincoat that reached to the ground was doing a song-and-dance act for them in the road outside. He held a small bowl in one hand. Coins rattled in it.

He sang and danced to 'Puttin' on the Ritz', his shoes tapping at the tarmac like machine-gun fire. He had a croupier's dark visor over his blind eyes, and a greasy dark felt hat. His hair was lank, and flopped around his shoulders as his feet tapped out the rhythms. When I dropped a two-bob bit in his bowl he doffed his hat to me, and sidestepped. The world wasn't quite back to normal; not quite.

Ming was still at the farm when I returned, but his feet were under the kitchen table, and a mug of cloudy cider was in his hand. He said, 'I forgot to tell you. A Yank turned up yesterday, asking for you. I think that he was an air-force sergeant of some kind. They have funny ranks, don't they?'

'Yeah, they do. Did he say what he wanted?'

'He wants you to look after a big parcel for him for a couple of weeks. He's going up to Ganda, and will see you on the way back. I had it put in your office, alongside the desk. Was that all right?'

I said, 'I suppose so,' before I thought it through. I'd looked after things for Tommo Thomsett before. I asked him, 'Just how big was this parcel?'

'*Big*: about three by four, and wrapped in brown paper. It wasn't at all heavy for its size, but something loose inside makes a very strange rattling noise.' Then a nasty thought crossed my mind. I should have listened to Dorothy Squires more closely when she sang 'There's Danger Ahead'. It was too late to do anything about it now. I just hoped that no one opened the package out of curiosity before I turned up on Monday.

'Anything else you forgot to tell me?'

'Yes. Joe Humm came by a couple of hours ago. He's going to a jazz club near Priors Norton tonight; at the back of a pub called the Good King Richard. He says it's six moonlighters from London bands, and that they're quite good. He says to join him there at eight to eight-thirty if you fancy it.'

8. *Snag It*

I was late, and the evening was drawing in. The pub car park was overflowing, so I parked close to a bridge nearby. It was still unseasonably warm, and there was a hatch of flies dancing a living cloud above the slow-moving river. Couples sat on the river bank, cooling their feet in the water. I stood in the car park for ten minutes, listening to the buzz from inside, and the music. It sounded brilliant. This had been worth fighting for. Was there a jazz club somewhere in Germany, with a retired night-fighter pilot lurking outside thinking the same? Joe was near the door with a mug in his hand. There was another on a narrow shelf alongside him, and he shoved it at me. 'Didn't think you'd resist, old son. Here – this one's yours.'

'What would you have done if I hadn't turned up?'

'Drunk it myself. Cheers.'

'Cheerio. What do I do – buy a ticket from someone?'

'Half a crown, up at the bar. Pay when you get your first round in.' He inverted his mug and added, 'And you can get your first round in *now*. This is Avril, by the way; she drinks sweet cider in halves.'

A pretty girl with her dark hair in bunches had been standing with her back to us all the time. Tapping her feet to the syncopated rhythms. She turned and said, 'Hello, Charlie. Joe said that you'd be here.'

Joe put his arm around her waist, and pulled her close. 'Go and find your own!' he warned me. 'My drink's a dry cider, by the way. I should go easy on it if I was you – until you're used to it. We'll get a dance while you're getting the drinks.'

When I returned from the bar the girl was still there. She offered me a de Reske Minor from a white fag packet: they were cheap, and popular with the girls. I shook my head, and put the drinks down.

'I usually smoke a pipe,' I said, having to shout to make myself heard over the music.

'I like men who smoke pipes. The smell doesn't cling afterwards.'

'I thought you wanted to dance.'

She shook her head. 'Joe did. I'm resting my feet. Besides, I was thirsty.'

Twilight had reached inside to touch us. The club was probably the pub's function room, and it extended towards the river. The only lights were above the busy bar, and the band. The rest of us hid in the darkness at its periphery, or jived it up in the centre. Avril was content to rest an arm against mine, sip cider and tap her feet until the clarinettist started up a slow number. Then she took my pint, set it down, and pulled me onto the floor.

'Dance with me. Don't worry,' she assured me. 'Joe won't mind.'

I still resisted. 'Can't jive properly; I don't know how.'

'Don't worry, we won't . . . and I can always teach you.' By then we were dancing anyway. Her head was on my shoulder, and the old man with the licorice stick was giving it 'When it's sleepy time down South'. I thought that I saw Brookie drift past, dancing with his tall WAAF, but they'd both been dead for years. I've often been troubled by ghosts on dance floors: you ask anyone from my generation and they'll tell you the same. A foot above our heads the smoke was layering out like fine cirrus clouds.

When I walked Avril back Joe said, 'Oh, good. There you are,' and he asked me, 'Good band?'

'Great. Who are they?'

'The band with no name. I don't think that any of them is supposed to be here.'

'I've heard the clarinet player before, on the radio. I was standing on the steps of a hospital at Bremerhaven at the end of the war. The programme came from Spa.'

'That's possible: he's a French guy. The trumpet player was an officer in the Grenadiers. Front-line job. Mad as a monkey.'

The man in question started another slow number. When his sleepy, brassy notes began to hang in the air in rows above us, we stopped talking to listen, and the dancers stopped moving. He had us. Afterwards I asked, 'What's that called?'

'"Snag it." Amazing, isn't he? I hope he doesn't burn himself out in a few years.'

I moved off from them during the next number: something ragtime. I was feeling a bit like a gooseberry. I saw a face I knew above a dark floral-print dress. She danced by with a boy who looked sixteen too. They stopped close to me.

'Hi, Charlie,' Alison said, 'this is Stacey. Say hello, Stacey.' Stacey mumbled 'Hello.' Then he shut his eyes and rocked on his heels.

'He's drunk too much, too quickly,' Alison said. 'Let's find him somewhere to sit.' We found him a wooden chair against the wall. He sat with his head down, clutched between his hands. He groaned.

'Sorry. Be OK in a few minutes.'

Alison said, 'He will be too, amazingly quick recovery rate.'

'He'd be better off outside in the fresh air.'

'No, that would finish him off, although I could do with some myself. How about you?'

I said, 'OK,' and allowed myself to be led by the hand back out into the car park. Alison watched me fill and light a pipe. I asked, 'Does Bella know that you're here?'

'Not exactly, Charlie. She didn't ask, and I didn't tell her.'

'That means she trusts you.'

She gnawed her upper lip, which probably meant I'd said something wrong. 'Time to go inside again. Stace will be coming to about now.' She was still holding my hand as we walked up to him, and let it go just before he noticed us. She whispered, 'Can you take me home if he gets too bad?' How bad was too bad? I wondered. And bad at what? But although I saw her dance past another couple of times during the evening, I drove home alone.

I slept alone in an empty house. The chicken serenade got into my room in the morning. A lot of chickens having breakfast make a lot of noise. So do excited dogs. I walked over to the bedroom window. Alison was in the fields, releasing the chickens from their long low houses. She was still dressed in her dancing frock, but was wearing wellingtons under it. After a minute she stopped what she was doing, turned, and waved to me, with a big smile on her face. Women seem to have an inbuilt radar that tells them when men are watching, and from where. I waved back.

Downstairs I did something that I hadn't done since before the war: boiled a couple of eggs myself, and ate them with lashings of salt, and toast soldiers. I felt the lightness of being about fourteen again. Alison walked in, made a pot of tea, and sat down at the table. Up close, the colour beneath her eyes told you that she'd been up all night. And up close you could just smell chickens. She had a couple of downy feathers in her hair: I reached over and took them. She whispered, 'Thank you,' blew on her tea to cool it, paused and added, 'But you won't tell Mum, will you?'

'You almost asked me that last night.'

'Did I? What did you say?'

'I think I said *OK*. Don't you think that Bella knows anyway? Mums are pretty good at that sort of thing.' I was suddenly lost for something to say to her, so I said, 'I've never been to a jazz club before: I suppose that I was always too busy.'

'You can catch up while you're staying with us. Take me, if you like. Mum would probably let me go if she thought that you were there to look after me.'

'Then she'd be making a mistake, wouldn't she? Besides . . .'

'. . . I suppose you're the sort of man who has a rule about that sort of thing.'

'Yes, kid, there's a rule. Shall I help you collect the eggs? I haven't done that since I was small.'

Do you know how many eggs a thousand chickens can lay when they've got nothing else to do all night? We collected hundreds, and then we had to wash them and stack them on trays in a cool shed. It took us most of the morning. I only broke two. Then I put on my new blazer and went out beer hunting.

On Monday there was a small queue of cars waiting to turn off the main road into Benhall at 0730. It was like turning up at a factory. I thought that I'd see what time my people got in for work. Both huts were already open: Mrs Boulder was sitting at her radio with the earphones over her head. It was a pity she'd never learned to smile. Sensing my presence, she turned, nodded, removed the phones and said, 'There's a big box of some sort in your room. It's wrapped in brown paper. I decided not to go near it.'

I decided that Boulder was brighter than she looked. Then she surprised me by saying two things. The first was, 'Would you like a cup of coffee? The kettle's not long boiled.'

'Thanks; I'll just pop over the road, and drink it when I come back. I'll only be a couple of mins.'

She looked embarrassed as she delivered the other surprise: embarrassed but determined to get her message across. 'Well done on Thursday night. You really took the bastard to pieces, didn't you? Mrs Miller said you were going to bring us luck.'

'Thank you, Mrs Boulder, but don't mind my asking . . . how do you know anything happened?'

'I was your angel on Thursday night. I heard it all. My third language is Russian.'

'My angel?'

'Didn't they tell you that you were being monitored?'

'Yes, but not from here . . . OK . . . I understand. Thanks, and yes, we really turned the bastard over, didn't we?'

When I said that the side of her mouth twitched. She was trying to smile. We'd have to work on that.

When I stepped into the other Hut 7 Weronka confronted me, and said, 'Was he a Russian you killed on Thursday, or a Pole?'

'A Russian, I think. That's what he was speaking . . . and I'm not sure he died. It was nothing to do with me, in any case.'

'No matter. You were there for us, so well done anyway. One to us.'

'Does it matter if he was a Russian or a Pole? He was trying to kill us first, and he couldn't fly for shit: he was a novice and all out of shape. He shouldn't have been up there.'

'If it had been a Pole I would have had a Mass said for him, but essentially it doesn't matter: no. Well done again.' Then she kissed me Frog fashion, on both cheeks.

'That's what Mrs Boulder said to me.'

'Then I'd better say so, too,' Miller said, and I felt suddenly warm all over.

She'd walked out of her office in her little grey suit. What was it that Kid Ory used to say? *Ashes to ashes, dust to dust: if the whisky don't get you, the women must.* It was one of the tunes I used to wake up with. Somewhere at the back of my brain a little voice must have whispered *here we go again*, but I didn't notice it. Not then. I just wanted to get the clothes off somebody else's wife again: situation normal.

'I didn't know that it would be Boulder listening out for me.'

'Whenever you're out there, one of us will be listening for you, sir. We always listen out for our own officer: it's the way it works. Make sure that you listen back if ever we talk to you. There's a huge parcel in your office: what's in it?'

'I'm just going back to unwrap it; why don't you come and see? Mrs Boulder's made me a cup of coffee.' I wanted her to smile and nod. She smiled and nodded.

'Thank you for the kisses, Ronka,' I said as we left. 'You can kiss me again tomorrow.'

The Pole had a raucous laugh. 'Kill another bloody Russian first.'

I had been right first time: bloodthirsty dames and hard work.

As we walked back to my hut Miller and I didn't speak, and that felt ominously comfortable. I wondered if Boulder had been listening in when they killed her lover in the cold sky somewhere over in the East. Maybe I could get to hate the Reds as much as I had the Fritzies. It would depend on how hard they tried to kill me.

In my office we moved the box against one wall before I unwrapped it. I told Miller, 'I saw the Boss on Saturday. I suggested that we flew on nights other than Thursdays for a while – it will be less exciting if the opposition isn't waiting.'

'The Russians will be very cross with you for that, Charlie.' I was pleased that she'd slipped into using my first name as soon as we were alone. I couldn't have kept the other thing going.

'There was a blind tramp in a long black raincoat dancing by the main gate.'

'That's Mr Summit. He's good, isn't he? He has a sort of timetable but I haven't worked it out yet. He appears in different places all around town at the same times every week.'

From inside the box there was a gentle rattling sound, like a dying man clearing his throat. Suddenly I didn't want to remove the paper. But I did. If the plexiglas had been broken in transit I was in trouble.

Then Miller screamed. She had that scream that some girls have; like a soprano in overdrive. But it tailed off; didn't last too long. I squatted down alongside Alice's plexiglas box. She rattled her tail *hello*, and then struck savagely. The plastic glass bulged with the blow, and then sprang back. I wondered if it gave her a headache. Clear poison streamed down it. Alice was a diamond-back rattlesnake.

I said, 'Hello, Alice.' Then I turned to Miller, who had gone white. 'I think she likes you, too.'

Miller said, 'That was a perfectly *awful* thing to do – not warning me.' Then she made curious little coughing noises. At first I thought that they were sobs; then I realized that she was laughing, and getting her breath back at the same time. She slumped into the spare chair. 'I've got to sit down, Charlie.' After several deep breaths she said, 'Don't do that again: not without telling me first.'

'Don't you like snakes?'

'Not very much.'

'Neither do I.'

'Then what's it doing here?'

'She belongs to an American I know. He's asked me to look after her for a couple of weeks. He didn't ask, actually. He just turned up, and left her here.'

'How did he know that you were here? This is supposed to be a top-secret site. And why is she moving around so much? Most snakes just lie there and sleep, don't they?'

'Tommo has a lot of contacts: I probably wasn't hard to track. And I think that Alice is hungry: she looks thin.'

Someone had fixed a nice little label on the top of Alice's box – it hinged out, and hung down like a pub sign. It read *Alice's Restaurant*. Her kills were painted in small matchstick figures on the glass alongside it. There were now six men, and a dog. The dog was new since I'd last seen her.

'What does the sign mean?'

'It means that she's often eating something in there. I'd like to take her out for a walk,' I joked, 'but I don't think that it would be safe.'

'Don't you bloody dare while I'm around, Charlie Bassett.' It was the first time I had heard her swear.

'Don't worry: just testing.'

Her smile wasn't like a girl's smile any more. It was a grin. Her chin stuck out defiantly. I went over and squatted in front of her, with one knee down. A splinter from the wooden plank floor went into my knee. I was very brave; I didn't cry out. Her eyes flicked to the door to check that it was closed, and then back to me. That was good. Get it right, Charlie. I gave her the eye-lock and said, 'I want to kiss you.'

The grin disappeared. But her eyes were still smiling – I think. They looked very grey. She said, 'Go and feed your snake,

Charlie.' That could mean anything, couldn't it? I almost said, '*That's precisely what I had in mind*,' but I stood up instead.

'I'll ask Ming: he'll know what to do.'

I turned as I opened the door, and looked back at her. She wasn't looking at me; she was looking out of the window. This time she was definitely smiling.

Ming came back an hour later with a live week-old chick. I didn't ask where it had come from. We lifted back the wire lid of Alice's box, and dropped the sacrifice in. Alice hit it before it touched the sand she slept on. Miller stopped to watch the hit, which surprised me. We shut the lid and tiptoed out, leaving Alice to get on with the messy bit herself. After Ming left, Miller asked me, 'Shall we go for a walk at lunchtime?' If the midday meal was called lunch where she came from, I was going to have to mind my p's and q's.

The big flat water bowl in Alice's box was dry, so I'd filled it with fresh cold water from a kettle in the small galley. I poured it through the top wire, and made a bit of a mess, but Alice didn't seem to mind: she immediately crawled over and took a drink. Then she sloshed around in it for a while before sliding into a corner alongside a rotten piece of wood and going to sleep. She had a bulge that had once been a chick about a foot back from her head; she had never looked happier.

Miller watched her over my shoulder. 'How long will she sleep?'

'Days.'

'How big is she?'

'About five feet long, and as thick as my arm in places.'

'And she's very poisonous?'

'I should say. She could kill an elephant with what she's got in her mouth.'

'I haven't seen any elephants round here lately.'

'Now you know why, don't you?'

'What are you going to do about her?'

'Can you borrow me a blanket from somewhere? I'll throw that over her house, and keep her in the corner until Tommo gets back. Lock the office door every time I'm not in here. Put a *Keep out: that means you* notice on the door.'

'Tommo's your American friend?'

'Our relationship is a bit more complicated than that. But you could say friend, yes. When are you going to tell me about the Jedburghs?'

I had tried to catch her off guard. My mistake.

'I'll ask the Commander when he gets back. He's away for a couple of days.'

'So. I'm your boss, but there are things that you can't tell me without the permission of someone really senior to me?'

'You got it. It's for your own good, really.'

'How come?'

'If you fall into the hands of the Reds you won't have anything damaging to tell them.'

I thought about that for a few seconds. 'You really believe that?'

'That you'll talk if they catch you alive? Yes. Absolutely.'

What I'd actually meant was, did she really believe that the Russians would get me some day? But then, she'd answered that as well, hadn't she?

*

Perce phoned on Wednesday, and Piers on Thursday. Perce and Piers: it sounded like a comic double act on a variety bill. I also signed a lot of requisition slips for equipment that I didn't need or recognize. When I asked Miller what the requisition numbers meant, she pointed me at a shelf of loose-leaf instruction books with an 'It would be better if you looked them up for yourself, sir.' I couldn't be bothered.

Perce had been out with another team the night before; the first trip all year that hadn't been done on a Thursday. He said that at the briefing they were told that the trips were being made on different days of the week 'on the advice of a battle-hardened professional'. I wondered how we'd forgotten that in less than two years, and what sort of morons were really in charge of the show these days.

'Was that you, Charlie? I got the feeling it might be.'

'Nah. I'm just a passenger, like you. Where'd you go?'

'Not allowed to say. I wasn't as scared this time.'

'Then you're halfway to being dead already, Perce. Stay scared, or give it up – it gives you an edge.'

'I wish you'd be serious for half a sec.'

'I *am* being serious,' I assured him. 'It's the curse of the survivor: no one believes us when we're being serious. Every time I climb a ladder I'm scared these days, let alone getting into a fucking aircraft.'

'Gotta go now, Charlie: good luck next week.'

Balls! He shouldn't have told me that either, should he? Perhaps he was just being kind.

For the first time in a couple of years I thought about my will. We were compelled to have one on the squadron, and the

Tuesdays created ours so that everything accrued to the survivors, until there was only one left. There's a name for that sort of will, and I used to know it. I'd have to change that now. I heard a noise from beneath the blanket over Alice's Restaurant: maybe a snore. *Do snakes dream?* I wondered.

Piers. I was surprised to have to admit to myself that I was actually pleased to hear him. He was obviously an evil bastard, but he interested me.

I said, 'Wotcha, Piers.'

'Don't do cockney, Charlie,' he advised me. 'I can do cockney, but you can't. You haven't got the voice for it.'

'What do I have the voice for?'

'Flight Lieutenant, if you stay with us: it's in my gift. That or the civil service equivalent, with a pension and a carriage clock after forty years. If you *really* cock up the King will give you an award. Order of the bleeding enema or something like that.'

I snorted. 'Not a bloody chance.'

'Nice pun. You still want out, then?'

'Definitely. As soon as the RAF will let me go: when is that, by the way?'

'In about six months.'

'That's what you told me about three weeks ago.'

'I forgot to start the clock. I'll do it as soon as I hang up.'

'You're fucking me about, aren't you?'

'If I am, it's all for the good of the country. Are you still going to go to Oz when you bale out?'

'I don't know; I'm going off the idea, but I don't know why.'

'How about hanging around, and then transferring to a civvy

airline as a radio operator? There are people around who fly to all sorts of interesting places. If you got as far as Oz with them and didn't like it, you'd still have the opportunity to come back again on the next flight. I could put in a word for you.' I didn't reply; I was trying to get my brain into gear, so eventually he asked, 'Charlie? You still there?'

'Sorry, Piers. I was thinking. Do you know, I think that that would suit me very well; as long as it was to nowhere very dangerous. Are you serious? What did you want, anyway – apart from to offer me a job I'd be very pleased to get?'

'Purely personal, old son. I wondered when you were coming up to town – we could have a couple of drinks or something.'

'Your *or somethings* land people in police cells.'

'Nothing like that, old son,' he said hastily. 'Anyway, you're not the type.'

'I might as well be; the luck I'm having with the girls up here.'

'That was part of the reason I phoned. The *girls* were asking after you as well, and asked me to tell you that you could bunk with them if you wanted to stay for a couple of days: they'll put you up on the sofa. Dolly goes all misty-eyed whenever your name is spoken. I think that they miss you. What about it, old man?'

'I'll ask Miller if I can get a forty-eight.'

'Who's Miller?'

'She's a WREN in mufti. She's a junior ranker who works for me, but I still seem to need to get her permission for anything I do. It's all arse about face out here, but I expect that you already knew that.'

'OK. Toddle off and get your forty-eight; then phone me back. Bring some of your clothing coupons, and some money, up with you. We'll pick you out some decent gear.'

'I already have some.'

'No. What you have is some dreary Old Farmer Giles outfit. I asked someone. It's time we had you looking like the man about town; maybe your strike rate with the fillies will even improve.'

'Strike rate?'

'American term. Originally from baseball, but now they apply it to killing things, apparently.'

'I don't want to kill things.'

'Then leave your bloody snake behind when you come, there's a good fellow.'

How come he knew so much about me?

'What number can I call you back on?'

'Just pick up your telephone,' he said confidently, 'and it will be mine at the other end.'

It was, as well. I still don't know how he did that.

Miller granted me a forty-eight for the weekend, and said that it would do me good. Miller could be a patronizing little git. She asked me where I would be staying, and noted that down on a card which she filed in a box on her desk.

It was my turn to pivot at the door. 'We're on next week. You might want to warn someone that they're in for a late night.'

I only did it to wind her up. If I was so picky about security I should have kept my mouth shut. Hers went into that screwed-up little shape that you can find on the seashore – it's called a Mermaid's Purse.

'You can't know that already. It's not the way things are done.'

I used a word she was fond of, and enjoyed using it.

'They are now – apparently.' Mrs Miller was not amused, and the set of her jaw said it. I felt that I had won that round on points, and rather enjoyed it. I rather thought I'd try it again. 'I'm going to take over from Elizabeth for half an hour. Just to keep my hand in.' I got the Mermaid's Purse again, and a quick response.

'You don't have to do that, Charlie.' *Charlie*, even although the door was still open and Jane was probably earwigging somewhere: Miller must have been ruffled. I gave her a cheeky grin.

'I know, luv. But I want to.'

I thought that I'd won the set, but I wouldn't have put money on myself for the match.

Elizabeth didn't trust me to function on my own. She sat in the corner, sipping her tea, crossing and recrossing her legs to distract me. It did. Eventually I turned my back on her, and once I did she chuckled. So did I. She went out and came back with a cup of char for me. The signal was intermittent, repeated say every ten minutes or so, and drifted. I compensated for the drift by flying with my left hand on the tuner all the time, and searching in towards the signal every time it faded. It was something that the old guys had taught me, and I'd used it over Germany in 1944. Elizabeth watched me closely. Then she nodded: she liked it. The string of letters and numbers was meaningless to me, but of course it was meant to be. I listened to four sequences before I handed back to her.

'Liz. What are we listening for?'

She leafed through the flimsies that I had copied my record onto. 'You did four signals, and they were all identical?'

'As far as I can make out.'

'What we're listening for is a single difference – one letter or one number.'

'What does that tell us?' I asked.

'Nobody's told us. Mrs Miller thinks that the single aberration is a trigger message of some kind. An initiator. Something that signals the start of a sequence of operational orders that have already been put in place. She thinks that maybe the intelligence people in London try to match the odd signal with something that other sources have told them about – military manoeuvres in the Soviet Bloc, for instance.'

'So that's not a Jedburgh?'

'No: nothing like. Shall I tip you the wink the next time I'm monitoring one?'

9. *Savoy Blues*

Piers was unimpressed by my clothing.

'Told you. Bloody Farmer Giles from Much Wankum or somewhere mudfully rural. You look bloody horrible.'

He and Dolly were squeezed into one of the small berths in the Printer's Devil. Dolly was wearing a pretty summer dress, and looked ravishing – or ravishable. Take your choice: the men with hopeful faces grouped around her end of the bar can't have been there by coincidence. I could make out a light dusting of powder on her shoulders. I wondered if she was dressed for one of Stephen's dates later in the evening. It was just after 1830. I had signed away from Benhall at lunchtime; nobody seemed to care. Would anyone notice if I failed to return? Failure to return was in danger of becoming another of my specialities.

I had dressed in a pair of twills and the tweed jacket over an open-necked checked shirt. I had thought that I looked quite the thing until I met them. Piers wore a lightweight pale blue suit and soft shoes. In his left lapel I noticed an enamelled badge in the shape of a tiny blue flower: a forget-me-not. An improbably slim belly dancer had been printed on his silk tie. As he moved the silk shimmered, and the girl danced. I asked him, 'What did you pay for what you're wearing?'

'About a hundred pounds – why?'

'You could have bought a house for that before the war.'

'It's not *before the war* now, Charlie, it's before the *next* war. Far East somewhere, if you wanted me to guess.' Piers sounded exasperated. 'Don't worry: I promise that we're all going to die far better dressed the third time around.'

I grinned on cue. I'd missed Dolly and Den. I'd even missed Piers. It wasn't as if there had been a clean cut-off between wartime and peacetime for me: I don't know why. It was as if peacetime was coming back bit by bit, and from time to time I noticed that. Somewhere deep in the back of my mind a grinning dwarf was once again reminding me *This is peacetime* and *It's good, isn't it?*

'So, good drive, old son?' Piers asked me.

'Terrific. I'll enter for Le Mans next year at this rate. I'll need some more petrol to get me back.'

'Dolly'll fix that up, won't you, Doll?'

Dolly looked down at the table and nodded. Her lips twitched. Then she looked up, and speared me with her eyes and her smile. Wallop. I knew immediately that she had dressed for me; there would be no other date this evening. I decided to try something. I leaned across the table, and lightly and briefly touched her hand. The important thing was that it was deliberate and in plain sight. 'You look wonderful; it's impossible to look at you and not want to go to bed.'

'Before supper?' Piers asked. 'Curb thyself. Get thee behind me, Satan.'

'Isn't that exactly how you get into trouble, Piers?'

'I'll pass over that catty piece of wit. We'll eat together at a little place in Wardour Street; it's convenient for a club that I'll go on to. Then you two can go off and do . . . well, whatever folk like you do.'

'Thank you, Piers,' I told him. 'It's very good to see you again. I never imagined that I would ever think so.'

'I hope that you like Chinese food.'

'Don't they eat dogs?'

'Only boxers. Revenge for the Rebellion, I expect.'

I didn't know what he was talking about then, and if *you* don't then you can always look it up.

Dolly said, 'It's lovely to see you too, Charlie – and to hear you sparring with Piers. But finish your drink and let's get moving. I'm starving.'

It was the first Chinese food I had ever tasted. Piers ate quickly and expertly with chopsticks. Dolly copied him, but clumsily, and dribbled food on the tablecloth now and again. I stuck to a fork and spoon. I ate pork pieces fried in batter and smothered with a sweet sauce that had a swift sour aftertaste. Something I said made Dolly start to giggle, and then to choke on her wine. It was that sort of an affair.

Afterwards the three of us walked in Soho Square I agreed to see Piers for some serious tailoring the next day. He seemed to think that my wardrobe needed managing. For some reason I was uneasy at the prospect. Maybe I was frightened I'd arrive back in Cheltenham kitted out like a Monty.

I was amazed at the variety of birdsong you could already hear in the centre of the capital. Dolly told me they were all coming back. 'During the Big Blitz virtually all of the birds, except the sparrows, starlings and pigeons just upped and left. We should have awarded medals to those who stuck it out with us.'

'A robin,' Piers said. 'On the twelfth of January 1944 I opened my bedroom curtain and knew that we'd won the war. I saw a robin perched on a spade in the garden: I hadn't seen one for three years, you see. Sentimental load of old twats, aren't we?'

'Where did you get that forget-me-not badge?' I asked him, 'Does it mean anything?'

'It's used by the club I'm going to, and *yes*, it does mean something to me, but I'm not going to tell you, OK?'

We left him there in Soho Square. I wanted to get a cab, but Dolly was in a strange mood, and wanted to ride on the top deck of a bus. She loosely held on to my hand for the whole journey, even when we walked the last hundred yards or so. The flat was empty, but even if it hadn't been I don't think that would have changed what happened next. We made love immediately.

I met Piers at the Savoy for breakfast. Stodgy porridge, then kedgeree followed by devilled kidneys. His treat, he said. The government must have been paying him too much. I left feeling half a stone heavier. I had expected him to try to palm me off with some smarmy Saville Row tailor, but that wasn't what he had in mind. We ended up visiting three small shops in the East End, and I chose a lightweight grey suit to take away, and a grey pinstripe that I was measured for. The prices were keen, and despite what Piers had said no one asked for coupons. They treated Piers as if he was an old friend.

We returned to Jermyn Street for shirts. They were all the same colour, an island blue, and too expensive by half, but I was too embarrassed by Piers's apparent expertise to resist. I insisted on choosing two ties for myself, both knitted – one in dark blue, and the other green. I looked at a silk kipper with the print of a bathing beauty, but decided that I hadn't got what it took to carry it off.

Back to the Savoy for lunch, where I was relieved of my parcels and bags by the cloakroom attendant. Grilled lamb chops, and grilled tomatoes. A bottle of claret appeared from somewhere. Piers addressed the waiters by their Christian names. He called one Hans.

'Jerry submariner,' he explained when I asked him. 'Bloody good waiter. Your Jerry is an excellent bod once you've taught him his place.'

The odd thing was that I felt uncomfortable both with having a Kraut as a waiter and with Piers being so patronizing about the bastard. It was like old friends getting off on the wrong foot. The last thing he said before we parted was, 'Fancy a walk on the Heath tomorrow morning before you go back, old man? Get some fresh air.'

Maybe it was the claret that made me say yes.

You must never take them for granted, must you? Women, I mean. When I got back to the flat Dolly was dressing up to the nines for an evening out, but not with me. I probably treated her to the upside-down smile. She said, 'Sorry, Charlie. I should have told you.'

I shrugged. 'No matter. I can find something to do – take in a flick, maybe. I knew a girl like you once. She had a lot of casual friends, too. I learned not to be jealous.'

'Good. I don't like jealous men: they panic me.'

'I won't ever panic you, Doll.'

'Yes, you will.'

'How?'

She whispered, 'When you leave for good, you fool,' and dashed into the bathroom, slamming the door behind her so hard that the bottles inside rattled on their shelves. *Now* what had I done?

When she came out her warpaint was on, and a brittle smile fixed in place. I might not have been jealous, but I could still envy the guy she was going out to see. He collected her at seven: a bespectacled middle-aged American in an army uniform. His ensemble looked tailored to me, even his topcoat. We shook hands. I said, 'Charlie. RAF.'

He had an engaging smile 'Adlai. Prosecutor's staff. War-crimes stuff.'

By then Dolly was ready. She had several dead foxes draped over her shoulders, gave me a peck on the cheek, and said, 'Don't wait up.'

I waited for Adlai to give me a peck on the cheek as well. He didn't: you never can tell with Americans. I turned on their radio. Bing and Rosemary were singing 'Don't Fence Me In'. That was OK by me.

Women. I've already said that you shouldn't take them for granted. But there again, anyone can make a mistake. When I was in my twenties the women I chased were like London buses: you waited half your life for them, and then half a dozen came along at once. I have a theory about that, but I'm not going to tell you. I didn't go to the cinema. I walked round to the pub we'd been at before, had a quiet couple of pints, and played two games of dominoes with the local parson. I didn't win either of them because God was on his side.

I had only been back a few minutes before Denys walked in and threw herself onto the leather sofa. She was dressed for going out, but hadn't overdone it.

'Strewth. They've reinvented afternoon tea-dances at the Guards, Charlie! My feet ache so much they're glowing. If you turned the light out we could read by the light of them.'

'Do you want a drink?'

'Not really, but if you make me a cuppa I'll have your babies!'

'Coming up,' I told her. I think I was referring to the tea.

I found a big old yellow tin of Coleman's mustard powder in the kitchen cabinet: it must have been pre-war. I stirred some into a basin of hot water while I was waiting for the tea to draw, and took it through to her. She asked me, 'What on earth's that for?'

'My mum's recipe for curing aching feet. Stop moaning, take your stockings off, and try it.'

I was back in the kitchen area when I heard her moan of pleasure.

When I returned she was leaning back with her feet in the basin and her eyes closed. I drank the tea myself because she went to sleep. I woke her when the water had cooled half an hour later: not because I was a spoilsport, but because I was afraid that her feet would be dyed a wrinkled yellow. She yawned. 'That was divine, Charlie. You're quite a find.'

'Even if I'm not too handy in bed?'

'Who said that?'

'You did. You told Piers. He told me.'

'I never said that! Isn't that funny? He must be jealous. Yer average in bed, if you must know. Most men are, just like most girls are; only men aren't happy with being average, are they?'

It was my turn to smile. 'No; I don't suppose we are.'

Den yawned again. And then again. She said, 'Thanks for the foot thing. Look – they've gone all white and wrinkly. I guess I'll drop into a bath for a while.'

I clicked the radio on. I had the choice between a brains trust on the redevelopment of the German industries, or Billy Cotton. Guess who won? It was just my bad luck that the first full number I heard was 'Somebody Stole My Gal'.

We went to bed for the form of it. As it happened, Den didn't want to, and neither did I, and I didn't mind. What goes around comes around. And around. We were slow to go to sleep, and lay there naked, whispering like children in the dark. I can remember sharing a cigarette with her in the small hours, lying on our backs and listening to Anne Shelton sing 'While the Music Plays on' from the small bakelite bedside radio. Before we slept she asked me, 'Do you think that we'll ever get used to the lights being on outside?'

'I'm not sure that I want to.'

Den hugged me. 'I'm glad that someone else feels that way too.'

I packed my small bag and was away before Dolly returned. I had agreed to meet Piers at Kenwood House, an old mansion on the edge of Hampstead Heath. At the garage on Highgate Hill I presented a WD chit that Dolly had given me the day before, and had the Singer filled up with petrol, topped off with a couple of shots of Redex. There was a public car park that was still chained off, because the house and grounds hadn't come back into use since the war. But Piers was there and he unfastened the chain and then locked it again behind me. He rode the running board down a twisted and slightly overgrown avenue of rhododendrons. I thought that they would have been a fine sight a month ago. We came upon the house suddenly, and I parked alongside a cream and red SS Jaguar coupe with cycle-type mudguards over the front wheels. Its headlights were as big as dinner plates, and were covered by mesh guards.

'Is that yours?' I asked him.

'Yes. Like it?'

'Part of me thinks that it's too flash. What can it do?'

'Good. It's meant to be a bit flash. I can get the ton and more out of her when I want to. Les Vieux gave it to me for my twenty-first.'

We walked through a tunnel in the rhodies at the side of the enormous house and came out into the sunlight on a gravelled path. The back of the house was all windows and looked out on lawns descending to a large ornamental lake. The lake was locked in with weed, and the water looked dank. A swan's corpse floated in it.

'What is this place, Piers? What's it used for?'

'Big Georgian house built for Lord somebody or other . . . Mansfield, that was it. It was used for all sorts of things in the war, but now it's reverted to the LCC. I think that they have plans to open it up to the plebs. Tea rooms and table tennis – that sort of thing. Pity, really . . .'

'Did you use it during the war?'

'I told you. All sorts of folk did. Let me show you something . . .'

The house stood on the rim of a landscaped basin fringed with dense woodland: specimen trees and shrubs – all gone over a little to the wild side. We had to push along pathways narrowed by bushes that brushed our shoulders. Eventually we came out into a small oval clearing. At one edge there was an old stone bench seat stained by lichen, and a couple of sawed-off stumps where two enormous firs must recently have been felled. Piers read my mind. 'Redwoods. They blew down in a storm last year. A real shame. What do you think of this place?'

There was something about the clearing, or about Piers, that was ringing all the warning bells. I felt the hair lift on my neck. That was odd.

'Suitably rural. The shrubs are so high that you can't see the house or the garden.'

'Almost, Charlie, almost. Now turn your logic back to front. The point is that no one in the house or garden can see *us* in here, which is how it's meant to be. This glade was designed into the original garden in the 1700s at the owner's request. It's the duelling ground.'

'Duelling ground? You mean that people were killed here?'

'That's right, it's a killing ground. It's what it was designed for. Smashing, isn't it? It's my favourite place.'

The duelling ground had a sombre, brooding air – even in the sunlight.

'When was this place last used?' I asked.

'A few years ago. We executed some spies here with Home Guard firing squads. SOE also brought some of their own people out here for the old bullet-in-the-back-of-the-neck trick; they'd gone to the bad, don't you know.'

'You brought me here deliberately, didn't you?'

'Yes. It only seemed fair. You see, Charlie, if *you* go to the bad this is where they'll bring you. I thought I should show you.'

'Do you think that I'll go to the bad?'

'No, of course not. But you *are* a bit of a loose cannon. I just want you to be very careful while you are still in the RAF. OK?'

'OK.'

I had read an article about labour relations in the *Chronicle* a week ago. The big new theory was called 'the carrot and the stick'. I suppose that lunch at the Savoy was pretty much the carrot, and a killing ground in Hampstead was the big stick. By the time we walked out into the sun and down to the lake, I had the blues.

I drove behind Piers out to the guard chain. I was chuffed to be able to turn my car around in a two-pointer down at the house, because Piers had hauled the Jag around in five. It was his own fault for driving a car that was thirty feet long. Once we were side by side on the other side of the chain Piers walked across to lean in over my car's passenger door. He had a folder in his hands, but first he pointed out a road which ran away down the hill to the north. There were big houses on one side, and ill-kept playing fields and allotments on the other. He pointed to the houses: 'That's The Bishops Avenue. Those are some of the places I was telling you about. Half of them have been occupied by squatters – a legion of them. Some of them were slated to become embassies, but what ambassador wants to live alongside the hairies?'

'I've seen castles smaller than some of those houses: they're massive. What are they worth?'

'Damn all at the moment.'

'That's the owners' fault, isn't it? Stands to reason that if a homeless family sees a big house standing empty, then they're going to move in.'

'That's how we saw it during the war, old man, but it's not during the war any longer, and the nobs want to come home. And now that the rubble rats have organized themselves it's become very political. If the police move in to evict them we could end up with another general strike. Old Clem's very iffy about it.'

'Clem?'

'Try to remember his name, Charlie: like everyone else in uniform, you work for him now – he's the Prime Minister.'

'It's got nothing to do with me. I already told you once.'

'One of our people was at a squatters' party in one of those big houses about a fortnight ago. Said he was a reporter, and took some great photographs to illustrate an article he's writing about the deserving poor. Nasty old world, isn't it?'

Personally I thought that he'd used the wrong word; it was a *Nazi* old world again. But I asked, 'And?'

'Loads of pretty girls. Some of them weren't wearing very much. I thought that if you took a look at them you might change your mind. You know – a picture's worth a thousand words, and all that?'

I laughed at him; not unkindly. I lifted the folder he had dropped on the passenger seat, and handed it back to him unopened. 'Fuck off, Piers. No hard feelings, but *no* means *no*. Let me serve out my time in peace; then I'll take that civvy job you talked about, OK?'

'Fine. You're sure you don't mind me asking?'

'Of course not; it's been a good weekend.'

Well – some of it had been. Piers was standing alongside his car, clutching the folder to his chest, and smiling like the cat that had had the cream. Tricky bastard.

The drive out of town took longer. I was baulked by a lot of flat caps and Sunday dresses in clunky old pre-war saloons, but once out of London I got up behind a couple of new upright Fords and was drawn along behind them at a steady fifty. Oddly enough I was looking forward to getting back to Cheltenham, Bella and Alison. I almost had a home again: that could be dangerous.

When I pulled onto the bricks in front of the Abbott house the sun was still shining. Alison was sitting outside on a kitchen chair, with a school textbook in her lap. She waved lazily when I drove up, and wandered over to greet me. She eyed the parcels stacked around my bag on the back seats. Then she reached into the car between the passenger seat and the door. 'You dropped a photo. Was this a party you were at? Lucky old you!'

She handed me the photo. Eight by six. I didn't know if that was the size that the press use, but I'd seen photo-reconnaissance pictures with those dimensions. This must have dropped out of Piers's folder, unless he'd poked it there deliberately. It showed a table at a party: covered by beer bottles and glasses. The people looked as if they were having a great time: about twenty of them, and all smiling. It looked like a wartime party from any camp you'd care to name. The men wore bits and pieces of uniform, overalls or dungarees, and the girls had party clothes and that joyful, reckless look in their eyes. I tell a lie.

The person at the very centre of the photograph wasn't smiling, and the reckless air was conspicuously absent. She was a small woman who wore a stained working vest and combat trousers; the same clothes I'd last seen her in.

Grace Baker: damn and blast her.

PART THREE

Reds

10. I'll Be Glad You're Dead, You Rascal You

I nearly tore the photo up. Instead, it ended up propped up on the small chest of drawers in my room. I was in a bad mood as I hung up my new clothes. When Alison walked in she took over, and smoothed them with her hand before she hung them. She said, 'I'm sorry I annoyed you. I thought that I'd say so immediately. We can't go around for days scowling at each other.'

At first I didn't know what she was talking about. Then I saw my thunderous face in the wardrobe mirror, and understood. I had to laugh at myself.

'Don't be silly. You did nothing. Someone dropped that picture in my car by mistake, and there's someone in it I knew years ago. It was a shock, that's all: nothing to do with you.'

'Was it one of the women in the photograph?' she asked me carefully.

There are times when it is best to tell the truth. 'Yes. Yes, it was.'

'Is she very pretty?'

'Not especially. Very striking.'

'Were you in love with her?'

'I thought I was: I'm less sure now.' There was nothing left to say on the subject so I stuck in, 'Let's go down and make a cuppa.'

Monday, Monday. Somebody wrote a song named that, a few years ago. Remember it? After less than three weeks I'd already found out that I wasn't cut out for an office job. My introduction to the morning had been Alison putting her head around my bedroom door. 'I'm off to school; it's eight-fifteen. C'mon, Charlie – *chocks away*.'

I think I groaned.

'Who taught you to say that?'

'Freddy did.'

I washed, and then emptied the pockets of my old clothes into the pockets of my new ones. That was when I found the code-pad flimsy on which I had written down the bursts of Morse I hadn't declared after my first flight.

In the kitchen Bella said, 'You're late; do you want me to phone and tell the gate?'

'No, thanks. Let them sweat. I was going to take some washing into town today: is there a laundry or something?'

'Providing you're not too embarrassed, your laundry's named Alison Abbott, and Monday's your lucky day. She'll do your washing for you, and you top up her pocket money – five bob OK?'

'Fine. What does she spend it on – Tizer and lipstick?'

Bella paused before she replied: she wanted me to pay attention to what she said.

'No: she's saving – for university. We don't want her married to a thousand chickens: not if we can help it.'

'Will she get there?'

'I think so, Charlie, if the amount of work she puts in has anything to do with it.' Then she said, 'I usually have a cuppa about now. Fancy one before you go to work?'

Later she walked out to the car with me. About three hundred hens spotted her and came rushing over; the dust and the noise was tremendous. She shouted to make herself heard. 'It's been difficult for Alison, growing up with glamorous RAF boys all around her. Sometimes they turned her head.'

'I'm sure that you both coped well.'

The lives some people lead. I wasn't going to make things more difficult for them, was I? She had a dab of dirt on her forehead. I licked a finger, and polished it away. Then I kissed the spot.

'Everyone should have a landlady as smart as you,' I said. Then I got into the Singer and told her, 'See you tonight,' as I drove away. As I bumped my old girl down the farm track, listening to her springs creaking, it occurred to me that maybe Freddy Timperley had been a bit of a snake, and the Reds had done us all a favour by knocking him off.

Miller was sitting at Weronka's radio sets, holding just one earphone to her ear. I was later to find out that that was her preferred way of listening in: she said that one ear was better than the other. They both looked OK to me. She looked over her shoulder. She didn't actually say, '*Phone me the next time you're going to be late.*' She said, 'I was worried about you.'

'Don't be. I'm like your bad penny: always turning up. Privilege of rank. Where's Ronka?'

'Sick. I'll stand her shift until Jane gets in.'

'When will that be?' I was asking officer-type questions and felt sick of them already.

'About twelve. They wanted us to do overlapping shifts today: start monitoring at eleven-fifteen, and go on until eight this evening. Just our luck.'

'What's the matter with Ronka?'

'She was mistreated during the war, and sometimes it catches up with her.'

'What did the Jerries do to her?'

'It wasn't the Germans: Lithuanians, I think. Eventually she had a baby, but she gave it up for adoption immediately. Now she can't have another.'

I turned away, saying, 'Do you want a cup of tea?'

'Camp, please; black, no sugar. Take them through to my office if you like. I'm only pre-tuning here: I'll be finished in a couple of ticks.'

I thought I'd try the chicory blend the way Miller drank it. I decided that I could get used to it eventually; in fact, drunk that way it tasted more like coffee than when you slopped the milk in. When she came in to sit behind her desk she made a steeple of her hands and looked at me over them as if she was making up her mind about something. Without actually bursting out of her clothes she somehow looked as if she was . . . like a ripe fruit preparing itself for the dive into the harvest basket. Maybe that was just wishful thinking on my part. It was an odd, tense, but not unpleasant moment.

She paused for about a six-beat before she asked, 'Do you have a raincoat, Charlie?'

'No. No, I don't.'

'Try the one behind the door.'

There was a man's raincoat hanging on the back of her office door. I tried it on, and found that it fitted perfectly – a short length, cut from a heavy khaki gabardine, with shoulder tabs, wide lapels, a belt and a deep collar. It looked like army surplus, bang up to date and brand new.

'It's terrific.'

'Then keep it.' Miller smiled at me. 'It's American. I bought it for Charles at a rummage sale on Saturday. He doesn't like it.' I somehow got the feeling that maybe she wasn't telling me everything. It was just like her to do something kind, and then talk it down so that she could keep you at arm's length.

'I'll treasure it. Thank you.' It was awkward. I've never known how to receive gifts graciously.

'Don't. Just wear it – but I'm pleased you like it.'

'Won't you let me pay you for it?'

'It only cost me half a crown. Buy me something back some day.'

'OK. What?'

She put on that little smile, shook her head, and looked out of the window. 'I didn't mean it.' When she looked back she said, 'I haven't got much to do until we start listening. Do you want another coffee?'

'I'd love one in a few minutes. I'll just pop over and say hello to Alice; what's happening over there?'

'Boulder's hooked into a Polish trawler that's stooging around off Scapa: just outside our sea limit. The Reds are using quite a few trawlers for the same sort of work that we do. One day they're going to be a nuisance.'

I produced the flimsy that I had found in my pocket before I left the Abbott place, and smoothed it out in front of her. 'Perhaps you'd like to look at that while I'm gone.'

'What is it?'

'Something I heard when I was out the other night, but forgot to tell them about. It sounded just like another signal I heard when they were testing me out over the Bristol Channel a few weeks ago. The Captain of that aircraft said that they were my Jedburghs.'

Miller gave me a very level look. 'One day, Charlie, you are going to get into very serious trouble.'

'Too late: I already am.'

'How's that? What kind of trouble are you in?'

'I think that I'm falling for a married woman.'

'That's dangerous: there's no future in it. You'll get caught.'

'I agree. Out. Dismissed. Leg before wicket. I always think that LBW sounds very sexy, don't you?'

'Stop messing about, Charlie.'

She knew exactly what I was talking about, and although she hadn't risen to the fly she hadn't flipped me a put-down either. That was interesting.

There was a pause in the conversation you could have launched a battleship into. Not a smile. Not even a twitch. Looking back I realize that there was a characteristic common to all the women I fell in love with before I was thirty: they lacked a sense of humour.

At first glance you would have thought that Alice was asleep, her head resting on her coils. Then you'd notice a beady eye watching your every movement. She could lie like that for days when the mood took her. I don't think that she had much of a sense of humour, either. I said, 'Hello, Alice. When's Tommo coming back for you?'

Her small forked tongue flickered out, as if in reply, but she really couldn't be bothered. The water in her bowl had disappeared, and the sand around it was damp – she'd probably been sloshing gaily around in it until she'd heard my footfall. Now she looked pissed off, and was trying to make me feel guilty. I poured some more water in through the wire lid of her box. She lifted her rattle and shook it at me, but I could see that her heart wasn't in it: she was sulking. Her attitude reminded me of Miller, when she didn't see a joke.

Miller herself came in an hour later, the inevitable brown envelope in her hand.

'Out tomorrow?' I asked her. I didn't say 'Told you so.' That would have been cruel.

'No – Wednesday. I'll leave a sandwich for you at the gate.'

'Thank you.'

Things were deliciously cool between us. I thought I'd try to break the ice.

'I'm a bit worried about Alice. She's looking a bit seedy.'

Miller went over and squatted down to look. Alice didn't rattle at her. Like recognizing like.

'I wouldn't worry too much,' Miller said. 'I think she's got the snake equivalent of time of the month. Her skin is dry, and peeling in places – haven't you noticed?' I went and stood close to Miller, but not too close. 'I think that she's shedding her skin: there will be a beautiful new one underneath.'

'I thought that you didn't like snakes?'

'So did I. I must have been mistaken. I came over to show you something, if they're still there.'

Boulder was still tied into the trawler. Liz was sitting in the corner of Boulder's office, flicking through a copy of *Picture Post*. Liz's own room was empty, and her radio array was silent. Miller led me into it, and fired the set up. I appreciated the economy of her movements. When she tuned into familiar bursts of Morse she handed me the earphones and moved away. I slid into her chair and chased the signal. Chased *both* signals: two remote stations chatting in brief regular bursts. It lasted for about ten minutes, and they went off the air simultaneously.

'Your Jedburghs,' she told me.

'You got permission to brief me?' That was a surprise.

'No. I'll tell you again, when HQ tells me to.' She shrugged, 'I made a decision, that's all. Do you know what the Jedburghs were?'

'No.'

'They were small teams of two or three commandos, dropped into Europe before D-Day and before we crossed the Rhine, to arm and organize resistance to the Germans. They were administered and trained by SOE and OSS but were not quite the same as either of those outfits and of course no one who was originally involved wants anything to do with them now.'

The penny dropped. 'So what are they still doing out there? The war finished two years ago.'

'Hunting Nazis. A few of the Jedburghs refused to come in at the end of the war – just like you did. They stayed out there to find specific Nazis; war criminals, if you like. Particularly those connected with actions against Jedburgh or SOE staff at the end of the war. They find out what happened to the people we lost and, if it was bad, bring the perpetrators to justice.'

'So they're working for the War Crimes Bureau now, then?'

'No. That's probably the point. They're working for themselves; particularly the Jewish teams – there are at least two of those. Investigators, judges, jurors and executioners – very economical little operations.'

'What's that to us?'

'The war's over. The WD wants them back: it wants them to stop killing people, and come home.'

'Won't they do that, once they've finished what they set out to do?'

'It's time they stopped now.'

I suppose that Miller was right. Neither of us knew what to say next. I switched off the radio set. One of the valves clicked as it cooled down – it would need replacing soon. Eventually I asked, 'What are we supposed to do about it?'

Miller sighed. 'We're probably a bit of a forlorn hope, because they must have people out on the ground looking for them as well. We're supposed to triangulate on their signals, if we can, working with an out-station at Southsea. It never works – they're never on air for long enough. You heard those short bursts. We were allocated listening watches on two of them. I don't know if any of the other huts have any; there can't be that many left out there. Sometimes we're asked to try to break into a transmission and get them to talk to us. That never works, either; they just shut down and move on. They're still very good.'

'So what happens?'

'We record their signals, and put them in the pouch with all the other stuff. Someone somewhere must scan them for clues to where they're operating.'

'All coded?'

'No; just mostly. Sometimes it's in clear, and sometimes it's in a simple Tango Charlie. We can read those with little effort, although we're not supposed to. It's a bit like doing a crossword.'

'Explain Tango Charlie, Miller.' I wasn't being funny; it was new to me. If it meant TC it wasn't the phonetic alphabet I was used to.

'Sorry, we've only just started using the phrase. TC means transposition code. Either the alphabet folded up on itself, or letters for numbers – that sort of thing.'

'And we're supposed to tell them "Come home; all is forgiven."'

'Something like that.'

'Bit bloody haphazard, isn't it?'

'If you say so.' Miller took the criticism personally, but that wasn't what I had intended. Change the subject, Charlie, before the upside-down smile comes back. I didn't see her again before I jacked it in for the day and returned to the Abbott house. It was overcast but I drove with the lid down, and in my new raincoat. It fitted over my working clothes as if it had been made for me.

11. Lonesome Mama Blues

On Wednesday afternoon Mr Summit danced outside the guardroom at the gate. He danced to 'Lonesome Mama Blues'. Ming ushered him to one side to let me through. The blind man skipped his shuffling steps sideways, drawing Ming after him. For a moment they looked as if they were dancing together. I probably had a silly grin on my face. I parked up in a space behind the gatehouse and collected my lumpy package of sandwiches. I wondered if Miller was paid to provide them, and if she'd made them up for Fearless Freddy. Then I stood outside smoking my pipe, waiting for my transport.

It wasn't late: when they're going to stick your neck out the RAF is never late. The same driver in the same crew carrier. The same cheerful, cheesy smile. What the hell – I was in a good mood myself. Miller was buying me clothes, and making me sandwiches – I guess that it was like being married, except that I couldn't help notice that something was missing. I had addressed an envelope to her, and put it in my own post box. That way they'd only find it if I didn't come back: I was getting back into old habits. In the bus I hugged the raincoat around me.

Joe Humm had a bruise on his forehead, and a small stitched cut over a cheekbone. I asked him, 'What happened to you, then?'

'Oh, that.' He touched the stitches and winced. 'I fell over last weekend.'

His navigator smirked. There was a story in there somewhere. Ten minutes into his short leg of my flight he began to hum a tune I recognized; it was 'Willy the Weeper'.

Waddington was locked down, but not for us: someone was already out – things were hotting up. More to the point, a strong wind was blowing a veil of rain across the runways. I almost didn't notice the wind because airfields are the windiest places on Earth anyway. I had the same SP escort sergeant as the first time. My face was slick with the fine rain; at least he had the jeep's canvas rigged. I asked him, 'What happens if we don't fly, sergeant?'

'I wouldn't know, sir, but I'd expect you'd wait over until we can.'

The same briefing in the same hut, from the same Squadron Leader, but with only one crew this time. I always hated waiting for them to reveal the place I was supposed to die in. I didn't mind so much this time. This time it was smiles of relief all round.

'We want you to go to Celle in Germany, gentlemen. Celle is still well inside our zone – marshalling yards, and a concert party. I visited it myself a few months ago. Didn't like it, actually; it's full of military policemen – you wouldn't like it either, so don't land there. OK?'

Polite laughter all round. The dour nav asked, 'Are we to stay inside the zone throughout the trip, sir?'

'Yes. Don't go near Brother Red. One of their top dogs is coming over to meet the PM this weekend, so we have to pretend to be friends.'

Someone asked, 'What about the met, sir?'

I looked around the room. The tousled Met Officer wasn't there. Why hadn't I missed him before?

'That's the only problem. You've got a hold for three hours. Then we'll look at it again. You'll have to stay in here, I'm afraid. Sergeant Ramsden will be here with you; I'll get coffee and things sent in. Can't use the radio – sorry. You can play cards or something.'

I'm convinced that the services have never been much good at alternative contingency planning either.

The wind and the rain conspired against us. The result was that I spent my first night in a proper officers' mess. And hated it.

I got a free breakfast and lunch out of it the following day, though.

Despite myself I was beginning to relax with the buggers. We were beginning to feel like a crew. Late afternoon I stood with the Skipper in the crew room while the others played pontoon for matches. We looked out of a window, peering across the runways. Somewhere out there a great black beast of a bomber was waiting for us. By then the rain and the wind had blown away into the North Sea and Europe; I just hoped that we wouldn't catch up with them later. I said, 'It's funny, Skip, but I went to Celle one night in '44. If the balloon goes up with the Russians, it will feel just like old times. They were always sending us back then, to clobber the same targets time and again.'

Tim touched my shoulder. I moved away slightly because I've never liked people touching me unless they've been invited to.

'I don't think the balloon's going up, Charlie. I think the Reds are as tired as we are. It's just a few old men posturing.'

'When old men posture,' I told him, 'young men get the chop. I was there once before – and this operation isn't exactly risk-free, is it?'

'You want to live for ever, Charlie?'

'No, Skip; just a bit longer than this. That would do for me.'

It was a different Linc: it smelled older. Out of habit I checked the fastenings on the fuselage door after Neil had dogged it shut behind us. He gave me the thumbs-up, and turned aft. I found my place and slotted in with my back to Perce, wondering which crew he'd flown his last trip with. As my radios came in, and the lights came on I felt like a stage magician muttering 'Open, sesame' above a magic casket.

Tim's voice brought me back, click, 'Radio check, Charlie?'

'OK, Skip,' and I started the call-through. The metaphor extended itself, because the words that ran through my mind were from that song, 'That Old Black Magic'. At just that moment I realized that by delaying the flight for a day the RAF was sending us out on a Thursday again. Bollocks.

Out over the North Sea, after Perce and I had calibrated our pre-tuning set-ups, we had time for a breather. With my old gaffer Grease in the front seat we might have risked a quick fag. Turnaway Tim was a different kettle of fish.

Someone once told me that all the best plans are simple ones. Anyway, our route was blessed by the virtue of simplicity. We were supposed to insert from over the North Sea between Brunsbuttel and Cuxhaven. Cuxhaven was an old U-boat base on which we used to unload our not so friendly bombs. Forget what you've been told about Slough. Our getaway was out over Osnabrück and Groningen, although it wasn't supposed to be a *getaway* per se because no one was supposed to be shooting at us. Perce's job was to plot the radar profiles of significant features on our way out: you already know what mine was. We were skirting south of Bremen when it became all too interesting . . . we should have known better than to fly on a Thursday.

Perce clicked, started to say something, coughed as if embarrassed, then started again. 'Skipper, this is Perce. We've going to have company.'

Click. 'Say again, Percy. We've done nothing to upset anyone this time. Are we still on the right side of the line?'

The nav broke in. The question had pissed him off. 'Nav. Skip, we're right on track. If Percy's got a Red closing on us, then it's a lost one.'

'OK, Henry. Give me a couple of easy course changes; we'll see if we can throw him off. Perce, tell me if he matches us.'

A minute later my bum gave me the message that Tim was turning us away from the Red Peril and back across the land of the free. Another five and we were turning back onto track, and the bogey turned with us, of course. I looked up out of the small window on my left just as I heard the voice in my earphones – up until then I'd had nothing except routine trade from the outside world. The voice said, 'Hello, English.'

It was a nice voice: gentle, a bit breathy and definitely a bit female. Her husky voice was heavily accented. A bit like Greta Garbo. When I looked up it was into the eyes of the pilot of a small fighter plane keeping station on us. It had no propeller on the front, so either it was in trouble, or it was another first-division job with a jet engine. I felt Tony, our top gunner, swinging his turret to bring his two hefty cannon to bear. The MiG didn't flinch.

Tony clicked and said, 'Shall I shag him, Skipper?' He wanted to sound cool, but his voice was suddenly about three octaves too high for that.

'*Her*,' I clicked, and stuck in. 'Definitely a her.'

Tim said, 'No, Tony; not yet. I rather want to know what happens next. Can I talk to her, Charlie?' Now he *did* sound cool. He was showing us the way.

'That wasn't very friendly, English,' the woman said. No need for a translator here.

Tim said, 'Sorry about that. What are you doing out here, my dear? Lost?'

'I'm just flying around, English. Looking for some company.'

'Are we going to shoot at each other?'

'I don't see why we should.'

That seemed to kill it for a six-beat. Then Turnaway Tim offered, 'You might be annoying a lot of people, you know – they'll probably send someone unfriendly up to look at you.'

'I know. I won't stay long. I just wanted someone to talk to.'

I turned to Perce and said, 'She's a nutcase. Keep an eye out for anyone else.'

He nodded, and asked, 'How did she get hold of a machine?'

'Come again?'

'She's a woman. How did she get hold of a kite like that?'

'They have women pilots in the Russian Air Force.'

'Oh.'

I could see her gently weaving her aircraft to match its speed down to ours. There was just a bit of a moon, and whenever she changed attitude her silver fighter would flicker like a Christmas-tree candle.

Eventually Tim said, surprisingly firmly, 'Time you went home, old girl.'

'Nowhere to go, English.' There was a terrible sadness in her voice. 'This is my last flight. I will be arrested when I return. They arrested my husband and my children this morning. Can you imagine that? Children are not yet four years old.'

'What did you do?'

'I am an officer. That is enough to be arrested for today.' The small jet must have been harder work than it looked, because we could hear her drawing deep breaths.

Tim said, 'You can always follow me. I'll take you in to one of my bases. We would look after you.' There was what is often called a pregnant pause, except that pregnancies don't last for ever, and this one seemed to.

Then she said, 'And leave my children, English? No; I do not think so. Goodbye, English . . . and good luck.'

Then she did a very professional wingover: Tony couldn't have followed her with his guns even if he'd tried. I leaned close to the window to watch her as she dropped away from us, until the silver blur became just a faint red glow from the jet exhaust, and finally nothing.

The stupid thing was that Tim said goodbye, back to her. Then so did I, and then the others, one by one. The sky suddenly felt very empty.

I said, 'Skipper; Charlie. I think we'll probably get a bollocking for that.'

'Then they can fly their *own* fucking aircraft, can't they?'

I smiled inside my mask, and fumbled in my flight bag for a packet of day-old sandwiches. I could probably grow to like him.

He clicked, 'Nav? Where are we?'

'Still on track, Skip. Next way point in . . . twelve minutes.' A voice totally devoid of emotion – like a mechanical man. Learning to like the nav would take more effort, and I wasn't sure that I was up to it. Brown-bread Spam sandwiches: the butter tasted genuine.

We landed at Wadders into the dawn of a fine morning. I was stiff as I stepped down the small ladder and onto the concrete. Ramsden was there to greet us with a flask of tea. I thought about the Russian pilot, and imagined her being escorted away from the last aircraft she'd ever fly, by a man with a Tommy gun. Would she see her children again? I shivered, even though it was not cold.

12. *It Don't Mean a Thing*

The Buddhists have this theory that every time you fuck something up you are reborn to do it again, and maybe again, until you get it right. That's what we call déjà vu. That's what I think, anyway. Is that why the RAF kept on bunging me back into aircraft over Germany?

Alison had tea on the table before I came down from my room and Bella soon put in an appearance. She'd had another successful foray into the big city – Oxford passes for a big city out there – and had a pocket full of denarii. But her Austin van had run out of petrol at the end of the track. She was flushed when she walked in. I told her I'd siphon a gallon from the Singer, and walk it down to her van later in the evening. She threw off her jacket, kicked off the army boots she wore most of the time, and sat down heavily in an old soft chair in the corner of the kitchen.

Alison handed her a half-pint of cloudy cider. Bella said, 'Thanks, love. Life-saver.' She slurped her first sip, and had to wipe her top lip. Alison asked me, 'Fancy putting the kettle on and making the tea, Charlie? I can do the rest.'

I hate it when someone tries to domesticate me, but I kept my trap shut; she was only a kid, after all. Later, when we were around the table, talking, playing cards and listening to a new jazz programme from London, I mentioned that I might drop along to Joe's jazz club on the Saturday night. Alison studied her cards, and said, without looking up, 'It's not going to be open. Someone at school said that some RAF guys got into a fight there, and the police have closed it for two weeks to teach everyone a lesson. It was over a girl.'

'It usually is,' I told her. 'That's why I'm staying single.'

Alison couldn't disguise her small frown when I said that, or Bella a small smile. I was holding my own. Just. And at this rate it was all I'd end up holding unless I could wangle another trip to London. Alison grabbed a book and sloped off to bed.

I awoke in the early hours as the bedroom light snapped on. I sat up immediately, reaching for a parachute that wasn't there. I said, 'What is it?' probably rather muzzily. Bella stood by my bed, wearing silky pyjamas. Behind her, in the doorway, I could see Alison. She wasn't smiling this time: she looked frightened.

'Are you all right?' Bella asked me.

'Yes. I think so.'

'You were shouting,' Alison said. 'You woke me.'

'It's OK,' I told them. 'I was in an accident once. I was dreaming about it. I should have warned you.'

My wits were remarkably slow at reasserting themselves. Where was chirpy Charlie all of a sudden? Bella looked back over her shoulder and said, 'Thanks for calling me, Alison. Charlie will be all right now.' And to me: 'Won't you?'

'Yes. Sorry. Did I frighten you?'

Both said no. Alison was lying. Her mother told her, 'You can go back to bed now, love. He's fine.'

After her daughter had left Bella sat on the end of the bed. I remember a woman in Manchester doing the same: aeons ago. Bella looked younger with her hair down, and pretty: you could see where Alison got it from. They looked more like sisters. I asked her, 'What time is it?' I was bathed in sweat, and shivering.

'Quarter past three. Can I get you a drink, or a cup of cocoa or something?'

'No, thanks. I'm fine now, I promise you.'

She smiled and shook her head. Nice one, Charlie. Getting it right for once.

I didn't tell her that I had been dreaming about a woman on fire. In my dream the woman's hair was burning, and she was beating the flames ineffectively with her hands, and screaming. You never want to hear screams like that. I'd seen her die years ago, and never knew her name. I lay awake for an hour before I slept.

The following day I walked a couple of miles across the fields, using a crude map that Alison had drawn for me, until I found a pub called the Lord Halifax. I drank too much cider, and slept it off lying under a tree in a meadow. I was awoken three hours later because my face was being rasped. Well, not *rasped*, exactly – say being rhythmically slapped, with an unusual amount of vigour, by about a hundredweight of tongue . . . which is what happens when you're being licked by a cow. This one had large dark brown eyes, and was probably a pretty cow, as cows go, but I was never going to fall for her.

When I returned to the farm the chickens had roosted, and Bella and Ming had gone off to his mother's house for the night, taking Alison with them. I wondered who had been lined up for the chickens in the morning. Maybe I was supposed to do it. One day I'd get round to telling them that I wasn't too keen on chickens – until they were in the oven, that was.

I didn't bother to make up the fire, just pulled on another layer of clothing, and sat and listened to the BBC Light Programme. After the usual variety show there was a dramatization of *Mr Standfast*, with Jack Warner and Valentine Dyall. I listened to them in the twilight, and smoked my pipe. I'd always liked Buchan when I had been at school. I had food and booze to hand, company in the pub if I wanted it, nobody was shooting at me, and I could do what I liked with my time. So why was I vaguely discontented with my lot when I went to my bed in the empty house?

Some rustic type I hadn't seen before let the birds out at dawn and collected the eggs. The chickens didn't like being roused by a stranger, made as much noise as George Frederick Handel on rum and fruit juice, and woke me up. I took the fellow a mug of char. He thanked me, but the look that came with it told me that he'd have preferred cider. He had string tied around his trouser legs under his knees. That was to prevent the chickens running up inside his trousers, I guessed.

Bella was very proud of the new telephone she had in the hall: I thought that the money would have been better spent getting electricity into her kitchen. Anyway, when the phone rang I ignored it. It would never be for me. Then it rang again, and curiosity killed the cat: I couldn't help myself. A local operator asked me if I was the number that I could see on the disc of paper on the telephone cradle. I was. I read it back to her.

'Please wait. I have a call from London for you.'

Piers came on the line as clear as if he had been in the next room. Perhaps he was. He said, 'Charlie! Where have you been?'

'If you don't know, I can't tell you.'

'Oh: *there*! Everything go off OK?' He wasn't really interested; he was just asking for the sake of it.

'It was rather sad, actually. I might tell you the next time I see you, if I get stocious enough.'

'*Stocious*. I like that. Very RAF. I was hoping that I'd see you sooner rather than later. In fact, I was wondering why you hadn't called.'

'What about?'

He paused before he replied. 'About a photograph I injudiciously left in your car. You *did* find it?'

'No. What photograph?'

Piers paused again. 'You're angry with me, aren't you?'

'Of course I am.'

'I'll need the photo back: everything in these files is numbered.'

'Put in a note saying that I destroyed it.'

'The B107 in your records is spot on, Charlie, do you know that? It says that you're an awkward little sod.'

'There you are, then. No use to you.'

I think that for a change I was one set up. Piers said, 'Unfortunately for me you're all I've got. Won't you change your mind about doing one or two little jobs for us? I'd see that it was worth your while.'

'I don't need money, Piers. I came into some during the war.' It wasn't exactly a lie.

'Money's not everything, Charlie. You've got no idea what we could do for you.'

Or to *you*, I thought. Piers continued, 'What about it?'

'Let me think about it.'

'The girls are missing you.'

'Tell them that I'm missing *them*: a cow kissed me yesterday, and I thought of them immediately.'

Piers laughed his hacking laugh. It wasn't a pleasant sound. 'You'll think about it, then . . . and phone me in the week?'

'If you like. Now bugger off.'

He said, 'OK,' and broke the connection.

I was left looking at the heavy handset: it growled at me. I thought about Alice. Had she shed her skin, and started moving around yet? As a pet, a snake has limited entertainment value. What I didn't tell Piers was that I'd already made my mind up. I wanted to see Grace Baker again; I just hadn't decided whether I was going to tell him about it.

I saw Watson on Monday morning, and asked him if there was any way of predicting when we were going to be asked to fly the weather flights. My excuse for asking was that knowing this would make my office work easier to plan.

'No. Sorry. Not unless you can get them to talk to you themselves. I get the same notice as you. I wouldn't get that if I wasn't first reserve if you go u/s or something. If you can't fly, I have to.'

'I didn't realize that, sir. Can you handle the radios, then?'

'Cheek of the fellow! I used to; years ago. How do you think I landed this job in the first place? It's all about minding a load of radios, women, locks and keys, isn't it?'

'Yes, that's exactly it . . .'

'. . . Sir.'

'Sir.'

'I hear that you're keeping a ruddy great snake in your office. The cleaners have complained, and they refuse to go in there.'

'Sorry, sir. I'm only minding it for a friend. It won't be there for long.'

'Good-oh. Fancy a snifter? Sun's over the yard arm.'

Watson had only one cupboard in his office. This was the first time I had seen it open. It was full of bottles. I'd had three proper Squadron Leaders in the RAF so far. The first went mad, the second was the one who had declared me dead, in order to tidy up my file – and the third was beginning to look like a drunk. I certainly could pick 'em.

Tommo Thomsett paid me the honour of a telephone call. He shouted, 'Hiya, Charlie. How's it goin'?'

'It's going well, Tommo, except that I'm sharing my office with Alice, and I don't want to be in the RAF any more. Why are you shouting?'

'To make myself heard over the wind. Can't you hear it?'

'No, all I can hear is you. Are you still in Greenland?'

'No. Iceland; speaking over the new link. You ever seen the broads up here?'

'No.'

'Man! Blonde bombers, every one of 'em. They all look like film stars, and they'll turn a trick for a hot dog.'

'What's that mean – *turn a trick*?'

'Come on, Charlie. Use yer imagination.'

'Don't you mean for the *price* of a hot dog?'

'No, Charlie. I mean for the real thing. You never seen girls eat like these ones.'

'Don't they eat whale meat for breakfast, and rub blubber all over themselves in the winter?'

'Not any more, bud: that's Eskimos. These people discovered the mighty dollar. The hot dog is their new national dish.'

It was time to get some business done.

'How long am I babysitting Alice?' I asked. 'She's losing her skin, and shaking her rattle at me. We're falling out of love.'

'Friday OK? We could have a few beers in the evening. I booked into that pub in Great Rissington. You could bring Alice. I kinda miss her.'

'What are you going to do with her eventually?'

'I keep trying to palm her off on a zoo, but I can't find anyone willing to take her. One of the German places said yes because they'd lost all their stock, but she bit a dog so I had to go and get her back again. They wanted their money back, but I told them to jack it.'

Tommo had inherited Alice from the first American whom she'd bit: he'd promised the dying man that he'd look out for her. Tommo could be a bit of a snake himself, and I'd heard that he wasn't averse to threatening reluctant payers with a visit from Alice. She was a pretty good enforcer. I didn't think that he'd get rid of her: he'd trailed her all around Europe so far. Selling a party an uncontrollable deadly snake and then offering to take it back off their hands for nothing sounded just like one of his scams.

'Look, Tommo. There's something you can do for me. Remember the day we first met? I gave you some bottles from Pete's stash – stuff you didn't have – and you gave me something in return?'

'Yeah; it was a cigar, weren't it? You want some cigars?' He was being coy. He'd also swapped me a pistol as well: a nasty great Colt automatic.

'No. The other thing. You know.'

'Why don't you come out with it, Charlie? You mean the gun.'

'I thought that someone could be listening.'

'I don't give a toss who hears me. I'm outside your jurisdiction. You want another gun?'

'Yes, please.'

'What happened to the first one I gave you?'

'Pete got it. How *is* Pete?'

'I'll tell ya when I see you.' That was interesting. There were obviously *some* things he didn't want to say over a telephone line. 'What happened to that dinky Kraut piece you had in Germany?'

'They took it away from me when I came back. Can you get me something discreet that won't look like a spare tit if I put it in my coat?'

He laughed. 'I like that, Charlie. I'll remember it.' Then there was a load of static, and the line went dead. Usually I'm quite good at static, but this wasn't one of my days. He hadn't said yes, either.

Miller had come in while I was talking. She asked, 'Who was that?' and when I stared at her, 'Who were you talking to?'

She was leaning against the office door jamb. I was getting better at girls leaning against door frames. I hadn't actually heard her arrive, and didn't know how long she'd been there or what she'd overheard. She was wearing a dress of dirty blue, and looked that way herself, in the best sense of the word. It touched in all the right places – just reached her knees, but left her arms bare. Maybe summer was a-coming in.

'The man who owns Alice. He's coming to get her back on Friday if I'm not out.'

'I'd like to meet him. He sounds interesting.'

'You can if you want to; we're going to have a few drinks at the Lamb.'

Pause. Six-beat, like Glenn's intro to 'In the Mood'. Maybe she was in the mood when she said, 'I'll think about it. Maybe.' She smiled. I smiled back at her. She wasn't carrying one of those damned brown envelopes in to me. God was in his heaven.

In the middle of the day we drove down to that place by the river. It was the only place I knew. We collected glasses of cider, and sat with our feet in the chill water: they quickly went white. I didn't say anything smart or funny: neither did she.

Miller talked about her schooldays and her friends. Then she told me about her family, and her father, whom she clearly adored. I told her about my family, and my friends on the squadron and how I missed them. I told her that having regular time off duty was difficult to get used to: that I didn't know what to do with my time when I wasn't working. On the squadron it had been so easy; there were always blokes to go on the skite with.

She didn't mention her husband once. I didn't tell her anything about women I'd been close to. We found that we couldn't stop talking, and were late back. She had a high colour when she left me; I was probably grinning like a gorilla. Alice stirred herself for a muted congratulatory rattle. Oh, Charlie.

Piers asked, 'Anything happening between you and Mrs Miller yet?'

'Like what, Piers? I thought that you didn't know her.'

'Of course we do, dear boy: we've a book running on you up here. The irresistible force meets the immovable object. One of you is really going to mess the other up, and we've placed bets on it. I'm not sure, so I've laid a couple off as well. Think of yourselves as amatory gladiators, entertaining the masses.'

'That's sick. Whose idea was that?'

'Dolly's, I think: her money is on Mrs Miller. Den's bet on you. But you didn't reply to my original question, did you?'

'And I'm not going to . . . that's not really why you called, anyway.'

'Clever boy. No. I wondered if you had forgotten to call me about that other matter.' Why was he pushing it all the time? *Something* must be in the air.

'No, I hadn't forgotten, I just haven't called. I'm still thinking about it, but if it helps . . . if you don't nag me, you might well get your own way.'

'Ah.' In the pause after that I ran the opening phrase to Major Glenn Miller's 'String of Pearls' inside my head – that five-and-a-half-beat. Then Piers added, 'You won't leave it too long, will you?'

'No, Piers: you'll be the first to know. Am I flying this week, by the way?'

'Wouldn't know, old chap. Sorry.'

'Yes, you do. Either you commission the flights in the first place, or you act as liaison between your department and the RAF when they tell you that they're going to fly. I haven't worked out which yet. Either way, you're in the know. Wasn't I supposed to work that out on my own?'

'Ah . . . no: not really.'

'Tough. Well, what about it?'

'What if I said that I think you can assume a pretty uneventful fortnight?'

'Thank you, Piers. Let's say that I call you every week, and put the same question to you?'

'Pretty irregular, old boy. Insecure.'

'But then you'd always know what I was up to, wouldn't you? You'd know if I was available to help you out with any other wee jobbie.'

'*Wee jobbie* – I like that.'

'I turn a good phrase, don't I? Can we leave it at that?'

'Anything you say, old boy.'

I already knew Piers well enough to feel unhappy when he

agreed with me. Miller was at the door. She and the door frame she leaned on must have been designed around each other. I wanted her clothes off. She knew it, and blushed; that was a first. She asked, 'Who were you speaking to?'

'Don't they call themselves GCHQ now? Our brothers in London; soon to be our brothers and sisters out here.' It was the first time I had used the letters.

'What did they tell you?'

'I don't know about the rest of you, but I'm getting an easy fortnight. Might take a few days' leave next week.'

'Go up to London?'

'Probably; want to come?'

She gave me the eye. It wasn't a friendly eye. Then she turned on her heel and walked away. Her hips swung like the stern of one of those stately Spanish galleons the man wrote about. *Swinging through the Isthmus*, wasn't it?

Tommo said, 'Look, Charlie, sooner or later you're gonna have to get this right.'

'What?'

'Broads,' Tommo explained. 'Start getting it right.'

'Why should I?'

'Because the rule is that the broad you sleep with always wants to run your life. If she happens also to be the one you work with, she'll want to run that as well. That's why you don't do it. You gotta keep part of your life fer yerself.'

'I haven't slept with her yet; in fact, I don't think that's going to happen. She keeps her knees together, and loves her husband.'

'She sounds like one of the dangerous ones. When they go off, they're like the atom bomb. Believe me.'

I spent a few pleasant seconds imagining Miller going off like an atom bomb. I probably had a silly look on my face.

'What's it to you, anyway?' I asked him.

'I like you, Charlie. I want you to profit by my mistakes.'

I was making my own already, because I'd told him about Miller.

Tommo was at the Lamb before me. He had a battered Bedford one-and-a-half-tonner in the courtyard. The driver's-side screen was missing, and the canvas tilt was torn and patched. Its unit insignia had been crudely painted over, but you could still see the faded Allied star on its doors. He shrugged when I asked about it. 'Got it at an auction. Ten English pounds. In fact I bought a dozen of them.'

'What for?'

'I'll put 'em up on bricks for a few years, and then sell them back to you when you get into your next war and get short of trucks. Say a hun'ed an' fifty each. Your government is selling off enough kit to equip a decent army.'

'That's because it's short of ready money.'

'I don't see how. What do they do with it all? Your friggin' taxes over here are as high as the friggin' Rockies.'

I looked at him pointedly. 'We gave it all to the Yanks in 1941, and then borrowed against everything else we owned. We beat the Germans, but lost to the Americans.'

'Don't blame me because your lot are bad businessmen, son.' Tommo never laughed in your face; he just used words that made you laugh at yourself.

'I'm not. You asked, and I told you, that's all.'

'Charlie,' he said, 'you didn't used to be this lippy.' He was grinning. I was grinning. He said, 'I got you a drink standing on the counter – next to my empty glass. Remember that cider and beer we used to drink in Thurleigh?'

'It's good to see you, Tommo.'

We lashed Alice's Restaurant down in the back of the Bedford, and covered it with an old carpet to keep her warm. Tommo laced the canvas shut. Any local tea-leaf taking his chance with Alice was in for a surprise. The bar was empty apart from us. We sat at a table in the corner, beneath which he handed me a canvas ammo pouch. It still had a lethal cargo.

'All I could get for you in a hurry,' Tommo said. 'Fifteen quid – all right?' A pistol and two boxes. The small automatic looked as old as the hills, but well cared for. It smelled of gun oil. 'Probably better today than the day it left the factory,' he told me.

'Tommo – it's a *woman's* gun!'

'Almost, but not quite. It's much bigger – can't you see that? It's a small nine point. It's a German artillery officer's pistol issued between the wars. Bloody wonderful piece. You got two big boxes of ammo, say sixty rounds, and spare springs and screws. Bargain.'

'Tommo, this is a museum piece! When was it made?'

'1919. What do you think?'

'I think beggars can't be choosers. Anything I should be careful about?'

'It's chambered for five shots but if I was you, I'd just load four. Make sure it don't go off in your pocket and shoot your goolies off.'

'Thanks, partner. Where's the safety catch?'

'Doesn't have one: when they made these bloody things, Charlie, nobody wanted them to be *safe*. They were supposed to shoot people.'

'What else?'

'The bullets go exactly where you point it. It shoots straight. Don't tell me what you're going to do with it, but just take care. We're pals, yeah?'

'We're pals, Tommo, all the way to the end.'

'Maybe not that far,' Tommo told me.

I was talking about Miller again when she walked in, straight up to our table. She said, 'Hello, boys. What can I get you?'

Surprised? I was. She had on the same off-blue dress, but wore a man's grey corduroy jacket over it and had heels that gave her another couple of inches. I'd like to tell you that my heart did a double somersault, except that it wasn't just my heart. She stayed about an hour. I think that she was only there to give Tommo the once-over. We drank too much too quickly. When Tommo was up at the bar I said, 'Thank you for coming. You look—'

'Don't tell me what I look like, Charlie. I know what I look like, and tonight I pass muster. Change the subject.'

'Where's Mr Miller?'

'He's at his club; he always goes to the club on Fridays. He doesn't know I'm here. Change the subject.'

'I want to peel that dress off your shoulders, and touch your breasts.'

'Change the subject.'

'I want to stand you up against that wall, and have you until bits start coming off.'

It was a phrase that Grace had taught me.

'Don't change the subject, Charlie.' I didn't know that someone with a mouth as small as hers could grin as widely as that. Her eyes gleamed. I'll bet mine did too. The odds were changing every minute. 'I said, *don't . . .*'

'I heard what you said . . .'

Then Tommo walked back with three jugs of cloudy mind's ruin.

'Am I interrupting anything?' he asked. We laughed. I suppose it was that laugh together that did it.

Tommo stayed inside when I walked Miller out to the car park. We raised the canvas on his truck, and she whispered 'Goodbye, Alice' into the darkness. I'm not sure, but there might have been a gentle rattle in response. Our hands touched as we replaced the covers. Hers was shaking almost as much as mine.

'I have to go now, Charlie.'

'I know.'

'I'm sorry.'

'I know that, too.'

She touched my face once; my cheekbone. Then she ran to a nice Standard saloon parked in shadow. She stumbled once, and recovered. I was still standing frozen, anyway. I didn't move until after the car had gone. All those emotional tricks I should have tried on her, she'd done on me first. Tommo was outlined in the lighted doorway of the bar. When I reached him he said, 'Nice lady.'

I nodded. 'I think so, too.'

He pointed a finger at me. 'She don't need no German pistol. She nailed you. Bang – you're dead.'

'Feels good, being dead,' I told him.

We got drunk together. Late in the evening I asked him, 'Tell me about those Icelandic girls again.'

'You never seen anything like them, Charlie. We got to get a posting over there. They're all Carol Lombards, with tits like Jane Russell.'

'What else do we have over there?'

'We have a fucking big base.'

'And the Icelanders?'

'They got no fucking base at all. They don't make war on anybody any more. They got over that a thousand years ago. They just eat, drink and copulate – and fight all the time. What you might call a seriously peaceful people.'

'They sound like nice folks.'

'They're magnificent drunks . . . I love 'em.' Tommo laughed at the memory.

'When do we go?'

'When you got your RAF off your back. OK?'

'OK.'

The bar was quiet all night. Whatever happened to Friday nights? We got to the stage when we began to drink ourselves sober. You know: one stage before you collapse, and have to crawl home on your hands and knees. I'm good at that. I remembered that I'd asked Tommo about Pete, and that he'd been coy. So I asked him again: 'How's Pete?'

Long pause this time. His drunk's grin slipped away like a fried egg skittering over the rim of a greasy plate. 'Dead. That Czech man got him.'

'Don't be dumb, Tommo. Pete can't be dead.'

'Why not? Nearly everyone else is.' I bought another round, waited until I could put together a decent sentence or two, and told him, 'He survived being shot at by the police, the Luftwaffe, and our own anti-aircraft people. Pete always walks away.'

Tommo shook his head. 'Not this time. You remember what he was doing last you saw him?'

It took a couple of seconds of alcohol-crippled recall.

'Yeah. He'd shifted into the Polish SPs – their military police – he was chasing down a Czech black marketeer in Germany.'

''Sright. The Czech got him. They faced off like gunfighters in a square in some ruined town last year. The Czech got him first. I saw it.'

'No: not Pete.'

'Don't take my word for it. Remember the black doctor we called The Cutter? He was there, too. Couldn't save him. We laid him alongside a statue in the middle of the square. I thought he said your name, but The Cutter thought he said *Tuesday*. That was the day he was killed on: do you think he didn't want to die on a Tuesday? Then he died anyway. The Cutter had to sign off the death certificate before the Red Cross told Pete's people. I tell you: we *buried* him. In a special coffin made of some funny wood he always wanted. It was called *Lipa . . . trumna lipowa*: that was it. Damned Poles! But he ain't coming back this time.'

I couldn't believe it, but I agreed. He wasn't coming back this time, and the last word on his lips hadn't been 'Charlie'. The Cutter had heard him right: it had been *Tuesday*. I told you already that *Tuesday's Child* was the name of the Lancaster we'd flown into Germany: we always called her *Tuesday*. She'd burned in 1944. Maybe she came back for him at the end.

'Can we talk about this again, Tommo?' I asked him. 'When I'm sober.'

'Yeah, 'course. Hey, I'm sorry, Charlie.'

I whispered 'OK', but it wasn't, of course. Neither of us said anything for a while. I filled a pipe, and lit it. It went out, and I said, 'Fuck it; life doesn't mean a thing,' which was nothing to do with the smoke.

Tommo replied, 'I know.'

'You off first thing, Tommo?'

'Yeah. Crossing from Folk-es-tone on Sunday morning. I'll give you this though.'

He tore the end from his packet of White Owl cigars, and laboriously wrote two telephone numbers on it. He had difficulty forming the letters and numbers, and cupped his left hand around the paper like a child. I don't think that it was the drink. It had never occurred to me before that writing or numeracy might have been a problem for him. It occurred to me now. Pete, our Pink Pole, was good at European languages, and had done a lot of Tommo's talking for him.

I said, 'You'll miss Pete.'

One of us picked up on the tense wrongly. He said, 'I already do.'

He gave me the numbers, and we left it at that. He said that one was his apartment in Frankfurt, and the other a pal in London who usually knew where he was. I drove back to the Abbott farm, with tears streaming down my face. I had the Singer's hood down, so that must have been the cold air rushing past my face.

When I awoke the next day I stank of the sweat that had dried on me, had a colossal hangover, and my cheeks were still wet. I guess I was all cried out, but nobody noticed.

13. Jazz Lips

My old skipper flew twenty-eight straight trips into Germany in 1944. We all went with him. Before he got up into the aircraft each night he used to tell himself '*Always expect the unexpected.*' You'd have thought that I would have learned that by now. I didn't expect to hear from Tommo for months, if ever – that's how it was with him. So I heard from him on the next Monday morning. I slouched into Miller's office just as she was telling someone on the other end of the telephone to get up. She laughed as she said it, and hung up. It must have been a comfortable conversation. I asked, 'Who was that?'

'My business.'

'I'm supposed to tell you who *I*'m speaking to whenever you want to know, but you get to keep yours to yourself? Is that it?'

'Yes.' The easy intimacy between us on Friday night was gone.

Weronka's voice over my shoulder said, 'She has to call her husband every morning when she gets in – to get him out of his bed. She says that if she doesn't call he stays asleep, and forgets to go to work. Then the country stops working because everybody starves. Isn't that so?' After a short pause she added, 'Or maybe he just wants to know where Mrs Miller is; just checking.'

I thought that was cruel, and was surprised when Miller didn't rise to it. I asked, 'What work does he do?'

Miller's mouth opened, but Ronka beat her to it. 'Ministry of Food. He's a local big cheese. That's funny, isn't it?'

I guessed that Ronka wasn't too keen on Mr Miller. Miller clearly didn't think it funny. Her mouth made the upside-down smile.

'Haven't you anything to do?' she asked the Polish woman.

And now Jane joined in, and there were three of us jammed in the door of Miller's office. She said, 'No, but the officer has – there's a call for him on my telephone.' Balls! I think that she only used the word 'officer' to annoy Miller – who was one too, of course.

The caller was Tommo, and the first thing he said was, 'I'm in a spot, Charlie.'

'Situation normal. Weren't you supposed to sail yesterday? Where are you?'

'London. Look, they won't let me go any further. Your cops have released me into the custody of the Snowdrops.'

The Snowdrops were the American Army Service Police – called Snowdrops on account of their white helmets, I guess. That, or because of their spotless reputations.

'What did you do?'

'I killed a guy I didn't mean to.' Pause. Eventually Tommo asked, 'You still there, Charlie?'

'Yeah, I'm still here, Tommo.' I took a couple of deep breaths, and then I felt better. 'Tell me what happened.'

'When I went out to the truck yesterday morning the canvas had been slit, an' Alice's box was on its side.'

'Christ, Tommo. She's not on the loose, is she?'

'Nah. She was under all that carpet. Not moving about much. I got her back in the box with a broom handle: she bit it twice – must be a bad time for her.'

'What does "not moving about much" mean?'

'I seen her like that before – after she bit some fella.'

'I hope that it wasn't a kid.'

'So do I, but that ain't the problem. I got outta there fast: skedaddled. You know what I mean?'

'I can imagine.'

'So I guess that I was driving too fast when I came over the top of a hill, and there was this guy dancing in the middle of the road. I yelled at him.'

'He have a long dark coat, and greasy hair?'

'That's the man.'

'What did you yell?'

'"*Wassa matter with you, bud? You blind?*"'

'He is.'

'I found that out after I killed him with the truck. He never got out of the way. I don't reckon he felt a thing.'

'What's the situation now?'

'Your country cops are gentlemen.'

'Don't let that fool you.'

'They let me out on bail to the Snowdrops. I think that was

because they didn't know what to do with Alice. The SPs've taken my passes and everything. All I got is my ID and my tags.' Some Yanks called the Snowdrops the Lootwaffe, but that was for a different reason, and was rather cruel.

'Did the police actually charge you with anything?'

'Nope. They said that when I came back to them I could be charged with causing death by driving, or somethin'.'

'Tell me where you are, and let me make a couple of calls.'

'Thanks, partner. I'm in a crappy little room in a crappy little ARC club for other ranks, in a place called Cadogan Square. It's not much better than a toilet in a knocking shop. Ancient women for rent are prowling the corridors in packs.'

'It has a telephone number, this club?'

Tommo told me. I fished out the scrap of cardboard he'd given me on Friday night, and added the number to the others he'd written down. We let it go on a low note: I didn't want to give him too much hope.

I went back to Miller. The others gave me some space and went back to their rigs. I closed the door on them. Miller's chin went up; maybe she thought we were going to get into a fight. I told her, 'I was just told that your Mr Summit is dead. Had you heard that already?'

All the fire went out of her. 'No; that's sad. What happened?'

'The man who killed him just told me; the man we were drinking with on Friday night. My pal Tommo.' At least I had her attention. She sat bolt upright, and didn't look as if she'd miss a word. 'Tommo was driving south yesterday morning. He drove over a hill, and the old man was dancing in the road. Bang.'

'What are you going to do?' It was interesting that she assumed I would do something.

'Phone Piers: from here if I may. You just sit there, and keep quiet.'

'Is that an order?'

'Yes – why? And why are you smiling?'

'It's the first direct order that you've given me.'

'Then get used to it; I might get to like it.' I guess that I was probably smiling too. The morning storm between us had blown over, and I still didn't know what it had been about. It's tight like that.

Piers was immediately businesslike when I spoke with him because I told him I could come to London for a few days to help him with a little project that he had mentioned to me if he could help out a pal of mine. And then I told him the story. He played hard to get, but it was all an act.

'He *will* come back for the inquest, and to face charges if necessary?'

'I can't promise that, Piers. He's a bit of a fast operator.'

'Aren't we all, dear boy? Can't wait to see him.'

'Is that necessary?'

'Absolutely. If we're going to scratch his back, then he'll have to scratch ours. And don't worry – he'll probably be on his way by this afternoon. He's taking that awful animal with him, I take it?'

'Definitely.'

'Good. There's no way she would have been given a formal visa.' Then Piers told me to be at the Cheltenham nick in my Number Ones in half an hour, with my pen in my hand in case I had to sign anything. I didn't tell him what this reminded me of, but decided to take Miller with me: back-up if I needed her.

I lifted Miller's uniform from the back of her office door as I hurried her away, and briefed her in the car. I'd rather have *de*briefed her, but that was another thing. We drove up to the farm; Bella was out chicken-herding. I stopped the car to tell her, 'We need somewhere to change.'

She nodded, smiled and then shook her head, as if I'd said something funny.

Miller and me. We changed our clothes in my room. Facing each other and watching each other. She had to take off her dark grey working suit. Once her jacket and skirt were folded and resting on the end of my bed I couldn't take my eyes off her. Before she stepped into her WREN skirt she grinned cheekily, and asked, 'Legs OK? Pass muster?'

'Christ, yes.'

She shook her head, but it wasn't a rebuff because she smiled as well. She made a little face and said, 'Put your trousers on – and next time take your socks off *first*; men look daft standing there in shirts and dark socks.'

I pulled on my uniform. Miller straightened my tie, and kissed me for the first time. She had jazz lips. I can't explain why she was so exciting and different. Her mouth had that musty sweet flavour that girls sometimes have.

Miller knew where the cop shop was: a yellow-brick Art Deco palace with big windows wrapped around wide rounded corners. Built in the 1930s, I'd guess; it looked like a cinema. The Station

Officer knew her; I should have guessed that too. He said, 'Good morning, Mrs Miller. Long time since we've seen you in uniform.'

After that it was simple, apart from the knowledge that for the second time in as many weeks I was signing for the good behaviour of someone over whom I had absolutely no control. If the copper noticed that I was familiar with the form he handed me to complete, and had breezed through it, he didn't say. He did say something to Miller, though, and it ruffled my feathers.

'And Charles? We haven't seen him recently.'

'Not all that busy. Everyone's behaving themselves.'

On the way back I asked her, 'Why was he surprised not to have seen Mr Miller for a while? What's your husband to do with the police?'

'I never talk about Charles's work.'

'Not even with the man you're going to sleep with?'

Pause. *Sotto voce*. '*Especially* not men I'm about to sleep with.' That was good. I let the silence hang.

It was a good thick overcast, but not cold, so I'd left the hood up but dropped the side screens into the back seat. The passing air, curling back into the car, ruffled Miller's hair. She said, 'You already know that he works for the Ministry of Food. He makes sure that the food produced in the county is officially accounted for; that people aren't slipping it onto the black market. He manages a kind of accountancy team: they visit businesses and see if the numbers add up. When he catches folk at it, he writes reports and has them arrested. It's always the same people, time and again.'

'We had a phrase for that sort of job on my first squadron.'

'What was that?'

'Pissing into the wind.'

Miller turned her head away and pretended to watch the passing countryside. I'd said the wrong thing again.

But you lose one, and then you win one. Back at the farm I hung back in the kitchen, and said to her, 'Why don't you use the room first?'

Bella was there, and I'd just saved Miller's blushes. But I hadn't, because she reddened anyway, looked down, and said, 'Thank you, Charlie. I won't be long.'

Bella and I stood outside with half-pints of cider. There was a veil of thin steel-blue cloud stretching across the horizon, and above that heavy bubbling cumulous clouds, brilliantly white. It wasn't until a tiny silver aircraft scuttled beneath them – a Lancaster like *Tuesday* – that you realized how big the clouds were. I said, 'Bad buggers.'

The chickens were uncannily silent; for a moment you could have heard that pin drop. Bella said, 'Aye; storm brewing.'

As she said it there was a distant flash of sheet lightning, and an explosion of thunder that rattled the tiles, rolled all around us, and seemed to go on for ever.

'Story of my life,' I told her.

I smoked my pipe until Miller came back.

We didn't speak much in the car, but it wasn't uncomfortable, and we parted as soon as we left it. My bum had scarcely touched my office seat before Liz bounced in, with a piece of paper in her hand. She shoved it at me and said, 'American fella phoned. That's his number.'

I recognized it as the London number that Tommo had given me for his friend. It wasn't Tommo who answered when I dialled it, but after a wait of a few seconds he came to the phone.

'Did you know that I'd have to sign up with your mob to get free of this thing?'

'Not at first. I didn't know what else to do.'

'What about you? Your neck stuck out over this?'

'Not too far. Did Piers come round to see you?'

'Yup – real freak, ain't he? Someone from my embassy came after that. I'm a kind of Deputy Honorary Consul in Frankfurt now, with a diplomatic passport. What you got me into, Charlie? I feel like a fuckin' Mason.'

'You can get in and out of the country again: isn't that what you wanted?'

'Yes it is, Charlie, and I forgot to thank you for it. Thank you.'

I nearly asked him, '*What are friends for?*' before I realized that I didn't want to know the answer. Instead, I said, 'OK, Tommo, why don't you get going? Give Alice my love.'

'Sure.' And that was it. When you know someone that well, a lot of things are never said.

14. No Name Rag

Miller's revenge was giving me several hundred paper requisition slips to sign before I left. Who used all this stuff? I was in the middle of them when Liz put her head round my office door and said, 'Your Jedburghs are signalling again, if you're interested.'

Mrs Boulder was also in the radio room when I got there. She was just replacing the telephone handset. 'Sorry, sir; we have to inform Mrs Miller whenever the Jedburghs are on.'

'That's OK.' It wasn't, but never mind. Liz was back at her rig; I said, 'Shift over and let me in.' She shifted seats, but remained sitting beside me.

I listened to the short rattles of Morse, and gently rested my fingers on the key. I knew exactly the right moment to roll the dice. The Krauts sometimes used to do it to us when we were somewhere over Germany. I broke in with the CFZ call sign I used at Bawne, and sent in open.

Hi, Jed, this is Charlie. I knew that I had just seconds.

Charlie who?

Charlie who thinks it's time you came home. I'll buy you a beer in—

Nice try, Charlie. NFO.

Then they were gone. Both of them. But one of them had acknowledged me. Now they knew I was there.

'What did *NFO* mean?' Liz asked me.

'*Now fuck off*. He must have figured that ladies could be listening.'

Miller was in the doorway: she was good at doorways. She asked, 'Did you get anything, sir?'

'I got told to fuck off. Perhaps they'll talk to me *next* time.'

'Never for long enough for us to establish where they are.'

'That was never going to work anyway. If you want them to come in, you'll have to make them *want* to. Give them a good reason. Get Jane to offer them sex, and a decent meal . . .'

That didn't amuse Mrs Boulder. Her mouth turned down at the sides. Then she said, 'Why only Jane?' and smiled. It was a good smile. I realized that I'd been had.

Miller said, 'I'll just go and tell the Boss.' I assumed that she meant Watson.

I was supposed to be the ranker here, but apart from the flying I was treated as if I was the office junior and that was beginning to piss me off. What could I expect? The fact was that I didn't really want the job anyway; I was just doing my time, and they all knew it. They were still going to be here with their ears to their boxes when Charlie was long gone: they all knew that as well.

I sat on the steps of St Paul's with the D girls, and cried like a child. Den sat beside me and Dolly on the step above: she massaged my shoulders as if she was a trainer working on a boxer between rounds.

They had taken me to visit John Donne, late Dean of St Paul's. In a niche high up on a wall in St Paul's Cathedral, his statue was smaller than I had imagined – say half scale – and was of an old man wrapped in his shroud preparing to die. Dean John was big on death before he died. I hated that. Where was the wild spirit who had written about love as if he had been exploding with it? I suppose that that's a bad metaphor under the circumstances.

The bad stuff started on the steps outside. Don't laugh, but that was precisely where and when the business of bombing Germany got to me at last. It pinpointed my scarred conscience, there on the scarred steps of St Paul's. I hadn't noticed it when we arrived, but afterwards, outside on the steps . . . well, there was nothing around St Paul's, you see: just acres of bomb-site. Cellars open to the sky, giving off a heavy foetid stench. Some had been screened by temporary walls or fences, to stop drunks falling into them in the dark.

St Paul's stood huge and sooty in a wasteland of smashed brick and stone. In places a pall of dust fouled the air, whipped up by eddying breezes as the wind learned new routes around London. I'd seen something similar in Bremen, but for some reason hadn't understood it then. What I was thinking about was the thousands of places we'd created in Germany which looked exactly the same, and the bodies that stank beneath them. What the hell had Krefeld looked like after we had finished with it? In a remnant of yard that had been cleared, I knelt behind a displaced headstone that had surfaced from somewhere, and was sick. No doubt the late Dean would have been pleased to see me on my knees at last.

I was wiping my mouth as I walked back to them. I said, 'Sorry. It's funny how things catch up with you.'

'What was it?' Dolly asked. I sat down, and that was when she began to knead my shoulders.

'I suddenly saw all this mess, and thought about Germany, that's all. I just didn't think about it at the time; not many of us did.' The wind had changed. Some of the dust drifted towards us, carrying the heady scents of urine and faeces. 'I never thought about mile upon mile of open cellars, and dead people.'

'Toilets,' Den said. 'Dunnees. It took the Germans nearly three years to knock this part of London down. It took us less than three months to turn it into an outdoor dunnee – can't you smell it? What are people like?'

I still felt I owed them an explanation. 'There are big holes in every city I've seen since the war. Nothing like this, though – except in Germany.'

'Liverpool,' Dolly said. 'They have pretty big holes in Liverpool too, and Glasgow, Coventry and Portsmouth. You haven't been down the docks yet, have you?'

'No.'

'Well, don't: not if you're going to get a fit of the 'abdabs. Around the docks is worse than this. What have you seen in Germany?'

'Bremen and Bremerhaven – that's its port. Parts of the North-West. There were thousands of people living underground. I expect there still are. I went into a cellar that had two hundred people in it. They were living on water flavoured with potatoes and cabbage.'

It was as if Dolly's fingers were reaching through the skin and muscle to my very bones. She said, 'Didn't you see this when you were here during the war?'

During the war and *in the war* were phrases that punctuated our vocabulary. Some people talked as if the events were as distant as ancient Rome, or Babylon.

'No. It wasn't like that. When we were up in town, we were out all night looking for fun, and a girl to get your leg over. Didn't get up until dinnertime, and then it was out to a pub again. 'S funny. It was almost as if we had become nocturnal animals – we only moved around in the dark; and we flew in it, of course. I remember that everyone in the crew had pale faces; like they had drowned. All a bomb-site meant to me then was a copper with a swinging torch, diverting our taxi. It had nothing to do with people. Not then.'

'And it does now?' That was Den.

'Yeah. Now it's got everything to do with people.'

She leaned towards me and kissed me on the cheek.

It took us nearly fifteen minutes to find a bus stop. From the top of the bus I could suddenly see bomb damage everywhere. Den asked me, 'What about the *atom* bomb, Charlie?'

'What about it?'

'If this is what London looks like today, and the German places you've seen look worse, imagine what those Japanese cities look like. Just one bomb, and no city any more. Hundreds of thousands dead, and hundreds of thousands infected with deadly rays and bound to die. Like a plague.'

'Is that what it's like? A plague?'

'I don't know. It's the only way I can think about it. I try not to think about the children but sometimes I can't think about anything else.'

It was just after opening time so we were the first into the bar of a pub in Camden Town that they wanted to show me. The Parr's Head. A tiny snug bar around the back, off a side alley, contained old sitting-room chairs leaking their stuffing, small low tables, a radio and a tank of goldfish. The licensee was a short, vivacious woman who everyone called Ma. The beer was Watney's – so good that even the girls drank it. Den drank pints, like a man; that was still unusual in a woman. There was something about the atmosphere of that little bar that made you reluctant to leave.

Den and I sat on their new leather sofa, and sipped American sour-mash whiskies. The girls never seemed short of drink, or new furniture.

'Can I ask you something personal?' I asked her.

'Sure – shoot.'

It was almost an appropriate response, because I asked her, 'Are you and Dolly *whores*, or whatever prostitutes call themselves these days?' I felt her stiffen, but she stayed jammed up close against me.

'What do you mean, Charlie?'

'What I said. Sorry I didn't dress it up in prettier words. Look

. . . you both have ordinary jobs, but you both get paid to go out with men that Stephen selects for you as well, and sometimes you sleep with them . . . I just thought . . .'

She just reached down and touched me. Then she kissed me under the ear, and asked, 'Thought what, Charlie?'

'Thought that I wasn't sure whether you were or not, that's all. It doesn't worry me.'

'I'm pleased about that, Charlie.'

'No, you're not. You're being sarcastic. I shouldn't have asked, should I?'

'Look at it this way: are you fucking anybody yet, down in deepest Gloucestershire?'

'No. Not yet.'

'Possibles?'

'One. Almost a promise, I think.' I probably closed my eyes, and put my head back. It's what some cats do if you rub them under the chin.

'What would you think if she gave you money, or a present, after she'd been out with you?'

I wanted to move. I dared not.

'She's already given me a new raincoat.'

'There you are, then. Does that make you a whore?'

'No. Of course not.'

She said it again. 'There you are, then. Do you want me to stop?'

'No.'

So she stopped immediately. She took my face between both her hands and turned me to look into her eyes. I squeezed my knees together. She explained: 'A whore would do exactly what you wanted: I'm not a whore, so I won't.' A six-beat pause. 'See?'

'Lesson learned,' I confirmed between clenched teeth.

'I fancy a jam sandwich. Shall I make you one?'

It was as if the rest of the conversation hadn't occurred.

They had a smart new gramophone, and the best record collection I had ever seen. If I named a singer or a band, she produced and played it for me. If it became like a competition, then she won, because eventually I listened to whatever she chose.

I remember her carefully dusting a record and saying, 'Benny Goodman – "Sing, Sing, Sing". You're a lucky man, Charlie. I only play this to the men I love.'

'You still love me, then?' We were sitting a yard apart by now.

'Figure of speech; don't get your hopes up.'

Goodman reached for the high notes one after the other. Den looked very beautiful.

She was alongside me with her head on my shoulder when Dolly came in at midnight. We had the radio tuned to one of the late-night dance-music programmes from Holland, and had the lights turned down low. Dolly frowned when she saw us, but replaced that with a weary forced smile. 'Did she seduce you, Charlie? Just my luck.'

'No; she was very cruel to me.'

'I left him for you, if you still want him. Charlie was asking some rather nasty questions,' Denys told her. 'So I played him music instead. Served him right.'

'I'll bet.' Dolly stretched. My eyes followed her body as her contours changed. Then she said, ‘I’ll bet it was about accepting money for our little expeditions. It always comes up. It’s no different from being married, Charlie.’

‘I don’t understand that.’

‘If I’m married and my husband is keeping me, I’m taking a man’s money anyway, aren’t I? What’s the difference? I cost less than a wife, and you know what you’re getting. If you’ve a better argument, beat that.’

‘I’d rather beat you; don’t some people do that?’

‘You can have him back, Den,’ Dolly said. ‘He’s getting a little peculiar.’

In the small hours I lay on top of Dolly in her comfortable bed, but I propped my weight on my elbows. Her eyes were closed but she wasn’t asleep. In the half-dark I could see that her cheeks were slightly puffy from our lovemaking. ‘That was beautiful. I loved that,’ I told her.

‘Is that why you love me?’

‘No. I love you because you’re outrageous in bed, but still use words like “golly” and “gosh” and “rotten devils”. Is that enough love to be going on with?’ It was just a game, I think.

She didn’t reply immediately. ‘I’m going to try very hard not to let you get under my skin, Charlie.’

‘Why?’

‘I don’t know; I just know that it would be a mistake.’

I kissed her on her nose. She smiled, and wrinkled it up. She still didn’t open her eyes.

‘I have to go and work with Piers in the morning; can I have you again before I go?’

She giggled. 'Can you come before you go? Is that what you mean?'

'Don't laugh at me.'

'Then don't ask, stupid. What do you think I got you here for?'

Not much sleep tonight, Charlie, I thought. What did Cole Porter write? *Just One of Those Things.*

Just one of those things that Piers asked me about was Alice. He was fascinated by the idea of her, despite himself. 'Has your friend taken his death worm out of the country with him yet?'

'I suppose so.' We drank expensive coffee from fine porcelain cups in his office. I was afraid that I would break one and lose a month's pay replacing it. 'What will happen to him?'

'The coroner will record a death by misadventure, and the police record will show that our gallant American ally was formally cautioned for driving injudiciously quickly over a blind summit: that's a hump in the road. I chose the wording myself: awfully good, don't you think? Amusing, under the circumstances.'

'I think you're sick.'

'Mmm. I probably agree. Something to do with one's school.'

'OK,' I told him. 'I'm here. I'm here because you'd already snared me with a photo of Grace. Was that kosher, by the way?'

'That's what I want you to find out. *The Lady Vanishes* and *Find The Lady*. Sound like films and card games, don't they?'

I wasn't in the mood for Piers's word games. 'They *are* a film and a card game. Just explain what you want.'

'Simple tasks for a man with your skills. I want you to study those photographs until you think that you can recognize the people in them on sight. Then go trolling down the Bishops Avenue until you come across them, identify them, and bring their names and locations back to me. I need to know exactly where the principals are living before we move against them. Find your errant lady into the bargain, and I'll give you a gold star for your exercise book.'

'I already have a medal from the French.'

'I know. They'll pay you a small pension for that when you retire. I'll bet you didn't know that.'

'No, I didn't. This isn't very RAF work, Piers.'

'No. It's not even very GCHQ work. It's *almost GCHQ* work.'

'You said "trolling down the Bishops Avenue": what does "trolling" mean? Is it a new in-word?'

'No, son; a very *old* in-word. Norse root; adopted by the Saxons, I should imagine. It means towing a baited hook behind a boat until a fish grabs it. I can't imagine where you went to school.'

'What's the bait I'll be trailing?'

'You and your errant woman. I'm betting she's as much an embarrassment to them as she is to us: Brother Ivan's not all that keen on poor little rich girls. I'm sure you'll be very popular once they suspect that you might be going to take her away with you. We want her away from them, and they probably want to see the back of her.'

'Why do you want her away from there?'

'Oh, the usual reason.' He waved his hand in the air. 'Her father still makes most of the bullets that our fine British Tommy marches to war with, so we don't want her face all over the front page of the *Sunday Pic*, do we? If you can lift her out of there without embarrassment, it will be the best of all possible outcomes for the largest number of people.'

'That's Benthamism, isn't it? I remember that from school. If you already know she's up there and you suspect they want to get rid of her, then you already have someone asking questions. Is that the man who took your photos?'

'A man who stepped off the edge of the world about four weeks ago; just about when you stepped onto the stage, Charlie. *Weren't* we lucky? We haven't got a clue what happened to him.'

'Why should she have anything to do with me? I followed her to Italy last year, remember, and she told me to bugger off.'

'You've got her baby, haven't you? Try that.'

I knew it: brutal little bastard once the gloves were off, wasn't he?

Piers parked me in a small office, gave me a couple of photographs to memorize, and a book on socialism to give me the flavour of the people I would be mixing with. It was entitled *A History of Socialism in Cromarty*, and it had been published in 1919. He said that it was the only book on socialism that he'd read. It centred on the life of a nineteenth-century stone mason, and was probably very interesting to other nineteenth-century stone masons. For my purposes it was utterly fucking irrelevant.

The pack helped, though. The office looked dead; as if no one had worked in it in years. In an otherwise empty dark green locker I found a tatty old army pack – probably from the First World War. In my mind I rehearsed what I was going to carry in it: a couple of old RAF shirts, well past their best, a change of smalls and socks. Soap and toothbrush. Oh, yeah – wrapped in there somewhere would be Tommo's pistol. If I was going to stick my head into the lion's mouth I wanted something that would convince the lion that I wouldn't be all that tasty. It was only as I was packing that evening that I began to wonder when I'd begun to think like that.

The next morning I took a bus out to the Spaniards – that is, the Spaniards Inn – and hoofed it from there. It might have been a circuitous approach, but I wanted time to think, and I think well on my feet. Kenwood House car park was open, and several cars were resting in it. A group of musicians and singers were limbering up so I wandered over and lit a pipe, putting off the evil hour. They were all in fancy dress, and produced the strangest music I had ever heard. Dark-haired women wore long red skirts that flew out into the shape of bells as they danced and whirled. A Scot who looked like Oscar Wilde told me that they were Bulgarians who had come over for an international folk-music festival being staged in the big house by the LCC.

'What do you think of them?' he asked.

'This lot, or the LCC?'

'Pardon? Ah! I see: joke. Funny.'

No – not like Wilde at all.

'Their singing sets my teeth on edge, and their music makes the hair on my neck stand up,' I told him.

'I know. Terrific, isn't it?' Oscar said. 'Would you like to come to one of their concerts? I've got some free tickets.'

I smiled at one of the women. When she smiled back I could see that some of her teeth were missing. Those that weren't appeared to have been filed to points. I didn't mean to shudder, but I couldn't help it. I settled for two tickets, but didn't guarantee to use them. Nevertheless the man had lifted my sombre mood, so I launched myself down the big avenue. The lime and silver birch trees had come into leaf, and I walked down a wide sunlight-dappled path. An ex-army pick-up drove slowly past me and dropped out of sight. The men dressed in uniform remnants huddled in the back of it gave me a quick once-over as they passed. One of them raised a hand to me. I didn't think that I knew him, but I was dressed the same as them. The tattered-uniform remnants of the new underclass: Charlie back in character.

The big houses were on one side of the street. There were three kinds: those occupied by their rightful owners, the unoccupied, and those taken over by our abandoned heroes – the people I was looking for. One house had a gardener weeding its freshly gravelled driveway, and a large dog chained to the front gate. It didn't look like the place for me, so I gave it a pass. The dog lifted her lip and sneered.

A big crumbling mock-Tudor mass looked more promising. There were kids playing in an unkempt front garden. A man wearing a tired Para smock sat on the front steps of an open door, smoking a big curved briar: one of the good guys. His accent said Newcastle or Gateshead: they get everywhere.

'Help you, pal?'

I put my old pack down, and stretched. I hoped I looked as if I was on the road. 'I was looking for somewhere to stay for a few days.'

He stood up so that he was between me and the door. 'Not

here, chook. We're full up. No room at the inn.' At least he was telling it straight.

I shrugged, and let my shoulders sag. 'Down the road?'

'You can always ask. I wouldn't know. Wouldn't think so.'

Well done, Charlie. Fallen at the first fence. I turned away from him, my mind racing behind what I hoped was something like a weary mask. I took about ten paces towards the gate when one of the kids, a boy of about seven or eight, went down on the gravel and set up a howl. He was sitting up by the time I reached him, grizzling and holding a hand over a bloody knee.

'You're a wounded soldier,' I told him, and gave him a hug. 'Come on, now; soldiers don't cry. Let me see it.'

It was just a shallow graze, but they can sting like blazes, can't they? All the boy needed was for someone to tell him what to do. Before the big man from the steps had arrived, I was kneeling to clean the kid's graze with his own spit and my clean but ragged spare handkerchief. The boy winced, but he didn't shout as I picked out the dirt with a fingernail. Then I tied the handkerchief around his knee. I said, 'There. Wounded soldier. Your dad'll be proud of you.'

'Dad was at Alamein,' the kid said, and drew himself up straight. He stuck his chest out. 'He never came back. He was a hero; I've got his medals.' How do you respond to that one? The Geordie was up to us by then.

'We can manage now,' he said. 'Thanks.' He hoisted the kid into his arms. Both of them were looking down on me now. 'Say thank you, Gary.'

'Thanks, mister.'

I grinned. It was because that was the first time anyone had called me mister.

'Bye, soldier. Watch out for the stones next time.'

Walking away from them was all that was left for me to do. As I turned away I saw a woman I didn't know at an upstairs window. She smiled and raised a hand. I waved back in a half-hearted sort of way. These people were good at hellos and good-byes, but not at what went between. What the hell, they'd probably all had difficult wars.

I was almost at the gate before the Geordie called out, 'Hey, mister. Wait a min.'

Second time the word had been used on me inside two minutes: not bad. I turned back.

He added, 'Go down to number twenty-eight and ask for the Secretary. He might be able to help you.'

'What do I tell him?'

'Say you're looking for a billet for a few days, and say Matesy sent you.'

'*Matesy?*'

'That's me.' He held a hand out for the ritual shake: the top of the index finger was missing. He said, 'Good luck, chum.'

The kid looked at me solemnly and echoed him. 'Good luck, chum.'

They grew up quickly in those days.

The house I had been sent to was bigger and uglier. Nineteen-thirties build – it reminded me of that police station in Cheltenham. This one had defence in depth: a couple of hard-looking buggers lounged near the garden gate, and another guy sat in a rocking chair by the double front doors, rolling a fag. I got as far as him because the hard buggers ignored me. I thought that meant that I looked as if I fitted in. *Wrong*, Charlie. The man in the rocker was a big serious-looking guy about my age. He had a moustache and beard around his mouth, and cheap, heavy specs. He said, '*You* took your time. Where've you been?'

For a moment I was thrown, and thought that it was all over before I put a foot over the threshold. Then the kid with the bloody knee moved out of the shadow of the hallway. Matesy had sent a runner around the back: the old ways were often the best.

'I had a look at some of the big houses on the way down. Why?'

The man looked down at his fag, and shook his head. He was making a rotten job of it, so I asked, 'Would you like me to do that? I learned how to in the mob.'

He handed over a tatty packet of Nosegay and a pack of Rizlas. 'Roll yourself one, too. What mob was that?'

'The RAF. That was years ago.'

'It seems like it, sometimes, doesn't it? Looking for somewhere to bunk down?'

'Yeah. There you go.' I handed him a fag and his kit. 'Thanks, but I use a pipe.'

'Can you pay your way?' he asked.

'I've a few quid. I can always get some more.' I wasn't lying: I had fifty pounds sewn into a shirt pocket.

'Not from round here, you don't,' he told me seriously. 'The rich folk all have dogs. And anyway, it's not my policy to upset the neighbours. Us living alongside them pisses them off enough as it is.'

'I'll remember that.'

He clearly took me for a thief. The odd thing was that he didn't seem to think any less of me because of it. 'And you can buy me a pint tonight.'

'I may not be here tonight. I have to speak to someone called the Secretary. I don't know what he's secretary of.'

'Secretary of the Housing Committee of the Highgate and Hampstead Branch of the CP. What a mouthful. That's me. I manage these houses for the People's Housing Cooperative.' When I didn't react he asked, 'Does that bother you?'

'Not if you have a room, or something, for me.'

'We'll find something for you. I'm Harry James – just like the bandleader.' He stood up. I had to do the handshake thing again. I said, 'Charlie . . .' And then I said something stupid, because it was much too close to home for comfort. 'Charlie Miller.' It was all I could think of by way of a surname at short notice.

'Welcome to Millionaires' Row, Charlie; make the most of it because they'll have us out of here before long, and they're the biggest houses *you*'ll ever sleep in. Hungry?'

I nodded. 'Yes, a bit.'

'Cut along to the kitchen; it's through in the back. They'll find you something.'

'How do I pay for this?'

'In good time. We'll find you something to do. Can you hold a paintbrush or repair a wireless set?'

I grinned. 'Yeah; I can do both those things for you.'

The kid, Gary, held his hand up. He said, 'I'll take you to the kitchen, mister.'

'Charlie,' I told him.

'Mister Charlie.'

I noticed that he no longer had my handkerchief: his knee had been properly cleaned and neatly bandaged. That was interesting: there was an organizing principle at work here. In one of the rooms off the corridor that led back through the house a radio was playing music. Benny Goodman was doing 'Memories of You'.

Gary watched me eat thick slices of bread and dripping and drink a mug of tea. The dripping wasn't as good as Miller's, but they'd probably started with less promising material. He shook his head when I offered him some. Things must be looking up in England if kids could afford to refuse a meal. He asked me, 'Were you in the RAF, Mister Charlie?'

'Yes, I was. How did you guess?'

'Didn't. I heard you tell Mister James.' He sniffed, and wiped his nose on the end of his sleeve.

'Don't do that. Use a hankie.'

'Sorry, mister.'

He looked as if I'd slapped him, and I realized that he didn't have one. I gave him my second, and last, handkerchief. It was clean but rumpled. He said, 'Thanks, mister. Can I keep it?'

'Yes, of course. You're welcome to it.'

'Mr Mates is making me a model Spit. Did you fly Spitfires?'

'No. Lancaster bombers.'

'Did you kill masses of Jerries?'

'Yes; I'm afraid I probably did.'

His hand suddenly bunched around the handkerchief in a hard little fist. He stared out of the window as if he could see for a thousand miles, and said, 'Good.'

The room they gave me faced a back garden half the size of a football pitch and neatly laid out with vegetables. I guessed that they had lived here a long time; maybe years. My space was about twenty by twenty – the biggest room I had ever had to myself – and had two large windows and a double-bed mattress on the floor. That had four sheets and three clean blankets neatly folded on it. There was a utility armchair which had seen better days, a small table and chair, and a flimsy wardrobe. There was a key on the inside of the door, and another hanging from a nail in the back of it. I asked Gary, 'Where did all this stuff come from?'

'Bomb-sites, Mister Charlie. You need anything else?'

'No. Thanks. This will do for me. Why aren't you at school today?'

'Half-term. I hate it, anyway. I should be out working, getting Ma a bit of money.'

'How old are you?'

'Nine.'

'Does she complain about that?'

'No.'

'Then wait until she does, Gary. You'll grow up soon enough.'

There was one missing window-pane. It had been replaced with a sheet of three-ply neatly puttied into place. If I had repaired that, and given the place a lick of paint, I could have lived the rest of my life there. There was a big bathroom, and a separate toilet along the corridor. I shared them with a woman who had three children and two rooms, and a girl who lived on her own in one. They were clean and tidy – there was no room here for my usual slobbish ways.

The pub that the Secretary took me to was the Parr's Head in Camden Town. What goes around comes around. Ma showed no sign of recognizing me from the night before. This time I sat in the public bar with half a dozen other men. I thought that I recognized two of them from Piers's photographs, but I couldn't be sure. They talked politics. The government had betrayed the returning forces, apparently, and the Nazis who had run England before the war were re-establishing themselves in all of the top slots. Your Working Man, who had done the bulk of the fighting, had ended up with less than he'd started out with, and something had to be done about that. I kept my head down, and asked the occasional question as if a new world was opening up before me.

We sat on the top deck of the bus going back that night. It had that musty smell of tobacco and old people: smoke, piss and sweat. Harry James said, 'They liked you. You can stay as long as you like.'

'How do you know they liked me?'

'I can tell. Would you roll me another fag?'

'Why don't I show you the knack?'

'I always wanted to write a book about politics. Something that would make a difference for working people – that would show them how to organize themselves and come out on top.'

'Yes?'

'Now I think that writing a book about how to roll a good fag would be of more use to them.'

'*The knack, and how to get it*,' I told him.

'I like that,' he said. 'You've been around, haven't you?' It was one of those phrases we used all the time in the Forties: it meant that you'd had some experiences – not all of them needed to have been good. I showed him how to dampen his forefingers and thumbs before he rolled a cigarette. He was a quick learner.

'Who were those men I met tonight?'

'Oh, just some committee. No one important.'

They'd been important enough to give me the once-over, and important enough to give me the nod. I remembered that in France in the 1790s they called themselves the Committee for Public Safety, or some such guff. They were the ones who sent you to the guillotine. That was interesting. I was on a bus with Robespierre.

The single woman I shared a bathroom with was called Wendy. She'd got through the war, and now she was an exotic dancer. She told me this over strong tea and wonderful home-baked bread in the huge kitchen.

'What's an exotic dancer?'

'Like the Windmill Girls.'

'You mean you take your clothes off? Striptease?'

'Yes, silly . . . I know that I don't look like much in the morning, but you should see me in the spotlights! Harry said that you'd give me a hand painting my room. That OK?'

'Sure. When?'

'How about now?'

*

I'd been in women's rooms before: you've probably realized that. Each one has its own characteristic smell. Sometimes it's the perfume she wears, or the make-up – nail varnish, powder or lipstick. Sometimes it's simply sheets that should have been changed a fortnight ago. Wendy's room was one of a kind: it stank of paraffin.

I threw the windows open, and said something like *phew* – you know, one of those strange noises they like in boys' comics.

Wendy said, 'Sorry. I don't notice it any more.'

'What happened? Did you have a big spill, or something?'

'Nah: it's the *exotic* part of the dancing I told you about. I'm a fire-eater.'

'Fire-eater? Like at the circus?'

'Yes.'

'You eat fire *and* take your clothes off? At the same time?'

'You got it. Wanna watch some day? It's very artistic.'

I shook my head: I'd been too close to a fire before, and it hadn't done me any good. Wendy's room was like mine, but bigger. Three windows and all of the panes were intact. As I looked around I noticed scorch and soot marks on the walls and ceiling.

'Harry says I can't practise in here any more. I have to do it in the garden. Just in case I burn the place down.'

Seemed fair enough to me. We were grinning at each other before we had finished shrouding her few sticks of furniture with borrowed paint-splattered sheets: she had as little as I. The paint was Ministry of Pensions puke green. Even its thin green label said *M of P*, and had the secret government mark, so it was the genuine article all right.

Wendy left me to push a light plywood chest of drawers over to the centre of the room and tuck it under the sheets. I had to pick up a framed photograph from its top, and glanced at it as I turned it over. And stopped. It was the photograph that Piers had hidden in my car. I still had it in my hand, and my heart had started beating again, when Wendy waltzed back in with a bottle of beer and two half-pint glasses: this girl knew how to paint a room. I looked up and asked, 'Party to remember?'

She took the photo from me and smiled. It had been a memory worth framing. A small modern wireless set on the floor in a corner was bashing out 'Storyville Blues' behind me somewhere. Time stopped, and Wendy remembered. 'That wasn't so long ago. It was the first real fun I'd had in a long time; I danced with all the men in that picture, and then *that* one asked me out.' She laid her finger on a face with a massive moustache.

I tried to sound disinterested. 'Who's the girl? The one who didn't smile?'

Wendy's smile stretched out. 'She won't tell us. She has no name.'

'None at all?'

'She said that we could call her Carla, but that it wasn't her real name.'

Carla. She had named her small boy Carlo, after the Eyetie she had been knocking around with when he was born. I tried to keep it casual. 'Does she stay here too?'

'No – why? Do you know her?'

Back off, Charlie. 'No. I rather fancied the look of her, that's all.'

Wendy laughed. 'So did all the other guys. Queuing up like

for ration books at the butcher's shop. I don't know what she's got, but I wouldn't mind some of it. I don't think that one often has a quiet bed.'

'Don't you like her?'

'No. And I don't know why – isn't that odd? She's in one of the houses around here; I don't know which one.'

'I'll keep my eye out for her.'

'You're a fly waiting for the spider, then: poor sod. Do you want the walls or the ceiling?'

'Ceiling. I was in the RAF once; I'm supposed to be good at heights.'

I finished my glass of beer. The band on the radio switched to 'No-name Rag'. If God existed somewhere, He was sending me a message. I'd caught the signal, but as with most of His messages it was the usual fucking gibberish.

I told Harry James that I needed to make a few phone calls if I was to stay in business. He cautioned me again about making my business too local. Then he told me where the nearest phone box was, and offered me change for it. The Bishops Avenue would have been called Mile End Road if someone else hadn't got there first. Even in a half-hearted smog you can stand at one end and not see the other. It took me ten minutes to reach the telephone, and I was sweating by the time I got there, so I propped the door open to cool down while I spoke to Piers. The other reason to prop the door open was to stop me retching: someone had crapped and pissed in the phone box the night before.

'You're still alive, then?' Piers said. 'Well done.'

'I'm learning a useful trade; I painted a ceiling this morning.'

'Don't tell the RAF; they'll want you to stay on even longer – or are we talking Michelangelo here? In which case don't tell the Pope, either. Have you found anything yet? I can't wait for ever.'

'Hang on a tick; I've only been here a day! I think that I've seen a couple of your faces – I'll need another shufti at your photographs sometime.'

'What about your woman?'

'I saw the same photograph of her in another woman's room. Apparently Grace is in one of the houses, but I don't know which one yet. God knows what I'm going to say if I bump into her by chance.'

'Do the same as any decent actor: rehearse it beforehand. And don't use names on the telephone, dear boy. You never know who's listening. Walls still have ears, and all that sort of thing.'

'These people are somehow under the impression that I pursue the honourable profession of thief: I didn't plan it that way, but it means that I can sod off for a week's thieving whenever I like without anyone being that worried – except that when I come back I will have to display a few examples of my ill-gotten gains.'

'*Swag*, you mean? That's colourful! Do you expect me to provide it?'

'If you would. I think that I'm just your everyday burglar: robbing Peter to pay Paul. I'm going to stay tonight, then go back down to the girls' flat and clean up, and then go back to Cheltenham. I never did wholly trust you, so I want to see if I still have a job there.'

'Getting to like it there, were we?'

'Sod off, Piers.'

It was just as well that my money ran out then.

Supper was a big affair in the kitchen large enough to house an aircraft. When you counted the kids there were probably twenty of us. Mountains of salty scrambled egg – the real thing, not powdered – chips, and fried slices of Spam. There were three bottles of HP Sauce, and five newly baked loaves on the long table. Back to wartime food, except for the eggs. This lot had probably never moved away from it.

'We've nearly a hundred chickens in the gardens here,' James told me. 'That's why I'm determined to hang on to the houses until the government gives these families somewhere decent to live. I can not only house them but feed them, and there's a school for the kids less than a mile away.'

I nodded. I'd seen more than enough eggs recently to last a lifetime, but in the Forties you never pushed your plate away with anything left on it.

'I've got to go away for a few days to do a bit of business. I'd like to contribute what I can, if you don't mind; otherwise I'm just stealing the food out of someone else's mouth.'

He shook his head. 'I told you. Money's not exactly a problem. I might even be able to lay my hands on enough to buy homes for everyone here, if only there were the houses to buy.' That 'country fit for heroes' the old man had moaned on about was still further away than before. 'Occupying the big empty houses encourages the government to fill up all those holes in the ground, and to start building decent homes on them. Building more houses means more jobs for more builders, of course, and "the music goes round and round".' He sang the last phrase: it was the title of a Tommy Dorsey number. 'You can have the room as long as you like because you're striking a blow for the workers by living in it. Get yourself a girl, and a proper job one day – it beats getting arrested for larceny.' James was a big innocent slob, and if I hung around there for too long I would begin to like him enormously.

'How about my contributing to some sort of political fund, then? Helping out in another way,' I offered.

He beamed. It was as if I'd switched a light on. 'That would be a fine thing to do, Charlie.'

'How much . . .?'

'A couple of quid a week is just about right for those who can afford it. You won't regret this, Charlie, I promise you.' Don't you hate it whenever anyone says that? 'You'll tell your kids about this one day.'

I handed over a few grubby pound notes. You would have thought that I'd handed him the Crown Jewels. He finished by telling me that my card would take a couple of weeks to come through, and I realized that I'd just joined the Party. Call me Red Charlie. My friend Pete, the Pink Pole, would have been very amused.

I finished my James Hadley Chase novel just before midnight, and banged my head six times against the mattress to remind me to get up early. It also reminded me to get a pillow from somewhere next time. My last memory before I slept was of the paraffin smell in Wendy's room, but eventually I drifted off.

That's probably why I dreamed I was over Germany in a Lancaster again. Germany was burning. So was the Lancaster. It never quite leaves you.

Den was in the mews flat next morning: she gave me a key. Before I went I telephoned Piers.

'How did that woman get a copy of Grace's photograph? Who did she get it from? Your guy?'

'You forgot to ask her, didn't you?'

Wise after the event; sod him. Den helped me bundle up my old clothes, pack them into a battered RN kitbag that she had, and stow them behind one of her two overflowing wardrobes. I kept hold of my battered American flying jacket to wear while I was driving. I pulled the hood of the car down, and wondered how far I'd get before it started to rain.

15. Once in a While

I got almost as far as Oxford before I introduced a three-inch nail to the front nearside tyre with sad consequences: they didn't get on, and the tyre deflated just as I reached a pub with a car park and beer garden. The beer garden was full of students, most of whom were ex-Servicemen toying with maths, science and engineering degrees. I know that because they did their best to help me to change the car's wheel, telling me that it was a simple matter of maths, science and engineering. You probably guessed that they hadn't a fucking clue.

Half an hour later a girl smaller than me – height-wise only – pushed through the crowd, explaining that changing a wheel on a Singer was more of an art than a science. She showed me how to do it. It took her less than five minutes. I hadn't looked at the spare since 1944 so the fact that it was still inflated, if a trifle soft, showed that someone up there was looking after me. We actually finished the job before we introduced ourselves.

'I'm Charlie Bassett, and that was very kind of you. Can I buy you a drink?'

'Madeleine, and *yes*, you can.'

Her brother had a garage, and he liked working on Singers: she helped him out sometimes. The party in the pub wound up out of nowhere: the best ones always do. It was like one of our parties in '44. I remember looking up suddenly, and asking where the *boys* were – my old bomber crew: that never quite leaves you either.

Rain. We had to hold my jacket over our heads to keep dry as we staggered to the car. The rooms she lived in were above her brother's workshop, and smelled vaguely of engine oil, petrol and exhaust fumes. I've always loved those homely smells. They remind me of my dad.

'We're home,' I told her, 'and you have triffic tits.'

'*Triffic?*' She laughed at me, and I didn't mind.

'That's what I said, wasn't it? Triffic. 'Xtremely triffic.' We were leaning against each other, holding each other upright. 'Christ; did I drive here without hitting anything?'

The god who loves radio operators had punched my ticket again, and lent me the goodwill of a good woman. I kissed her mouth for the first time at the foot of the stairs leading up to her room. In bed she made me use a French letter. That was probably the first time that I didn't mind about that. Afterwards I kissed her lightly on her nose. Innocent as babies. In the morning she asked me to give her my old leather jacket, which I did without a thought. Easy come, easy go.

The next day was my special saint's day: Hangover Sunday. We made plans to meet again. She was going to call me, but deep in our hearts we both knew that would only spoil it. She didn't call. We didn't meet, and sixty years later I can write about her now, with a smile still on my face. I hope that she is still around, and smiling somewhere too.

The first thing that Miller said to me on Monday morning was, 'Where's your old flying jacket?'

I usually hung it on the nail in the back of my office door. Women are like that; they notice bloody everything. If you plucked a hair from one of your eyebrows they'd comment on it the next time they saw you.

'I don't need it now that you've given me a new raincoat.'

'That's sweet, Charlie; did you leave your old jacket in your rooms?' She wasn't going to let it go.

'I gave it to someone I met yesterday. They needed it more than I did. Why?'

She stuck out her lower lip. 'I rather liked it; that's all.'

'It once belonged to James Stewart, the film star. Did I ever tell you that?'

'No; that only makes it worse.' Then she smiled and said, 'A few days off have done you good: it's brought the colour back to your cheeks.' I'll swear that she was a bloody mind-reader.

I didn't like to tell her that I'd decided it was time to go to war: so I just called a meeting. The others filtered in shortly after that, at my request. Four sat on chairs, but Jane sat on the end of my desk and flashed her stocking tops at me. Miller didn't like that. I did.

'I've been thinking about those two Jedburghs,' I told them. 'How long have you been trying to pin them down?'

'About eight months so far.' Jane produced one of those

odd-shaped stilettos and began to file her nails, but it was just displacement activity. She uncrossed her legs, then crossed them the other way. Miller frowned. No one likes discussing their failures. Perhaps no one was supposed to tell me anything. After all, I was only supposed to be in charge, and I'd spent the last four years keeping as much as possible from *my* bosses.

'Well, I reckon they've got our measure, don't you?' No one would meet my eye, so I went on, 'And I don't want you to get all down in the mouth about that. I just want us to put them on their back foot for a min.'

Liz made a sound that came out halfway between a raspberry and a giggle, and then said, 'Sorry. I mean, *how?*' What she meant was '*Better men than you have tried, Charlie Bassett.*'

'Work out their schedules and probable frequencies, and keep jumping in first before they broadcast. Let's really piss them off.'

'Rattle their cages?' That was Weronka. 'Isn't that what the Yanks say?'

I just waited for Boulder. She said, 'I think I need a cup of coffee. Anyone else?'

Now that might not sound like much, but they were all in the same conversation at the same time, you see. For the first time they began to sound to me something like a team. Boulder came back with three cups of uncut Camp. One of them was for me. I said, 'Thanks,' and got a little twitch around her lips back for it. That was good, but she hadn't quite finished. Boulder looked at me. 'We're supposed just to monitor the frequencies that London gives us, but not supposed to keep notes of anything we do, other than any we hand in to Mrs Miller at the end of each shift. It's security; London says so.'

'That's right,' Miller said. 'I have to give them a certificate every month.'

'I lie to you,' Boulder told her nervously. She sat with her knees pressed tight together and looked down. It was as if she had tossed a hand grenade into the room. 'I've a bad memory . . . so I need to keep some things written down if I'm to remember them an hour later. I have a small notebook. I think I've got a record of each of the frequencies I've heard the Jedburghs on.'

I was grinning fit to split my face. If Boulder had looked up she would have seen that the others were, too. All except Miller: you could see the battle between keeping the rules and making a match of it all over her face. The match won: thank God for that. She gave in. 'If you tied that into my book you've probably got close to what you want.'

'What book?' I asked.

'The logbook: our *legal* one.' That was a bit mean. 'Every time I send off a flimsy I keep a numbered record. When the call was intercepted, call sign – and which of our operators copied it. One signal for every line in the log. The Commander calls it our *defensive* record. It means that London can't deny they received a signal copy from us. Periodically an independent officer arrives to compare my log with a list of signals that London says they've analysed.'

'But not the frequencies or the radio profiles?'

'No. I'm not allowed to keep that. Standing orders.' Miller looked pointedly at Boulder.

I said, 'I'd better read those SOs one day.'

'I don't think you can, sir. I don't think that your clearance goes that high.'

'But yours does? Even if you're technically my number two?'

'Yes, sir.'

'In that case stop calling me *sir*,' I snapped. 'It's bloody insulting.'

Miller coloured. Two bright pink patches just below her cheekbones. I'd never spoken to her like that before, and now I'd done it in front of the others. Bugger – that wasn't going to get her on her back, was it?

Liz didn't help. She said cheerfully, 'It's confusing, isn't it? I think that they do it on purpose.'

So I turned on her. 'Who's *they*?'

She was made of stronger stuff so she just shrugged and said, 'The toerags running this operation. They were born with silver spoons up their arses, I guess. Are you going to fire me for saying that?'

I had to laugh. 'No. Don't you mean silver spoons in their *mouths*?'

'No, Charlie. I know the difference between a mouth and an arsehole: it's something most girls learn quite quickly, if they don't want contradictory sex lives. What I mean is that we got the runts of the litter for our bosses. They can't fight, and they can't think; so they wangle their way into an Intelligence manager's chair because they haven't any. It's always been that way: Intelligence'll still be like it in fifty years' time.'

'You don't really like it here all that much, do you?' I said.

'Don't mind me – I just had a touch of BTD.'

'Bored to death,' Jane explained. 'It's like flu: we all get from time to time.'

'Then why do you stay?' I asked Liz.

'I made a mistake a few years ago, and this is my punishment. Piers says that I've got to stay here until they've forgiven me.'

'You know Piers, then?'

'*Everyone* knows Piers.'

'What was your mistake?'

'I'm not going to tell you, sir.' It was the first time Liz had used the word, and she was using it to tell me where to get off. 'What was yours?'

The silence that followed that wasn't an uncomfortable one. Honours even; but nobody was going to help me out. Eventually I said, 'We can't *all* have fucked something up?'

Jane sniffed and looked out of the window. 'I wouldn't be surprised,' she said.

We were on the verge of playing that childhood game of *you show me yours, I'll show you mine*, but I could see that Boulder and Ronka weren't comfortable and wanted nothing to do with it. Time to settle for what I had, and draw the threads together. Even better: Miller got there first. She said to Mrs Boulder, 'If you're not booked for anything this morning, Jean, I'll bring my log over and we'll see if we can slot something together for Mr Bassett.' *Jean*.

Boulder glanced up and looked her squarely in the eyes. 'For God's sake, Mrs Miller, call him *Charlie* – the same as the rest of us.' And that was how Boulder began to call me Charlie. Then she looked at me and winked. It nearly knocked me over. I'd thought it before, and I had been right the first time: there was something the matter with the women that week.

Miller hung back as the meeting broke up. Unfinished business.

I started with, 'I want to ask you something.' She glanced at the open office door. 'No, it's all right. I wanted to know if you could use one of those chitties of yours to get me another flying jacket. A decent lined one to keep out the weather?'

'You'll miss your old one.'

'I know I will. That was a mistake. A spur-of-the-moment thing.' Then I said, 'And I also wanted to apologize to you for snapping at you in front of the others. Even more than that; it was ill-mannered. I'm very sorry.'

Pause. Eye lock. Smile. I liked that smile.

'That's all right, Charlie. Boss's prerogative.'

'Does the boss have other prerogatives?'

Miller shook her head. She had this way of shaking her head and continuing to smile, which confused me.

'Sorry again,' I told her. 'I'm not much good at this sort of stuff. Put it down to bad breeding.'

Miller spoke so softly that I had to strain to hear her. 'I think that your breeding will probably be just fine, Charlie.'

'But not at work?'

She nodded, and blinked her eyes. It's not so much that I'm so stupid that I can't understand women: it's more that I'm too bleeding clever to try in the first place.

*

That was Monday. They thought the signal schedule they prepared for me was a bit iffy. It ran like this: *If the northern Jed call sign initiates signals on, say, a Tuesday, it will use this profile, or that profile, and will probably be active between this hour and that.* It was actually a lot better than I had anticipated, but I didn't tell them that. I'd let them sweat it out for a few days.

Miller came back late afternoon. She had a signals flimsy in her hand, but it wasn't one of ours. I asked her, 'What's up? We flying?'

'No – it's from London, Ming brought it over. Piers wants you up there for a few days – to work on a new signals manual for the service, apparently. There's a travel warrant waiting for you at the guardroom.' She looked puzzled.

'What's the matter?'

'It's not happened before; that's all. I don't like surprises – that's part of my character.'

'Inflexible, you mean?'

'If you like.' Miller's bottom lip went out. It was one of her things. I don't think that anyone had ever told her not to sulk. I would have to work on that. I gently punted my office door shut with my toe.

'I like; very much indeed.' At least I got a grin for my efforts.

But all she said was, 'Not now, Charlie. Do you want me to pick you up in the morning and take you to the station?'

'That would be good. Thank you. I'll phone Piers and find out what the score is.'

I asked for a number that Piers had given me weeks ago. The woman who answered said there was no one of that name working there, but asked me to wait anyway. That had happened before. When Piers came on the line I asked him, 'Why don't you use the same phone all the time? It would make things easier for the rest of us.'

'Need-to-know, old boy.'

'You lot are away with the fairies, you know that? The sooner I get away from you the better. That clock *is* running now, isn't it?'

' 'Course it is old son. Ticking away like a time bomb.'

'What's this nonsense about a manual? I'm not a signals clerk.'

'Gives you an excuse for being away, old son. Your coven will soon rumble that you're up to something if you keep slipping away from them, won't they? There isn't a dud one among them, you know. I picked 'em myself.'

'I know you did; they told me earlier.'

'So: there you are. I've given you a decent alibi. Say thank you.'

'Thank you, Piers. But why now? I've only just got back. I'm spending half my life up and down the sodding Great West Road – it's getting tedious.'

'That's why I wired you a rail warrant. Sympathetic beggar, ain't I?'

I asked it again. 'Why now?'

'Because your landlord was back at his pub last night.'

'So?'

'And he took a khaki lady with him this time.'

I paused. 'You mean . . .?'

'Yes, Charlie. I mean *her*.'

'Balls.'

'Yes, Charlie. Frequently a common denominator. Wayne will meet you at the station and bring you here.'

'Why?'

'I have some trinkets for you. Props. I adore them already – it's going to be difficult to surrender them to you.'

'I'm not happy about this, Piers.'

'Don't ever mistake me for someone who gives a fuck whether you're happy or not, old boy. Needs must; needs must.'

I didn't like him. All over again. Right first time.

One last thing that Monday. The projected schedule for Jedburgh broadcasts gave us a window that very day. Boulder wanted to launch immediately, so we all waited to listen in to the fun. They had anticipated a broadcast at eighteen thirty-eight our time. I was surprised that it was the first time they had tried to predict a Jedburgh. We sat around Boulder's radio rigs and watched the second hand on the big clock on the wall above her sweeping round. At eighteen thirty-seven and fifteen seconds Boulder started to give them brands of English beers on a frequency they had used before . . .

Bass, Worthington, Flowers, Ind-Coope . . . as soon as she broke off a station was snapping back at her: 'Who is this? PI?'

'PI?' Miller queried with me.

'Please identify yourself. That's a very old short code. Pre-war.' Then I told Boulder, 'Send *Charlie*.' She did.

'*Leave us alone, Charlie. Fuck off.*' This all came back in clear; as indeed it had to if they wanted us to read it immediately. Then they were gone.

'I lost him,' Boulder said. She quickly switched to the other profile, but there was nothing there either.

'That'll give them something to think about,' I told them. 'Well done, everyone. Now they know we can really mess them about.' Smiles all round. I asked, 'Are there any orders for tonight, or is that it?'

'No.' That was Miller. 'That's a stand-down. Do I log that call, by the way?'

'What do *you* think?' I could see from the upside-down smile that she didn't like that, so I jumped in with, 'Anyone fancy a pint on the way home? I won't see you for a few days; I'm off to London again.' They surprised me by running for their coats. I wish those magic words had occurred to me weeks before.

Jane looked at me over a half-pint of cider. 'I was a WAAF teleprinter operator on a station,' she explained. 'I used to see the target list about four hours before your lot did. You heard of the Le Panioque mutiny – October 1943?'

'No, that was before my time. I was still training then.'

'Le Panioque was a factory in France – your blokes used to call it "Panic Stations". There was a call for a daylight early-evening low-level raid by Halifaxes. Suicide job. I warned my boyfriend, who didn't fancy the trip; so he reported sick. The problem was that he didn't keep his trap shut, and half the squadron agreed with him. They also went sick. There was a secret inquiry, of course – closed-doors job – and it led back to me. So here I am: serving my time. What about you?'

'I forgot to come home when the war finished,' I admitted. 'I was a little late.'

'How late?'

'Earlier this year.'

That made Jane laugh and spill her drink. 'Christ, Charlie – that's nearly two years. What were you doing?'

'Driving around Europe mostly; looking for someone, and seeing what was left. Cheers.'

'Cheers. *Was* there much left?'

'You'd be surprised.'

'That's why they gave you a team monitoring a couple of lost Jedburghs.'

'That's what I think, too. There must be a line in my file that says "good at finding lost people". Set a thief to catch one: I can't seem to get away from it.' I switched my focus. 'What did *you* do, Ronka?'

She said, 'I killed someone. You killed people, Charlie?'

'You're the second person to ask me that recently. Yes. Loads, I suppose, and I killed two German soldiers about a week before the war ended. That was different.'

'I killed a Lithuanian SS man about six months after that. I recognized him. He was living in London as free as a bird – working in a butcher's shop. Can you believe that?'

'Yes. I can believe it.'

'Ronka strangled him with her stocking,' Liz offered. 'I always thought that was kinda classy.'

I looked at Boulder, who shook her head and looked down. Liz just looked away. They would have to wait for later.

Miller came back from the bar with a tray of drinks. When I looked up at her Liz snorted, and said, 'No; not Gloria; she's the jailer. She has an untarnished record, don't you, dear?'

Miller's smile didn't dip for an instant, but something happened behind her eyes. I'd have to watch her, but I didn't mind that: she wasn't exactly hard to look at.

PART FOUR

Last Orders, Please

16. Temptation Rag

When she met me Dolly was wearing a light linen dress, a wedding ring, and a small cardy over her shoulders to fend off the breezy wind around the station. She gave me a peck on the cheek and fiddled ostentatiously with the ring; we must have looked like a couple of newly-weds. She had one of those new upright nippy black Fords.

'Piers is getting twitchy,' she said. 'You never know who's watching.'

'Would you *like* to be married?' I asked her.

'Mmm . . . eventually. Not at the moment – I'm enjoying myself too much. It would be nice to have a couple of children in a few years' time, wouldn't it?'

'I suppose so. I never give it much thought. Where to next?'

'Round to the flat so that you can change. Piers is coming round to see you there. I'm not staying, I'm afraid: work to do.'

'Anything to do with me?'

'No. De Gaulle's coming over in a few days; his first visit since he forgot to say thank you to us for getting his country back for him. We want to get a calculated insult to his pride properly rehearsed.'

'What's that?'

'He wanted to bring six beefy bodyguards. Legionnaires. We've vetoed that, and said that we'll provide for his security ourselves. What he doesn't know yet is that the bodyguard we'll provide him with will be one unarmed WAAF. Me.'

'And that's a calculated insult?'

'It tells the world that one unarmed Englishwoman is more than a match for six heavily armed Frogs. I think he'll get the message, don't you? So will the newspapers – they'll love it.'

'Piers's idea?'

'Of course; he really knows how to get under someone's skin.'

Dolly didn't even get out of the car in the little mews. I didn't get another kiss, either.

Den wasn't at the flat. In fact, the place had that indefinable sense of having been abandoned for a few days. There was a sort of staleness in the air, so I opened the kitchen windows and let the zephyrs in. I recovered my old clothes from Den's room and changed back into them. I suddenly missed my old leather jacket and hoped that Miller would hurry up a new one for me.

Piers let himself in an hour later. I wondered just how many folk had keys to this place. He was carrying a bottle of wine that still had beads of moisture on it, and he even knew which drawer to find the corkscrew in without searching. It was delicious: white and slightly sparkling – like champagne without that awful bite at your tonsils that the cheap ones have.

'Cava from España; it's all the thing with the county set. Like it?'

'Delicious. It really hits the spot.'

Piers snorted. 'No flash words about bouquet or colour from you, eh, Charlie? Just "it really hits the spot".' Then he told me, 'It comes from Catalonia. If they send us this you can almost forgive the dagos for being a load of sad old fascisti, can't you?'

He gave me a battered old music case that he'd carried in.

'What's this?'

'Greeks bearing gifts. Your swag. Will it do?'

Inside there was a mixture of jewellery and valuables, wrapped in a large piece of grubby brown velvet. There were gold and silver bracelets, pendants on chains, rings and watches. I was particularly struck by one woman's ring, although it probably wasn't all that valuable. The ring was fine, and gold. Its large oval green stone had been polished flat, and was flecked with other colours, pink and blue hues which seemed to gather and then scatter the light. The stone had a number of small chips around the rim – it had been worn and loved by somebody.

'These will do fine,' I said. 'Where did you get them?'

'Someone bought them in Rotterdam yesterday, and had them flown over for me. Probably stolen from the Jews five years ago.'

'How much?'

'Do you need to know?'

'I think that if push comes to shove I'll be expected to know what the stuff I'm stealing is worth.'

'About two hundred pounds.' Piers's bottom lip was out; he hadn't liked telling me that.

'Thank you, Piers. I'll try to look after them, but if I have to lose any I'll account to you for them afterwards. I'll complete all the right paperwork.'

'Sometimes I forget precisely how much of a *beginner* you are, old boy: a paper trail leading back to you is precisely what we don't want.'

After we'd finished the wine Piers asked me, 'When are you getting away?'

'As soon as I can; don't want to keep the Party waiting, do I?'

'Where's your old jacket?'

'I gave it away.'

'Pity; I rather liked it.'

Bollocks.

Matesy was in the kitchen listening to a piece of classical music on the radio. Whatever else the Party was short of it wasn't radios: they were everywhere. There was even one in my bathroom. The music was sombre and chilling – spectral, almost.

It suited my mood; I don't know why.

'Char?' Matesy asked as if I hadn't been away. Cups of tea were the new currency; it must have happened while I was AWOL.

'Thanks. Ta. Milk and two, if that's all right.'

'Like music, do you?'

'Yeah. How did you guess?'

'Your face changed as you came through the door. You play anything?'

I laughed.

'Me? No. Tone-deaf.'

'Can't be; not if you like music. I used to play my uncle's squeeze-box when I was a kid. I often wonder where that got to.'

I sat a while with him and let the music wash over me. It helped me become someone else. Matesy said, 'Gary's been asking for you. You know: the kid who left his dad at Alamein. He's looking for another one, and his mother's rather pretty too, so you'd better watch your step.' Matesy obviously found it a bit amusing, because he was smiling in a gentle sort of way.

On reflection so did I; I found it touching too. I said to him, 'There are too many widows around at the moment, aren't there?'

'Aye. Do you think the bastards will ever notice, and realize what they've done?'

There it was again. The *they*. *They*. The people in charge, I guessed. The people responsible. The *bastards*.

'No.' The way I said it sounded sharp and ugly, even to me. 'No. They'll do it again and again if we let them.' Harry James would have been proud of me. I was.

The door to my room was unlocked. I was sure that I had locked it behind me before I had left. The only things that I had left there were the two concert tickets that the strange Scotsman had given me – on top of an empty chest of drawers. Now there was only one. There was also a small upright mirror that wasn't mine. Alongside the mirror someone had pinned a drawing on the wall. The drawing was childish, but skilful: it depicted an airman standing in front of a recognizable Lancaster bomber. The airman looked like me. I rubbed my chin; it felt smooth.

The mirror would come in handy if ever I needed to shave again. Alongside my single concert ticket was a nearly finished lipstick. It had been expensive once. There was a tap on the door, and when I turned Wendy was standing there with some material draped over one arm. 'Can I come in?' she asked.

'Of course you can.' I was smiling.

'I found you some curtains.'

I asked her, 'It doesn't matter, but I thought I left my room locked . . .?'

'Harry will have unlocked it. It's part of the fire drill. Any empty room is left unlocked so we can check it quickly if we have to run for it. A girl stayed here for a night. I hope you don't mind?'

'No. 'Course not. She folded my sheets up for me.'

'Clean ones, by the look of it,' Wendy sniffed. 'You should learn to tell the difference.'

Then it was Harry James. Wendy left after helping me hang the curtains. Each was a different colour, material and length. I liked that bizarre effect, and promised to try it myself if ever I had a place of my own. Harry sniffed and laughed: 'That Wendy – she must be colour-blind.'

'I kind of like them.'

'Don't take offence. I just came up to apologize for not asking you to leave your room open whenever you're away. You needn't worry about losing anything; nobody steals from you here, just borrows. It's part of my fire drill – I'm scared of losing one of the kids.'

I thought, but didn't say, *In that case somebody* borrowed *a concert ticket from me*. The concert was the next day; if anyone intended to return it they were running short of time. I told him, 'Someone drew my picture.'

'That would be Gary. He draws all of us. Did he ask you how many Germans you'd killed?'

'Something like that.'

'He always asks that. If we're not careful we'll end up with another generation of kids without dads who can't wait to go to war with Germany, just like the last time. I wonder if anyone knows what to do about that?'

I shook my head. James asked me if I'd got my business done. I'd left the brown velvet cloth opened on the mattress. He walked over and studied the valuables.

'It could be difficult for me if the police raided here and found all this stuff,' he told me seriously. 'They'd have a reason to turn everyone out.'

'Would it be better if I stowed it elsewhere?'

'If you wouldn't mind, Charlie. That all right?'

'No problem.' Then I added, 'It's legal, you know; I buy this stuff, and sell it on. Buy low, sell high – that's me.' He didn't believe a word of it, and that suited me.

'That's the curse of capitalism,' he told me. 'We should have a chat about that one day.'

'How about me giving you an assurance that no one is going to starve because I have these things?'

'I'd be very pleased about that, Charlie.' James picked up the ring with the green stone, and said, 'Hey: this is very pretty.' But he was good at resisting temptation, and put it back into the hoard.

'Yes: I thought so too. I might keep it.'

'We're having a bit of a party tonight. You'd be more than welcome to join us downstairs. Young Gary's been telling everyone that you're some kind of Robin Hood. Robbing the rich to feed the poor.'

'What gave him that idea?'

'Word gets around. People need to believe that someone's fighting back.'

'Is that what *you* think?'

'I believe in the cliché that whispers to us that desperate times breed desperate people. But, in answer to your question, I shouldn't mind if you were – providing you didn't jeopardize the folk here: they have problems enough of their own.' Then James asked me, 'Why are you laughing?'

'I was just thinking that when I sit down after you've gone, and run through this conversation in my head, I'll realize that I've actually been given a severe talking-to . . .'

He grinned back. 'Party tonight, then?'

'Do you need any money?'

'Just a couple of quid for whatever you drink; later will do.'

Welcome home, Charlie. The silly thing is that it really felt like that.

Party. One at which staying relatively sober was more of a priority than any I had previously attended. It was in a room big enough to hold a dance in, so that's what we did. The booze standing on an old dresser was beer and wine. The ladies drank the wine. The children drank home-made ginger beer and lemonade from the kitchen; they might have had the best of it. The beer was Worthington IPA again, and a bottled dark stout that poured out like liquid licorice. I can't remember what it was now; it might have been Mackeson. It was the wine that interested me – about a dozen bottles with familiar labels: Cava again. I started to calculate the odds of there being no connection between the bottle I had reduced with Piers and the ones in front of me, but gave up. I asked the woman I was dancing with, 'Where does the wine come from?'

'Harry's got a contact in the docks, I think; we've a lot of party members there. Harry's got contacts everywhere.' Then she determinedly changed the subject with, 'You're quite a good dancer, for Robin Hood.' She was trying too hard: the truth is that I'm an abysmal dancer.

She was Gary's mother, and Matesy had been right. She was dark, very pretty and uncomplicated. Probably vivacious on good days. But there was a residual sadness that you found in a lot of the women in those days, and I was not prepared to shoulder that lot yet. I got very hot with the dancing, but couldn't take my jacket off because I had my pistol in a pocket. Robin Hood would have understood. Sometime after midnight I gave Harry his couple of quid, and left with Wendy. He winked. It wasn't a conspiratorial wink; it was a friendly one. At least another couple of faces from Piers's photographs had been there, and this time I introduced myself and got their names. One lived just up the road. He wasn't terribly comfortable with me. Another was a port tally clerk at the Royals, who had a place of his own in Stepney and hinted that he was good at moving hot property. Somebody must have pointed me out to him. Instead of lying to people I was merely evasive, and by the end of the evening I think they were accepting that as part of my character. I was worried because it made me sound just like Piers.

This time I left the door open. Wendy knocked gently, just like before. This time she had a pillow for me. She didn't offer to stay, and I didn't ask her. I slept eventually, but must have dreamed, because when I opened my eyes the door was still open and a ragged little girl stood there. She had a dirty tear-streaked face, and a wonderful smile. She had something I couldn't make out in her hand. I had one of those dreadful moments when you know that you should move, but can't. Then I drifted off to sleep again. The little girl was still smiling. In the morning she had gone.

In the morning I helped wash up the party dishes and earned myself a few points. Wendy dried up the plates that I washed, and after a few minutes Gary's mum walked in and joined us. I had one woman on either side of me, lunging for anything I rinsed. I couldn't keep this up for ever, so I walked down to the telephone box and made a couple of calls. I called Piers, told him the two names I'd obtained, and gave him the guys' descriptions. He didn't like us speaking the names aloud, but he had no choice because I turned down an invitation to meet him. Miller, when I called, was similarly disturbed. She said, 'Charlie, this line isn't secure.'

'None of them are, love. Just tell me. Have you run the profiles again?'

After a long pause she whispered, 'Yes.'

'Speak up. Even if you are being overheard no bugger can know what we're talking about.'

She cleared her throat before saying, 'Yes. We did.'

'And?'

'Nothing from one, and a very annoyed respondent on the other. Boulder says that it was the same sender. Same signatures, she says.'

'She's almost certainly right. Good old Boulder. Good-oh.'

'What's that mean?'

'*Good-oh*. We said it on the squadron all the time if we were pleased.'

'What do you want us to do now?'

'More of the same, please. That's also how I feel about you.'

'Oh, *good-oh*.' Sarcasm.

'Tell me what you're wearing.'

She didn't. She broke the connection. Miller knew I was up to something. I was sure of it.

Kenwood. The choir of singing vampires in their bell-tent skirts was simply awful. The Scot I had first seen them with pointed out their patron and introducer to me. Their patron might have been the BBC poet, Dylan Thomas, because he looked drunk. He stubbed his foot against the low stage, and stumbled. I think that he was trying to tell me something. Something like *run*. I should have listened, but I had difficulty in making out what he said. That might have been because he was drunk, or because he was Welsh. Both conditions sound similar to an untutored ear. The voice which came to the audience was like a turkey gargling with tar. He recited a couple of lines from his most recent poem. It was the usual gibberish: God probably understood him, and everyone applauded anyway. A woman in a knitted dress exclaimed in ecstasy, and slapped her hands together like a performing seal long after everyone else had finished. The Bulgarians looked bemused.

The screeching of their vampires set my teeth on edge again. Their men played large odd-shaped guitars which sounded like unharmonized machine guns. That set my teeth on edge too.

Grace slipped into the empty seat alongside me and whispered, 'We could have found a better place than this, couldn't we?'

Time stopped.

17. *Goose Pimples*

The husky sound of Grace's voice gave me goose pimples. She was dressed in the same olive KDs and a khaki vest – and a scruffy duffel coat and laced American boots, even though it wasn't cold.

'There's a room like this in your house,' I said to her. I meant the orangery in the mansion at Crifton. 'I saw your mother riding a horse around it once.'

'Just like mummy; I'll bet that she was squiffy. For a few months before the war we held dances there every week. They were really gay affairs: I suppose that we all knew that there was a war coming.'

'Hello, Grace.'

'Hello, Charlie.'

'Aren't you mad at me any more?'

'No. Not particularly. Not any more. How about you?'

'I'm still mad at *you*. Every time you pop up, my life seems to stop. I want to get on with things; get moving.'

'Without me?'

'Yes. Without you.'

'Don't you still love me?'

'Of course I do; I'm not a traitor.'

There was a six-beat pause, and then Grace said, 'What odd things men say!' She said it too loud, and the Scotsman lurking in the shadows said, 'Sshh . . .'

Grace whispered, 'Fancy a walk?'

I nodded. We sidled out in the middle of a Bulgarian primal howl. The Scot frowned. The Bulgars never missed a beat, but their mournful stares followed us to the door. What can they have expected, making a noise like that? I was only surprised that the rest of the audience didn't follow us. The poet was already sitting asleep on a chair in the passageway outside.

I took Grace along the paths to the duelling patch that Piers had shown me. It was better disguised than I remembered, and reaching it was like finding my way to the centre of a maze. She loved the spot immediately; I didn't tell her what it was. We sat on the stone bench. Grace produced apples for us, one from each coat pocket. She said, 'I was a bit surprised to find out that we were neighbours again; I thought that you'd have given up on me by now.'

'I had: then I had to start again. How did you know that it was me, anyway?'

'A couple of the women were discussing a man who'd recently turned up – you. When they described you my stomach turned over.'

'How can you recognize me from a verbal description?'

'Charlie, when are you going to realize that you're attractive to women?'

'Don't try to flatter me, Grace: that isn't kind.'

She shrugged. 'As you like. This place is *glorious*, Charlie. How did you find it?'

'Somebody showed me. You didn't answer my question. How did you know it was me?'

'I didn't, not for sure: not until I went into your room. Then I *was* sure. Even though it was empty it was like you'd left something on the air. Like a fox.'

'Thanks.'

'Don't worry. I didn't mean anything bad. I took one of your tickets, and wondered if you'd take the bait. Why are you using the name Miller, by the way? Are you on the run?'

'I've been on the run ever since I met you, Grace.'

'Sometimes, Charlie, you say the nicest things.'

'I didn't mean it to be.'

'I know; that's what makes it nice. You followed me all the way to Italy after you'd promised to leave me alone: they'll arrest people for that sort of thing one day.'

'I know. I'm sorry. I was asked to catch up with you. First of all it was because your parents wanted you back, and then it was to make sure that you *didn't* come back. They're probably disappointed that you've turned up again. I didn't want to chase you; it was just the best of two bad options.'

'I don't understand.'

'The war was ending, and it was either find you or be posted to a death-and-glory squadron to get the chop in the last few weeks. Guaranteed.'

'Is that what they told you?'

'Yes. *Hobson's Choice*.'

'Poor Charlie. I always loved that film. The girls came out on top, didn't they? Was that Charles Laughton?'

Then nothing. Just the sound of two people munching apples, sitting on a bench in a glade in the sunshine. Tension flowing out of them into the ground. Eventually she asked, 'Good apple?'

'Yes. Very. Thank you.'

'I think so, too. They come from South Africa – they weren't that easy to get in the war, were they? You don't want me to tell everyone that you're Charlie Bassett the war hero, I suppose?'

'No, of course not. *You've* read Pete's tosh too? I was never a hero.'

'It's in the papers, darling: it must be true. Couldn't miss it. Do you know that almost the last thing you said to me in England was that Pete was *dead*? Why did you lie about that?'

'I didn't: I just thought he was. Then I met him again in Holland and Germany. Anyway, he is now. Somebody told me last week.'

'I wouldn't depend on it.'

'Oddly enough, I agree with you this time.'

She leaned her head against my shoulder; intimacy always came easy to Grace.

'Why are you here, Charlie?'

'To see you again – sorry. Someone showed me a picture of you taken at a party, and I couldn't resist it. I pretended to be homeless like the rest of them, and waited for you to show up.'

'Are you telling me all of the story?'

'No.'

'Why not?'

'Because you wouldn't like it.'

Another pause. The pieces of the jigsaw began to click into place for her. Click, click. I was aware of a fragment of apple wedged between my molars. It annoyed me.

'So someone asked you to find me again? Daddy?'

'No. That's not how it works.'

'The same people that asked you to find me in France?'

'More or less . . . I think. I'm not sure.'

'Why?'

'They don't want you to be caught with this lot and get your face in the papers. That would embarrass far too many people. They want you to come away with me: I'll take you home.'

'Never more to wander?'

'Something like that.'

Another pause. Then Grace said, 'You know, when I saw you I really hoped that it *was* daddy who had sent you.'

I thought that she was shivering, but as soon as I turned to look at her I realized that she was crying. I had only ever seen Grace cry once before, and it had moved me then as well. I did what I had resisted doing minutes earlier: I put my arms around her, and hugged her to me. Poor Grace. Poor Charlie. I don't know how long she cried. It seemed like hours. Not a huge earthquake of noisy weeping: just a quiet dumping of all the tears she had.

Afterwards she moved away from me, and mopped her face with my clean handkerchief. If I wasn't careful I would be running out of them before too long. I realized that I shouldn't produce too many clean handkerchiefs in the presence of the Party: it would have been out of role. Grace looked very young all of a sudden, gave me a sheepish grin and said, 'Sorry. I haven't cried like that for years; I wonder what brought it on?'

I couldn't tell her. I stood up, took half a dozen paces, then turned so that I could look at her. Before I could say anything I focused on where her coat fell open, and the thin shirt that clung to her breasts. Grace's not-so-secret weapons. She noticed me noticing, and lifted it. Her breasts were exactly as I remembered: small and perfect. She said, 'You can look, Charlie; you know them as well as anyone. Thirty years old, and I still don't need a bra. What do you think?'

'I think that you're beautiful, Grace. I always thought that you were beautiful. I always will.'

We all get it right, sometimes, don't we? Her face softened, and the rough colour from crying faded as I watched her.

'Good man, Charlie Bassett.'

'Someone else told me that a few years ago.'

'It wasn't me; I probably didn't know then.'

'But you do now?'

'Yes, and I'm pleased to see you after all.' She stood up, walked directly at me, grabbed me and kissed me. Every woman's kiss is different, isn't it? Grace's kisses made you feel as if there wasn't a stitch of clothing between you – as if she was holding nothing back. That was ironic: because once you got to know her you realized that Grace held *everything* back. Even so, you wanted them to go on for ever; you wanted to die kissing.

'Suddenly I want you to fuck me more than anything else in the world, Charlie.'

Even though I was hard, I said something strange. I said, 'I'm not sure that I can, Grace . . . not now. I'm sorry.'

One of the nice things about Grace was that she rarely asked you for an explanation, and never took a refusal personally. Welcome back, Grace.

We walked around the paths, through the rhodies, the woods and across their lawns for hours: holding hands, and catching up. Anyone who saw us would have sworn that we were already lovers again. The swan's body had gone from the lake. When we had finished walking we found that the gates had been closed, so we climbed through a gap in the outside fences. She linked her arm through mine as we walked down the Bishops Avenue and asked, 'Are you staying?'

'Yes, but I don't know for how long.'

'Can I stay with you tonight?'

Did she honestly think I could refuse her?

We made love all night. I'd never done that before. Grace's body was flatter and sparer, and still tanned. She said that I was more muscular. We fought against each other until we could see light coming through the gaps in the curtains. Then we slept. The Krauts had had a phrase for it: *Strength Through Joy*. Lovemaking wasn't what they meant, but it was nice to know that they didn't get everything wrong. When I awoke an hour later Grace was sitting up beside me, talking about dead babies. She was still asleep. Her spine was ridged like an animal's. I touched her back. She started, woke up, and immediately asked, 'Was I jabbering? Sorry. I've done that a few times in the last couple of years. Mostly when I'm relaxed and safe – that's a bit odd, isn't it?'

I yawned. 'Not as odd as opening your eyes and being instantly awake. I'd forgotten that you did that. Are you all right?'

'Yes.' She cuddled back down into bed and snuggled against my shoulder.

'You were shouting about children.'

'Yes. I always do. I was caught in a raid at the end of '44. I was driving past a school that was hit.'

'I know. Tell me about it if it helps.'

'It won't.' I suppose that neither of us spoke for three or four minutes, and then she said, almost as if there had been no pause: 'The first thing was that the car turned over onto its side quite gently, as if a giant had just reached out and pushed it over. None of the windows were even cracked. I simply opened the door, which was now above my head, stood up and climbed out. Everything happened in slow motion. It took a great effort to move my arms and legs, even though I was completely unharmed.'

'I think that was the blast affecting you. I've heard that it does odd things.'

'I've heard that too.' Again, she didn't speak for several minutes, then: 'The air was filled with dust, like a pea-souper of a fog, and all around me I could hear bricks falling as walls collapsed. They rumbled down for ever. Then a little girl walked towards me out of the dust. She was very pretty – hair in pigtails – she was carrying something, which she held out to me. It was a child's arm. A very little arm. Then she gave me a dazzling smile and said, "*My little sister.*"' Grace whispered it again: '"*My little sister.*" Then I looked around, and saw that there were pieces of children everywhere.'

I hugged her as tightly as I could. All I could say was, 'Oh, Grace.'

'I took the arm in one hand, and her hand in another, and we walked out through the dust to the end of the road, where I found an ARP man crying. I took him with me as well. All that time, it seemed, inside the dust the bricks kept falling.'

'What did the girl you rescued look like?' It was one of those questions that as soon as you've asked it you wonder why.

'She was about eight, I suppose. Lovely dark hair in pigtails – I told you that. Her face was smeared with dirt, with streaks where she had cried. Her clothes were a bit ragged. She had a cut on her head. Why did you ask?'

'I saw someone like that. Not long ago.'

There was another one of Grace's pauses. Then she sighed, and said, 'I know. I don't seem to be able to leave her behind.'

I left Grace upstairs. A man with a huge moustache sat at the other end of the kitchen table and glared at me. I almost recognized him. When I was on the squadron huge moustaches were all the thing: you saw less of them these days. Mainly poets and artists who borrowed the mantle of the warrior, now that the real fighting was over. I wondered whether to thump him before or after my first cup of tea. I don't know why I felt so feisty that morning; I'm not usually a morning person.

'What have I done to *him*?' I asked Harry.

'He's Edward Morney – the poet. You've bedded at least one of his birds in the last couple of days. Last night's was mine as well, come to that.'

I cast around in my mind for the name that Grace was using, and found it after a while.

'Carla isn't anybody's bird: she's an owner-driver. If you worry about who she's sleeping with now, you shouldn't have done it in the first place.'

'Happens that I agree with you . . .' He handed me a mug of tea.

'Ta.'

'And you already know that "Carla" isn't her real name – it's all over your face.'

'Yeah. I knew her before, from when I was in the RAF. How did *you* find out?'

'I recognized her from a photo that was in the papers just before the war. She'd flown solo to some godforsaken Middle Eastern country or other, and back: something heroic, I suppose. When I said I knew, she told me that she was trying to get away from her old life.'

'Anybody else know that?'

'Not unless she's told anyone. Shall we keep it between ourselves for the minute?'

'Why not? I'll have to go away again, anyway. I have to follow my business – I'll take my stock with me, don't worry.'

I finished the tea and then poured another mug to take up to Grace. I carried it in my left hand as I walked out of the kitchen. The poet had big feet, and stuck one out in front of me as I approached. He'd intended to trip me up, but moved too quickly and telegraphed it. All I had to do was step on the inside of his ankle to turn his foot over before I put my weight on it. He screamed like a girl as I walked away from him. Upstairs again, I sat on the edge of the mattress, enjoying the sight of naked Grace drinking the tea I'd brought her. Wendy went past the open door on her way back to her room, and called, 'Hi, Charlie,' held back a half step and added, 'Oh. Hi, Carla.'

We grinned back at her. When I told Grace that I was off again she asked, 'Off to report? Can I stay here while you are away?'

'No: you'd only bring somebody else in here. Mess up your own place until I get back.'

'Spoilsport.' She carefully put down the mug, and just as carefully pulled me over onto her. All she had in mind was a kiss. As we pulled apart she said, 'Don't turn me in, Charlie. Not yet.'

'If you don't turn me in either.'

We both thought about it. Grace said, 'OK' first. Then so did I.

The smiles we fired at each other seemed genuine enough. I presume I was aware of something like love, and yet no longer wanted to spend my life with her. I suppose that it had been like that for Grace from the start. She watched me put my few possessions into the pack, and was still naked under my blankets as I turned to leave. I asked her, 'What are you thinking?'

'That I need a bath. I'll get up once you've gone.'

'Don't bathe too often or they'll rumble you.'

I fished in my pack until I could feel the ring with the green stone and held it out to her. 'Here; have this. It will look very good on you.'

Her fist closed around it, and she turned away from me so that I couldn't see her face. She didn't speak to me or look up as

I left . . . and I knew that I'd got to her for the very first time since I'd met her: I was sure of it.

Harry James was at the door to see me off. He asked me, 'Can I contact you if the cops are sniffing about asking? I wouldn't put it past that Edward to rat on you.'

'No. I don't do calls in; only calls out. I'll be careful.'

'Just make sure you are, for all our sakes.'

'Is there anything you'd like me to bring back?'

'Any spare radio valves you come across . . .' Then he caught himself and grinned: 'Fuck off, Charlie.'

'Yeah,' I told him. 'Time to go.'

The flat was empty, but I had a key now – remember? I stripped off, stashed my old clothes and lay in a hot bath. It was a proper man-sized bath; in fact, you could have shared it. The soap was trademarked Paris, and smelled of brothels. I towelled myself down vigorously to get rid of the scent – I didn't want to give the wrong impression.

Piers wasn't at his office. The person who answered the phone didn't know him, but told me that a message could be delivered. That was an improvement, I suppose. I asked her to tell him to call me. I called Cheltenham and told Boulder that I was on my way back. She didn't sound exactly thrilled by it. Stephen turned up, and offered me a lift to Paddington in a bright orange two-seat Ulster Austin Seven that he threw around like a racer. When I think about it almost everyone I drove with in the Forties threw cars around like racers: it must have been the war. Unfortunately

Stephen wasn't a professional; he was a poor amateur. We mounted the pavement twice, once narrowly missing one Chelsea pensioner pushing another in an ancient wheelchair. Their fading cries of alarm were drowned out by Stephen's cackles. He was either a quite terrible driver, or already drunk.

Paddington station is a shite-hole with but one saving grace: it is within walking distance of a pub named the Fountains Abbey which I already knew from my aircrew days. I had time for a couple of pints before my train. I had travelled up to town in a suit that Piers had chosen for me, and Miller's raincoat. They must have worked, because when the ticket collector looked at the return part of my rail warrant he invited me to occupy a First Class compartment. I realized that I would be expected to tip him as I disembarked: little Charlie was in a new world.

I changed trains at Oxford and got the clunker to the edge of the known world. What surprised me was that Miller was there to meet me. She was wearing a smile that made her mouth look twice its real size. I didn't ask why, I asked, 'How did you know what train I'd be on?'

'Deduction, intelligence work and the railway timetables. We have them in the office, you know. How was the signals manual?'

'What manual?'

'The one you went to London to help write.'

'Oh. That one.'

'I think you left your brain behind on the platform, Charlie. Shall we pop over to Lost Property and ask?'

We were in her car by now, side by side; I slung my bag on

the back seat. Miller laughed and said, 'I love you, Charlie,' while she was still laughing: as if it was the most natural thing in the world to say. I spoilt it by saying nothing back, leaving a silence that stretched like elastic. Miller said, 'Sorry. That just popped out. I don't know why.'

'Did you *mean* it?' I asked.

'I don't know. I don't think so. I'm just pleased to see you back, but don't actually know why.'

We were still in the station car park, which was now empty. Miller looked around to make sure that no one was looking and hit me with a kiss like a limpet mine. After my breathing got back to normal I asked her, 'Did that just pop out too?'

'No. I've wanted to do it for days. It's not my fault; it's the way you look.'

'How do I look?'

'As if I should kiss you. You're the first new man I've kissed since Christmas; do you know that?'

'Do you want to kiss me again?'

'Almost.'

I was leaning facing her anyway, and didn't give her another chance. I put my hand between her knees as I kissed her: no further. She squeezed gently. I had never wanted a woman more, but I didn't push it. When we pulled apart I asked, 'Can you have a drink with me before you take me home?'

She glanced at her wristwatch. 'Just one; is that all right?'

'Nothing was ever righter.'

Her smile told me that I'd thrown a six again. I was making a habit of it. Almost. There was a small place up a side street called the Star Bar. It was empty except for us. The barmaid was big and bouncy and happy. Miller was happy. I was happy. I found that I'd missed the taste of freshly brewed cider, and that I'd missed her. Halfway through my pint I had a thought that I had to share with her.

'It's just occurred to me,' I told her.

'What has?'

'My Christmas came early this year.'

Miller looked away. Her face wore a smile. Good-oh.

18. Big Butter and Egg Man

By the middle of the next week I'd interdicted four Jedburgh calls. Halfway through they tired of the game and switched their profiles, but because they were a hundred miles apart they had to send a new key, and because I was listening I knew it as quickly as they did. They should have worked that one out, but were beginning to sound seriously pissed off with me anyway.

It was fun until everything stopped for Tommo's inquest.

Piers knew its date and locus before anyone else, and called me after he'd spoken to Tommo. That irked me and I'm not sure why. We had an anxious ten-minute wait on the steps of the small courthouse they held it in, but Tommo rolled up with another ten to spare. He wore his laundered and pressed, but old, Master Sergeant's olive drabs. With his big round sad face and rolling gait, he looked every inch the innocent US farm boy caught in the net of English law. When we went in and took places reserved for us at the front, I saw some of the women in the place turn to stare at him. I think they liked what they saw.

A local magistrate sat as coroner. He looked a thousand years old and gaga with it. He heard Tommo's evidence, and that of the police witnesses. They hadn't measured the skid marks because they couldn't find any. A local doctor told us what a body looks like after it has been hit by a truck. Not nice.

Then they heard me. I don't suppose that I would have bothered to attend if I hadn't been cited as Tommo's character witness. What I can remember of the exchange between the coroner and myself went like this. I told him that Tommo and I had had a professional meeting the night before the accident, but declined to tell him anything about it. It was the first time I played the official-secrets card. The coroner simply didn't like that. He looked at me, glared, leaned forward and asked, 'Good character?' He had a voice that sounded like gravel being shaken in an enamelled bucket.

'I've had good reports so far, sir.'

'Not you, ninny. The accused.'

The clerk coughed and intervened. 'There is no accused, sir. This is your coroner's court.'

'Really? Why didn't somebody tell me?'

The audience howled. Miller giggled every time she met my eye. It was a fucking circus.

After an hour of it there was a verdict that precisely reproduced the wording that Piers had quoted to me earlier. I believed him now: he'd actually written it himself. Tommo had driven over a blind summit and killed a Blind Summit. Damn shame, really.

The three stooges who went to the Star Bar: Tommo, Miller and I. It was doing a roaring trade because there were already at least two people there before us, propping up the bar. We took our glasses to the table that Miller and I had sat at the week before. It will surprise you that neither of us had spoken about what had happened that night. And I had kept my hands off her. I'd done that because I thought that she was edgy around me, and it made me feel uncomfortable. I said, 'It's OK, Tommo. You can come back now. Be your devious old self. That's your bit over.'

'I'm off the hook?'

'What hook?' Miller asked him, and squeezed his knee. 'I didn't see one.'

'That wasn't a trial,' I explained. 'It was just an inquiry to establish why he died. If the coroner had decided that you'd acted unlawfully, *then* there would have been a trial.' Something had been troubling me for a while. 'Did you slow down at all when you saw him in the road in front of you?'

'How could I? I had all four wheels off the ground. I was still in the air when we made contact.'

I was glad that no one else had asked him that.

Miller stood up and said, 'My round. Same again?'

You can fall seriously in love with women who know when to ask that question.

Bella dragged Ming over to our table in the Star. She said, 'Introduce us to your friend, Charlie.' They'd been cheering in the audience, but I hadn't seen them. I did, and they joined us.

It was the signal for Miller to jump up. 'Must go now.'

I was disappointed, but I couldn't show it. Tommo winked at me: he was draining pints of cider as if it was water. I felt a decent night coming on.

Tommo looked at Bella: the old *sharp* Tommo. 'You do

chickens; Charlie's told me. I could be in the market for a thousand eggs. That, and half a ton of butter.'

Bella said, 'I don't do butter, but I know a man who does. We can talk eggs whenever you like.'

They talked eggs. I was glad that Miller had gone. She wouldn't have liked the conversation carried out in front of her. She would have worried what her husband would have made of it.

'What were you doing there, anyway?' I asked Ming before the cider turned my brain to mush.

'Report to the boss. We write a report on any of our people that end up in court.'

'Even as a witness?'

'Especially as a witness.'

'Will it appear on my personal record?'

'They'll stick a copy in there, yes.'

'Then be gentle with me.'

For some reason everyone thought that that was funny. Tommo nearly fell off his chair, and I thought that Bella was about to wet herself. Why don't we say that about men?

Later, when we were really stocious, Tommo asked me, 'What did the old guy mean about a *blind summit*?'

'That's a very English description of a hump in the road.'

'But it was also the dead guy's name . . .'

'Don't labour the point. He was telling a very poor joke. We English are good at them.'

Tommo held his pint up and squinted as if he could read the future in it, found he couldn't and drank it instead.

*

Ming stayed overnight at the farm. It was the first time that had happened since I'd been there.

Tommo found a small hotel, and in the morning took off for London while the going was good. I saw him off. He was driving the same truck. I don't know whether that was a brazen declaration of independence, or just plain bad taste. He gave me a hug – he did that sometimes – and said, 'Thanks, buddy. You came through again.'

'That's OK, Tommo. But I lumbered you with Piers at the same time.'

'Don't worry, I can ditch him whenever I'm minded. He may come in useful. Anything I can do fer ya when I'm over there?'

I don't know why I hadn't thought of it before.

'What do you know about the Jedburgh special units we sent over to Europe to fuck the Krauts up while we invaded?'

'Americans, weren't they?'

'All sorts. Americans, Brits, Dutch, French – you name it. Seriously funny dudes.' 'Dudes' was a word he'd taught me: I liked it.

'What about them?'

'A couple are still out there, in France and Germany – gone native, and won't come back.'

'Why not? What they doing?'

'Clobbering the bad guys. Catching war criminals, giving them field trials and field punishments. Fatal hangings, or the old bullet-in-the-back-of-the-neck trick.'

'Is there a problem with that?'

'Yeah, Tommo. Sooner or later an armistice has got to be an

armistice. The opera's not over until the fat lady sings, and a war's not over until the shooting really stops. They've got to come home. They're really scaring the Reds.'

'Where do I come in?'

'My little team has been asked to contact them and talk them down, but they won't talk to me. I've got a sort of one-way dialogue going with them, but it's taking bloody weeks.'

'I s'pose that this isn't unconnected with the fact that you were a little late coming in yourself?'

'The bosses probably think that. If I got their names and unit identities, and knew the localities where they were supposed to have been working, is there any chance you could get a message to them?'

'Mebbe: they got to get their stores from someone. Won't somebody have already tried that?'

'Probably. But no one with your contacts.'

'What good would it do, anyway?'

'It gives me two strikes. They might actually send a reply, and also it tells them that I can get to them when I want to, doesn't it? That might upset them enough to make them start talking.'

'Or they may just shoot the messenger.'

'Send someone they won't; that German girl with the great legs you had.'

'I found her with another guy. She was a goddamned chocolady on the side.'

'What's a chocolady again?'

'Women who do it fer Hershey Bars. Maybe cigarettes or stockings.'

'I'm sorry.'

'Don't be. The only problem was she didn't tell me – so sayonara, señorita.'

'What about it then?'

Tommo thought about it. Then he said, 'You still got that London telephone number I gave you?'

'Yes, Tommo.'

'Phone it if you get the names. He'll tell you what to do with them.'

'Thanks.'

'Don't get me wasted now.'

'OK, Tommo, strictly business.'

'I knew you were learning things from me, Charlie. Be a pal and find me some butter, won't you? I got a coupla base customers in Lin-coln-shire who can take a lorryload in a coupla weeks.'

The way things worked out my Jedburghs made the first move anyway. Pawn to my king's knight. That was after I'd phoned Piers and asked him to get me the Jedburgh names. He laughed and put the phone down on me. Dead end.

19. *Bye-bye, Blackbird*

The next day Miller walked into my shrine, waving the old brown-paper envelope. The office seemer larger now that I wasn't sharing it with Alice, although it was scruffy because the cleaners still wouldn't venture over the threshold. I was hung-over.

'When?' I asked her.

'Cheer up: tomorrow, but it's not what you think.'

'What is it, then?'

'Fly from CFS to Thurleigh. Transport laid on to drive you to a police station near Bedford.'

Bollocks. I didn't want to tell her that I'd been in this movie before. 'Why?'

'A man walked in there yesterday and asked for you. He's come from France. He says he's with our Jedburgh.'

'Want to come with me?'

One of her six-beat pauses. Then, 'OK. Yes.'

'Number ones, then, and bring an overnight bag.'

She did it again – six-beat pause, then, 'OK' – and turned on her heel.

Just like that.

*

Alison scowled at Miller when she opened the door to her. I could see that from the back of Alison's head: I had been a bit slow off the mark. Miller was driving the jeep, which meant that she'd already been into the station. I wondered what she had told Watson, and whether he'd care. He must have used the jeep himself from time to time, because his battered panama lay in the rear-seat footwell. Miller was collecting me from the Abbott farm: she was in her WREN number ones with regulation sheer dark stockings. My oh my. I was in my walking-out blues, and wore my US raincoat over them to give the RAF a twitch.

Bella gave me a quick peck on the cheek when I left, and said, 'How long?' She probably thought that I was going out to pay the piper again.

'Back tomorrow, probably; but if I'm not here don't put anything in the oven for me.'

In the jeep Miller asked me, 'Has her daughter got a crush on you?'

'No, not yet. I'll move out if that happens: too complicated.'

'Do you always work things out in advance?'

'No, almost never. I wait for things to happen – never a dull moment, me. Do you like that?'

'To *be* with, yes; to *live* with, no.' That was me being told, wasn't it? 'What do you do when you go up to London to work with Piers?'

'We're rewriting a signals manual. You knew that already.'

Long pause. Then Miller said, 'Saying that you're not going to tell me something would be better than lying to me.' Her lips were set, and her mouth looked so small that I couldn't have forced even a pencil through there.

'Are you looking for a fight this morning, Mrs Miller?'

'Yes, I suppose I am.'

'Stop the car, won't you? There – that will do.'

'There' was a narrow strip of common, opposite a long row of picture-book country cottages. Smoke speared thin and vertical from a couple of chimney stacks. As soon as she stopped I could hear the sounds of the birds and the bees. That's what you could hear in the jeep as well, because even as we stopped I pushed her back, kissed her and touched her knees. They moved apart as if they were spring-loaded. I took a breath and said, 'I know this is difficult for you, but don't think it's easy for me either.'

'No?' Her voice was so quiet that I almost couldn't hear her. Sardonic.

'No, but you can get off whenever you like. It won't matter.'

'What do you mean?'

'Drop me off at the guard block at Little Rissington if you want, and then go back. Take the jeep. I promise you it won't make things any more difficult between us – and what's more, I'll behave myself until they demob me.'

She actually laughed as she pushed me away. Then she said, 'I've had *better* offers than that, Charlie!' Yeah. You guessed it. Odd creatures. It was as if a sharp summer storm had passed. 'I can be a proper bitch at times.'

I realized that I'd been holding my breath, because what I wanted to say was '*I want you more than I've wanted any woman in my life: you make me tremble.*' I let the breath out slowly. 'I think that I like women who can be bitches at times.' I swung my feet out of the jeep, and got out. The grass was still wet with dew. I had to duck my head to miss knocking my cap off on the canvas. When I went around it to stand alongside her she was repairing her lipstick. I said, 'Shove over. I'll drive. It feels a bit poncy having you drive me everywhere.'

'Order?' she asked. The smile was back. I wanted to kiss the lipstick off her again – I loved its taste.

'Order.'

'You're getting better at giving orders, sir.'

'Then get used to it; and if you come with me get ready to get on your back tonight, and stay there until the sun comes up.'

Even that didn't wipe out the smile. I looked around the sky before I got behind the wheel. There should have been a rainbow somewhere.

The SPs in the guardroom at Little Riss kept us waiting until after they had made a call; then they waved us through without any paperwork. I got a very smart salute. I think that they were trying to impress Miller. She stayed in the jeep, and held on hard to the seat frame. It would have been difficult to prize her off it. It was time to get things settled so I told her, 'This is where you get off. It's all right; I meant it. I wasn't put on this world to turn your life upside down. I'll see you tomorrow, maybe.'

Miller looked away over the airfield. All she said was, 'I wonder where our aeroplane is?'

As I drove us down to the Transport Command hangar I couldn't believe where she put her hand. After I collected the jeep from the double zigzag it had somehow got me into, I pulled Miller's hand away. Sometimes the old phrases are the best ones: actions do speak louder than words.

There was no sign of the silver Hudson, but there was that familiar unmarked olive-drab Airspeed Oxford sitting in the Hudson's spot. It matched the familiar olive-drab pilot in his battered US flying jacket who was sitting on its step . . . and I had a familiar fluttering in my stomach. I parked up, and we went over to him. I tried to take Miller's bag as well as mine, but she took it firmly from me, and smiled as she did so. Later she told me that it was like taking control of her own life again. I didn't exactly see what she meant, but I understood there was something behind the words that made sense.

The pilot settled us in. Me alongside him; Miller at the radio training station behind us, facing a well-used 1154/1155 rigged set-up. She asked me, 'Is this what *you* used, sir?'

'Yeah. They're not as good as the American jobs we use on station, but they are more robust, and easy to repair.'

'It's hard to imagine you here, over Germany at night.'

'I wasn't. The aircraft I worked in were larger than this – it makes the radio sets appear smaller, although they're not.'

The pilot coughed. He said, 'When you're ready? You both strapped in?'

'Yes.'

'Yes, sir.' Miller, was bloody hamming it up for all she was worth. She was right. She could be a proper bitch at times. When I looked back her knee was cocked, giving my eyes the come-on, and her own eyes gleamed.

The pilot was either navigating by the railway lines or the roads. Grace had once told me all about that. I suddenly wondered how Grace was without the flying. It had been all her life to her. I asked him, 'How long?'

'Less than an hour. They have a nice new runway at Thurleigh – long and wide.'

'Not like that grass strip near Inverness.'

'Beggin' your pardon, sir?'

'I could swear I've flown with you before.'

'Not me, sir. I'd have remembered you.'

'Didn't you fly me from Twinwood to Ringway in 1944, and from Croydon to Scotland earlier this year?'

'Not me, sir. You got me mixed up with someone else.'

'I don't do that often.'

'First time for everything, sir.'

'Isn't your name John Morgan?'

'Nossir. It's Randy, sir. That is Randall. Randall Claywell. I'm just a contract pilot for your War Department. I drive VIPs in a hurry.'

'I'm not a VIP.'

'But I guess that you're in a hurry, sir.' Then he looked briefly over his shoulder, saying, 'Enjoying the flight, miss? Have you flown before?'

That was my lot.

It was one of those flights when no sooner have you reached your operational height than you are descending again. That's what it seemed like. Claywell was a big man, and an enormously competent pilot. You also got the impression that you wouldn't want to cross him. He left the aircraft before we did, but not until it was on the ground: anything other than that would have been irresponsible. Claywell was not an irresponsible man. He helped Miller down from the small ladder, and she gave him leg up to the stocking top. I was momentarily angry, but then I smiled, because I realized why. Jealousy. Our transport had come around the peri-track: it looked like we had jeeps to spare these days.

Claywell touched my arm to delay me briefly as Miller went to the vehicle. He grinned. 'Glad it worked out for you, bud.'

Then he climbed back into the aircraft, pulled up the ladder, and shut the door – leaving me on the other side of it. Just before he shut the door he winked.

The guardroom at Thurleigh wasn't interested in paperwork for us, either, although we had to sign for their jeep and promise to bring it back. The civilian who had driven it out to the Oxford shook my hand and said, 'I'm very pleased to have met you, sir.' I was getting used to that.

I asked Miller, 'What *did* Pete write about me?'

'Haven't you seen it?'

'No.'

'Not even in the papers?'

'No.'

She laughed. 'You're a bit of a fool sometimes. Remind me to show you when we get back.'

They'd given us a map to St Neots but I could have driven the route with my eyes closed, because I'd flown my war from around there. As I turned down towards Thurleigh village Miller asked, 'What was all that chat with the pilot, about having met before?'

'He's not who he says he is. I flew with him before. He was piloting Glenn Miller then.'

'In that case isn't he supposed to be dead? Weren't they drowned in a plane crash in the English Channel?'

'I can't answer you, but now I think that I saw their aircraft too – in France in 1945: a bit smashed-up but definitely not wet. That's interesting, isn't it? One day, when I've time, I'm going to think about it. Maybe go back and look again.'

Eventually Miller held on to the grab handle with her right hand, and held her cap on with the other. The air rushing through the open jeep ruffled the skirt around her knees. I concentrated on staying on the road, and tried not to think about them. It didn't work. It hardly ever does.

The St Neots police sergeant remembered me. So did his wife. She made us cups of tea and fussed around me. I could see that Miller was mystified, but I wasn't prepared to go into explanation mode so I asked the copper, 'When did your new guest arrive?'

'Day before yesterday, sir. He walked in off the street bold as brass and told me that he was an AWOL British serviceman; just like you did.' We both smiled at the memory. It must rank among the more stupid things that I've done in my life, and we both knew it.

'And he asked for me?'

'That's right, sir.'

'How did he know that I'd been here?'

'He hasn't said, sir. In fact he hasn't said anything else yet.'

'When are the monkeys from London coming to pick him up?'

'After you've finished with him, sir. I have to make a call.'

I sipped my tea. That was to buy thinking time. Eventually I said, 'Nice tea. I suppose that we'd better finish it and see the bugger, then.'

I wonder if I'd looked as bad as he did when I'd come in. If I had it wasn't surprising that no one had believed me. I was looking at an emaciated, uniformed twenty-three-year-old who looked at least seventeen years older. I suppose that that wasn't all that unusual in the Forties, if you think about it. His greasy brown hair needed washing, and cutting, and someone would have to do something about the rash I could see on every exposed part of him. It even went up into his hairline. I said, 'You need a doctor.'

His voice was cultured: thin, like him. Slightly accented. 'I saw one this morning; courtesy of our kind jailer. She said that I was starving, and need nourishment. I'd rather have a cigarette.'

Miller coughed quietly. It was to attract my attention. When I looked at her she raised one eyebrow, and when I nodded she produced an unopened packet of Players Navy Cut cigarettes and a box of B&Ms. They were making a comeback now that Norwegian spruce was becoming available again. Our man pounced on them and didn't say anything else until there was a layer of thin blue smoke in the air above us.

'No words. You're very good, you two. Have you worked together a long time?'

'No,' I told him. 'It only seems like that.' All three of us fired up smiles, so I risked asking him, 'What's your name?'

'Ari Spelling.'

'Really?' I noticed that Miller had magicked a notebook from somewhere, and was demonstrating that she knew better than me what to do with it.

'No, not really. My name is Aaron Joopeman. Ari. I'm Dutch. When I was recruited by the British, the officer asked my name. I told him Joopeman, and he said "Spelling?" So I said, "Yes, that will do." We both found it amusing.'

He spent more time looking at Miller than at me. In his place I would have done the same, so I had to ask him, 'Why did you ask for me?'

'Because you're messing us about, Mr Bassett, and my boss wants to know what for. You're making our communications very difficult.'

'I meant to. I wanted to get your attention. Why did you report *here*?'

'Snap! It's where you gave yourself up. We needed to get *your* attention. The boss said that your curiosity was bound to get the better of you.'

Whoever his boss was knew too damned much about me. 'Who's your boss?'

I didn't expect him to answer, but he said, 'Lieutenant Roland Rolfe – Roly Poly. It's all in the files; no secret. We call him "Father" because he's such an old worrier.'

There was a light tap on the door, and the copper came in without waiting. It was his charge room in *his* police station, I suppose. He brought in a plate of freshly baked ginger biscuits, and said to me, 'Excuse me, sir, but the gentleman was sick as soon as he'd finished his breakfast this morning, and the doctor said to give him little and often, and maybe he'd keep it down.'

The sergeant's interruption had done me no favours, but when I cast back in my memory I remembered that he'd been good to me too. He took his responsibilities seriously.

I waited until he'd gone away again, and gestured at the plate.

Joopeman took a biscuit and sniffed it. 'I haven't seen one of these in years. In the Netherlands we put a few drops of lemon juice in the recipe. It brings out the flavours.' He took a bite, and smiled.

Miller wrote something in the back of her notebook. I'd ask her about that later.

'OK,' I told him. 'I'm Charlie Bassett and you're Ari Joopeman. Now, *here is the news*. Our government wants you to pack up and come back. It is grateful for what you've done, and for your sacrifices, but enough is enough and it's time to stop. I'm authorized to offer an unconditional amnesty, demobilization and help with resettlement, if your people come in.'

I counted five clear seconds before he replied, 'No, you're not, Mr Bassett. Your beautiful colleague's eyebrows climbed at least an inch when you said that. It was news to her too.'

'She doesn't know everything I know.'

'But enough, I think.'

Stalemate. We didn't try to stare each other down, but we didn't break eye contact either.

'OK. I was going to go away from here, and negotiate that back to my bosses. I was going to tell them that those are your conditions for coming home. They will agree.'

'Home? My home was in Groningen.'

'When were you last there?'

'1942.'

'Then it's time to go back, isn't it?' I didn't say it was time to go back to his family. If he had been a Jew living in Holland there was a good chance that he no longer had one.

He considered what I had said. Then: 'So – you intended to speak up for us?'

'If you had agreed, yes.'

'We will remember that when we come in. You could be useful.' That's what Tommo had said of Piers. *Thanks, pal!* 'But I am afraid I can't speak for the units over there. Father will know what to do when I inform him. You may go now.'

'Thanks.' That was me. Even Miller thought that Joopeman was coming it a bit rich. You had to laugh: he was handcuffed to a table, and was telling *us* what to do. 'Tell me something.'

'If I can.'

'How did you know who I was?'

'You use "Charlie", and a personal call sign that was issued to you in 1945. I expect Father got someone to look it up.'

'Someone over here?'

'I couldn't say that.'

'How did you know that I'd reported *here*?'

'I expect—'

I waved him silent. 'OK. I get the picture. Are they all as hungry as you?'

'We're always short of money. In France there are good people who help us, but in Germany it's difficult. No one has that much to spare. What will happen to me now?'

'What they gave me was a few weeks in an old aircrew-interrogation centre in London. That was uncomfortable. Then they locked me up in a prison in Scotland. That was even more uncomfortable. I think I saw Lord Haw-Haw there.'

'That's not possible. He's dead. He was hanged.'

I'd wrong-footed him for the first time since I'd opened my mouth.

'OK. Then maybe it was his ghost.'

'Why are you telling me?'

'It's what your lot do, isn't it? Your job? Catch war criminals, try them and execute them. If they send you to the same place I thought you might be just the right guy to check it out. You could earn a big tick from the teacher.'

Joopeman leaned back in his chair. He spoke to Miller. He said, 'You didn't write that down in your book, did you, miss?'

'No, Mr Joopeman.'

'Good. No reason why we should all get in trouble.' Then to me, 'Now: shall I tell *you* what will happen to me?'

'If you like.'

'I will be back with my unit by this time next week.'

'You'll be too late. You'll find that friends of mine have already been knocking on its door.'

I was bluffing: I didn't think that I could bring Tommo into play that quickly.

Joopeman called me. 'Care to bet on that? Five pounds English?'

'Why not?'

His right hand was free. We shook on it.

'Leave the stake with the police sergeant. I will collect,' he said.

'What about yours?'

'I have no money. You will trust me.'

'I'll have to, won't I? If I have any more questions I'll be back tomorrow.'

'I won't be here, Mr Bassett.'

Cocky little sod, wasn't he? Despite that rash. The police sergeant insisted on giving me a receipt for the five-pound note I left with him.

Miller showed me how to put up the canvas on a jeep. I'd never done it before. Women with that sort of practical skill can be a little unnerving. I bet she knew how to change flat tyres as well. When we sat inside it she shook her head, and smiled.

'We've been trying to get close to those Jedburghs for a year, and within weeks you're sitting down and talking to one. Are you always that lucky?'

'No. Personal magnetism. No one except you can resist me for long. What did you write down in the back of your notebook?'

'Nothing.'

'Show me.' She shrugged, and passed it over. She had written: *Drops of lemon juice in ginger biscuits* and *Bring out the flavours.* 'Good,' I told her. 'I wouldn't like to have forgotten that.' Her tight mouth showed it all: I'd forgotten that women didn't like being laughed at. 'You can drive if you like; then you won't have a hand free to slap me with.' That didn't work either.

Miller drove us less than half a mile: to a building that called itself the Bridge and which looked out on St Neots market square. It was old, and couldn't make up its mind whether it was a hotel or a pub. I couldn't see a bridge anywhere. I like places like that; they bring out the child in me. I asked her, 'You think we can get in here?'

'We already are. I telephoned yesterday. It's a place that the RAF uses at the moment. We have a small room for me, and a big one for you – benefit of rank.'

'Are we going to use the small one?'

'Not unless you snore.' I just wished that she looked happier about it.

Miller carried our bags, and walked behind me as we went up the steps to reception. I would have to be careful or I could get used to that. At the desk she took charge, signed the book, and presented a chitty that seemed to open all sorts of doors and wreathed the landlord in smiles. He looked like a *Monopoly* player who'd just bought Park Lane. I wanted to find my way straight to the hotel's small bar, but had to go upstairs with her and the landlord while he showed us the ropes.

My room overlooked the square. It was lined in dark wood boarding, had a window seat, and windows with heavy curtains. It was big enough to play rugby in, and contained a four-poster that you could have fitted at least one of the teams into. The floor was so uneven that if you'd put a golf ball in one corner it would have found its way to the opposite side and end of the room by gravity alone.

Miller's room was about as big as the average kitchen cupboard, had no windows, and a bed the right size for an immature Japanese. I hope that I didn't smirk.

Mine had a telephone on a small table alongside the bed. A small Bible lay on the thick brocade counterpane. I made a mental note to look up one of the Ten Commandments before I slept.

When I mentioned the telephone our host said, 'A lot of your senior officers stay with us, sir, and they need to keep in touch with their stations. It's not the same telephone number as the hotel, so I'd be grateful if you could give me a note of any call you make before you check out – not the number, only whether it's local, trunk or abroad. Just for the account, you understand?'

I didn't tell him that it was the first time I had seen a telephone in a hotel bedroom. I said, 'Of course; I'll make sure that my assistant has a note of that. Thank you.'

Behind his back Miller pulled a face as if she was being sick. I enjoyed that. After he left us, walking backwards and tugging his forelock, I asked Miller, 'Did you bring civvies with you?'

'Yes.'

'Go and change, then, and I'll take you out.'

She nodded once, slowly, and before she turned her back she smiled.

From a man's point of view, a problem with Miller was that she could step out on the street wearing nothing but a pair of last season's old football socks and still look stylishly dressed. Some people have got it, and some people haven't. When Miller came into a room you always felt dowdy beside her. I don't think that this was deliberate – it was just that she put everyone else in the shade, and didn't realize it.

She came down in a pair of slinky black trousers with flappy wide legs, a cream silk shirt and the corduroy jacket that I had already seen. There were two other men in the bar. One was in his eighties, I'd guess, and the other a harassed council official of some kind – he had the look. The glances they gave her as she walked in said the same thing: they wanted her clothes to disappear. I made another mental note: to ask her if she knew that. I know. It's ridiculous, but I was pleased.

I took her to meet Black Francie at Everton. He's my favourite corpse. We drank pints and ate pies at the Thornton Arms – and then sat outside in the graveyard on a seat in the sun. I knew how to show a girl a good time in those days.

The row of RAF graves was longer than I remembered; Tempsford must have had more bad luck before the end of the war. It looked as if one grave marker had recently been removed. Mine, maybe. I wondered if there was anyone down there. Francie's grave had a proper stone now with *Per Ardua Ad Astra* and the old badge on it. *Through adversity to the stars.* No stars for Francie: he was rotting under our feet – cut into bits somewhere over Germany. There was a small dried-up bunch of violets on him. I had seen that before, and wondered who his girl had been.

When I told Miller about him she said, 'That's a sad story. There are millions of sad stories in the country at the moment.'

'I didn't mean to make you sad. I thought that you'd be interested.'

'Because you knew him?'

'Yes, I suppose so.'

The sun warmed our faces and our hands. In the village behind us someone was practising with a muted trumpet. The song was 'Bye-bye, Blackbird'. The melancholy music swung. From further away the occasional voice in the air told us that a cricket match was in progress nearby. Music, beer and cricket: any government which provided that for the English wouldn't go far wrong.

Miller suddenly chortled. It seemed so out of context that I asked, 'What?'

'Do you know how many men have propositioned me since I was married, Charlie?'

'Several thousand? When were you married?'

'When I was eighteen. Too early, really. No, not thousands – don't be silly. Although more than I realize, now you've made me think about it.'

'What about them?'

'Well . . . what you men always try is something *interesting*: something that makes a woman focus on you, or makes you stand out from the crowd.'

'So?'

'You're the first man who's tried to seduce me with a pie, a pint, and a corpse.'

'A very superior class of corpse,' I said firmly, as if it was the only thing which mattered. I wasn't going to let her put Black Francie down. I let it lie there, then, 'Did I succeed?'

'Maybe you did. Tell you later.'

'Would you like to walk on down to the airfield? There's an old sunken lane just over there.' There were also some huge patches of long grass, I thought. But she didn't take the hint.

'Would you mind if we didn't? Why don't you find us a river to walk by?'

I took Miller to Granchester, and then to Cambridge. I showed her the pool in the Cam where Byron swam, and Rupert Brooke's

Old Vicarage. Kingfishers flashed above the water. But we couldn't get away from it completely. In the pub I chose Grease had burned his name onto the ceiling in the back bar, and I couldn't resist showing her.

We didn't go down for supper. She stood by the window of my room in nothing but her stockings, and my hands shook.

When I opened my eyes in the morning she was sprawled across me, already awake, and smiling. *Bene.* I yawned, and smiled back, 'If I thought that this was the last time I'd be with you . . .'

'Don't: it won't be.'

'You love sex, don't you? I didn't realize . . .'

'Is there any reason why I shouldn't?'

'No. There never will be. Did I tell you . . .?'

'Don't tell me anything, Charlie; just roll on your back – over here. Girls on top.'

Being ridden by Mrs Miller before breakfast is something close to going to heaven. My every sense was so heightened to a strange level that I'll swear I could hear and see a hundred miles. Then she did something. Without breaking the pace she leaned over and placed her finger across my lips. She had long fingers; did I tell you that already? She murmured, 'Sshh,' and picked up the heavy telephone handset.

She didn't brain me with it; she phoned her husband and woke him up, wherever he was. Their exchange of words was affectionate. I don't remember them exactly because I was rolling my head slowly from side to side, and my eyes were closed. We both came as she was saying 'Goodbye', and she collapsed with her face cuddled into me. I could feel our perspiration sticking her cheek to my neck. Her fringe was plastered to her brow. She let the telephone receiver slide onto the pillow beside me. Perfect. There was a bird singing out in the square: a blackbird or a thrush. Bye-bye, blackbird.

When I opened my eyes again I said, 'Thank you.' So did she.

My neck was still slick with sweat. I felt loved again, even if I was deluding myself. Sometimes life's tight like that.

20. *Blues for Percy*

The Lord giveth, and the Lord taketh away. The rotten bugger took Percy, which was a bit of a bummer. Even now I can remember the exact sequence of events. Our dour navigator had just click, clicked, cleared his throat and said, 'Norwegian coast, Skipper: five minutes.'

Turnaway clicked back, 'Anything, Charlie?'

'Negative, Skip. There's a bit of gobble gobble, but unless the Russians are doing Norwegian these days it's not them.'

'Just say *no*, Charlie.'

'*No*, Skip.'

'What? Oh, forget it!'

It was a particularly rounded *oh*. From one of those posh schools up in the bogs of Haggisland, I'd guess. There was a guffaw from somewhere. It was unusual to hear someone coming on air just to laugh. It turned out to be the last noise that Perce ever made.

Something bumped against my right shoulder, just like someone tapping you to get your attention. When I turned round I found that it was Perce's head. He was sitting upright in his seat but his head was lolling sideways and back.

'You OK, Perce?'

Tim came in with, 'What was that, Charlie?'

'Wait one, Skip. I think Percy's passed out on us.'

For once both the aircraft and Tim seemed to be in sync and not dancing about, so it wasn't difficult to get out of my straps, stand up and turn round. Perce's head still lolled. His eyes were wide open; he looked astonished. That wasn't surprising because he was astonishingly dead. When I touched one eye he didn't blink. I took off my silk glove and touched his exposed face. It was cold; colder than mine, I thought. So was the skin of his neck when I felt for his pulse. It was gone. I felt perspiration break out all over my forehead. That was pure funk – I could sweat at the North Pole if I was scared enough. I turned back to my station and clicked the office. 'Charlie, Skip. Just how important *is* Perce to this trip?'

I'm really good at the stupid questions: we were taking Perce and his radar array to the Kola Peninsula – really pissing in the Reds' pyjamas this time.

'Crucial, Charlie, you know that. Why? Isn't he OK?'

Click, 'No: he's dead.'

'Say again . . .'

'Dead. He just died on us. Pegged out. Can anyone else do his work?'

After a silence that stretched a bit Tim clicked, 'Can you come forward a min, Charlie?'

It was a beautiful night. We flew up a fjord. I could see farms, acres of trees, and beyond them the high ground and a ridge of mountains clad in gleaming snow. Perce would have liked to have seen that. Except in Lincoln bombers at night he wasn't particularly well travelled. Too late for that now. The cabin heating was working for once, and Tim was flying in his shirt-sleeves. He said, 'Silly question, I know, but are you *sure*, Charlie? Perce is dead? We can't do anything for him? You've seen dead people before?'

I decided to change the sequence. 'I'm sure. He's gone: I don't know why. I've seen some dead people before, *yes*, and there's absolutely nothing we can do about it.'

Tim tried the navigator, Henry Morgan. I always thought that Henry was a neat name for a navigator, even if I didn't like the bastard. Don't worry; you'll get it eventually.

'Nav, can you operate Perce's station?'

'Negative, Skipper. I can manage with the radio, but not the radar station.'

'Don't look at me, Skip,' I told our driver. 'The RAF didn't think I needed to know.'

The bomb aimer, Lambert, had been following this. He said, 'It doesn't help, but you can count me out as well. That radar-mapping kit is under development . . . it means bugger-all to me, sir.'

The engineer, up in the office with us, shook his head. That left the two gunners and Tim didn't even bother to ask them. Henry broke back in: 'What's going on?'

'You heard,' I told him. 'Perce is a goner, and we're fucked. Give the Boss a heading for home.' I shouldn't have taken Tim's decision for him, but someone had to. 'OK, Skip?' I asked.

'I'm fine now, Charlie. You can go back to your radios.' It

wasn't what I meant, but who fucking cared? The truth is that Tim wasn't cut out for this kind of flying, and everybody in the bloody crate knew it.

It was a long haul back. It always is when you have dead or injured on board: the ninety-minute-hour phenomenon. Somewhere over the North Sea I tuned into a radio station broadcasting jazz music from Holland. After the first slow number Nutty Neil came on and said, 'That's Louis Armstrong playing "Skid-dat-de-dat".'

Turnaway Tim didn't reprimand us, although I expected him to. Henry surprised me. He said, 'No; it's "Blues for Percy".' He was only making it up, but how come everyone except me knew so much about jazz all of a sudden? Behind us the eastern sky was lightening already, but we were flying at a narrow front, heavy with rain.

I couldn't argue about Tim's flying skills. He put us down on the long runway at Dyce so smoothly that I wasn't aware of the actual moment of touchdown. That's a rare skill. The runway was very wet. We bowled along it in a dirty great ball of spray to be met by a civvy police car and the Aberdeen police surgeon. Both were sopping wet. He came on board to verify that Perce was dead, and examined him in his seat. I stood over them and watched. The surgeon said, 'Yes, he's gone. You knew that, of course.'

'Yes. What was it?'

'I don't know. Your own surgeon will find that out, I expect. What exactly happened?'

'Nothing. I made a joke, and he laughed. Then he bumped against my shoulder, and when I turned round he was dead.'

'I've always wanted to put that on a death certificate.'

'What?'

'Died laughing.'

I had thought that he'd looked ex-services the moment I saw him: now I was sure. But I wasn't sure whether that was funny or not.

What I did know was that he'd scrounged a load of thermoses from somewhere, and had brought tomato soup and coffee onto the aircraft for us. A couple of service policemen with ineffectual rain capes stayed at the aircraft: one at the fuselage door, and one by the escape hatch under the nose. They made sure that we weren't going anywhere. We were topped up from a National fuel bowser marked up for a local Scottish airline, and an hour later we climbed back up through the rain for the long drag south. It was a sombre homecoming. Perce was lying on the floor at the back, wrapped in a tarpaulin bag. The Aberdeen doctor had given me a sealed envelope for the Station Commander at Waddington; it flew tucked into the top of my flying suit.

Nobody talked much. Even Henry's voice, giving the Skipper his navigation coordinates, was an intrusion. I found myself turning a couple of times and looking at Perce's empty seat. All the lights on his equipment were still showing. Occasionally they blinked, as if looking for some direction. I didn't even know the sequence to power it down. Tim flew three low circuits around Waddington when we got there. It was almost as if he didn't know what to do next.

I clicked, and told him, 'Put her down, Skip. It's time Percy went home.'

'OK, Charlie, as you wish.'

It was still raining, but not as heavily. The wheels squealed as we touched down. We were met by three ambulances: one for Perce, and two for the rest of us – the station doctor had insisted. Henry touched my elbow as we waited to climb into one. He said, 'Thank you, Charlie.' It didn't change the way I thought about him, but it helped.

I nodded because I didn't feel like saying anything.

Waddington stayed locked down for the duration of my visit, which turned out to be longer than planned. Just before I climbed into the ambulance I had seen Joe Humm and his navigator preparing to board the silver Hudson they had brought me there in. They were fifty feet away, but I waved, and he waved back. He must have recognized me, and someone must have already informed him that I was going nowhere. He was ferrying the empty aircraft back to Little Riss. I watched his take-off before I climbed into the ambulance. The small silver aircraft disappeared into the rain, and I suddenly felt lonely and abandoned.

They kept us locked up in the isolation unit at Waddington for three days. It was like a greenhouse with a wooden roof and a wide veranda, and was located as far from the other station buildings as it was possible to get. The hefty nurse who stayed with us told us that it was their old TB ward. We had separate rooms, and time on our hands. I played chess with Henry, and got to like him better. You always like men you can consistently beat at something or other.

The place had a good library, and I found some poetry by an American called Whitman. I didn't understand a line of it, but found I liked the way that inappropriate word linked with inappropriate word to make a logical sequence of sound. We were also interrogated to pieces, of course, and I was subject to the most intense medical examinations of my life. The third time I saw the doc he said, 'Do you want the good news first, Charlie, or the bad?'

'Give me the good news, sir.'

'We've tested your specimens. You're definitely not pregnant . . . and we don't think you have VD.'

These medical bastards are just like coppers: they all fancy themselves as comedians – you noticed that?

'And the bad news?'

'We still haven't got a clue what happened to your radar operator – and we can't let you go until we do know.'

'You don't know *anything*, sir?'

'Not much. I know that his heart stopped, but I'm damned if I know why. Some clever bods in the RAF wing at Ely have speculated that you flew into something like a beam weapon.'

'You mean the Norwegians zapped us with a *death ray*, like in the *Superman* comics?'

'Mmm. Something like that.'

'That's ruddy ridiculous, sir! They're on our side. Anyway; then why haven't the rest of us died?'

'That's the point. I'm hanging around just in case you do. In the meantime the station's locked down, and nobody can go on leave. You lot are about as popular as pox in a nunnery.'

'Couldn't he just have had a stroke or a heart attack, sir? Whatever it was, it happened very quickly. He was laughing at a daft thing I said, there was a brief bit of interference, and then he died. I wouldn't mind dying laughing.'

The doc was still working on his notes, and didn't look up. 'What interference was that? I don't think that you mentioned it before.'

'I've just remembered it. Just a quick crackle; it happens all the time. It wasn't your death ray – or if it was then I've flown through hundreds of them.'

'So what was it?'

'Static, probably. It's not supposed to build up in the radio frames – they're insulated to prevent it, and properly earthed – but you can never screen it out completely. It has to earth through something.'

He was supposed to be seeing Bombs after me, but suddenly the doctor shut his notebook with a snap, grinned and said, 'Apologize to Lambert for me, will you, Charlie? I've just remembered something I have to look at.' Then he almost *jumped* up, and ran to his jeep. Funny man. Lam wasn't disappointed: he was in a card school with three of the others.

The doc came back after lunch, and signed us off. Just like that. He carried a pair of dirty white silk gloves into our airy recreation room. When we examined them we saw that their finger tips were discoloured. I asked, 'What's up, doc?'

'Burn marks. Carrington got an electric shock from the metal table he was working at. Probably not a very big one. Not even a jolt, I expect – but it was enough to interfere with the electrical impulses which kept his heart pumping. *Bang*. There you go.' To the others he said, 'Charlie remembered a short burst of static just before it happened. His radios picked up the discharge.'

'So Perce had a weak heart?' Tim asked. 'Simple as that?'

'*No*, Flight Lieutenant. He had a braw heart. It was one of the best I've seen. No: there was something wrong with his electrics, that's all – and that little charge was enough to shut the pump down.'

'Could we have done anything, sir?'

The doc frowned, and sort of stroked his chin. Eventually he said, 'No. No, I don't think so.' But I knew that he was lying.

The others were all on a squadron there anyway, and they wasted no time. They made for their messes, or their quarters. Perce and I had been the only outsiders. Perce wasn't going anywhere, was he? The doc told me that transport had been laid on for me; someone was driving over from CFS who wouldn't get in until evening. I'd seen enough of the others for the time being, so I turned down invitations to the bar and waited where I was. There were plenty of books, a radio and a gramophone. I'd been wrong about the nurse. She wasn't that much of a hard case because she showed me a cupboard containing a crate of beer before she signed off, and told me to help myself. I had a party on my own in an empty TB sanatorium. I drank too much. That's probably why I looked up when twilight was closing in to see a tall thin sergeant standing in the shadows outside the glass, watching me. He was touching his chin the way Perce had done as he spoke, but it can't have been Perce. I'd seen people like him before. I glanced briefly away, and then back . . . he was no longer there. I unscrewed another beer, and silently toasted the space he'd been in.

Miller had used her own car, but had dressed in uniform. I was sitting on the veranda under a single light when she arrived. Moths must have been Japs: they were crashing into the light like kamikazes. Bats, lurking like night fighters at the light's extreme limits, picked them off one by one. My packed bag was on the stoop alongside me. I don't know who I had expected, but it hadn't been her. She ran up the three wooden steps and hugged me so hard and for so long that I thought we'd get stuck that way. I was out of breath as I spoke into her hair: 'I can have you here, now, or on the way home. No real choice; but *your* choice, anyway.'

'In a hotel, Charlie. Fifteen minutes away. We're already booked.'

'What did you tell Charles?'

'Exigencies of the service.'

She didn't say anything else, because I kissed her.

Miller's idea of a hotel matched mine: an old pub with bedrooms. The landlord was about thirty, and walked with a limp. Even so, he insisted on carrying our bags, and before he left us pointed out a battered biscuit tin on the dresser: it was full of candle stubs.

'We're getting electricity cuts all the time,' he told us. 'Use as many as you like.'

After he left Miller lit about a dozen around the room, and turned the light off.

'I love your legs.' I kissed Miller's stomach, just below her navel. Her tummy wasn't flat, and I liked it for that.

'I'm glad. I like you loving my legs, but they're a bit on the short side.'

'They're shapely. I love their curves. I knew a girl with straight legs once: stilts.'

'Is that the girl you go to London to see?'

It came out – just like that.

'I go to London to work with Piers. I thought that you knew that.'

'And to see a girl.'

'I know some girls there, yes.'

'The way you know me?'

'Not any more. Not until I've stopped knowing you.'

Miller had kept her eyes closed throughout the exchange and now, at last, she smiled. I'd said something she wanted to hear, but she couldn't resist teasing me. 'You'll stop knowing me one day, then?'

'You'll kick me out eventually, won't you? Maybe after the novelty has worn off.'

'You think that?'

'Yes. I daren't think otherwise, or I'd be lost.' She smiled again when I said that. I wondered if she knew that she was smiling. 'There's no telephone in here. What are you going to do in the morning?'

'Creep downstairs, and use the one in the bar.'

'Why not let it go for once?'

'Not a good idea. Charles would wonder if I was with a man.'

'And you're not, of course?' I kissed her stomach again. She put a hand on my head, and combed gently through my hair with her fingers. Without looking I knew that her eyes were still closed; it was like being explored by a blind person.

'No: I'm meeting with a group of other WREN officers to discuss careers for women in the Navy. Charles actually wants me to leave the service, settle down and churn out babies.'

'How would you react if you found *Charles* with another woman?'

'Feel a bit insulted, I suppose. I always feel that I should be enough for any man.'

'And what do you feel about being married?'

'Being married isn't quite enough for me, Charlie.' Miller's fingers tightened in my hair. 'Do you want to go down for a drink now? We could see if he has anything left to eat. I'm starving.' Apparently making love always made her hungry.

As she went down the narrow stair ahead of me she stopped suddenly and turned. 'I forgot. Piers Fortingale phoned a couple of times. He sounded quite concerned.'

'Thanks. What else did I miss?'

'Joopeman radioed in – from France, he said. He wants to talk to you.'

I'd lost a fiver.

All four of my hens clucked sympathetically over me. Boulder brought me coffee. She was putting on weight, and was wearing a very red lipstick. Whatever the treatment was, it appeared to be working. I wondered who the doctor was.

Watson wanted to see me. 'Fancy a spot of crash leave, old son?'

'We didn't crash. Are you trying to get rid of me, sir?'

'Perish the thought, Charlie. We're just getting used to you. Air House was on the blower a couple of days ago asking me if you could be persuaded to stay.'

'But they're not really in charge here, are they?'

'No: they were just speaking for whoever pays our salaries.'

'Which is?'

'The people round here have been told that we work for the Foreign Office.'

'But that's not true, either.'

'No. What is it that Winnie said? The truth has to be defended by a bodyguard of lies – don't you like that?'

'No, sir – and I don't like flying out over the Soviet Zone every week or so, either. It's like putting your hand into a cage of rattlesnakes, waving it around and hoping they'll miss.'

'You'd know about that, old man, wouldn't you? I hear that you're quite good with rattlesnakes.' Someone had moaned again; probably the cleaners.

'Piers offered me a job with a private airline when I've served my time here.'

'Good man; pleased to know you're still on side. Fancy a snifter before you toddle off?'

It wasn't hard to work out what Watson had done to fall into Piers's clutches the same as the rest of us.

My car wasn't behind the guardroom where I'd left it. Ming had gone into Capability Brown mode and was weeding a rose bed, so I asked him. He led me to a building as big as a bus garage, and showed me where it was parked up in a corner with a dust sheet over it. I pulled it off to find I had a freshly polished automobile: it looked quite the thing. Gleaming. The dark paintwork shone and even the leather seats had been cleaned and polished.

'The Motor Section did it,' Ming explained. 'They serviced it as well, and changed the front brake shoes – you were almost down to the metals.'

'What do I do, Ming? How do I say thank you?'

'It was no big deal: the lads had nothing else to do – and it was probably a nice change from working on big Humbers, or trucks. A bottle of Scotch would probably be very well received, if you could find one. It's still pretty scarce down here.'

'OK. What would have happened if I hadn't come back?'

'They would have said nothing to no one, most like . . . and if no one came asking for it in six months they would have flogged it.'

'Same old army, then?'

'Yes, sir. Don't know why I would ever want to leave.'

'Can you thank them for me?'

'Thank them yourself, sir. They're in the small office against the wall, having a brew-up.'

I got away an hour later. They gave me tea in a chipped enamelled mug, and wanted to know about what it was like being in Germany on the day the war ended. I had Pete to thank for that. They even produced a copy of his book, and asked me to sign my name on the page where Pete first mentioned me. It was depressingly close to the beginning.

Alison met me in the yard behind the Abbott house. She was carrying a galvanized iron bucket and was wearing a pretty dress, Wellington boots and a khaki infantryman's blouse from which the buttons had been removed. She asked me, 'Why are you smiling? Are you laughing at me?'

I had been smiling at the memory of a girl I had met in Germany: or, to be strictly true, the wonderful tits of a girl I had met in Germany. The first time I met her, she too was wearing a soldier's jacket stripped of its buttons. Only hers had been field grey.

'No. Don't be cross, but I was remembering a girl I met in Germany: she was wearing a soldier's jacket too. Where's Bella?'

'She's in Oxford, silly. It's Friday. I told her I'd feed the chicks for her.'

'Have you finished?'

'There are still the paddocks behind the house, the broilers.'

'I'll do one for you; you do the other. Then we'll have a cup of char.'

I waited until I was alone. Alison was cleaning out one of the low roosting sheds. That entailed digging out the accumulated hen pen of the previous few days. I think that she was just putting off the evil hour until she had to open her books again. I phoned Piers's number. The woman who answered said she'd never heard of him, and put the phone down on me.

I needn't have worried; a minute later it rang almost under my hand, and when I answered Piers said, 'Back in the land of the living? I'm glad that you're away from there.'

'What do you mean? I wasn't hurt.'

'TB clinics, old son: revolting places. People go to die in them – even healthy men die in those places. The TB bacterium forms a spore that lives for years, just like anthrax. It can jump up and bite you on the bum when you least expect it.'

'I didn't know that, Piers.'

'I know you didn't. You need someone like me looking out for you until you grow up.'

I gave it a six-beat, and then said, 'I'm pleased to hear from you too. Were you really worried about me?'

'I was worried that you wouldn't be able to finish the jobs you've started. Clem's getting ready to do something about the Rats, and I haven't got long to make the most of it. Can you come down here again next week?'

'The Gaffer offered me a few days' crash leave, so I don't see why not. Can you make sure I'm not wanted for flying?'

'Probably.'

'I had a thought about Grace that might help.'

'What was that, old son?'

'When I first knew her,' I told him, 'she was nuts about flying: it was all she did.'

'So I heard: it's all in her file. What about it?'

I didn't reply; I waited for the penny to drop.

'Oh my God! You want me to offer her a job, don't you? Just like I did to you. Why didn't I think of that?' Piers said.

'Can I offer her a flying job with one of your tame airlines or not? It might do the trick, and get her moving.'

'By all means. Offer to make her a Marshal of the WAAF if you have to; just get her out of there.'

'What else do you want me to do?'

'Just another couple of faces. I'll brief you next week. Tuesday?'

'I suppose so.'

'See you in the flat on Tuesday morning, then. Have a nice day, now.'

The last sentence was something we were copying from the

Yanks. It was delivered with all the irony that Piers could muster. Which wasn't much: he hadn't the voice for it. He sounded like a constipated cocktail waitress.

Bella looked dispirited when she returned from Oxford. I knew where the cider was stored: the bottles stood in an old stone sink in the pantry. I brought a couple out and poured them for us. Bella said, 'Thanks, love,' and raised her mug to me. Then she saw Alison hovering at the door, and told her, 'Yeah, get yourself one: you're old enough.'

'So what's the matter?' I asked her.

'Your Mrs Miller's husband's the matter. He's a bit of a creep. He followed me around town all day trying to catch me selling off record.'

'*Did* he catch you?'

'You think I'm stupid? It just means I didn't get rid of all I wanted to. It's a problem, because if I declare what I didn't sell in next week's white sales he'll ask me why my production level has suddenly shot up.'

'White sales?'

'In food production there's the *white* market and the *black* market. You know what the black market is – your pal Tommo is up to his sweetbreads in it.'

'And what are your Oxford sales?'

'I like to think of that as my *grey* market: neither one thing nor the other.'

'So what can you do?'

'Bleed in this week's excess bit by bit over the next few weeks and hope that no one notices. It's just a pain in the backside: juggling what to hold back, and what to feed in. Some are bound to addle in the long run. It depresses me: I hate waste.'

'What about Tommo?'

'Not ready for my eggs for another three weeks. That's what we agreed.'

'Why don't I phone him? You never know.'

'Do you really want to get involved, Charlie?'

'I am already, aren't I?'

I phoned Tommo later that night: Charlie Bassett, egg baron. When I put it to him he asked me what the split was. At first I didn't know what he was talking about.

'I'll take this load of eggs,' he explained. 'Ten per cent less than I agreed with her in your seedy pub.'

'It's not a seedy pub, Tommo, it's just English. I thought that you were used to them by now.'

'What's the split?' he asked again. 'What you getting outta this?'

'Nothing yet; I hadn't thought about it.'

'After this it's got to be twenty boxes a week to make it worth our time, OK? Is she good for that?' That was two hundred and forty eggs.

'Of course she is.' I crossed my fingers behind my back, as if he could have seen me otherwise. I passed Bella the telephone so that she could make the delivery and collection arrangements.

I danced with Avril on Saturday night. The band was Nat Gonella and his small band – maybe half of his Georgians. His cheeks puffed out around his trumpet's punchy stream of notes. She saw me watching and said, 'It's the pressure. Their cheek muscles go slack eventually. That's what Joe says.'

'Where is he tonight?'

'Working, I think, but he hasn't come for a few weeks. He caught me dancing outside with someone, and got into a fight. He might have been banned.'

'I thought you said that dancing with someone else was OK.'

'I think I might have got a bit carried away as well.'

'Why don't you go to the pictures with Joe instead?'

'On Saturdays I dance.'

'And get carried away?'

'If you like.'

It was as easy as that. Perhaps that's why I left her, and walked outside for a smoke. It was a fine night and I'd left the car in the car park alongside the pub, with its hood down. I sat in it in the dark, and let the heavy smoke from my pipe dribble from my mouth and up into the night sky. After a few minutes Alison climbed into the seat alongside me. She was wearing the dress Ming had sketched her in; it must have been her best. She smelled of soap.

'Hi, Charlie.'

'Where's your boyfriend? Stacey, wasn't it?'

'Dancing with the girl those men fought over a couple of weeks ago. He's very immature.'

I couldn't help myself: I smiled. In the darkness she couldn't have seen me. There were more stars than you could count. In the war I knew a girl who thought that they were the souls of dead aviators.

'You're not?'

'No. Women are more mature than men, year on year. Didn't you know that?'

'No, I didn't. Come on – I'll drive you home.' The tune of 'Polka Dots and Moonbeams' rattled through my head on the short journey. It was the number being played when I walked out. Alison was so quiet that I thought perhaps she had gone to sleep, but when I stole a quick glance she had her head tipped back and was watching the stars rush by.

Bella was still up when we walked in, playing *Monopoly* with Ming by tilley-lamp light on the kitchen table. They both looked very content. She asked, 'Where did you two bump into each other?'

I decided to let Alison answer: I was interested to see if she would tell the truth.

'The jazz club over at Priors,' she said. Bella raised an eyebrow, but said nothing. Alison scurried on: 'I went with Stacey, but he danced with someone else all night, and we fell out. Charlie spotted me, and brought me home. Saved me the bus fare.'

Bella smiled at me. 'Thank you, Charlie. Who was playing?'

'Nat Gonella. He's not what he once was.' I remembered his dance music.

'And a bit screechy for me. Do you two fancy a game of cards before we go to bed? Ming's got to go in half an hour.'

We played pontoon, but it was really *Happy Families*.

PART FIVE

Chasing Shadows

21. Chasing Shadows

The front of the red-brick farmhouse was half smothered by some plant or other. It wasn't until the buds began to form that I realized it was a rose: the largest I'd ever encountered. I pushed my bag into the footwell in front of the car's rear seat. Bella reached over and lodged four bottles of cider alongside them, 'for the journey'. She gave me a peck on the cheek. 'Not long now, Charlie. You'll soon be demobbed, and a free man again. How long you going to be away this time?'

'Less than a week. Don't take any chances while I'm away, but if you do get into trouble phone Tommo.'

'I have Ming.'

'Ming's a policeman. If he sticks his neck out too far for you someone will cut his head off. Please remember that.'

'OK, Charlie. I'll remember.'

This wasn't the same as saying that she'd do what I said. Deep down inside, women like taking risks: I've never quite understood why.

I called in at the office. Watson was at a meeting somewhere, and Miller was sulking. I don't know if she was sulking because I was going up to London again, or for another reason, because she didn't tell me. One of her inexpertly wrapped packages was on the corner of her desk. She sniffed and said, 'That's for you. For the journey.'

'Dripping?'

'Yes.'

'Marvellous. Thanks.'

She suddenly looked bashful, and I found that I liked that.

'Come back soon.' She came round the desk and kissed me. I am sure that if I had tried to do that she would have pushed me away. It's best not to try to understand them. Miller wanted to know what she should do about Joopeman and the Jedburghs while I was away.

'Keep disrupting their signals traffic, OK? I want them completely fed up with you by the time I contact them.'

'OK: anything else?'

'Marry me?'

'No. I'm already married.'

'Why won't anyone marry me?'

'Maybe you're not the sort of man that girls marry, Charlie – too much fun in small doses for that.'

'Fuck me, then.'

'When you come back; so don't come back exhausted.' It was always silly to underestimate Miller, because she always came back at you. Then she paused and asked, 'You're not really going on leave, are you?'

'No – but I'm not flying either. So you needn't worry.'

'What makes you think that I will?' Smiling.

'Vanity.'

'I love you, Charlie.'

'No, you don't.'

Trust me to spoil it. Her mouth dropped into the upside-down smile again. She turned away. 'Suit yourself. Call me if you can.'

I said, 'OK,' but it was only a way of disengaging. I hadn't said what she wanted me to.

There was a brand new flying jacket hanging on the back of her door – all sheepskin and smelly leather. Miller helped me on with it: she'd ordered a size too big for me, so it fitted over my clothes perfectly. When I tried to say thank you she just waved me away as if it was nothing. It wasn't the best note on which to say goodbye.

You never can tell what will happen if you walk away from a witch, having left her with a sense of grievance. That was the first thing I thought when my car stopped spinning. Then the tops exploded off the cider bottles with gentle pops, one after the other, leaving me sitting under a golden shower of something I'd rather have been drinking. I had thumped my chin against the steering wheel and nearly dislocated my neck.

I had cleared Oxford, and exhilarated by watery sunshine and an empty road had just let the car open up. On a gently cambered curve, with the speedo needle nudging seventy, I met the biggest pothole in the west coming the other way. Well, that's what it felt like at the time: it was three feet wide and nearly a foot deep in places. I know because I inspected it afterwards.

The problem with a car that starts to fly is that it hasn't the aerodynamic profile and lift to maintain level or ascending flight. I know that: I was in the RAF. I think that I lost the front nearside wheel when we hit the ground again. The impact felt as if it had loosened my teeth. Then the car started to spin in great loops: off the edge of the road, through a hedge and dropping down into a meadow. The wheel chased me, but kept going in long hops after the car and I stopped. In the silence that followed, the song of a skylark lifted into the air. It didn't give a damn.

A farm worker walked slowly up to me; I think he wanted to be sure that the accident had ended before he spoke. Two small Jersey cows followed him. I thought that they looked very sympathetic.

He looked like a halfwit, but observed, 'The wheel's over there; in t'corner of t'field if your'n interested.'

I wasn't. And I wasn't ready to say anything yet, so he added, 'I told 'em to fill up that darned hole weeks ago, but they never listen.'

They: the council, the people supposed to be in charge. And that was the whole story really, in a single sentence. Here's another: bollocks!

The cows began to lick the car. The guy said, 'You all right, then, sir?'

'Yes. Sorry. My head was spinning for a moment there.'

'Not as many times as your car did. I'd sit there a couple of mins if I wast you. Your wheel's—'

'In the corner. Yes. You said.'

It wasn't only the wheel. I walked around the car. Cider was drying on it in the sun. That was what the cows were licking: they worked their way methodically around it. The nearside front wing was hanging from a single twisted bracket, and its front light had disappeared completely.

'They should put up some temporary warning sign,' I said.

'They did but some of the young RAF boys from that school stole it. They'm mad buggers. There's a phone at the farm. Boss'd let you use it for an emergency.'

I stopped momentarily to look at the car as we walked away. I suppose that I wanted to fix in my mind just how lucky I had been. My chin hurt, and so did my forehead. One of the cows reached into the back of the car, found Miller's sandwiches and ate them: brown paper, string and all. If the dripping was beef dripping, she was discovering the joys of cannibalism.

There was an AA badge on the car's radiator grille, so I took a chance and phoned them. The farmer stood alongside me in the hallway of a solid-looking farmhouse. The farmer's wife had bustled off to make a pot of tea. She told me that a cup of tea would ward off delayed shock. I gave the AA the car's registration number, and the man who answered their telephone asked, 'Would that be Mr Abbott?'

'No: I'm a friend of his – I'm just driving his car.'

'That's all right, sir; Mr Abbott is a life member.'

An afterlife member actually, I thought – the original owner had fallen into Germany in 1944, but I hadn't got round to telling them yet. This wasn't the time, either.

The man went on: 'I'll direct the nearest patrolman to come out to you; he'll arrange for the car to be moved to a garage – and we'll have a go at the council about the hole in the road.'

Better late than never, I supposed.

What goes around comes around. The mechanic summoned

by the AA patrol looked very familiar. He told me, 'I love Singers. Works of bloody art.'

He was a strong, cheerful-looking young fellow, with a scarred jaw. I wondered if I should tell him that I'd probably slept with his sister not too long ago. In the end I didn't have the nerve. Then he said, 'But it will cost a bit to put her back together again, sir.'

'How much?'

'About seventy-five quid after I touch up the paint. I've probably got most of the parts we need back in the workshop. I cannibalize wrecks.'

'Don't cannibalize this one: she's not ready for the knackers yet. Seventy-five would be fine.'

We shook on it, and arranged that he would deliver the car to the Abbott farm in about a week's time. He had a mechanic's oily hands. The AA man took pity on me and broke the rules, which was why I arrived at Oxford railway station on the back of his combination, riding a folded-up towel over the rear mudguard. My bag was stowed inside the curious sentry-box-shaped sidecar. He even saluted me as he left: you'd think that after men got clear of the services they'd want to drop the bullshit, wouldn't you? But without thinking I threw him one back.

I had half an hour's wait for a London train so I telephoned Miller from an old wooden call box on the up platform. Someone had pinned a used johnny to the ceiling. It hung shrivelled and perished over my head, moving gently in the breeze from a broken window. I kept eyeing it as I phoned; ready to jump aside if it fell.

Miller was stiff and impersonal until I told her where I was and why, and then she turned on the emotion tap.

'Don't try to sound sympathetic,' I told her. 'As I spun to a standstill the first thought I had was that you'd wished it on me for not being nicer to you. You're a ruddy witch and, what's more, a cow ate your sandwiches.'

After a pause she laughed. It was a low, gentle laugh of conspiracy that said everything. The sort of laugh that lovers share.

'I love you, Charlie,' she said.

'I love you too.'

'I know you do. Sometimes you fall in love with someone precisely *because* they love you.'

'Does it matter who loved whom first? Which one of us?'

'I don't know; I keep changing my mind. All I know is that this is going to end in tears, and I am pretty powerless to do anything about it.'

I wished that I didn't agree with her. 'It's like a card game,' I told her. '*Chase the Lady*. Once the cards have been dealt to you, you have to play them out. Right to the very last hand. I'll play them as well as I can.'

'I know you will, Charlie.' That six-beat pause I was used to, and then, 'So will I.' She said it so quietly that I almost missed it. There was nothing much left. I asked her to phone Piers and tell him that I would be late. I didn't ask if she had his number, and she didn't ask for it. The last thing she said was, 'Bring me something back from London.'

The last thing I said was, 'You can count on it.' Then the pips told us to pay up or shut up. We put the phones down at the same time. I felt warm all over: wasn't that odd?

Piers met me at the station. I hadn't expected that. He had a dark blue jeep, and was wearing an RN Commander's uniform. I hadn't expected that, either. He drove right onto the platform and up to the train, and looked quite the thing. I flung my bag in the back. 'You look very smart today, Piers. Where are we going?'

'To a grubby consulting room in Battersea where we retain the services of a struck-off doctor. He'll look at your ugly mug and see if there's any permanent damage.'

'I don't need a doctor. I need a drink.'

'You'll see our doctor and like it. Piers takes care of his bods; surely you realize that by now?'

'You didn't take care of young Percy, did you?' That was a bit cruel. 'Nor either of my predecessors. Which one took the photographs, by the way? And what happened to him?'

Piers shook his head.

'Peter Williamson. Pete. Sweet man. RAF Film Production Unit, until we borrowed him. As to what happened to him – I simply don't know, old son. He dropped off the radar just before I heard that you were up for grabs. I'd like you to find out where he's got to before you clock off, of course . . . if you can.'

The surgery looked a thousand years old; there were instruments in there that looked as if they'd been dreamed up by Michelangelo. So did the doc: stringy grey hair and a closely clipped grey beard, like a picture of Edward Longshanks from my school history textbook. He told me to rub a cut potato onto my chin and forehead, and take it easy for a day. Then he charged us thirty-five pounds.

'Thirty-five quid for that is daylight robbery,' Piers said.

'Aye, laddie,' replied the doctor. 'Learn the first law of diagnostics.'

'What's that?'

'Commence your examination by emptying the patient's pockets.'

Comedians: all of them.

Piers didn't like it, but he gave me the next day off. He was working to a deadline, he said, but we must have been inside it because he certainly wasn't panicking. He left me to my own devices for the rest of the day as well.

I picked up a girl in Foyle's Bookshop and took her to a pub near St Giles. I enjoyed her company because the meeting was never going to go anywhere. She had long wavy hair the colour of polished brass, and swigged her gin like a sailor.

I spent the night in the flat on my own. I didn't know where the girls were or whether they expected me. Piers phoned to ask how I felt. He sounded as if he was drunk, and there were nightclub noises in the background. I could hear Noël Coward playing the piano, and singing 'Dance Little Lady'. It was washed in and out by a static noise of chat and laughter, like a weak signal . . . but it still sounded like an epitaph for a lost generation, and it upset me. I read *Eyeless in Gaza* for a few hours, until a headache got the better of me, and then chose Dolly's bed.

*

Don't laugh, but next day I went to the zoo. The sun shone through broken clouds, and my head only ached now and again. The captive animals and birds looked hungry and listless – and there weren't as many as I remembered from a visit before the war with my mum, dad and sister. In particular there was only one toucan now: where were all the others? Eaten during the hard times, or simply flown? They were still working to repair the bomb damage to the Clock Tower and the Giraffe House. The Ravens' Cage looked smashed beyond redemption, and the east tunnel still had its 'Bomb Shelter' sign.

The pretty middle-class woman who I invited for a cup of tea at the terrace cafe turned out to be a war widow. She accompanied a stocky little girl of about three, and pressed her address and telephone number on me before we parted. Her desperate need for adult company cut into me like a knife, so I walked down Parkway to Camden High Street under my own cloud.

I found what we would now call a wine bar: it was a pub licensed to sell only wine – I hadn't seen one of those before. In 1947 it was probably unique. I went two steps down from the street into a cool interior with a long bar and tiled floor. A big raised platform at the rear had long tables, benches like church pews and free newspapers. The sign on the wall over them said *Silence*, like in a library, and *Men Only*. Grace would have chucked something at that.

I didn't know what to drink, but a friendly barman started me off with a cold white burgundy, and that seemed to do it for me. How had the French concealed it from the Germans? I drank three glasses of the thin lemony wine, remembered drinking it at pavement cafes in Paris in 1945, and read the papers.

Only the *Daily Mirror* told it the way it was. In the others the politicians were already jockeying for position, even though Mr Attlee's government had only been in power a couple of years. The barman turned on a radio over the bar, and I noticed that it was an old air force tuner. That made me smile: there was that theme again – swords into ploughshares. A music programme was broadcasting a *Glenn Miller Hour* recording made by an American station before the war. 'Serenade in Blue': the trumpet solo on that still lifts the hairs at the back of my neck. I lingered over the Jane cartoon. The page was so creased that others must have done the same.

The following morning I dressed down and went out to meet Piers at a licensed cafe at Smithfield. I remembered it from years before. The Smithfield porters worked around the clock, and had somehow convinced the local licensing board that the nearest pubs and cafes needed to be able to serve booze twenty-four hours a day to keep up with them. I went back there on a nostalgic trip in the 1960s, and found that little had changed. We had steak sandwiches, and pints of stout that Piers insisted on calling 'blackstrap'. He was still in his uniform, which now looked a bit rumpled, and he hadn't shaved. He didn't look like the best advertisement for the senior service.

'What a night,' he told me. 'What a day and another night.'

'You look as if you haven't been home yet – or back to work.'

'Correct, old son.'

I bit into my sandwich. The steak was exquisite. Its juices ran over my fingers.

'What do you want me to do this time, Piers?'

'Get that bloody woman away, of course. Apart from that, not much – though any more names you could put to faces before we lift them would be useful. Find out where young Peter went. Same as before: easy stuff.'

'*Lift them?*'

'Arrest them; toss them in the pokey. Then throw the key away. Bang.'

'What for? They aren't doing anything.' A picture of the boy, Gary, formed unbidden in my mind. They'd taken his father already; would they take his mother now?

'For trespassing, and being very inconvenient to His Majesty's government. And there's bound to be deserters like you among them.'

He was just being a bastard, so I let it go.

'There must be a hundred or so of them in the Bishop's Avenue . . .'

'No. Only the men, old son. Just the men. Don't worry.'

'What will happen to the women and children?'

'Separated, I suppose. The kids will go to children's homes and Borstals, and the women will be told they can have them back once they've found themselves somewhere of their own to live, and a legal means of supporting themselves. Neither of which will be readily available. It's a hard old world. Barnado's will probably get a bit of a boost.'

'How will that help? Didn't you say that there are thousands of them in London?'

'Yes, but the Bishops Avenue is the jewel in their grubby little crown; if we take that back from them they'll realize just how nasty the new world order is prepared to be: the others will panic, and disappear like . . . like . . . what is it the Tykes say?'

'Snow off a dyke.'

'Correct, old son.'

It was the second time that he had said that, and I had liked the satisfaction in his voice on neither occasion. Piers *was* a bastard, although I wasn't sure whether he was a shallow nasty bastard or a deep nasty bastard. It wouldn't matter to the kids banged into children's homes without their mums and dads, would it?

'Who's *we*?'

'Told you. You, me, Clem, the king, and all the other government wankers in bowler hats.'

'Can I offer Grace a flying job?'

'Affirmative. Pathfinder Bennet will take her on as a second pilot. He's started a newish mob called British South American Airways, or something like that. It will keep your Grace gainfully employed, and thousands of miles away from England most of the time. Good result. I wish I'd thought of that.'

'Did you speak to Bennet?'

'No – out of my league. Grace's Pa did the needful, but don't tell her that.'

'Thanks, Piers, I wouldn't have worked that out by myself.'

'Don't be sarky, Charlie; it doesn't suit you. Why are you looking so down in the mouth?'

'What you just told me. This government is going to behave as badly as any that went before it. *We* are the Nazis now.'

Piers looked at me in astonishment. 'Why on *earth* should you have thought otherwise, old boy?'

I looked away from him, concentrated on finishing my sandwich, and imagined him in a black uniform. It was not that difficult to do.

22. Limehouse Blues

Harry James looked genuinely pleased to see me. 'Look what they gave me,' he said, laughing. He always wore bits of suits that didn't match; now he flipped his jacket open to reveal a sheriff's star from a kid's cowboy outfit, pinned to a pinstriped waistcoat.

'John Wayne or Gary Cooper?'

'I always feel I should be on Jesse James's side. Probably something to do with my name.'

'You wouldn't say that if you'd known him. He was probably a bit of a shit.' I thought I'd better show some professional interest in our last encounter. 'Did the cops come round looking for me?'

'Just the once; after that they sat outside the gate in their car for a day. Young Gary used them for target practice with his catapult, and got a ticking-off. After that someone must have called them off. We can do without that sort of attention.'

'Sorry. It won't happen again.'

'I know it won't. I won't let it.' It was as well to be told, I suppose. 'Want a cuppa?'

'Terrific. I brought some sugar and tea. Here.' Bella would wonder where it was until she found my note.

The huge kitchen was full of light and happiness. I realized now how much I looked forward to coming here. One of the radios was on a high shelf, its thin copper-wire aerial stretching out of the window. Roy Fox and his band were giving it 'We'll all go riding on a rainbow'.

This was all going to be over in a few weeks. I kept reminding myself that these people were not my responsibility. I sat opposite Harry at one side of the long table. The radio switched to the Squadronaires doing 'Something in the Air'. Damn. He didn't have to remind me, did He? I already knew that, and wished that I didn't.

Harry grinned, and held something out. 'Your card. It's official now, *Comrade* Miller. I'm really pleased for you, Charlie.'

Comrade Judas, more like. I produced some crumpled fivers I had lifted from Piers.

'I've been thinking about that. I know that you said that money's no problem . . .'

'That's right, Charlie – we have our sources.'

'I still want to pay my own way around here if you'll let me.' There were six of the notes. I divided them into three pairs and pushed them over to him in sequence. 'I thought that these should go into some political welfare fund – you would know what was best – and *these* would cover what I've eaten. The last ten will cover what I eat this trip and maybe kick-start one of your parties, if you had time.' Thirty quid. Grimly appropriate, wasn't it?

Harry put his hands down flat on either side of the money, and looked at it. When he made eye contact again I thought that he was about to cry.

'What's the matter?' I asked, worried that I'd somehow upset him.

'It's nothing. You're too good, that's all. I don't expect this sort of thing.'

The CP membership card was lying on the table too. I lifted one of his hands, and put it down over the money. Then I put mine over the card. 'Let's just call it a fair exchange.'

In my room the first thing I noticed was a bunch of fresh flowers in a cracked vase on the small chest of drawers. The second thing I noticed was another drawing pinned to the wall – it was of a Lancaster bomber. It was trailing smoke, and bombs fell from its open bomb-bay. A series of sharp dashes were the machine-gun bullets arcing away from the rear turret. The curtains were drawn, and there was someone in my bed. I was still throwing sixes: one after the other.

Grace lay across me, her face at my shoulder. Against my chest her nipples felt huge and hard. They always looked huge. They weren't: her breasts were small, so it was all a matter of perspective. She said, 'Look at me, Charlie . . .'

When I didn't move she reached a hand up and turned my face towards hers. 'Don't worry about it. It happens to all men sometimes. You can't be *en garde* all the time.' I didn't reply. 'Look. It happens to us too. Do you think that women are always that desperate for a knee-trembler? The difference is that we can hide it when we're not, whereas you can't. A hole is always a hole, and I can always do what Mummy told me: lie back and think of Derbyshire.'

'Don't you mean England?'

'No, I mean *Derbyshire*. It's one of the few places that makes England worth being in.'

That was interesting. I smiled, but still didn't have anything to add.

She kissed my shoulder and asked, 'Still love me?'

I suppose that I didn't answer quickly enough. 'Of course I do. But it's not enough, is it?'

'No.' Grace shook her head. Slowly. 'I'm glad you've realized that. I love you a bit, too, but that's not enough either.'

'Someone else told me that about her marriage recently. She said that it wasn't quite enough.'

'That doesn't necessarily mean that she'll throw her lot in with you, either.'

'That's what *I* thought. But I can't help hoping.'

When Grace spoke again she sounded sad. 'You do that, Charlie. Never stop hoping.' She slid off me, and lay on her back alongside. 'If it helps, *I* love just two people, and one of them is you.'

'But not enough?'

'That's right, love: not enough.' She turned her back. ' 'Night, Charlie.'

I slid my arm under her neck. She moulded her back against my side.

' 'Night, Grace.'

*

Morning.

‘’Morning, Charlie.’

‘’Morning, Grace.’

Smiles all round. I realized that in all the time I had known Grace we hadn’t actually woken up in the same bed all that often. It wasn’t bad. It made me grin. ‘Darby and Joan’ was a phrase we used all the time in those days; you hardly ever hear it now. Grace said, ‘Go and take a bath. You smell sweaty, like a dog.’

‘And you don’t?’

‘Ladies don’t sweat; they glow. I was taught that at the school at Lausanne I was sent to – it didn’t do a bit of good. I was too far gone by the time they got hold of me. Go now.’

‘Join me?’

‘No.’ The definite negative.

I didn’t tell her that I liked to start the day with a bath or a shower anyway. I didn’t want to give her the satisfaction of being right.

In the kitchen Gary and his mother sat on either side of Matesy. It looked absolutely right. Matesy turned his brown eyes from me for a moment, and smiled. He knew it. So did the kid.

Gary said, ‘The cops came for you, Mister Charlie, but we didn’t tell them anything. Then I broke their car headlight with my catapult. Brilliant shot.’

‘Brilliant shot,’ Matesy confirmed. Gary smiled. His mother somehow laughed and frowned at the same time. Mothers can do that.

‘Don’t congratulate him, Daniel; it will only make him worse.’ *Daniel.*

'They suspended him from school for a week,' she told me, 'and gave him work to do at home.'

'And that's punishment?' I asked. 'If I'd known that when I was his age, I would have been out with my catty every day.'

'You're as bad as Dan.'

Matesy said, 'I was applauding the fact that Gary stands by his pals – that was all.' It was uncanny; he had this huge, still presence. 'Maybe attacking the coppers was going a mite far.'

'A mite far,' the woman echoed. It looked to me as if Gary had got his new dad. I was glad that I hadn't queered the pitch for them.

Breakfast was huge hunks of warm bread and marge, with dollops of crystallized honey 'from our own hives'. Half a dozen other folk drifted in and out. Jokes and snatches of song bounced around, and the sun came out. Does a good spring drag a good summer along behind it? Grace showed up eventually, still rubbing her hair dry.

They were somehow just not quite the same with her there – even Gary kept his distance. That was interesting. I was leaning against one of the ovens; Grace came straight over and kissed me on the lips. That was interesting too. Whenever Grace did that sort of thing she was saying something. The problem was working out exactly what. I'd known her long enough not even to try.

'Take me for a walk?' Grace asked.

Kenwood again. Her idea. We sat on a long slatted chair at the back of the house, looking out over the lake and the sculptured woodlands. It bore a new bronze plaque dedicated to the memory of a Second Lieutenant Clare who had died in Africa with the Long Range Desert Group. Apparently he'd spent his earlier life sitting on this very seat composing poetry. I wondered if he was looking down on us now, thinking that he'd wasted his fucking time.

'These dedications are all over the place,' Grace said. 'People aren't satisfied with a name on a war memorial any longer.'

'I think I can understand that.'

'Yes. Maybe.' She shut her eyes and leaned back. 'Sitting with the sun on my face reminds me of Italy.'

'I didn't know that it could be as hot as it was out there.'

'I did; I flew to Egypt in the 1930s. Even hotter.'

'Do you miss flying, Grace? Being able to fly?'

There was a definite catch in her voice when she answered. 'Yes. Very much. It's almost unbearable, so I don't think about it.'

So there it was.

'I can get you a job flying; you'd be one of the very first female commercial-airline pilots. All you have to do is say yes.'

Grace actually said nothing. She looked away from me and into the distance. Eventually she looked back at me, said, 'There has to be more to it than that,' and sighed.

'Do you remember that I told you I'd seen a photograph of you at a party here . . . and that was how I knew where you were?'

She nodded.

'Who took the photograph?'

She frowned as if she needed to dig into her memory, but I knew Grace. I knew that it was an act.

'Peter . . . something or other. He lived up the road.'

'Peter Williamson?' Another Pete. I left it for a moment and then asked, 'What happened to him, Grace?'

Grace said, 'Ah . . .'

She stood up and stretched in the sun. I've seen old cats doing that. One arm and then the next. Then she walked away from me, and across the path to sit on the grass looking away from me at the parkland. She sat there alone for twenty minutes.

When she stood up she went through the stretching routine again.

She sat beside me. 'I get it now,' she said quietly.

I was smoking my pipe. It was an American tobacco that Dolly had given me: very sweet and a bit hot – a little like Dolly herself, I suppose.

'Do you?'

'You're still in the RAF, aren't you? And they've sent you to find out what happened to Peter, just like they sent you to find me in Germany. Getting me away into the bargain would be a bonus for you.'

I didn't say anything.

Grace asked, 'I'm right, aren't I?'

I played at sending out smoke signals with my pipe. 'You bought me this pipe, years ago. Do you remember? It's probably on its last legs: you'll have to buy me another.'

She didn't respond, and when I looked at her she was crying. That was the third time I saw Grace cry. I put my arm around her, and she laid her head on my shoulder. She didn't cry for long. Then she asked, 'How long have we got?'

'What do you mean?'

'Harry told us that although the government actually *wants* to build new houses for everyone who's living rough, they will be afraid to be seen to be giving in to pressure. Ordinary people would see it as common sense, but the government and the councils would call that anarchy. Harry says it means that they'll have to break us up before they do anything. If you want me out of here, and he's right, that means that they're coming, doesn't it? So – how long have we got?'

I didn't duck it this time. 'About a couple of weeks, I'd guess, but I can't be sure.'

'It's such a happy place, Charlie.'

'I know that; I love coming here . . . It's the way people were meant to live. No pressure. I'm sorry.'

We walked around the lake, holding hands again. On the small bridge that crossed its outflow we stopped, leaned on the parapet and looked at the water. They had begun to clean it up. Grace said, 'It's a place before its time, that's all: everyone will want to live like this one day.' Then she asked me, 'Why did you tell Harry that you were a thief?'

'I didn't. He made an assumption, and I didn't correct him.'

'Poor excuse, Charlie.'

'I know it. What happened to Williamson?'

After one of those six-beat pauses when a conversation can go anywhere she asked, 'Do you trust me, Charlie?'

I thought about it, and told her, 'Not bloody likely.'

'What if you had to?'

'Then I'd bloody well have to. But I wouldn't like it.'

'Then get used to not liking it. I'd tell you not to worry but you wouldn't believe that, either.'

'Exactly what are you saying, Grace?'

'That I'm not going to answer your question now, but I might later. Either way you're going to have to trust me, or bugger off. Who did you get that offer from, by the way – of a flying post for me?'

'Pathfinder Bennet. He's landed himself the licences to open a commercial route to Rio and the Caribbean. You'll be suntanned all the year round.'

Pause. She still hadn't given me the yes I wanted.

'I have to go now, Charlie. Walk us home?'

'Of course. What happens next?'

'You're a bad spy, Charlie. So you can run . . . or you can trust me and hang around to see what happens next.'

'I'm gonna run.'

'No, you're not.'

Grace was right most of the time. I bloody hated that.

I made myself useful by giving Matesy a hand in the garden: weeding.

'What are these, Matesy?'

'Early lettuces. The knack is keeping the slugs away from them now, and the butterflies later on.'

'Are you good at this lark?'

'Fair. My father was a gardener up at a big house near Gateshead when I was a boy. The sons were all killed in the war, so it's a golf clubhouse now – can you believe it?'

'Yes. Times change; sometimes it's hard to keep up.'

'I was just starting my apprenticeship when war broke out. I've been catching up ever since.'

Every time we filled a wheelbarrow with weeds I took it to a big compost heap against a fence. Matesy would take a breather and walk with me.

'You still see your old man?' I asked him.

He shook his head. 'Mum and dad ended up down on the coast at Norfolk. He got a job on a farm, and was in the Home Guard. He went out on patrol one night and never came back; none of them did.'

I hadn't heard about Home Guard casualties. 'What happened to them?'

'Either no one knows, or no one's saying. Ma's convinced that they were captured by a German raiding party, and he's gonna turn up from some camp in Germany sooner or later. It sent her a bit loopy.'

'Is that what *you* think?'

'No. I used to, but since I've seen the way the Boss Class have behaved since the war I think that he copped it in some brilliant cock-up that will remain for ever an official secret to protect the guilty.' Then Matesy asked me, 'Why are you smiling?'

'You said the "Boss Class". That's what my old man always called them. He brought me up to hate anyone with authority.'

'That can't have been very handy when you were called up . . .'

'I did get into bother now and again . . . but eventually you learn how things work. I was aircrew so they had to make me a sergeant anyway; then I lived too long, and they had to make me an officer. It was a bit of a laugh . . .'

'Irony,' Matesy told me. 'It was *ironic* – time for a smoke break?'

'Why not?'

We were still smoking when Grace came out. She was wearing the olive KD trousers I remembered, a thin khaki vest shirt like the Americans favoured and a sleeveless leather tank jacket on top of them. She looked like the heroine from a comic book. She told me, 'I've got to go down to the docks near Limehouse. Do you want to come along?'

'Someone told me that it was pretty knocked about.'

'Yes. That's right. It will make you feel less bad about what you did to German cities once you see what they did down there.'

Grace had got a small ex-Army Hillman Tilley similar to the vehicle in which I had crossed from France. Someone had given it a quick coat of livid green paint.

'Whose is this?' I asked her.

'Ours. Belongs to all of us. I think that we have three vehicles in the street. You just take whatever's free.'

'I think I saw one the day I arrived: a small lorry with half a dozen bods in the back.'

'That would be right. They'd have been coming back from work.' When I looked at her she added, 'Just because they've nowhere to live it doesn't mean they can't work. We've got some men rebuilding the Tube, and some are working on the roads or the bomb-sites.'

Grace was a competent driver: better than me. Being a passenger gave me the chance to take in what I saw. Acres of terraced houses reduced to rubble. On one pulverized corner site the bricks didn't even look like bricks, just misshapen chunks of red stuff. Burned-out warehouses. One family was moving its possessions in three prams. There was a small street market on a road of bombed-out shops. I had a sudden memory of the feeling of futility that I had experienced at St Paul's. It made me angry, but I had no one to be angry with.

Grace stopped at a crossroads to ask a coloured guy directions to KG Five: it was a dock. Grace might as well have been speaking a foreign language, because he turned out to be a GI, on leave and rubbernecking. He had a camera around his neck, and couldn't help us. Grace offered him a lift in the back of the Tilley, but he smiled and refused 'No. Thank you, ma'am, but no. I guess I'll walk.'

Grace nodded.

The insidious sweet smell of the unburied crept into the cab from the bomb-site alongside us. She wrinkled her nose and wound the pick-up window shut.

'When do you think they'll finally bury all the dead?' I asked.

'Years. When they finish finding them. It's the dead children they still find that upset me. They make me numb inside.'

'And yet you haven't asked me about your own.'

'I know. That's a bit strange, isn't it?'

'We're all a bit odd. I think it's on account of all the killing.'

'What's happened to Carlo? Did you put him in a children's home?'

'No. I brought him back with me. I also had a five-year-old German kid who I sort of inherited. They're both with my old Major down on the South Coast. He has a pub and a restaurant down there: the last I heard the kids were doing well. I send them money.'

'You don't go to see them?'

'No. That's right: me neither.'

'Fat lot of good we are.' Grace said it ruefully.

'We can't be good at everything, can we?'

'No, Charlie, we can't. But you'd think that we could be good at *something*.'

I needed to change the subject. I asked, 'What are we going down to the docks for?'

'I'm doing a favour for Harry. A ship's captain he knows is taking his ship into the Med for the first time. I was volunteered to check his charts and make sure that he'd got everything he needed.' Grace was A1 with maps. I remembered that.

A uniformed man, with a single ring on the end of his dark sleeve, directed us around the dock to the vessel we were seeking. He wasn't too smart, but he was cheerful – and that counts for a lot. He caught my glance at a group of massive brick arches that had been exposed by a bomb.

'They were wine vaults built by Napoleonic prisoners of war in the 1800s. We used them for air-raid shelters, and never lost a single person.' He sounded proud of it. 'They'll still be here when I'm gone.' An optimist.

The ship was named the *Polly B*. Underneath her name, on her old-fashioned raked stern, Boston was shown as the port of registration.

'*Polly B* what?' I asked Grace.

'*Polly B* good, perhaps?'

A man I already knew was sitting on a pile of hatch boards near the end of *Polly B*'s gangway, which was a steep set of light metal steps leading up to a gap in the ship's rail. The port tally clerk. Why hadn't I expected that? Grace parked up alongside him and we got out. He banged the bent pipe he had been smoking against his boot heel and wandered over.

Grace said, 'You two have already met . . .'

We performed the ritual of the hands. If he was a Mason then he wasn't letting on this time.

His eyes twinkled like a weasel's – we had not only met, remember, but he had offered to fence for me.

'I'll take you on board and introduce you to the Old Man,' he said. 'After that it's up to you. OK?'

Grace said, 'Fine. Thanks for taking the time.'

'Think nothing of it, *comrade*.' It was just the way he said it that made us all grin. He was the first person I'd met who saw the funny side of being a Red.

The captain of the *Polly B* was an eighteen-feet-tall red-headed Dutchman named Herman. He had scars all over his big hands, and from the moment we were shown into his small day cabin I was aware that he had a way with the ladies. I could feel Grace blossoming alongside me, even without looking at her. We drank thick clear Dutch gin with him and, despite what he had said, our dock worker stayed for a couple of rounds.

'You're registered in Boston: is that Boston, Lincs, or Boston in the USA?' I asked Herman.

'Nobody knows, Charlie – which is good for me. Maybe both.'

'Herman owns this ship,' Grace explained. 'He's an owner-driver. He just takes it wherever he pleases. Tramping.'

'And he pleases to go into the Med now?'

Herman waved a finger the colour and size of a beef sausage

under my nose, and told Grace, 'Your friend asks too many questions. He a policeman?'

'No. He's not long out of jail.' Had I told her that? I couldn't remember.

'OK.'

I said, 'No more questions. I was just making conversation. I didn't mean to offend.'

'Why not?' The Dutchman changed tack again. 'That's the problem with you English; you too afraid of offending someone. You steal someone's wife, or take his money or his life, you don't give a damn. You *offend* someone, and you get worried.'

I had had enough. I stood up, and even then, standing over him where he sat, wasn't that much bigger than him. 'I could get very pissed off with you . . .' It must have been the gin.

Even Grace smiled at that. I must have looked like a mouse threatening an elephant.

Herman laughed a series of slow explosive laughs – like, *ha . . . ha . . . ha*. Then he said, 'Sit down, Englishman,' and when I didn't: 'Sit down. Have a drink. You're safe here.'

He produced another bottle from a small cupboard alongside him. Rum. The label said Four Bells, and *For export only*. He asked, 'You like this?'

'I don't know.'

'Let's find out. You ever been to Netherlands?'

'Only once. In 1944.'

'Ah!' Herman said. 'A liberator. It would be impolite to offend a liberator.'

I wasn't sure whether I liked this big man or not. But I liked his rum. He was married and had a huge family, he told us. He went to sea to get away from them. He had a girlfriend on board; a Portuguese girl named Victoria. She must have been sitting in his sleeping cabin, because she came out from behind a hanging bead curtain that guarded it as soon as her name was mentioned. She was about eighteen years old, had straight black hair that hung to her waist, and skin the colour of milky coffee. She was stunningly beautiful.

Grace's mouth dropped open, then went immediately into the upside-down smile. Herman said, 'Victoria's a nurse from the English Hospital in Oporto. They let her come on this trip to get drugs in England. Things they run short of in Oporto.'

That didn't help. Grace lifted a lip and asked, 'But can she read maps?'

Herman grinned at me, and shrugged. It was his show, and I wasn't about to let him off the hook. 'Probably not. Would you care to examine ours now?'

We left Victoria in the cabin sipping a hefty slug of rum that she had diluted with ginger beer from a stone bottle. She hadn't said a word. She hadn't stopped smiling at me since she'd shown up, either. Herman's mouth made the upside-down smile too, only it was bigger than Grace's, and nastier. 'You too, Charlie,' he told me. 'Not safe to leave you here. She eat you alive.'

Up on the bridge he turned and grinned at me. 'Ain't she something, Englishman?'

'Can she speak an intelligible language as well?'

'Don't know. I never asked her. Mostly she makes moaning noises.' Then Herman roared his loud staccato laugh.

'I prefer my girls a bit older than that,' I said. 'And a bit more experienced.' I was tipping my hat to Grace, but it didn't work because she swung round and glared at me. You never can tell.

The chart house was a small windowless room aft of the bridge. It had just enough room for a chart table with wide drawers, and a high stool. Grace ignored the stool. She dragged out the charts one by one, scrutinized them, and seemed to pay a lot of attention to their publication dates. She screwed one into a big paper ball and tossed it in a corner, and made a list up as she went along.

Herman sat on a high chair at the rear of the bridge and smoked a cigar. He still had rum in the glass that he had brought with him. 'How old you think the *Polly* is, Charlie boy?'

I had been keen on ships when I was at school, so I reckoned in her raked stern, her high bridge that stretched from beam to beam, straight narrow funnel and vertical bow, took a chance and said, '1920. Maybe 1921. Clyde-built.'

'Very good. Very, very good. 1919, actually. She was a dirty ship until 1942, and then your government paid for the conversion to diesel engines. That was done in New York Yards.'

'Were you with her then?' Ships are like beautiful paintings: no one owns a ship – you're just *with them* for a time. If you're lucky, that is.

'No, we came together a year ago. I saw her in Lowe's Yard in Ipswich; laid up. Love at first sight, you say. Bought her with a loan against reparations the Nazis owe me. I already paid it off.'

'What will she do?'

'Fifteen knots, eighteen. A nice steady lady.'

'Who was *Polly*?'

'You ask too many questions, Charlie.'

'You've already told me that. The rest of the world agrees with you.'

'Polly was a widow I knew at the time.'

'Nice steady lady?' I asked with a grin.

'You take your chances, Englishman.'

'I know. I can't seem to help it.' I couldn't see Grace's face because she had her back turned to us, but I knew that she was grinning. 'Would you mind if I had a poke round, while Grace works?'

''S long as you don' poke round my Victoria it's OK.' And he laughed that huge laugh again. I had heard anti-aircraft guns which sounded like that in the war.

'You need a guide?'

'No. I can find my own way around.'

The *Polly B* was a five-thousand-tonner, or thereabouts. She was sleek but deep, and not too broad-beamed amidships: a good deep-sea ship. I knew what the Dutchman meant: love at first sight – some girls are hard to resist, and *Polly B* fell into that category. Despite her age she was in prime condition: even her engine-room brasses gleamed. Her forward hatches were off. Maybe they were the pile of hatch boards on the quayside. The forward hold was clean enough to eat a meal in. They'd obviously started to load the cargo: piles of mattresses strapped together in bundles of ten – most of them second-hand – but none stowed properly yet, a couple of tractors, four demobbed jeeps, a couple of trailers and some agricultural equipment. By the time I wandered back half an hour later I fancied signing her articles myself.

Romantic tosh, of course.

Most of the crew were ashore, but I met a small round man who introduced himself as Galliano and bowed. He was the cook, and wouldn't let me away from his spotless galley until I had sampled his coffee. It was terrific. This guy Herman had it made. He was still on the bridge when I returned. Grace had disappeared.

'She's a terrific ship, skipper, and your cookie makes terrific coffee.'

He grinned. 'I think so. She's my third ship. I scrapped the last one, and the first was torpedoed under me in '43.'

'U-boat?'

'Nah. By a British MTB. She was a German coaster. I had a spruce cargo from Norway, so she floated herself ashore even with her back broken. She was still there the last time I passed.'

'I thought that Grace said you were Dutch?'

'I am. What you worried about? I sail anyone's ship for them.'

Yeah, I thought. *Why not? Then claim reparation.* We would have called him a Flash Harry type a few years later. The new post-war world was full of them.

Herman walked me to the rail. Grace was down on the quay talking animatedly with the dock worker we'd met before. She looked excited rather than argumentative. The skipper said, 'She knows her business with charts, your friend.'

'She's always been good with maps,' I told him. 'She's flown all over the world. Solo most of the time.'

'Ah. That was it – I felt something wild about her. I only need three more charts for where we're going; she wrote them down.' He had a small piece of crumpled paper in his hand. 'I'll get the chandler to deliver them.'

'I saw your cargo. Where will you take those old things?'

After a pause he said, 'Italy. There's a lot of war damage in Italy. They'll buy anything there.'

No. He wasn't telling the truth, but whatever *that* was it was *his* business, not mine.

Smuggler, I reckoned. But he gave me a couple of tins of tobacco and a bottle of rum before I left, so who was I to knock it?

I could have excused myself that evening, walked down the road and phoned Piers, but I didn't. I don't know why. I just didn't. Grace disappeared after she dropped me off, and I spent the evening reading, and the night alone. The water had leaked out of the cracked vase and the flowers had died. *Eyeless in Gaza* was just a bloody miserable bunch of words. I threw it aside without finishing it, promised myself the original Milton, and started in on Mr *Gatsby*. He was like an old friend, and I liked him immediately.

23. I Can't Give You Anything But Love, Baby

I made myself useful by giving Matesy a hand in the garden: he was weeding, and we reran the earlier scene.

'What are these, Matesy?'

'Early cabbages.'

'The knack is keeping the slugs off them now, and the butterflies later on,' I told him.

'How did you know that? Are you good at this lark?'

'Fair. I have a pretty good teacher.'

Matesy laughed at me. There was a heavy dew, and the ground steamed moodily in the sun.

When I had half a bucket of slugs for the compost heap we washed our hands under an outside tap and stopped for a smoke. The principle of the smoke break is the British Army's greatest contribution to the industrialized society. The tobacco that Herman had given me was that old Sweet Chestnut. I hadn't been able to get it for a year. I savoured its marvellous nut-laden smoke, more convinced than ever that God is a pipe smoker. We were still sitting there when Grace sauntered out.

I started with, 'Hello. Where did you get to?'

'Had to see a man about a dog.'

'The man was a giant redhead, I take it, and his throbbing dog was probably as big as my arm?'

'You're just plain jealous. Anyway, it didn't work out. Victoria chased me off the ship with one of the cook's knives. The cook stood there laughing.'

'His name is Galliano,' I told her. 'You can't win them all, Grace.'

'I can have a bloody good try. I told Herman that she'd better be off the ship before I—' She stopped in mid-sentence: most un-Grace-like.

'Before you *what*, Grace?'

'Oh . . . before I see him again, I suppose,' she told me evasively.

I suppose, my arse! Grace didn't tell that many lies, but when she did you saw them coming on like a 157 bus. But it was always as well not to challenge her, because she would only get stroppy and make your life a misery.

'So what about you? How long are you going to stay for this time?' she asked, her voice laden with sarcasm for some reason. She had this terrific ability to completely sod something up and then blame you for it. I've met other women who can do that.

'Maybe later today or tomorrow. I'm waiting for news of an old friend.' I gave her the look, and for once it was Grace who dropped her gaze first. That was interesting.

*

Grace flapped around me a bit, but there's no one more irritating than someone who's not that hard to get *playing* at it – if you see what I mean? So I got my things together and pushed off. Before I left I found Matesy in the kitchen and gave him a quid for the kid: two ten-bob notes.

'I meant to get him something, but I don't have time,' I explained.

'That could be more than he's ever had in his hand before – they were never well off.'

'You'll help him with it then?'

''Course I will. Thanks.'

'You don't have to say it's from me.'

'Yes, I do. He needs to know who his friends are. That's more important than the money when it comes down to it.'

He was already sounding like a father. Or rather, how I supposed a father *should* sound.

I had decided not to phone Piers from the usual box, and that was a good call because not long after I had turned away from it I met Harry walking in the opposite direction. He still looked glad to see me, so I guess that Grace hadn't grassed me up yet.

'Off again?' he asked. 'You cover more miles than a lace-underwear salesman. Where you going?' He produced a tup-penny bag of aniseed balls, offered me one, and tossed one up in the air to catch in his mouth. It hit his teeth as he lunged for it.

'Just up-country. Perry Bar, near Birmingham. Someone told me about a big house-clearance; you never know what's on offer.' My gran had been in service there before the First World War: it had been the first place that popped into my head. Harry didn't believe me – which was all right because I wasn't telling the truth, was I?

'Back next week? We could have that party then.'

'Yeah. Why not? If I've made a decent profit I'll have something to celebrate.'

'OK – and us: you know about Matesy and Susannah, don't you?'

'Susannah?'

'Gary's mum.'

'Oh, yeah. I was pleased. They all look happy.'

'They are: one of my success stories. We should celebrate for them, too.'

Later I realized that there had been one of *His* little clues in there for me, but as usual I bloody missed it: the name's everything. I walked away from Harry, feeling like a louse. Well, that's what traitors are supposed to feel like, aren't they?

I walked to Kentish Town for the exercise, and phoned Piers from the public call box in the Tube station. The girl who answered the phone had never heard of him, of course.

'I don't care!' I told her. 'Just tell him Charlie's gone back to the flat and will wait there until he hears from him.' Then I put the receiver down on her.

Both the girls were out, but the flat had signs that they were not that far away. There were dirty dishes in the sink, and clothes were spread around the main room in gay abandon, although maybe we're not allowed to use the word that way any more. I enjoyed tidying them up, and identifying which belonged to whom, until I reached a man's Aertex double act which I dropped in the waste bin under the kitchen sink. That was mean-minded, so I fished the items out again and tossed them into the bathroom laundry basket. That reminded me to bathe. I lay in a bath for an hour until the water cooled around me. The soap made it smell like the Windmill Girls were in there with me.

Even Piers noticed when he sloped in. 'Get yourself a decent cologne, old man. You smell very cheap. Mister Crabtree's Sandalwood is probably about your mark; they've just started making it again.'

'Have you noticed how often everyone uses the word "probably" these days?'

'It's *probably* because no one is sure of anything any more. How did you get on?' Before I could answer he added, 'Thanks for the Williamson thing, by the way. Very neat. Startling, but very professional. I'm no longer sure that I should let you go.'

'What Williamson thing?'

'Don't be so coy, old boy: he phoned me this morning. You must have set it up.'

'So he's OK?'

'Of course he is. If being in Geneva is all right: it's where he called from.'

'What's he doing over there?'

'Fund-raising, he says. Then he resigned from the Empire, and sent us his best wishes.'

'Fund-raising for whom?'

'He wouldn't say, but it's got to be for your little band of malcontents, hasn't it? I always wondered where their dough came from.' The word 'dough' didn't come easily to Piers. He must have been rattled.

'Are you sure that it was him?'

'Definitely. He called me all sorts of authentic names. I remember them well.'

'And are you sure that he was in Geneva?'

'Absolutely. The cunning old dear called from a public phone in the main railway station, then held the telephone away from him so that I could hear the station announcements. Swiss German and French are exceptionally ugly languages; the first time I heard spoken Swiss I was reminded of drunks vomiting in a lavatory.'

'So that's cleared that up. I wonder why he ran.'

'They turned him, of course. Your old Commie can be a real clever clogs when he puts some effort into it: make sure that he doesn't turn you too.'

'Fat chance of that,' I said, and sniffed.

'Mmm . . .' Piers made that steeple of his fingers and watched me over them. He obviously wasn't as sure as I was, and I felt curiously vulnerable. 'How *did* you manage to get him to call in, old man?'

How could I say 'Search me'? The bugger probably would have done.

'I dropped a couple of hints to Grace,' I said. 'That was all. I didn't expect a result that quickly.'

'Bully for you, old man. Bra-vo.' Others have said 'Bravo' to me in the past. It had always meant quite the other thing. Piers said it quietly, and for that reason it sounded very threatening. 'Has your woman agreed to take that job with Bennet, by the way? He won't keep it open for ever; loads of bods want to fly with him. God knows why – the man's distinctly dangerous.'

'I'll get an answer from Grace within the week,' I assured him.

'That might be a bit tight, old man.'

'That's up to you, Piers. Do you want her out of it before you strike, or not?'

He held both hands up in mock surrender. 'Whatever you say, old cock; only don't take too long. My masters won't withhold the whip for ever: one way or the other she'll have to take the fence.'

'Do them good to wait for once.'

'Dare say you're right, old man.'

'I'd better be,' I told him. 'Otherwise I'll get my arse kicked again, won't I?'

Piers didn't deny it. He'd brought a suitcase with him: one of those nice battered leather ones covered in travel labels. It might have been a dozen times around the world.

I asked him, 'Where are you off to now?'

'Back to the office, I suppose. The case is for you. I had one of the drones pick up all the clothes you ordered last month. I knew you'd forget.'

'Thank you, Piers. What do I owe you?'

'Not much – and forget it, anyway. I'll set it against your first expenses claim.'

'I didn't know that I had any.'

'Oodles, old son . . . oodles. Dolly will run one up for you; just sign it in the places she shows you, and don't question any of the detail.'

'That sounds a bit crooked, Piers . . .'

'What was it you were telling me a little while ago? "We are the Nazis now" . . . I expect you're right, old boy: they were pretty crooked too, weren't they?'

'I'll get the suitcase back to you.'

'Don't bother, old chum. We found it on a bomb-site with a dead baby in it. Washed it – the case, that is – of course, but you can keep it if you like.'

I'll tell you something that made me feel stupid. I went to the station by way of a small shop in the West End and bought a bottle of their sandalwood cologne. It cost nearly a week's pay – but it was only money.

I slept on the train, was in Cheltenham by mid-afternoon and took a taxi to the funny farm. At least the sun had stopped shining. The driver refused payment once he knew our destination; he presented me with a small book of receipts to sign. I could get used to working for Piers if I didn't have to pay for anything for the rest of my life.

Ming met me at the guardroom. 'I thought that you were on leave for a week, sir. Didn't we tell you not to come on duty when you're not expected?'

'Ming, I come and go as I please. It's one of the rules.'

'What rules would they be, sir?'

'*My* rules. Either the RAF obeys them, or finds someone else to sit in their aeroplanes.'

'I don't think that you'd risk that, sir.'

'And I don't think that you'd risk me trying it on.'

'I'll sign you in. Nice to see you again, Mr Charlie.'

'And you, Ming. What time are you off today?'

'1815, sir.'

'I'd appreciate a lift home, if it doesn't take you out of your way.'

His big face creased up like a great smiling sun. 'My pleasure, sir. I'll be able to claim the petrol.' Were all these buggers at it?

Miller was sitting at my desk. She scowled when I came in. 'I thought that you were off for a week.'

I threw my hands up in the air in disgust. 'Why isn't anyone pleased to see me?'

'At least the Commander will be . . .'

'I'm pleased about that.'

'Because now that you're back you'll be flying on Friday,' she added, frowning. She pushed the brown envelope across the desk to me. 'He thought that he would have to do it himself, and he gets airsick these days.'

Sometimes I remember the things I'm supposed to: I had made more than one purchase at the pong shop. I pushed the small wrapped box, containing a stone jar of perfumed cream, across the desk to her. I kept my hand on it. I said, 'I bought this in Town. I hope that it doesn't embarrass or compromise you. I hope that you like it. The salesgirl said that it would last for a year if you were careful.'

One of her pauses, and then Miller put her hand over mine. 'Thank you, Charlie.' The good old Prince of Denmark again: *A hit, a very palpable hit.*

I didn't push it with her. I left her at my desk, and wandered off to see Old Farmer Watson. She'd been right. He was pleased to see me.

'Hello, Charlie. You back?'

The RAF always picks people who are quick on the uptake for command rank: have you noticed that? It works every time.

'Yes, sir. London was a bit quiet. I didn't know what to do with myself. I smashed my car up on the way there.'

'So I heard. The MT section was a bit miffed after all the work they'd done on it.'

'I managed to get them a couple of bottles of Dimple Haig . . .' In fact, I'd nicked three that belonged to the girls. They had so many that they'd never miss them. If they did, I'd pay up, and apologize for forgetting to tell them. 'Has anything happened while I've been off, sir?' I asked Watson.

He mumbled a bit, and thought about it. 'You know that there's a listening station down at Southsea, don't you?'

'Yes. They're supposed to triangulate the Jedburgh signals with us, to see if we can get a fix on their location. It never works.'

'Quite so. They have another comfy little job. They relay the Navy meteorologist's shipping forecast to any naval vessel in home waters twice a day.' I didn't see which way this conversation was going, so I just looked intelligent and nodded. It always fools them. 'The problem is that their weather signal has been temporarily and deliberately blocked by one of your ruddy Jedburghs for the last few days. Tit for tat. On the one occasion Southsea were able to ask why, they received the big kiss-off, and were told, "Ask Charlie." Want a drink?'

'Yes please, sir. While you're fixing it, I'll try to work out how much I can afford to tell you if I want to keep my rank.'

'Good man.'

I escaped an hour later. I still had my rank. Watson thought that it was a bit of a lark. So did I. I always feel uneasy when I find myself in agreement with superior officers. I like the fact that the acronym for superior officers has always been SO – just like the one for *sod off*. I spent great chunks of my service life just wishing that they would.

Miller hadn't left yet. Both huts were monitoring Red trawlers. The Red trawlers were probably monitoring us. At least that made it nice and cosy. I had this picture in my head of radio-monitoring officers all over the world listening to each other's silences through headphones, each waiting for the other to speak first, like a shy couple out on a date. When I stood alongside her I could just get a faint whiff of the perfume. Jasmine or roses – I couldn't make up my mind.

'I want you to come out with me. Properly. For dinner and a show up in Town. Something like that.'

She looked at her feet. 'No, Charlie. You know I can't do that.'

'Why not?'

'Because it wouldn't be right. I can't explain.'

'You can sleep with me, but not go out with me?'

'Yes. That's it. Do you understand?'

'No, I don't. But it doesn't matter.' I shrugged. It actually mattered an awful lot, but I wasn't about to tell her that. I could see Ming coming up the path. 'That's my lift coming. See you tomorrow.'

'Fine,' she replied shortly.

Charlie had buggered it up again. Neither of us left happy.

*

I had a smaller jar for Bella. I gave it to her in front of Ming so there would be no misunderstanding.

She flushed with pleasure. 'What's this for, Charlie?'

'Dabbing between your whatsits, they tell me.'

'Don't be daft. I mean what's it *for*?'

'It's for being an ace landlady. Thanks.'

Ming said, 'Nobody brings me presents, do they?' He was just pulling my leg. I produced the third bottle of Dimple. 'Yes, they do, Ming. There you are. Thank you for looking after me.'

'Thanks, Charlie. I can see I'm going to have to have a proper word with Mr Watson.'

'What about?'

'Ask him to send you on leave more often. This is just like Christmas.'

We drank cloudy cider around the table until the world took on a rosy glow.

Of all the Lincolns I had climbed into in the last couple of months this old lady, under her blanket of drizzle, was the oldest and most careworn. She showed us what she thought of us right from the start, when her port inner refused to fire up. The huge prop turned over a couple of times in response to a few weak coughs from the exhaust stubs, but that was it. The smoke that dribbled out of them was white: she had elected a new Pope. Maybe this one wasn't a Nazi.

We all piled out again, and stood in a huddle under her wing waiting for the bus to collect us. Turnaway Tim was still doing our driving, a quiet new Welsh bomb aimer called Walters sat in the greenhouse at the front, and there was Perce's replacement, of course. He was another Welshman: overweight and voluble – a real Land of My Fathers type. He told us his name was David, but that everyone called him Dai – short for Dire Straits because he brought bad luck to anyone he flew with. He told me that as we were introduced, and I wished he'd kept his trap shut. He was right, though: the aircraft must have turned against him before he even threw a switch on the radar array, because it had refused the first fence.

I asked Tim, 'They'll have a replacement kite for us, won't they, sir?'

'You'd have thought so.'

'What does that mean?'

'That I don't know, so shut up, Charlie, and wait and see like the rest of us.'

The crew bus smelled of fresh vomit. I was beginning to get a bad feeling about flying today. We were taken back to our ready room: a small Nissen hut not too far from the dispersal. Someone had run the stove up so hot that the larger droplets of drizzle hissed and evaporated on the hut's metal outer skin. It was wreathed in steam.

'I'm not going in there,' I told them in all seriousness. 'When aircraft get that hot they bloody burn.'

'Don't be such an old woman, Charlie.' That was from Morgan the Navigator. I still didn't fancy him much, and if our aircraft needed to be abandoned in the cold night sky I didn't fancy his chances of getting to the door in front of me. 'We'll leave the door open for you if you like. Just let's get in out of the rain.'

'Rain is good,' I muttered. 'Kites don't burn so well in the

rain. I love the rain. The SS ran their crematoria at lower temperatures than that room.'

'*Charlie* . . .' That was Turnaway Tim putting his oar in again.

'OK, Skipper. I know when I'm outgunned.' I stood just inside the door.

'Run this past me again,' Dai Straits asked us. 'Explain why we are recording ground radar profiles in deepest France.'

Tim told him, 'The French are our allies, but if Ivan decides to roll west our Gallic friends will put up just as firm a resistance as they did last time. They will surrender immediately: it's what they're exceptionally good at.'

'So we'll bomb the brown stuff out of them?'

'No. Whether we'll bomb them or not is something I don't know . . .'

'I'm all in favour of it,' I said. 'I met some artists in Paris who paint with their tadgers: we ought to stamp *that* out, for a start.'

There were muffled guffaws from the rest of the crew and a 'Shut up, Charlie' from the boss. 'Even if we don't bomb the Frogs,' Tim explained, 'we'll need to overfly their country to bomb somebody else, won't we? So we are profiling the navigation Way Points that we'll need to plan missions against the Hun. Sorry – slip of the tongue – I mean the Russians. That's the theory of it, anyway.'

'If the French are just going to surrender again,' I asked him, 'why did they bother to accept their country back in the first place? Why don't they let some other sods run it for them, and just live there for free?'

'I don't know, Charlie.' There was impatience in his voice. 'I'll get Nye Bevan to ask them the next time he's over there.'

'And if we're only out there navigation profiling, why do we always take a bomb aimer?' *Let's see how he gets out of that one*, I thought.

'Charlie, why are you being such an obnoxious little shit tonight?'

'I don't know, Boss. I think that it's something to do with not wanting to fly with you any more. Can I go home now?'

'No, you bloody can't. You're bloody well coming to France with me.'

'It's because we're doing target profiles as well, isn't it?'

Pin-drop time.

Eventually Tim said, 'I warned you, Charlie . . .' But he wouldn't look me in the eye. He shuffled his feet around, and watched them moving.

'Warnings don't work with me any more, Skipper,' I told him. 'They must have told you that. I've been inside worse prisons than you could ever dream of, and if you threaten to ground me I'll kiss you for it. Do the French know that we're coming?'

'This is insubordination, Charlie . . .' Tim was almost blustering now.

'And frankly, my dear, I don't give a damn: I'm almost demobbed. I heard something like that in a film once. Do they *know* we're coming, Tim?'

He whispered, 'No.'

I didn't whisper as I turned away. I said, 'Fuck it.' Then, 'And fuck the brass, and fuck the Frogs.' I swung back on him angrily. 'Can you give me one good reason why I should carry on with this mad lark, sir?'

My old skipper wouldn't even have bothered to explain that orders are orders: he would have clouted me one, and carried me onto the aircraft under his arm. Tim didn't. He looked at me, and did something more effective. He said quietly, 'Because you'll be letting us down if you don't, Charlie.'

Pin-drop time again.

'You're a right bastard, sir,' I sighed.

'Good. I've always wanted to be one of those.'

The crew bus splashed up to the door again, and Sergeant Ramsden stood in the door like a Labrador, shaking the rain from his cape. He spoke formally to Turnaway. 'The reserve aircraft will be ready in about five minutes, sir. We've been asked to get you over there. The bomb load has been transferred over.'

I spoke to Walters for the first time. 'What bomb load?'

He blushed. 'We sometimes fly with a bomb load, didn't you know? It shows the Reds that we mean business.'

'But not this time,' Tim butted in. 'This time we have a load of paper, just for ballast. Is there anything else you need to know before we fly, Charlie?'

'How about how to say "I give in", in French?'

'Something like *je cede*, I think, but duck before you say it: the French aren't all that used to taking other folks' surrenders yet. They'll probably mess it up, and shoot at you first. Can we get on now?'

In the bus Dai Straits asked me, 'Why is it important that the French do or don't know that we're coming?'

'Because if they don't know who we are they'll assume the worst, and start shooting at us.'

'They'll think that we're Russians?'

'No. They'll think that we're English. That's much worse.'

'I don't understand.'

'That's because you've never been liberated. Don't worry – Tim will probably get us back.'

So we were an hour or so late for Death. Death wasn't all that amused: he must have spent far too long in the company of Queen Victoria.

This is how it happened. We were held on the strip for another half-hour waiting for the weather. In my experience that never does much good. It gave me time to light up my boxes, check them until I was bored and then move up to look over Morgan's shoulder. He was friendlier now than the first time we'd sortied together, but ours was always going to be a marriage of convenience.

'Isn't it odd? You're called Morgan, but you're about as English as they come, and our Welsh bomb aimer is Walters . . . which is pretty English.'

'Norman French, actually, after the Fitzwalters who came over with William the Conqueror. Walters will feel at home where we're going.'

'Where *are* we going this time?'

'Weren't you listening at the briefing?'

'No, I was looking up the skirt of the WAAF who came in with the CO. I regret that now.'

'We're going low-level to Hamburg. We refuel there; some kind of practical exercise to see if it would be possible to do it with a squadron. Then we fly down the jolly old border we're so familiar with already. Then turn west and fly across France at our maximum ceiling, finally turning north to dear old Blighty. Your oppo will be plotting and profiling all the way, of course. No peas for the wicked.'

'How far down the border are we flying?'

'To Zicherie and Bochwitz. They used to be German villages joined to each other once, but now the border cuts between the two of them, although everyone's been pretty relaxed about that so far. They must be important to somebody, because we have to dive just across the border if no one's looking, and approach them from the north as if we were doing a bombing run. It will probably scare the shit out of somebody.'

Yeah, me, I thought. 'What about the bombing height?'

'Ask Walters. 'Bout fifteen thou', I think.'

'I wish we wouldn't do that sort of thing. If I was a Red, this would really piss me off.'

'But it keeps Ivan on his toes, doesn't it?'

I didn't want Ivan on his toes; boxers get up on their toes just before they clobber their opponents. The problem was that I didn't know how to put that into the simple words that Morgan would understand.

Hamburg was all right, although we opened the back door on a fine veil of drizzle. Just like England. I realized that I had no way of knowing where we actually were, because one airfield looks pretty much like another, you know. Maybe Tim had flown us cunningly to a big redundant airstrip in Wales or somewhere.

I stood under the raised canopy of the Red Cross canteen wagon that had come out to refuel the crew. A harassed-looking ground crew refuelled the aircraft. Nutty Neil stood alongside me and blew on his mug of coffee.

'How do we know we're in Hamburg, Neil? We could be in Iceland for all I know.'

'No. It's snowing in Iceland, and the girls have bigger tits.'

'How do you know it's snowing in Iceland?'

'It's *always* snowing in Iceland.'

'And how do you know the girls have bigger tits? Have you been there?'

'Nah, but I know some Yank who has. You know that it's dangerous to shag outdoors in Iceland?'

'Why?'

'As soon as you withdraw your plonker it freezes solid. Then you have to be careful not to knock it off. One guy had a hard-on for eleven months.'

'Why eleven months?'

'That's how long the winter lasts in Iceland. The odd month is spring, summer and autumn all rolled up into one.'

'You're nuts, Neil.'

'Flying with you, Charlie? I must be.'

'You like a hot dog, boys?' the Red Cross girl serving us asked.

'Iceland's national dish,' I told Neil.

He leered, but at the girl, not at me. She was dark, tall and a bit on the rangy side. She looked tired and hungry, and I wouldn't have made fun of her.

Neil asked her, 'If I buy one, can I put my hot dog in your roll?'

She had a quick grin. 'That's *clever*.' Somehow she made one eyebrow stand to attention: that was a neat trick. 'I haven't heard that one before. I was only serving hot dogs for two years, and I never heard that joke before.'

'OK, OK.' Neil waved his free hand. 'It's an old joke and I'm sorry – and yes, please.'

'Please?'

'I'll have a hot dog.'

I asked her, 'How do we know this is Hamburg, and not some other city?'

'When the rain lifts you can still smell the smoke from the buildings you burned; OK?' OK. She was sharp enough.

'If I come back can we have a date?'

'No. You're too small.'

'I could grow up if you waited.'

She shook her head and smiled. 'No, you RAF boys never grow up.' That was all we were going to get.

Twenty minutes later you could have seen a huge ball of spray belting along the runway. I was somewhere inside it.

We flew through the weather front and out the other side. A late moon cast a cold light on a damp countryside. The Lincoln droned south like a drunk in a coma. It was quite like old times, but something was not quite right. It took me half an hour to work it out: there were *lights* visible on the ground. Towns and cities. So, *no*: not quite like old times. I heard an aircraft on the other side talking to his controller; he seemed to be pacing us, so whoever he was he could fly slow and still stay up in the air.

I clicked. 'Skipper, it's Charlie.'

Click. 'Yes, Charlie?'

'There's someone out there. I can smell him.'

'Bears?'

'No. Jerries.'

'Does he bear us ill will?'

'Don't know, Skip. He seems to be pacing us, but over on their side.'

'Let me know if he does anything . . . Dai, wake up. Can you see him?'

Click. 'Yes, Skip. I have him now. Something big like us.'

'Is he a beacon? Anything smaller homing in on him?'

'No, Skip.'

'Let me know if he does anything – and bloody well stay awake.'

'Yes, Skip.'

I turned in my seat and tapped Dai on the shoulder. He lifted the side of his helmet so that he could hear me.

'Sorry, chum. I should have asked you first,' I told him. 'We didn't have people like you in my day.'

He grinned. 'Don't worry about it.' He put his finger against a vertical blip on one of his small screens. 'There he is. He'll turn away from us in a few minutes. Back towards Berlin.'

'How do you know? Have you seen him before?'

'No. I just know: it's a feeling I get.' As Dai spoke the blip started to move across the screen and away from his finger. I turned away from him and got back to work.

Click. 'Skip, it's Dai.'

Click. 'Aye, Dai.'

Someone clicked, and sniggered. I think that it was the engineer.

Turnaway snapped, 'Shut up, that man. What was it, Dai?'

'It's OK, Skip. It's turned away. On his way home.'

I clicked. 'Charlie. His signal's fading.'

'Well done, chaps . . . tally ho.'

Prat.

When I was a boy we had an ancient Airedale dog. He was named Rip, because he came from Ripon in Yorkshire. He was so bad at catching the mice in our kitchen that every time he lunged for them with his great open mouth they would jump through his jaws as if engaged in some bizarre sport. His mouth would snap shut with a *clack* as his teeth met on nothing, and I would look up from my book knowing that Rip had missed another one. In my opinion we were just about to try the aviation equivalent of that: a quick dash into Ivan's territory and out again before his jaws snapped shut on us. The AVMs wouldn't dream up such stupid bleeding stunts if they had to do them themselves.

Morgan warned the Skipper of our course change about three minutes before it was due, and told him to turn to it 'on my mark'. Surprisingly, it worked. Almost immediately he clicked and said, 'We are in enemy airspace.' *Enemy*? Since when? That had been a turn to fly almost due east. Four minutes later we turned south, and Morgan sang out, 'OK, Bombs. She's all yours.'

Walters ran through the drill that came back to me from a couple of years ago. *Fly right, left, up a bit, down, down*. That didn't upset me. What upset me was when he clicked and said, 'Bomb doors open' in the middle of it.

Tim responded with 'Bomb doors open.'

And a minute later Walters clicked and shouted, 'Switches on. Red light; green. Bombs gone. Close bomb doors.'

'Bomb doors close,' confirmed Tim.

Almost immediately Morgan sang out, 'Friendly airspace . . . *now.*'

I had distinctly felt the old cow lurch upwards at '*Bombs gone*', so whatever had been in the bay was now in Germany, and *we* had just attacked the Soviet Zone.

Fuck it.

I clicked, and heard someone breathing very deeply. I worked out that it was me. The hairs on the back of my neck would have stood up if I hadn't been wearing a helmet.

'Skipper, it's Charlie. Permission to come forward?'

'Later, Charlie. Just make sure that no one is talking about us first.'

'Roger.' I wondered what the difference was between mutiny and wresting command from a mad pilot and his bomb aimer. There was a problem: if Tim took the huff and went on strike there was no one else who could fly the damned thing.

He let me into the office as we crossed the German border into France. Morgan clicked, 'C'est le Nav. Ici la France!' He sounded euphoric. I couldn't see what about: his French was atrocious.

I couldn't believe that we had made it this far without someone shooting back at us. On the way up to the office I looked over Morgan's shoulder as I asked him, 'Where are we?'

He laid his finger on a line drawn on his map which crossed into France north of Haguenau, in miles of open country, and grinned as if someone had told him a joke. He was taking us deep into France over Nancy, Sens and Orleans before turning north for home and brekkers.

The office was almost a haven of peace and tranquillity. Tim was munching a Piccalilli sandwich, and had a thermos top of coffee in his hand. The engineer patted me on the back as I squeezed in. George, the automatic pilot, was flying the kite and we were up in the cold stuff at twenty-three thou. I couldn't understand why they were all so terribly pleased with themselves. 'Skipper, snap out of it! We just attacked the Soviets. Were we *supposed* to start World War Three, or was that just something you thought up on the spur of the minute?'

'Nobody's going to start anything, Charlie. Don't be such a windy old woman.'

'We just bombed a village in the Soviet Zone—'

'With Bibles.'

'What did they do to deserve . . .?' My question petered out as I took in what he'd just said.

'Two villages with one vicar; split in two by the new border. The vicar asked the RAF to drop a load of Bibles for the ungodly on the other side.'

'And the RAF risked our lives for that?'

'The RAF is always on God's side, Charlie. Go back to your boxes now, and have your supper. Sing out if the Frogs start talking about us.'

He seemed calm and collected, and directed a very level gaze at me.

'Yes, Skip,' I said. 'Sorry.'

I had just strapped into my seat, rubbing backs with Dai, and was unwrapping a neat package of sandwiches. I never had time to discover their filling. There was an enormous explosion somewhere up front, and the gale that was suddenly blowing through the fuselage blew my food out of my hands. I knew it; I *had* been in this film before. The aircraft began pitching up and down like a roller coaster. I locked down the Morse key into transmit, and struggled forward.

We were tilted slightly down, so must have been losing height. In the office the engineer was still on his seat, but hunched forward with his hands over his eyes. The noise was tremendous, and the air rushing into the aircraft was pushing me off my feet. There was nothing in front of Tim's feet except his pedals. Nothing at all. Just cold French air. Tim was covered in blood from head to foot, and there was a lot of it sloshing around everywhere. He shouted, 'Not mine.'

I shouted back, 'Where's Walters?'

'Blown up. Flak, I think.' Tim's eyes were very wide and bright. 'Give me my 'chute, clip his on –' he nodded at the engineer 'and fling him out. Get everyone out, and go yourself.'

I must have frozen for a moment. Blood was blowing into the slipstream in strings of globules from where it had accumulated on the surfaces around us. There was an arm in a flying jacket behind the Skip's seat. I'd have sworn that it was still clenching and unclenching its fist. '*Now!*' Tim screamed.

I did it without thinking. The front of the Lincoln, with Walters's glasshouse and the front turret, had gone completely. English flak had taken off *Tuesday*'s rear turret just as neatly in 1944. Now it was the bloody Frogs. I clipped on the engineer's 'chute, put the ring in his hand and rolled him forward. He simply disappeared. I touched Tim's shoulder as I went back. He was still flying the kite as well as he could. Morgan had already gone, and Dai was going. I helped the mid-upper gunner down, and pushed him in front of me. I had forgotten his name. As they jumped I hammered on the rear turret door. There was no response, but I noticed that the gunner's 'chute was missing from its stowage. Neil hadn't hung around waiting for the order.

That left me. I couldn't remember clipping the 'chute on, but it was there, so I swung my legs over the sill and was pulled away by the slipstream before I knew it. I flinched as a huge dark rudder fin slashed past my face. I tumbled for a five-count, and then lost my nerve and pulled the ring. Another five-count, or so it seemed, and then there was a soft bang, and when I got my breath back and looked up there was a round silk canopy hanging above me in a starry sky. I couldn't help myself: 'Oh you beauty!' I shouted to it.

I seemed to swing up and down, going nowhere. Occasionally the canopy tipped a bit and obscured the moon. My feet were cold. I couldn't remember how I'd lost my boots. My face was wet. That was because I was crying. I thought about pushing Miller against that office door and lifting her skirt. I know that I should have been thinking something useful, but that was what I was thinking about when I hit the deck. To each his own, I suppose.

I landed in a grass field alongside a black slow-flowing river. The field had a ruined shed in one corner. I hobbled over to it, pulling my 'chute behind me like a bridal train, too tired to unhook myself. The shed had once contained something like fine hay, and there was still a heap of it in one corner. I wrapped my parachute around me and went to sleep there.

24. Down by the Riverside

When I awoke in the morning an unfriendly girl of about seven was staring down at me. She held a three-pronged pitchfork about ten sizes too big for her.

'*Je cede*,' I told her.

She let me drink from the river before she turned me in.

The seven-year-old explained that she wanted me to walk in front of her by prodding me with the bloody fork. I carried my parachute. We went across the field and onto a country road. The single-street village she took me to was only a mile away, but I was through the bottom of my socks by then – men aren't designed to go far in bare feet. It got so that I was wincing with every step. She did an odd thing as we came onto the village street; she came up alongside me with her fork over her shoulder like a sentry's rifle and took my hand. That was the way I arrived at the small Gendarmerie: hand in hand with an agriculturally armed child. As I began to climb the three concrete steps to the building's blue door the girl relieved me of my parachute and walked away with it. Even when they're seven years old girls get their priorities right, don't they?

Police forces all over the Continent are overly fond of dark blue uniforms: have you noticed that? It must be a kind of club they belong to. The gendarme at the small desk was a heavy-set man with thinning brown hair and a small moustache. He was not Claude Rains, and his eyes did not twinkle with suppressed humour. This was not one of his Anglophile days.

My feet left bloody streaks on his grey linoleum. When I first spoke he waved me to silence, and concentrated on a form that he was completing. He wrote slowly and gnawed his lower lip.

I finally lost my patience and said, 'I'm cold, I'm hungry and I'm tired.'

He looked up from his writing for a moment and observed, 'You are also under arrest.' Then he went back to the form.

Fuck it! At least I should be used to being arrested, not like the other poor sods. For the first time I realized that I had assumed they had all made it. Now I began to wonder if they had.

The little girl had been kinder than I thought, because the local quack walked in minutes later with his nurse, who wore her number one whites. She had something like a wimple on her head. It had a small red cross on it. Maybe she sold hot dogs on the side, like the girl in Hamburg. They sat me in a hard old chair in the corner. The doctor examined me, and tut-tutted at the old burn scars on my shoulders. The nurse washed my feet, and anointed them with a strong-smelling yellow ointment. She bandaged them. The doctor produced a pair of canvas-topped soft shoes from his bag. They were too big for me, but the bandages filled the spaces.

Then something odd happened. When I went to stand up I

found that my legs had turned to jelly. The nurse grabbed my arm. The doctor moved the chair to face the policeman and his desk, and they helped me into it. The odd, literally legless feeling persisted for a few minutes. Then the doctor went to stand behind the policeman. Apparently 'You are also under arrest' had all but exhausted the gendarme's English vocabulary. The policeman spoke: the doctor translated for him. I replied, and the doctor translated for me. I probably could have managed more or less in French by then, but I wasn't about to tell them that.

The copper asked, 'And *you* are?' I rather liked the emphasis; it implied that one or more of the others might be around.

'Charles Aidan Bassett.'

'English?'

'Yes.'

'Royal Air Force?'

'Yes. Pilot Officer.'

'Your service number?'

'22602108.'

'You were the pilot?'

'I'm sorry, I can't tell you that.'

'When did you arrive in France?'

'I can't tell you that either. Name, rank and number. That's all I can say.'

Fatso had a sour look on his face. What he said next was fast, and sounded insulting. The doctor said, 'The officer wishes you to cooperate. He asks me to inform you that the war finished three years ago, and that when it did we were allies.'

'In that case please ask him why you shot down my aircraft.'

I got the first glimmerings of smiles. From both of them.

'He will put you in a cell now,' the doctor said.

I looked the copper in his piggy little eyes. 'J'ai faim,' I told him.

'Vous parlez Français?' The surprise in the piggy little eyes said it all. He would have been less startled if his dog had begun to sing the Marseillaise. I shook my head. I didn't want him to get carried away.

'Comme un enfant.' I shrugged a Gallic shrug, and smiled a rueful Gallic smile. They were both put-ons. You may not believe it, but in 1945 Picasso was among those who taught me how to do that. The copper didn't know that, so he emptied my pockets, took my ID tags, and locked me up.

They put me in a cell with Nutty Neil. Normally he was just the sort of cell-mate you would choose, but he stank of animals, and his uniform was caked with what looked suspiciously like shit. He had removed his flying jacket and was sitting on it. He had a black eye. After we got over being pleased to see each other I asked him, 'Did they beat you up?'

He shook his head and looked embarrassed. 'I fell into a pigsty. A pig kicked me; but that wasn't the worst thing.'

'What was?'

'The fucking thing tried to mount me. If the farmer hadn't come to see what all the commotion was about I would have been raped. How about you?'

'I was captured by a little girl who stole my parachute. Have you seen anyone else?'

'Tim's here. He's in a terrible state. He's got a head like a football.'

'What happened to him?'

'I don't know. He hasn't said anything – I'm not sure that he can. I think he's dying.'

There was a plain wooden bed under the single high barred window. I could just see out of the window by standing on the bed on tiptoe. I was looking out onto a narrow side street or alleyway. There appeared to be a few people about: it was probably the rush hour. Anyway, I shouted out to them, 'Au secours! Au secours! Je suis un aviateur anglais – *Au secours!*'

'Is that French?' Neil asked.

'No, it's something *like* French,' I replied. 'I just want to create a fuss. *Au secours!*'

You'll have realized by now that I'm not at all bad at creating fusses: in fact, I'm a natural. Our captors stormed back into the cell. The gendarme pushed Neil aside, dragged me down from the window, and bounced me across the cell and into a corner. I didn't take much bouncing. He was bigger than me. The doctor said, 'He wants to know what the matter is. Why are you shouting?'

'I want to see my Skipper. Mon capitaine. I know that he's here, *ici*, and I know that he's hurt.'

He translated that, then told me, 'The officer says no. He also says that if you keep shouting he will beat you until you are not conscious.'

'Please tell him that he will have to beat me every time I wake up. I will not stop shouting to the citizens until I see my officer.' I remembered that 'citizens' is a very big word in France.

Neil said, 'Blimey, Charlie.'

I quickly hushed him. 'Shut up, Neil. This isn't your show.'

By now my breathing had slowed to normal; so had the gendarme's. The doctor said, 'He wants you to speak French.'

'Tell him I would like to, but that my French is far worse than his English. We would not understand each other.'

The doctor translated this for me, and I don't know what was in the sentence but it worked. The copper gave his twitchy little smile again. Then he shrugged. Then he beckoned me to follow him. The doctor came too. Neil stayed in the cell. They let me see Tim through the bars of a cell down the corridor. He sat at one end of a wooden bed identical to the one on which I had been recently standing.

Morgan sat on the other end with his feet up, hugging his knees. He perked up when he saw me. 'Was that you, making all that noise?'

'Yes. You OK?'

'Not bad. Twisted my ankle a bit. How about you?'

'Fine, except I cut my feet walking here. Neil's with me. A randy pig gave him a black eye. What's happened to Tim?'

Neil had been wrong. Tim's head was bigger than a football. Most of the bulge was on his left side, and was lividly bruised. His left eye bulged too. He was staring ahead.

'I don't know. He doesn't say anything, and I think the swelling's getting worse. I've asked them to do something about him, but they just pretend they can't understand me.'

'Tim,' I tried. 'Speak to me, Tim.' He didn't even twitch. I'd swear that he could neither hear nor see me.

I turned to the doctor. 'This man is very badly injured. I have seen injuries like this before: if he doesn't go to hospital he will die.'

'Maybe. Where did you see a similar case?'

'I was one myself. I am telling the truth.'

The doctor spoke to the gendarme. Then he told me, 'He has instructions from the Ministry of the Interior to hold you all here until officers arrive from Paris. You flew a heavy bomber aircraft from Germany into France without notice or permission. It is a serious and difficult matter.'

So he knew that much already. I wondered how much else.

'You shot us down,' I shouted. 'Also without notice or permission. A little warning would have been nice. That is also a serious and difficult matter. We are supposed to be allies. This is a diplomatic incident and eventually it will be disposed of by diplomats. There is no reason for anyone else to die. Please tell the officer that if he will permit my captain to be taken to hospital to be treated at once, I will answer all of his questions. Paris will think him a hero; an ace interrogator.'

'Ace?'

'Exceptionally skilful.'

The copper was like me; he understood a lot more than he let on, because he immediately nodded, said, 'Oui!' and beckoned the nurse forward from where she had been standing at the end of the short corridor. Tim was walked away between her and the doctor. Morgan and I were locked in the cell with Neil – and I hoped that I'd done the right thing.

Where the fuck were the others?

Morgan said he didn't like it. 'We're not supposed to say anything, Charlie. Not even under torture or duress.'

Bugger that for a game of soldiers.

'I'm not prepared to let Tim die for dropping a box of Bibles into Soviet Germany. There are nobler causes to die for than that: we should save him for one of those. If the Boss Class wants to court-martial me for *that*, it's up to them: I don't care. It's not Tim's fault that the blokes in charge don't have a spare brain cell between the lot of them. What happened to you, anyway?'

'I was blundering around in a wood and stepped into a snare. Then I was caught by a gamekeeper looking for poachers. He had a bleeding great blunderbuss: I thought I was a goner for a moment.'

'Charlie was captured by a kid who stole his parachute,' Neil said. 'I was nearly shafted by a ruddy great pig. Do you think they'll let me sponge my clothes down? The stink makes me want to throw up. Does anyone know what happened to the others?'

'Walters blew up,' Morgan said. 'I still can't believe that I saw it without getting hurt myself. I had just leaned back, and was looking forward. I could see through the office to where Walters was sitting in the greenhouse with his back to me. There was a sudden flash – not a very bright one – and everything else happened in slow motion. Walters's body just seemed to get bigger and bigger. Then he exploded. I think that the shell actually exploded inside him. He went everywhere. Christ, I'm thirsty – have they given you anything to drink yet?'

'Walters, Walters everywhere,' Neil said, 'and not a drop to drink.' It was just the way he was. I should have seen that one coming. So should you.

'What about Dai?' I asked.

'He passed me on the way down,' Morgan said. 'His parachute

had candled, and he was doing a couple of hundred miles an hour. He looked as if he was singing.'

'That's the Welsh all over.' That was Neil again. 'Any excuse for a song. He didn't make it, then?'

'I don't see how he could. What about old Tone?'

'Never saw him.'

Tony: the mid-upper's name came back to me. 'Neither did I,' I told them. 'What about what's-his-name, the engineer?'

Neither had seen him.

I sat on the floor near the bars and contemplated my future. It had just disappeared on me – but at least it had lasted longer than Walters's. I thought of the uncomplicated girl I slept with once, in that room over the garage near Oxford. I missed her already. It's a funny old world.

My little captor turned up at noon and brought me some dinner: a hunk of grey cheese, a rough loaf of bread and half a bottle of an even rougher red wine. I thanked her gravely, wondering how I was going to divide it into three, when Neil's pig farmer walked in. Neil got the same sort of bread and the same sort of wine, and a paper poke of ends of ham. The gamekeeper brought Morgan a couple of slices of cold game pie. When the doctor looked in on us after lunch I asked him, 'Why are those people being so kind?'

'They're not. Under French law the person who apprehends a criminal is responsible for their well-being until the examining magistrate brings a charge. They are only doing their duty.'

'I shall ask the King of England to send them a personal note of thanks.'

'You shouldn't laugh at them.'

'No. I shouldn't laugh at them.'

'Would you like to go for a walk?'

'All of us?'

'No – just you.'

I glanced at Morgan. He nodded. 'OK.'

There were no handcuffs or anything like that. The copper was eating at his desk as we went past him. He too had bread and ham, but he was spreading marmalade on it and was making a bit of a mess. He just waved a hand and nodded. Outside in the street only the children stared. The adults flicked quick glances at us and then looked away. I asked, 'Aren't you afraid I'll run?'

'You wouldn't get far with feet like that. Besides, you wouldn't desert your comrades, would you, comrade? Why don't we walk down to my house? It's just down there.'

We sat in the doctor's small consulting room and drank brandy from small glasses. He had two dark wings of hair below a shiny bald pate, although he wasn't an old man. With his large black-rimmed pebble specs and strangely formal clothes he looked as if he'd walked in from the last century. I don't know much about brandy, but it tasted all right to me. He called the small glasses his 'day glasses'. He also showed me his other brandy glasses: great bulbous bowls that could take about half a pint.

I asked him, 'How's Tim?'

'Tim?'

'My Skipper. My boss.'

'Ah. *Boss*. So *he* is the pilot. You were right, of course. The swelling has been drained, and he is conscious. I believe he will make a full *physical* recovery.'

'Can I see him?'

The doctor paused before he said, 'No.'

'Why not?'

'Because it would do neither of you any good. He is talking fluently, but in a sing-song accent – you say that? *Sing-song*?'

'Yes. We say that. What do you mean?'

'He sounds like a Caribbean calypso singer. It is very entertaining. We haven't seen this before: he is very convincing – already a celebrity in the hospital.'

'You mean that he's gone barmy? Mad?'

'Yes. It is exactly what I mean. I wouldn't let him near an aeroplane for the time being. You say *time being*?'

'Yes, we say *time being* too.'

'Shall we have another glass?'

'Why not! Cheers. Why have you brought me here?'

'The officers from the ministry will not arrive until tomorrow. You offered information in exchange for your comrade's life, but, alas, our gendarme has very little English and has asked me to interrogate you. The Interior Ministry gave its permission.'

'So here you are, and here I am.'

'However, I made a telephone call to someone of my acquaintance before I came to get you, comrade. He asked me to cooperate with you.'

'With me? Not the gendarmes, or the ministry?'

'That is correct, comrade.'

'Why?'

'Why do you think, comrade?'

Sometimes I have these *slow* days: days when my brain never gets into gear. The day after an aircraft accident is often a slow day, in my experience. He had had to use the word four or five times before the penny dropped. He was looking into my eyes as it did, and leaned over to offer me his hand. 'Welcome to France, Comrade Bassett.'

My brain stopped altogether. All I could think of saying was, 'I was in France before: in early 1945 before the surrender. I met Picasso in Paris.'

The doctor smiled, and shook his head. 'Do not tell anyone else; knowing an artist is not a thing to be so proud of. I was with the Maquis.'

'Was?'

'*Am*. As you see, there is still work to do. Keeping the comrades out of the clutches of that fat pig of a policeman, for instance. I will relish his first heart attack.'

'I'm not going to tell you much.'

'I don't want you to tell me anything. I will make up a story to satisfy him, and you will refuse to say anything else. Perhaps then they will send you home.'

'How did you discover that I was a . . . a comrade?'

'The card you have in your wallet. I have a similar one myself, although I keep it in my safe. You should be a little more discreet . . .'

'I will; but carrying it on my person seems to have worked out this time.'

'But if I had been a *Petainist*? I would have shot you and claimed that you tried to escape – not so lucky then.'

'I understand.'

'Good. After I saw it, I made a call to someone who can check the identities of Party members. I do not know how. You are a recent member?'

'That's right. London: a few weeks ago.'

'In that case, congratulations.' Then he said, 'Excuse me,' and belched. It made him more human. 'Another brandy? In the old days, physicians swore by it.'

We probably got through the best part of a bottle. His nurse joined us after half an hour or so, and brought a plate of pickled walnuts. We sang 'The Internationale' and the 'Marseillaise' with brandy glasses in our hands before he took me back to the lock-up. I wasn't sure the two songs sat all that comfortably alongside each other, but I just la-la'd along with the tune. The nurse kissed us after that: I loved it. She had big soft rubbery lips. Then the doctor kissed me on both cheeks: that wasn't so hot. He slobbered a bit.

The copper was still eating when we got back. He wiped his moustache on the back of his hand as we walked in, and stood up. A shower of crumbs fell like snow.

'Ça va?' he asked the doc.

The doctor replied with six rounds of rapid Frog talk. He was too quick for me, but I knew enough by then to work out approximately what he was saying. Tim was the pilot, and I had cooperated, apparently. He said that he would put it all into a report for the next morning.

Fatso turned and beamed at me. He loved me. He said, 'Merci, m'sieur.'

'In that case, may I have my possessions back?'

The doctor translated for me. The gendarme shrugged, opened

a table drawer and from it gave me back my wallet, my loose change, the usual grubby handkerchief and my tags. Then he had second thoughts, took the tags back and pulled one off. That went back in the drawer. He grinned and tapped his nose with a fat finger. He wanted me to know what a clever fellow he was. I smiled. I could go along with that. I held my hand out for the survivor.

In the cell Morgan asked me, 'What did they do to you?'

'Bribed me with brandy.' I breathed out, close to his face.

'Jammy bastard. What did you tell them?'

'A load of old tosh.'

'What will happen when they find out?'

'They'll probably give us a bit of a scragging.'

'Don't worry, Morgan' – that was Neil. 'You'll say nothing – even under torture or duress.' Then he asked me, 'Did they tell you anything about the boss?'

'On the mend, apparently, but talking like a Jamaican.'

'He'll be having them on.'

'I wouldn't be too sure of that; the doctor isn't. He thinks that Tim's brain has been hurt.'

I could see that Morgan was already worried about being questioned: he had begun to bite his fingernails.

Our captors came back with supper for us: they'd obviously got together on it because we shared a decent rabbit stew, and one of those long narrow loaves of over-sweet bread. Fatso split us into separate cells for the night, and gave us blankets. Look on the bright side, Charlie: at least you're full, warm and safe for the moment.

*

Wrong.

They came for us at about three in the morning. Like thieves in the night. That's almost what they really were, I suppose. Fatso unlocked our cells. His white face was almost luminescent with fear. I had just about enough time to slip my feet into my soft shoes. We were ushered out into the gendarme's office, blinking in the artificial light. I was right: he looked sweaty and scared. I felt that way myself. That wasn't surprising because the three soldiers already there all had guns in their hands. I've told you before: there is something quietly impressive about these buggers in khaki who carry guns and *walk* everywhere.

The biggest one, who appeared to be in charge, carried a pistol. The other two had Stens. I'd fired a Sten before: it could spit out ten bullets before you'd finished a decent fart. The big fellow looked at the copper, and deliberately cocked his pistol. I supposed that this sort of thing had been commonplace in the war, because the gendarme clearly knew what was coming next. He impressed me by drawing himself erect, and looking his executioner in the eye.

Neil impressed me even more. He stepped between the two, and said to the pistolero, 'I don't know if you can understand me or not, chum, but there's no need for that. If there *is*, then you'd better do me as well – and here, too, because I ain't going anywhere if you have to kill him for it.'

One of those frozen moments that I have come to treasure. The big man and Neil tried to stare each other down. Neither won, but the former broke the spell by snarling, 'They told me that there was a mouthy one: you'll be Bassett.'

'No,' Neil told him, 'I'm t'other mouthy one: there're two of us. I'm the compassionate mouthy one you haven't been told about. Sorry.'

'OK. It's your funeral. Lock the cunt in his own cell, and then get yourself outside: your carriage awaits.'

It took me seconds to take in that he was speaking English. Well . . . Novocastrian, which is more or less English. He was probably used to giving the orders. 'Chop-chop.'

I went outside with Morgan, and one of the Stens. There was an American Dodge ambulance at the foot of the steps. One of the things I've learned not to like is an olive drab vehicle smothered in red crosses. Too many people have bled too much in them. But I liked this one, because the guy standing at the open back doors was someone I recognized.

'Good morning, Charlie.'

It was Joopeman. He looked healthier than at our last encounter.

'Hello, Ari. Where did you spring from?'

'About sixty miles south. Sorry it took so long to get up; the roads are full of holes, and they still haven't repaired all the bridges you lot knocked down in '44.'

'I mean, how did you know we were here?'

'Some clever booger left his kit on *transmit* as it fell out the sky, didn't he? I wonder who that was? Your office thought that I'd like to know where it landed. Gloria sends her love, by the way, and says get well soon.'

'I'm not ill. Gloria?'

'Third Officer Miller.'

'Oh. Miller . . .'

'She's promised me a date if I get you home.'

My head had probably stopped spinning, because I told him, 'I'd accept if I was you; I've been trying to get her to come out with me for months.'

Joopeman smiled. 'Get in the wagon, Charlie, you're holding things up.'

As I climbed in, half pushed by Morgan, Ari and finally Neil, I saw that Turnaway Tim was already there, strapped to a stretcher. His head was bandaged, but the bit of face I could see looked normal: he was snoring, and smiling like a cherub.

'He'll sleep until we're in England,' Joopeman said. 'He had the big needle.'

Dai was sitting jammed up into a corner. 'I sprained me knee,' he complained. 'When I fell into a sewage farm.' He'd managed to survive falling fifteen thou, with a fucked-up parachute, and somehow still saw the darker side of things. 'Do you think they'll give me a medal?'

'I fell into a pigpen,' Neil told him. 'I didn't exactly come up smelling of roses, either.'

'How are you going to get us out of France?' I asked Joopeman.

'Piece of piss.' His grasp of our vernacular wasn't all that bad for a Dutchman.

I might have worked out the exit strategy for myself, but I didn't, because I was still having a *slow* day. I should have worried about that; they didn't usually come in twos.

They told me later that the pick-up was near a small town

named La Petite Pierre. In 1947 we still had people who were good at that sort of thing.

You'd have thought that the war hadn't ended. We stood at the edge of a big grass field that was surrounded by trees. The Stens and their big man stood out on the field at the points of an imaginary letter L, and each turned on a torch aimed vertically into the sky as soon as they heard the aeroplane.

It was a battered old Hudson, patched and painted black. It bore no national markings, and bounced only once as it was put on the ground. The pilot gunned it round for take-off immediately. Whoever the bastard was knew his business, and didn't want to hang around.

Joopeman drove the ambulance up to the aircraft. I sat beside him, and Neil and Morgan rode the running boards. I could tell that the pilot was desperate for the off by the way he gunned the motors. We scrambled in, leaving Tim to the professionals. They shoved him onto the floor, and scrambled in after us. It looked like we were all going back together. After Neil had dogged the fuselage door shut, I pushed past everyone up to the office and took my seat behind the pilot and nav in the small radio bay. I did it by instinct. The only moment of misgiving I felt was when I saw the tree line rushing at us, outlined by the dawn behind it. The Hudson freed itself with a hop, a skip and a jump: not a conventional take-off, but any one that gets you into the sky is OK by me.

We circled the field once as we climbed away: the ambulance was already burning. It looked like a bright orange beacon below us. The navigator mumbled to the pilot on his left. That was probably the first heading. He looked as old as Wilbur or Orville, and worked from creased old maps in his lap. You knew that he was one of those types who had been around for ever, and who did it the old way.

There was something familiarly competent about the pilot. I waited until he had settled the noisy old bag into a gentle climb – to the east, oddly enough – and asked his back, 'Excuse me, sir, but after I say thank you for the rescue I've got to ask you: have we ever met before?'

'No, we ain't, son: not unless you're always getting into trouble. I'm forever pulling folks outta the holes they get themselves into.'

'But we haven't met before?'

'That's right, son, we haven't – and we'll never meet again. Even if we do.'

I suddenly twigged. 'Thank you, Randall.'

'That's all right, son.'

It was like an old boys' reunion.

The French would be looking for us at the coast, the navigator told me, and he didn't want to embarrass them. So they took us low-level back into Germany, and to Hamburg.

When we refuelled, the same tired old Red Cross canteen wagon came out to the hard standing. The same tired German woman was trying to shift her hot dogs.

'I told you we'd be back,' I told her.

'Yes, you did. But maybe you forgot your aircraft – and somehow there are not as many of you as went out, I think.' She must have been psychic. I was the only one who had stepped down for a cup of coffee. She looked sad. Maybe she always looked sad.

'What about that boy who joked about putting his hot dog in my roll?'

'He's OK. He's on the aircraft, sleeping. We're all very tired.'

'You tell him that next time he comes through Hamburg we'll talk about it.'

'OK. I'll tell him that.' I blew on the surface of the coffee and sipped it. 'What's your name?'

'Marthe.'

'You are a very pretty woman, Marthe.'

'I know.' But she still looked sad.

'How about giving me a date?'

'No. I said before.'

'Maybe I'll have a hot dog this time.'

That didn't work either.

The airfield they took us into looked familiar. They all do. If you've spent time in the RAF anything with runways, hangars and Nissen huts looks familiar. This one was on care and maintenance: it had been mothballed for at least two years. It was populated by ghosts: a *Mary Celeste* of airfields.

I've told you before that Claywell was an enormously accomplished pilot: he put the heavy Hudson on the deck as sweetly as silk drawers dropping away from a French stripper. Memories are made of landings like that. We were met by two RAF ambulances – sleek new Daimlers – an Army one-and-half-tonner, and one of those malevolent brown Austin staff cars.

Tim was whisked away first, in one of the blood wagons. He had woken up, smiled dreamily at everyone, but didn't know who he was. When I leaned over him to say goodbye he was humming a tune: I think it was a calypso. Neil, Dai and Morgan were ushered into the other one. The last I saw of Neil was his hand waving from a window. An Army officer got down from the lorry, and before he reached the aircraft the Jedburgh had drawn up in line on the tarmac. They came to a very smart *attention*, and their big guy saluted.

The officer saluted back. All he said was, 'Well done, Roland.' Then, 'Stand easy, boys, and welcome back.'

The genuine pleasure in his voice made you want to weep. Then I realized that we had done what he'd wanted someone to do for months: we'd got his team back. That was the good news. The bad news was what and who we had left in France in order to do so. I wondered about the top gunner whose name I had forgotten. Tony. Was he still evading on his own, or was he just a man-shaped hole in the ground somewhere?

The staff car was for me, of course. Dolly sat behind the wheel, trying not to smile. Piers was in the back, glowing with anger.

'What the fuck *happened* to you people out there?' he asked me. It was nice to be one up on him for a change.

25. Pasadena

Bella fell upon my neck, the way they do in books. Ming poured me a glass of cider – their stock seemed inexhaustible, and I never asked about it. Alison burst into tears and ran away to her room. I wasn't back from the dead, but I might as well have been Lazarus Bassett.

When I eventually went up in front of Watson he said, 'Funny old job, isn't it? No man can serve two masters, and all that.'

'Isn't that what we do most of the time, sir? We work for Piers on one hand, and the WD on the other.'

'Don't you think that Piers is War Department as well?'

'No, I don't,' I told him truthfully. 'I think that he's with some people way out on their own, somewhere halfway between GCHQ and the RAF. Some unit where the services dump their unreliables – which includes us, by the way. Where's Mrs Miller, sir?'

He ignored the question.

'I never asked about Piers myself,' he said gruffly. 'I thought it safer that way.'

I nodded impatiently. 'The need-never-to-know system? Where's Mrs Miller, sir?'

Watson studied the desk in front of him. 'You are going to get your wish, Charlie: you're going to be demobbed. I understand you've secured a senior radio operator's job with one of the new airlines. Congrats: wish that I was coming with you.'

I started to lose it. 'Sir, where's—?'

He cut me off. 'I heard you the first time, Charlie. I'm trying to phrase an answer. Shall we have a drink while I think about it?'

He wanted to know what it was like to visit France by parachute. I told him it was a bit rough-and-ready; not my idea of a Cook's Tour. When I got to the bit about the Jedburgh he said, 'They weren't a real Jedburgh, you know. I don't know who they were, but they weren't a *real* Jedburgh.'

'Can you explain that, sir? Unless it will take too long to phrase an answer.'

He gave me the look. I'd only said it to tell him that I hadn't forgotten.

'Real Jedburghs were just what you've already been told. Gallant gentlemen who linked up with partisans behind the lines in order to harass dear old Jerry. Your lot was something else: one of several groups that landed from a submarine in 1944, deliberately lost themselves, and then went Nazi-hunting – they forgot how to stop, that's all.'

'They were proper soldiers. I saw the officer who met them. He was old army – one of the old school. Anyway, I thought that there were at least two teams operating out there?'

'There were. The thinking is that the last chappies will jack it in off their own bat, now that they're on their own. I know that you didn't plan to finish it this way, Charlie, but there are a lot of people at the War House rather pleased with you.'

'I've just noticed what you said before, sir. Our German enemy is now *dear old Jerry* . . . whilst our Russian allies have become the dangerously threatening Reds.'

'Yes. The Red menace or the Red peril. I've heard talk of both. It's because you notice things like that, Charlie, that you'd be better off out of the service . . . although there's another reason.'

Ask me another. I didn't ask: Watson was going to tell me anyway.

'When a service aircraft is lost in peacetime, the law of the land demands a board of inquiry into the loss. It's not like when we're at war and dropping them all over the place every day.'

I thought about the CFS at Little Rissington, but didn't mention it. 'What about when personnel are lost?'

'Then too; but they're more worried about the aircraft, actually. The *point* is that if you are still in the service when the board convenes, you will be ordered to attend. If you're not – then it will be up to you whether you attend or not . . . even though you'll still be a reservist. Kingsway thinks it might be just as well to demob you as quickly as possible, to give you a choice.'

I suppose I laughed cynically. 'You mean Piers doesn't want me to appear and give evidence?'

'That's what it looks like, but the real answer to that is yes and no. If it looks as if you will be unavailable to the formal inquiry, standing orders require you to be examined by a personal board before you demob. They will decide which of your evidence is relevant and should be submitted to the inquiry.'

'And I expect that Piers or someone like him would be on my personal board, sir?'

'I should expect so: head it up, probably.'

'They get you all ways, don't they? What happened to Mrs Miller?'

'Suspended, Charlie. She used her initiative: very bad form. She'd been warned about it before, apparently. She should have asked permission before she passed information about your crash to the Jedburgh.'

'Which wasn't a Jedburgh.' I looked out of the window and then back to Watson. 'It wasn't a crash either, sir. The Frogs shot us down.'

'I think that you'll find it *was* a crash, Charlie. I wouldn't be surprised if the pilot and navigator had become disorientated in bad weather over Germany and had strayed unintentionally over the border into France where the aircraft crashed.'

'The weather was perfect. You could see for bloody miles.'

'Weather can be a funny thing, Charlie.'

'Both the pilot and the nav survived.'

Then Watson said it: 'Then *they*'d better be careful too, hadn't they, Charlie?'

A few ordinary little words can change your world-view if you let them.

I kicked my heels with damn all to do, and the girls did Russian trawlers. Russian trawlers did us. Mrs Boulder had taken up knitting: she was knitting a man's scarf the colour of venous blood. Elizabeth had painted her finger- and toe-nails the same colour. We all pretended not to miss Miller, but without her the station felt as if it had had its lungs ripped out. Jane sat at Miller's desk, answered her telephone, and made out the requisition slips that I had to sign. I hadn't ever bothered to check an item number, so I still didn't know what I was signing for. It would be good to find out that I had just requisitioned a brand new battleship for a bored sea cook stationed at Scapa. Anyway, Jane sent me far less than Miller had done, and the answer to that mystery wasn't too far away.

After about a week I received a formal signal from the WD saying that an unexpected opportunity had occurred to advance my demob. It did not leave me feeling unloved. I received another telling me that I would be examined informally before then by a panel of officers who would report on to the board of inquiry investigating the loss of Tim's Lincoln.

Then my new boots arrived: it was the highlight of that week. If old men like me look back on their service lives for you, the bits they forget to tell you are the excruciating periods of boredom. The little box radio in my office took a bashing: Wilfred Pickles and Mabel were almost on first-name terms with me after a while. One afternoon I sat with my feet on the desk and a glass in my hand, heard an old recording of Florrie Desmond singing 'The Deepest Air Raid Shelter in Town' and never stopped laughing. The BBC had just started censoring risqué songs again, so I guessed that the song's days were numbered.

I helped Bella and Ming brew cider in a steading I hadn't been allowed into before. She confessed that she made more money from selling cider to the local pubs than from her chickens. So I was living with a bootlegger. I told her to stop being mean in that case, and buy a new van to replace the wreck she drove around in. She said the wreck was part of her image of abject poverty. Together with a thousand scraggy chickens and their associated chicken shit, it deflected the attention of the tax collectors. Unfortunately it attracted the attention of Miller's number one, but she could live with that.

Eventually I asked Ronka, 'Do you have an address for Mrs Miller? I can't find one.'

'Yes. But she made us promise not to give it to you.'

'Watson made me promise not to contact her while she's under investigation. I'm not very good at keeping promises.' OK. That was a lie. I just wasn't very good at keeping *that* promise.

'*I* am, Charlie, but I can hardly keep you away from the telephone, can I?'

'Did she ask you not to give me her telephone number either?'

'No, she forgot to do that. She may have intended me to understand that when she asked me to refuse you her address, but I am foreign, you see. English is my third language – I still take words at their face value.'

'You speak better English than I do.'

'I have the better brain.'

'Thank *you*, Weronka.'

'But a brain that is curiously bad at remembering telephone exchanges and numbers. That's why I write the important ones in pencil on the wall above my radio.'

*

'Hello, Miller,' I said quietly.

'Hello.' I noticed that she didn't use my name. She sounded small: defensive.

'Are you alone? Can you talk?' One of my old bosses had cautioned me against asking the second question before getting an answer to the first, but Miller knew how to cope with it. She was more experienced at this sort of thing than me.

'Yes. But I'd rather not.'

'So put the phone down.'

'No.'

'You saved my life.'

'No. Your parachute did that; I think the company that made it will send you a little gold caterpillar badge to celebrate it. I only called the taxi.'

'And you are being investigated because of it.'

'Is that what they've told you?'

'Yes.'

'Oh . . .'

'The Jedburgh, or whatever it was, came back with me. We don't need to mess with them any more.'

'I know. That was the deal. If they brought you back, no one would ask what they'd been doing for the last couple of years. Ari Joopeman came to see me last week; he took me to lunch.'

'That was part of the deal, too; he told me. I was jealous. When can I see you again?'

'You can't. I was allowed to stay at home on condition that I should have no contact with potential witnesses if they prosecute me.' That was too stupid. After a pause – neither of us seemed to know what to say next – she said, 'Charles has got to go to

Town for a couple of days next week. Maybe I could see you then, and explain.'

'When?'

'Monday night.'

'OK. Where?'

'That pub we were at before, the one near Little Rissington. Where I met your friend Tommo.'

'The Lamb. OK.'

'Don't be angry if I'm not there.'

'Don't ask the impossible, Miller.'

I kept on expecting a call from Piers: not about the board of inquiry, but about Grace. It didn't come, which made me vaguely uneasy. The truth was that whenever I thought of that great lump of people living on the Bishops Avenue a slow smile came to my face. I hoped they'd been left in peace, and I wished them well.

I phoned Dolly from the farm one evening, when Bella and Alison were out at a church concert. I'd lent them the Singer. Bella looked the very example of rural propriety as I showed them to the car.

'Hello, Dolly – it's me.'

'Oh. Hello, Charlie. Hail the conquering hero.'

'Don't take the mickey; it's not fair. When can I come round, and come again? And again and again: if you see what I mean.'

Her pause wasn't a refusal.

'Weekend after next? That sound OK? I'm pretty tied up until then.'

'I didn't realize that you did that sort of thing. Is Den in?'

'No, Ike's here. They're up in Scotland somewhere. I think that they're giving Ike a castle, or something. Leave it until Saturday week. Give me a call first.'

'OK. Is Piers saying anything about me?'

'Whenever he does, he jolly well swears a lot. I'd wait until he cools down if I was you.'

'I didn't know that I'd done anything especially wrong.'

'That's always the problem with Piers, isn't it?'

When the call came it wasn't exactly a yorker. It was a medium-fast delivery that strayed out on the leg side. I got my bat to it, but the second slip was waiting. I was leaning on one of the paddock fences watching Alison and the dogs herd chickens. Bella came to the door wiping her hands on a towel and called out, 'Charlie – phone . . .'

When I picked up the handset a voice from a hundred years ago asked me, 'Mr Charlie?'

'Barnsey?'

Barnes was the butler from Crifton – the barracks block of a house near Bedford that Grace's mother shared with her stepfather. It was as big as that new aircraft carrier HMS *Eagle*. The first time we saw it we called it Fuckingham Palace. I won't say that Grace's parents didn't exactly get on, but being in their presence was like sitting in the Emperor's seat at the Colosseum. The real thing, I mean; not that bloody theatre in London.

'How are you, Mr Charlie? Mrs Baker mentioned that you are recently back from another trip to France.'

'That's right, Barnsey. How did she find out?'

'It's the circle she moves in, Mr Charlie. You know how people talk.'

'Worse than Old Mother Riley.'

'She wouldn't like to hear you say that, sir.'

'But it made you smile, didn't it?'

Barnes had been good at his job too long to answer a question like that. 'They want to see you, sir. They thought that you could drive down on Saturday, and stay until Sunday.'

'Do I have much choice?'

'Probably not, sir. That's the burden of the underclass.' At least he'd worked out that we were both on the same side. 'Mrs Barnes will look forward to your being with us again.'

'Tell Mrs Barnes that I look forward to her cooking; especially breakfast in the kitchen on Sunday.'

'That may be in order, Mr Charlie.'

'Dress for dinner on Saturday?'

'I'm sure that your best uniform would be appropriate, sir.'

And that was bloody that. You get it, don't you? They were the last people I expected to hear from, and it's always the one you don't see quickly that gets you. Caught at second slip, I'd say.

I have never got away from the idea that Crifton glows in the sunset, but less and less as each evening falls. It's like the light fading as you turn the gas down: like some bloody great metaphor for the British Empire, I suppose. I had intended to drive around to the back and slide in unannounced, but Barnes must have been on the lookout for me – he was out under the portico as I drove out of the trees and onto the wide gravelled road that went down to the house. You could build one of those new towns on the sloping lawn in front of it. Mrs Baker once told me that she'd married her husband in order to get someone wealthy enough to support the house and estate: she couldn't bear the thought of giving them up. Peter Baker once told me that he'd married her because she had the house, and was a better poke than Grace anyway. They were a complicated bunch. What annoyed me was that there was a side of me which actually liked them.

Barnes started with, 'Welcome back, Mr Charlie.' The grins on our faces possibly said it all. 'Mrs Baker wonders if you would join her for tea.'

'In the bloody Orangery again, I suppose.'

'Just so, sir. You remember the way?'

'If I'm not back by Tuesday, send out the search party.'

'No need, sir. Nancy will take you.'

Nancy must have been listening, and appeared as he spoke. She looked about seventeen, had short dark hair, heavy top hamper, and wore pre-war black to the knee, with a white pinafore. She gave me a quick curtsy.

'There have been some additions to the staff since your time, sir,' Barnes said.

'Good morning, sir.' Nancy had a nice smile but didn't hang about, spinning on her heels and marching off. She clearly expected me to follow her. Times change. The last time I was there, any servant under sixty-five was considered one of the youngsters.

The Orangery was full of plants: just like orangeries should be. There were giant trees like palms, and bamboos. It was like a bloody jungle. The temperature was high enough to have bred monkeys in. I had last seen the huge room in wartime, when it had been empty apart from a large ill-tempered horse kicking chunks from the polished pine floor. Mrs Baker sat on freshly painted garden furniture in a clearing cut into the centre. She was wearing a light summer dress. A couple of brightly coloured birds argued in the foliage. Condensation ran down the windows and walls. I took off my flying jacket and dumped it on the floor as I approached her. She held her cheek up, and closed her eyes for a kiss.

'Charlie, darling.'

'Mrs Baker.'

'Adelaide or Addy, Charlie. I'm sure that I told you that before.'

'Addy, then. You were drunk; I wasn't sure that you meant it.'

'I was always drunk, wasn't I? We're very proud of you, you know.'

'I don't know why. Are you still drunk?'

'No; I'm cured. I drank my way through it, and out the other side. I stick to champagne these days.'

'And Lord Peter? Do you stick to him as well?'

'Don't be silly, darling. That would be stretching the point too far.'

'Where did you get all these trees? The place was empty when I was last in here.'

'Some of them came from Kew on loan; Peter twisted their arms. The others were given by the Germans, I expect: war reparations. We got some tremendous stuff over there – especially paintings. We were just told to go over and pick out what we wanted.'

'You mean you stole it.'

'No, darling; heaven forbid. Everyone with a house this size went over to help themselves. War reparations for being good. I brought eight Germans back as well, to work on the farm and in the house.'

'And I suppose that everyone living in a council house in Streatham was given the same opportunity.'

'Do they *have* council houses in Streatham? Don't be a prude, Charlie. Each of those grubby little soldiers coming back from the war had his own kitbag full of loot. Why shouldn't we have had our share?'

'Because your lot's share is invariably larger than anyone else's. Besides: they fought for it. They *earned* it.'

'So did I, Charlie.'

'How?'

'I can't remember that much. I think that I was looking after the Americans, remember? Gave them a warm bed on a cold night, happy memories of Old England, and a belief that their cause was worth dying for.'

'How many of yours *really* died, Addy?'

'Three, actually.' She was immediately subdued. 'I still dream of being in bed with them. How can one dream of making love with dead lovers?'

'Is that American, Washoe, still around?'

'No – he went home to his wife, children and a legal practice: a *tradesman*! Ugh! How could I?'

'I'm sorry, Addy.'

'So am I. Maybe he'll be my last. Would you like a cup of tea now?'

'No, he won't be your last: nothing like . . . and *yes*, I'd love a cup of tea. It's good to be back again.'

'You're a strange man, Charlie Bassett. The rest of us feel trapped here, and we can't wait to get away.'

The only thing that we had in common was Grace, and neither of us had mentioned her. That was funny.

They put me in Grace's room, which was unfair. I had memories of play-fighting her on that heavy wooden bed under its dark canopy. Making love with Grace could be like fighting her. She would strain against me sometimes, and punch my chest as if the act of love was an act of violence, and I was her worst nightmare. Who knows? Maybe I was. Then something would happen inside her face, and her arms would loop around my neck, and she would love me again. Yes: unfair memories.

Nancy had pressed my uniform. It lay across the bed like a corpse. I think that there is something about Crifton which plays to the dark side of my character. Maybe that's where Grace belongs too.

Dinner was a strained affair. I sat at a round table which wouldn't have fitted into any house I've ever lived in. I was placed between Lord Peter Baker and his secretary, and Adelaide and her secretary: the umpire's position for a set of mixed doubles. It hadn't occurred to me that a woman without a job would need a secretary.

Lord Peter's secretary was a tall bosomy woman in her early twenties. She had long blonde hair, and laughed at his jokes.

Adelaide's secretary looked like a young Guardsman. He was tall and muscular with closely cropped fair hair. His slight accent made me suppose that he was one of her new Krauts. He laughed at *none* of Lord Peter's jokes. The two secretaries obviously fancied each other . . . so I guess that it was a draw.

Peter Baker told us that the Labour Party was ruining the country, and selling the Empire for a handful of beads. Adelaide Baker told us that the Conservative Party was organized to promote the interests of pederasts and fascist peers.

He said that the Labour Party would end up in the hands of trade unionists, or maybe teachers and lawyers. She parried that the Tories would end up represented by crooked car salesmen, or maybe doctors and lawyers. They'd both obviously had a recent problem with lawyers: it was all they agreed on. All women were sluts. All men were lechers.

The secretaries looked down at their plates, smiled and shovelled away: they'd heard it all before. *How early can I get away tomorrow morning?* I asked myself

Adelaide took the women away. She could have concealed her eagerness to leave us a little better. Lord Peter's secretary wore a bouncy cream cocktail dress: she flung a lingering smile back at the men as she left, but it wasn't for me.

Peter Baker poured me a whisky big enough to swim in, and took me over to stand at the fire. We could have stood inside the huge fireplace. I enjoyed the heat from the logs radiating through my trousers. Addy's secretary stayed at the table. Baker said to him, 'Karel?'

'Yes, Lord Peter?'

'Get lost – there's a good chap.'

'Yes, Lord Peter.'

We waited for the door to close behind him.

'Can't bear that fellow, Charlie. Think he's tupping Adelaide.'

'Aren't you?'

'Good lord, no! A filly my own age? Give me credit!'

'Then it's not all that much to do with you, is it, sir?'

Nothing. Then Baker laughed. It was a new thin, reedy sound which surprised me, coming from him, because he was six and a half feet tall. Had he always laughed like that, or was he simply getting old?

'*What?*' I asked him.

'Forgotten that you spoke to me like that.'

'Does you good now and again, sir, I expect. Do you want me to shove off now?'

'You're a little bastard, Charlie Bassett.' But he smiled as spoke.

'I hadn't noticed that, sir. I hadn't noticed I was *little*.' He laughed again. I asked him, 'Does that radio I repaired for you still work?'

'I don't know, Charlie. I haven't been up to that room since the war ended. We won't need it again until the next war, will we?'

We sipped the whisky. It had been fiery before I'd slopped some water into it.

There was something on Baker's mind. I suppose that if you were that wealthy there would always be something on your mind. After a while I felt the tension I'd brought into the house with me ebbing away. Whisky can be good at that sort of thing.

I said, 'You *did* invite me here . . .'

'Did I? Are you sure that it wasn't Adelaide?'

'Yes, Lord Peter, I'm sure. She wouldn't mind if she never saw me again.'

'You're probably right. First I wanted to say sorry for the mess we got you into in '45. We made some terrible choices, and you suffered.'

Was that how things worked in their world? You just said sorry, and made friends again? One of their bad choices had been asking an American copper to kill me, and the bastard had nearly succeeded.

'I also wanted to say thank you for getting Grace out of the hands of that bunch of parasites she was staying with last month. Before we saw her arrest splashed all over *Pathé News* or the *Mirror*.'

'They weren't parasites,' I told him. 'Just ordinary people without roofs over their heads. There are thousands of them, and she was helping them out.'

'Well, now she's gone and so are they. I don't know how you managed it, but that was a brilliant resolution. Thank you.'

'That's all right, sir. You did as much as me. Where will she be based: here or overseas?'

Baker looked at me as if I'd said the wrong thing. 'Sorry, Charlie; I didn't follow that. What did *I* do?'

'Got her a job flying for Donald Bennet. Her eyes lit up when I told her, but she hadn't said yes before I last saw her.'

'She didn't say yes at all, Charlie – didn't you know? She sailed off to Palestine with some hairy great Dutchman. They'll build the new state of Israel there, if only we'll get out of the way and let them.'

The noise that I heard inside my head was the sound of a penny dropping. 'Let me guess: they took a ship called the *Polly B*? I was on it with Grace, but I didn't tell anyone. It was loaded with all sorts of odds and ends.'

'That's right: I knew that you must have had something to do with it. They took a load of homeless people as well, and ran the blockade in the Med. They ran their ship straight up onto an empty beach . . . and unloaded it before the Allied patrols reached them.'

I shook my head in wonder at Grace's scheming. 'I didn't know they were going to do anything like that.'

'People may not believe that, Charlie. Some departments are furious. They feel they've lost face, and your old civil servant doesn't like losing face: it's worse than if you ride his missus. You could be in for a rough one – ride, I mean.'

I probably nodded glumly. I do that sort of thing at times of stress.

'It doesn't matter if Grace is safe and happy, does it? Can I have another drink?' I needed to think. No: cancel that. I needed to *drink*.

'You're a good man, Charlie. Help yourself.'

I didn't feel like a good man. I felt like a fool again. At least I knew why Piers was spitting red stuff: our next meeting would be interesting. I refilled both our glasses from the ship's decanter on a side table. Baker kicked one of the logs; sparks danced in the fireplace and swirled up the chimney.

I said, 'When I was a boy my mother would tell us that the sparks were fairies, and that the wandering red lines you sometimes saw on the soot at the back of the fire were fairy writing.'

Baker didn't respond to that. He said, 'There were civil servants who got it all wrong. They thought that the Commies organizing homeless people to occupy big empty houses was less about getting new homes built quickly in London, and more about getting Communism another toehold in the LCC. It wasn't, of course: they fooled us. Being Commies wasn't important to that mob at all. It was all about getting breeding stock together for a new country in the Middle East. They have enough men over there for the time being, apparently: most of the survivors of the death camps were young males. What they lacked were functioning wives and families. Women who knew how to make homes, and children who would grow up to work the farms and carry guns. Seed corn.'

'I wonder how they convinced them to go?'

'Offered them husbands, and fathers and land. Somewhere of their own for free. Land's a powerful pull, you know: everything is different when it comes to owning land. You'll kill to keep what you have. Way of the world.'

'I'll take your word for it.'

'If Grace is in the middle of all that, and if it comes off, she might even be remembered as a heroine one day.'

I let that lie for a bit before I trusted myself to reply. I know that I spoke quietly, looking at the fire, not at Baker. He had to lean closer to hear me.

'Don't you realize that she already *is* a heroine? For Christ's sake, sir – she flew deliveries for the ATA for five years, until she was exhausted. Then she flew trips over Germany with us, after our own gunner had run away. Then she nursed her way across Europe as Germany collapsed in front of her. She *is* a heroine: the genuine article. The only one I've ever met.'

'You really believe that, old man?'

'Of course I do, Sir Peter. She's remarkable: the most remarkable person I'll ever know, even if I live for ever. One day someone will make a film about her, and she'll be famous in the best possible way. Every teenaged girl in the country will want to be just like Grace then: you'll see.'

Baker prodded the logs again. One tumbled, but he kept it in the grate with his foot. Sparks careered upwards and out of sight. He flicked something away from each of his cheeks, looking away from me. 'Wish her mother had heard you say that.'

But Adelaide's voice behind us said, 'She did.'

Karel can't have completely closed the door behind him, and neither of us had heard Addy come back into the room. She crossed over to the fireplace and stood on tiptoe to plant a kiss on Baker's cheek. 'Silly old thing. Why don't you two come in and join us? I'll put some music on and we can dance.' Try a little tenderness.

If I didn't know better I could have sworn that they were still in love. I remembered how Grace had cried when she'd learned that Sir Peter *hadn't* sent me to bring her home. Maybe they all deserved each other.

Someone had beaten Addy to the draw: the music came towards us as I followed them to the door. An old 1920s dance band was playing 'Pasadena'. There was a glorious rising trumpet solo at the end of the second chorus.

That was how I learned that they'd begun to establish the State of Israel, despite my best efforts. Not many people know that. I still had to face Piers, so life is never that simple.

In the morning I had breakfast with the staff. It was a noisy, cheerful bun fight in the kitchen, with Barnes singularly failing to keep order. Afterwards, I walked up over a flat hilltop where Grace had once found the body of a wireless operator whose parachute had let him down when he'd most needed it. That made me think of the jump that I'd just made, and the missing gunner whose name I forgot. Maybe God had owed the Bakers a wireless operator.

Barnes accompanied me. The only concession he made to being outside was a pair of wellingtons over his formal working clothes. He looked comical. The field had just been ploughed when the late WO crashed feet first into it, killing himself and turning into Toulouse Lautrec at the same time. It didn't bear thinking about. Now it was down to grass: a lush green hump that dominated the countryside. The dew hadn't burned off, and my feet inside my shoes were soon wet.

'Miss Grace loved coming up here when she was younger,' Barnes puffed. He was too old to work, really, but no one would have dared to say that to his face.

'I know. She once told me that you could see into three or four counties from here.'

'Three.'

There was no marker in the field to show where the airman had fallen, but there was a faded bunch of flowers tied to a gatepost. I stopped to check it on the way back down. Its cardboard label bore a man's name, rank and number and RIP – all in childish handwriting. There was also a drawing of a cross that looked like a medal. It had been done in indelible pencil, and must have been rained on a few times, because the cross stood out as a stark, purple-black shape on the curling card.

'Was that him?'

'Yes, Mr Charlie.'

'Who put this here?'

'His mother, and his very young brother. They came to see where it happened.'

'He was a decorated man, then?'

'I believe not, sir, but I supposed they felt that he deserved one.'

'They all did, Barnsey. Every last one.'

'Madam has ordered that it is not to be taken down.'

'Never?'

'That's right. She says that the weather will take it in time. God will decide when.'

A lark rose from the grass and began to pipe out its song above us.

'A long time ago someone told me that you were a Commie, Barnsey: you don't believe in God.'

'Not only do I believe in Him, sir, but I am convinced that God is also a Communist. It is the only way that things make sense.'

Barnes insisted on carrying my travelling bag to my car. I was frightened that his arm would come off, but he was one of the old school – you did things *his* way. The last thing he said was,

'What did the Master want with you this time, Mr Charlie? If you don't mind my asking.'

'He wanted to say sorry.'

Barnes looked away and then back, and closed the car door for me. 'About *fucking* time if you ask my opinion, sir.'

Addy wasn't up yet, Sir Peter was chasing the serfs around the manor on horseback. I turned the Singer north and west. I found that I couldn't wait to get away from the bloody place . . . and it wasn't the first time that had happened, either.

26. *Goodbye, Dolly*

I waited in the doorway of the Lamb until Miller drove up in their Standard. She parked away from the light. I walked up to her, kissed her and wrestled her into the back seat where we went at each other like tigers. She left scratch marks on my neck. When I got the power of speech back I said, 'I love you, Miller.'

'Christ, that was *good*, Charlie! I'll miss that.' Then she added, 'I love you too.' Bit of a bloody afterthought.

'Leave him, and come away with me.' I didn't have to say who I was talking about.

'No, don't be stupid. I can't.'

'Why not?'

'Because I promised. Don't you ever make promises?'

'Yes, but sometimes they're mistakes.'

'Mine weren't.'

She pulled her knickers up and smoothed her skirt down as if they were the most natural actions in the world. A stocking was starting to ladder down from the button of a suspender. She said, 'Damn!' Then, she said, 'Take me inside, and buy me that drink now.'

Maybe I'd already been filed away in that glorious head, in a box labelled *mistakes*, but I couldn't very well refuse to return the favour, could I? Come on, *you* work it out: you used to be quicker than that.

It would have been surprising if we hadn't sipped cider: me, and the prettiest girl I ever saw – just like in the song. No straws, though.

I asked her, 'Why did they suspend you from duty so quickly?'

'Didn't you ask the Commander?'

'Yes, I did, but because he only knows half of what goes on around here his explanation was less than complete.'

'First of all they weren't pleased that I told Ari Joopeman that you'd fallen into France. I should have waited, apparently.'

'Why didn't you?'

Miller laughed bitterly. 'If I'd waited for HQ to do anything about it the civil servants would have got involved, and you would still be there – you know what they're like. Someone needed to *do* something, and Joopeman was the only one I could think of who might have been close enough.'

'He was. They moved bloody fast. I was behind bars for less than twenty-four hours. Thank you. Thank you from all of us. You saved us from a fate worse than death.'

'What was that?'

'French cooking: they eat their horses over there.'

Being funny wasn't going to work with Miller tonight. She actually looked uncomfortable. 'That's all right. I cried myself to sleep that night; I couldn't stop thinking about you. But it wasn't the only problem. There was another one; with some of my stores requisitions. Items which went missing.'

'I can fix that. Stores go missing all the time; ask Tommo, he ends up with most of them. How much, incidentally?'

'About twenty-five tons, more or less: mostly in bits and pieces.'

'Jesus Christ! What happened to it?'

'Somebody sold it on; but it's not what you think. The money was used to finance operations that the department couldn't afford to do otherwise. I think they called it unofficial funding. Someone else must have found out.'

I could have had a fair stab of identifying who: the Paymaster General's office had a number of investigating auditors. They used them on Lloyd George when he started selling off nobility, didn't they? And they won't do *that* again.

'Do you know who did this?'

'Yes.' Miller looked down at the table. 'Of course I do.' The bar was suddenly chilly.

'Who?' After a long pause I asked her again.

Her mouth set into that narrow straight line like a horse refusing a fence, and that was that. 'I'm not going to tell you.'

'*I* signed those requisitions.'

'They know you never read them,' she told me. 'You probably got the job because someone thought that you never would. All you wanted to do was put your feet up, fly as little as you could get away with, and wait for demob.'

'Until I met you, that is. Then all I wanted to do was have you.'

'Well, you did that too, didn't you?'

Waspish and bitter. It sounded like regret in there. Why? I

didn't know what to say; neither did she. Eventually she said, 'I'm sorry, Charlie.'

'That's all right. What for?'

'For disappointing you. You weren't supposed to love me. I thought that you wouldn't.'

'My mistake.'

'Yes. But I'm glad that you made it, in a funny way.'

'What will happen now?'

'Mr Watson has already told me that they'll let me resign with a clean sheet, as long as I sign all the right forms. Civvy Street, the same as you.'

'Sworn to silence?'

'Yes. I suppose so.'

'What then?'

'Babies, I suppose.'

'You didn't tell me you wanted any.'

'I'm not sure yet that I do. Charles does, though.'

'I've wanted no one but you since the first moment I saw you.' OK, so that was stretching it a bit. 'Can't I change your mind?'

Miller shook her head. Her hair bobbed.

'That would be another mistake, Charlie. No: I don't think you can change my mind.'

'OK.'

It was as if she'd turned off the love tap; like someone turning off the water at the mains. Can normal people do that?

What was the point of trying? I had nothing to offer, and no argument that would cut any ice. Then I had another thought, and fell back to my reserve trenches for a last stand. I asked her, 'At least tell me before the last time we'll ever make love; so I'll know how to make the most of it. I'll want to remember that all my life.'

Another one of those bloody great broody gaps. Then, 'Just start remembering now, Charlie, because that was it.'

'Just like that?'

She spoke very softly, and didn't look at me. 'Yes. Just like that.' Then she added, 'I can't bear it any longer.'

Bear what? I shrugged, and walked out. At least she let me do that. It was a clear night with stars beginning to show; maybe there would be one last touch of frost. An old man walked briskly by on the other side of the street. His studded boots rang on the stone paving, and he whistled 'Tipperary'. I listened to him until he was out of sight, and the song had died.

I spoke to Bella as I threw my bag into the back of my car the next morning. It was a glorious day; perhaps I could make it all the way to London with the hood down. I was in a decent uniform, with my flying jacket over the top. Bella said that I needed a haircut.

'Do you want me to trim it before you go?'

'No, but thanks. I'm going to let it grow until my demob, just in case they begin to change their minds and want to keep me. They usually let the scruffy ones out first.' I filled and lit my pipe. 'It's all winding down. I have to appear in front of a board in London tomorrow morning. They're inquiring into the accident in France. After that, all I have to do is wait. Jane is doing my job now, and Elizabeth's doing Miller's. It wouldn't surprise me if they leave it that way to save money.' I'm sure that you picked it up: I was using the word *accident*. That was a new European definition of being shot down by the French. 'I probably shouldn't have told you.'

'I knew anyway: Ming told me. Mrs Boulder is going out with your CO. Did you know that?'

'Dirty old bugger!'

'No, he's not: he's just learned our lesson. Grab it while you can.'

'I'll quote you on that every time a girl tells me I'm being too pushy.'

'Good. Will you come back here?'

'Of course I shall. It will all take another few weeks, I expect.'

We left it at that. Ming came out in his shirtsleeves. He needed a shave, and nodded to me. I grinned back. Things were looking good for them. Bella gave me a kiss.

London always looks good in the sunlight. I parked up behind the Major's old safe house in Highgate, and walked around the front. There was a key under the mat of the basement front door. The house smelled musty and unlived-in: Stan and his family had moved out. But everything was still there upstairs. It was like a newly abandoned hotel. I opened some windows to let the air in, and helped myself to a bottle of Worthington from the small bar. I picked up one of the telephones; it was still connected. I dialled the flat, and Dolly yawned when she answered, 'Hello?'

'Why aren't you at work?'

'Oh, it's you, Charlie. I was at work all night chaperoning

Den with some dusky Air Minister from the Middle East. They have very curious ideas about women.'

'Don't they want you to put some kind of sack over your head when you climb into bed with them?'

'Don't be silly, Charlie. You don't have to put the sack on until you get up in the morning. Are you up in Town?'

'Yes, for the Air Accident Board. You heard I ran into a little trouble?'

'Yes, we did. Denys cried a bit – that's the first time I've seen her do that. I told her you'd turn up; just like a bad penny.'

'And I have. Someone else said that about me a long time ago.'

'Me, probably. Do you want to come round?'

'No, I want to take you dancing tonight.'

She must have counted to six or seven, then with what sounded like a smile in her voice she said, 'That will cost you, Charlie. You pay to dance, remember?'

'I think I can afford it. I want to go to a Palais somewhere, just like I did when we were at war. Do you know any?'

'*Hammersmith*,' she laughed. 'I haven't been there for years. Are you really sure about this?'

'Never surer,' I told her seriously. If anyone could help me forget Miller, it would be Dolly.

I turned up for the board the following morning with sore feet, a clear conscience and twenty minutes to spare. I took my flying logbook. The board read it: two senior officers, and a benign civilian with white hair. He looked old enough to have had his telegram from the king. They told me that I was a brave officer with a distinguished record. Actually, they wouldn't have recognized a brave man if they'd woken up in bed alongside one. The strange thing was that they weren't in the slightest bit interested in what had happened on Turnaway Tim's last flight. I drank coffee with them, and made polite conversation. If this was how officers spent their time maybe I should stay in the service. The whole interview boiled down to two or three questions, and they weren't about the flight that left me hobbling around in France.

They were about the flight from which Percy came home dead. A Squadron Leader Kinsman squirmed about a bit on his seat, like someone with a bad case of worms, and then said, 'No gentleman likes to speak critically of a fellow officer, I realize that, but I have to ask you a couple of things about that aborted sortie to the Kola Peninsula. OK?'

'No problem, sir; shoot.'

'I'm not going to put you on the spot, Pilot Officer, so I'll tell you that some of the crew, including the navigator, have been interviewed already, and there are indications that during that flight you took over the decision-making for a time. True?'

I didn't want to answer. I'm not a grass. I shook my head, but they just let me hang there. 'It wasn't quite like that, sir.'

'What *was* it quite like?'

I took a deep breath. If Tim had been there I would have kissed him, because I've already told you that friendships or betrayals should be ended with a kiss. 'The aircraft captain hadn't had the experience of losing a crew member in action before, sir. I had: that was all. I recovered from the shock quicker, and advised him what needed to be done.'

'Advised? Not ordered?'

'Advised, sir. It would not have been proper for me to order him.'

'Quite.' Kinsman shuffled the papers in front of him, then looked up and asked, 'Did he lose his nerve?'

'No, sir,' I assured him. 'I was closer to losing my nerve than he was. He just shut down a couple of times; it was only because that sort of thing hadn't happened to him before.' I was aware that I was repeating myself.

He looked down at his papers again, shook his head almost imperceptibly, and smiled.

'Thank you, Pilot Officer.' That was it really. A puff of smoke in an otherwise cloudless sky. 'Have you any questions for us?'

'How is he, sir – and the rest of them?'

'He's ill; but you knew that, of course. He'll be in hospital for a long time, and will probably never fly again.'

'Can I visit him?'

'There's no reason why you shouldn't, but, at the same time, no point. He won't know who you are. He doesn't even know who *he* is.'

'And the others, sir?'

'Returned to active service, as far as I know. Morgan, the navigating officer, has taken the option of a ground job – he'll never fly again, either. One of the gunners died of injuries before he was found, and the flight engineer is still missing. Anything else?'

'No, sir.'

'You're due to be demobbed soon. Joining a civvy outfit, I understand?'

'Yes, sir. Halton Airways. Based at Lympne in Kent, with long-haul freighters.'

The old man with the white hair coughed into a gleaming white handkerchief. The cough seemed to echo around his lungs for ever. It sounded terminal.

'I'm Geoffrey Halton,' he told me when he'd stopped wheezing, 'your new employer; so welcome aboard. I know a friend of yours: Peter Baker – Lord Peter, that is.' The bastards got everywhere, didn't they?

The third board member hadn't spoken directly to me yet. He seemed to be taking the notes – he must have been the junior hand. Now he gave me a friendly glance and said, 'I think that's all we need from you, Pilot Officer; why don't you cut along now, and make the most of your time off in London? It's been an honour to meet you.'

Now you don't say '*Don't talk wet*' to a senior officer, so I said, 'And you, gentlemen,' as I stood up. In fact I don't know why I said that either. I turned at the door, cap on, and gave them the best and last salute of my service career. A1 stuff. The bastards didn't even look up.

I got an even smarter salute from the corporal who met me just outside the door. He handed me a note that said Dolly was waiting for me with a car, and that Piers begged the pleasure of my company in the evening. Actually, it was a bit terser than that.

Dolly drove me to a pub in Greenwich – the Trafalgar Tavern – where we lunched on plates of whitebait and pints of Watneys, and watched ships passing up and down the river. Suddenly I longed to be on one of them: outbound for anywhere.

'It was called the George once, after some king or other, I suspect,' Dolly told me. 'I always bring visiting Americans here: they love it.'

'I'm always surprised that anything near the river survived the bombing.'

'I think it was cracked by a near miss, but they never stopped serving.'

'I think that's what beat the Germans eventually: that attitude. It was nothing to do with what we did to them.'

'You could be right.' Dolly lit a Passing Cloud, and blew a stream of smoke towards the ceiling. Cigarettes are very sexy; that's what people forget about them. 'You could call it the Windmill attitude; after the theatre. You know: *we never closed*.'

'Wasn't that only the Windmill Girls' legs?' I said, grinning.

'You can be very crude at times, Charlie. Do you know that?'

'Sorry, Dolly.'

'Apology not accepted; I'm going to take you home and give you a bit of a doing-over.'

'You can be very crude at times, Dolly. Do you know that?'

As it happened she didn't give me the doing-over, because I didn't fancy it. Dolly didn't mind. She sprawled on the carpet, lit a cigarette and asked me, 'What's the matter now?'

'I don't know. For the last few weeks I've been absolutely nuts over a woman, which hasn't stopped me jumping the bones of every other girl I met. It's been super.'

'I've always wanted to know my place in the world, Charlie,

and now you've told me. Just a collection of *bones*. Nice one. Thanks.'

'You've got a very decent bunch of bones; I'll never forget them. Anyway, she gave me my marching orders a couple of days ago. It's not the first time I've been given the bum's rush, but this time my brain's stopped. That's stupid, isn't it? Maybe it's a cumulative thing!'

'What did she say?'

'At the end? She said, "I just can't bear it any longer", or something like that. Then I buggered off.'

'That was very flattering . . .'

'I don't understand.'

'A man wouldn't.'

There was nothing much left to say after that.

Dolly drove me. I think that Piers wanted to make sure that I'd be there. I was still in my number ones with my flying sheepskin on top. There was a nip in the air, which meant that we were on the edge of a clear night. I asked her, 'Where are we going?'

'That LCC place he sometimes uses. Kenwood.'

'Why not his office?'

'Piers moves in mysterious ways his wonders to perform. We're a bit early – we can drive around if you like, or stop for a drink.'

'You can take me somewhere first,' I said, and gave her directions.

Dolly parked up under a street light, behind a cop car. She told me to wait and went out to talk to the policeman. When she came back she said, 'It's OK. They're just making sure that no one moves in to fill the vacuum. The owner takes repossession at the start of next week. You can go in if you like. Do you want me to come with you?'

'No.'

I walked up the driveway of number twenty-eight. The gravel still needed weeding. No doubt its next occupier would be able to afford to have it done. The front door opened to my touch, and the lights went on at the switches. The electrical supply was still jury-rigged to the street lights outside . . . and the table and chairs were still in that big kitchen. Someone had swept up and left it clean and tidy. Some ex-serviceman, I thought. My feet echoed past the big room where we had danced, up the big staircase and along the corridor. I thought about the boy, Gary, and his mother: in Palestine the sun shone every morning, didn't it?

My bed had been made and the blankets left folded on the end of the mattress, as if to await my return. The bunch of flowers in the jar on my cabinet had been changed. There was still some water in the jar, but the flowers drooped. They were old, and I had been away too long. I topped the water up before I left to give them a last chance. The two drawings were pinned to the wall where I had left them. I took them down, folded them, and buttoned them into my breast pocket. Alongside them on the wall someone had painted the words *goodbye Mr Charlie* and *good luck* in white paint. Some of it had run before it dried. Alongside it was the painting of a star, in heavy blue lines. The letters were in a childish hand and at about eye level for an eight-year-old boy. Going back down the stairs I thought about the way people said goodbye.

'I've been thinking,' I told Dolly. 'For the last few years all of my life seems to have been about saying goodbye: to people and places and things. I want to change all that.'

'I've been thinking too, Charlie – while I was waiting for you. Maybe you shouldn't meet Piers tonight. Maybe you should just go away. He's in a funny mood, and seems really venomous about you.' I understood *venomous*: Alice had given me lessons in it. Dolly explained: 'He will be very vindictive if you let him: mess up your new job or something like that. Give him a few weeks to get over it.'

I said, 'I don't think I can do that.'

'I thought you'd say that.' She sounded miserable.

The chain guarding the Kenwood driveway was down. We bumped across it.

Rhododendrons brushed against our car. Piers's big SS was parked alongside the house where I had seen it before. Then so were we. Dolly had a small WD torch which we used to find our way around the building. Our feet thumped hollowly on wooden-board floors in massive empty rooms. There was a single lighted candle stub in the centre of the room in which the musicians had howled their awful songs. In every room we had walked through Dolly had shouted out 'Piers' or '*Piers*, where are you?' What had come back was an ugly echo.

Now I told her, 'I know where he is. Lend me your torch, and stay here with the candle: it'll last at least half an hour. If we haven't come back by then, just go home. And go to work in the morning as if nothing has happened. OK?'

'OK, Charlie.' Suddenly we were whispering, but I suppose that's what people do when they're wandering about in the dark.

Then she leaned towards me, and quickly kissed me. 'Take care.' I've already told you about kisses like that.

I lost my way on the paths twice. Piers must have heard me blundering through the bushes but he remained silent. Eventually I broke out onto the killing ground. He had hung storm lanterns in two of the taller trees, giving the duelling patch a strangely festive air. He leaned against a tree under one. He was wearing a dinner suit, and smoking a thin cheroot. The air was still. I could smell both his cigar and his cologne on it. Neither insect noises nor the scuffling of small predators disturbed the silence. The stars were beginning to show. I heard an owl hoot a mile away.

I said, 'Hello, Piers, late for supper?'

'They'll keep it for me: nice people. Classy people.'

'Not like me?'

'No, not treacherous little slugs like you. That's right, Charlie.'

'You'll have to explain that, Piers.'

'Will I, Charlie? Explain your betrayal?' He put a hand into his pocket and produced the pistol I knew that he would have: a small silvered automatic. I'm sure that Les would have called it a proper lady's gun. 'Maybe. But not until you've stood under the other light; over there.'

He motioned with his pistol: sideways slashing movements. I felt as if I was an actor in a film: Leslie Howard would be in the bushes, waiting to spring to my rescue. No, he wouldn't: this was Charlie's world, remember, where everything got buggered up. Anyway, Leslie drowned in a plane in the Bay of Biscay years ago, didn't he? So I was on my own. I complied, stood where Piers wanted me to, and pushed my hands deep into my jacket pockets. I remembered that Miller had got me the jacket: so she was still with me at the end. Her and Tommo.

I asked him, 'Who am I supposed to have betrayed?'

'Me. Everyone. This whole fucking operation went tits-up the moment you joined it. You couldn't resist warning your old girlfriend, could you? Which meant that the jaws of the trap we'd been promising our dear Prime Minister sprang shut on precisely nothing and nobody. A police operation supposed to put the Commies and the *untermenschen* back in their places now so botched up that it's made me an utter laughing stock. The pink papers are full of it, and Scotland Yard suddenly wants damn all to do with me. It'll take us years to win back their trust.'

'Do you deserve to? Anyway: how was I to know what they were up to?'

'You must have known about the ship.'

'Yes. I visited it with Grace.'

'You see . . . and you *chose* not to tell me?'

'I suppose so. I didn't ask them where it was going, if that's what you mean. I didn't see the connection, so it didn't seem to be your business: you didn't need to know.'

It was ridiculous, but even staring, as I was, at his small pistol, I enjoyed using the words. It was like a little payback.

Piers snarled, 'You little bastard. You told her when we were going to move in.'

'I might have done; but not in so many words. They were homeless people, anyway, Piers, not the fucking Wehrmacht.

Now they're off your hands; gone away; not our problem. Forget it.'

He could have asked me to try telling our soldiers being murdered in Palestine that it wasn't our problem. But he didn't. He smiled without making eye contact – and the smile had a frightening quality. At that moment it occurred to me that he was completely off his fucking trolley. All because of a sly smile. I knew that there was to be no reasoning with him in any meaningful sense of the word.

'What happens now, Piers?'

'I warned you what happened to people who went to the bad, didn't I? I brought you here, and warned you.'

'I haven't gone to the bad, Piers, although I rather think *you* may have done.' I was thinking about someone else taking the rap for tons of missing stores, and what he might have used the money for. 'But forget that for a minute – *yes*, you warned me.'

He frowned and said, 'Well, you know what happens: we fight a duel; just like the old days, old boy. Always wanted to do that.' The first *old boy* of the evening might have been a signal that he was getting himself together again.

'What kind of a duel?'

'The kind of duel where I win and kill you; because I have a gun and you don't.' He had a moment of doubt, and asked, 'I say, old man, you *don't* happen to have a gun, do you?'

I saw no reason to lie to him. 'I've carried a gun since soon after I met you, Piers.'

Piers looked at me for a long moment. He was making his risk assessment. Finally he smiled and said, 'No. You haven't the stomach for that sort of thing, old man. Dropping bombs on kids from twenty thousand feet is more your mark. You were never made for the old *mano a mano*.'

My dead pal Pete had taught me never to give a bad guy an even chance, so Pete was here at the end as well.

I watched Piers's pistol, not his face. As soon as it began to move I took my museum piece from my jacket pocket, cocked it as I lifted it, and shot him through the throat. It wasn't a particularly good shot; I'd aimed a foot lower. His head flopped immediately to one side. The look in his eyes was worth a million. Utter surprise, and then mortification. His arm fell back to his side, and with it the little silver automatic. Then he dropped the pistol, and collapsed gently in the other direction, ending up on his side facing me, with his legs under and behind him – like a man felled in prayer. I could smell the burnt propellant in the air.

I went over and squatted by him. My legs were shaking as much as my voice. I said, 'Sorry, Piers. You'd already made up your mind. No matter what I said you weren't going to let me walk away from here, were you?'

He could neither move nor speak. All he had left were his eyes, and from those I knew that he was dying. There was a lot of blood. What was left of his breath was a bubbling sound. I looked very closely at his face: he didn't panic.

I asked him, 'Do you want to know why I might get away with this?' There was a spark left in his eyes, so I carried on. 'When you're dead I'm going to remove your trousers and leave them folded very neatly under a tree. I will leave your pistol where it is. With one of your fingers I am going to scratch the words "lovers' tiff" in the soil close to you. The police will look back into their record of arrests, and draw their own conclusions, won't they?'

If you'd thought that my words might have provoked a last flash of anger in his eyes, you would have been mistaken. If there was a look there at all, it was one of amusement: the dying bastard found it funny. The flickering lantern caught the precise moment that the light flared and died in Piers's eyes. Just before that I leaned over, held his hand and said, 'Goodbye, Piers; happy landings.' Then he was gone.

One of last year's leaves finally gave up its hold on the tree and spiralled down incredibly slowly to land on his face. I brushed it away. In an odd way the words that I scrawled on the ground alongside him weren't all that far from the truth.

Dolly had gone. It took me an hour to walk back to Highgate. I was overtaken by a slow wet front coming up the Thames Valley and watched as, one by one, the stars overhead went out. A fine drizzle clung to me before I walked up the front steps. I drank several bottles of Worthington before I went to bed, and I slept without dreaming.

I should have been asked a million questions. I wasn't asked one. Either no one knew it had been me, or no one cared. I waited two days for the knock on the door, or the telephone call from the flat. I thought about Piers a lot, and a couple of times lifted my hand for the telephone to call the police. But I didn't. If I hadn't killed Piers he would certainly have killed me, and Mrs Bassett didn't raise a stupid son. The knock on the door, or the telephone call: neither came, so I packed up and drove back to Bella. Goodbye, Dolly.

The following Friday Alison stood in the doorway of my room, leaning against its frame. What goes around, comes around. I remembered that Miller used to do that, and I realized that there were already some days when I didn't think about her. That was sad. Alison's right hand was stretched up to touch the top of the door frame in a Jane Russell pose. She was dressed in her dark blue school uniform. Alison could give Miller a run for her money any day of the week, but didn't know it yet. In a few years' time somebody would tell her. She said, 'You could always marry *me* instead, Charlie.'

I laughed, and shook my head. 'No.'

From the radio downstairs a dance band was swinging out with 'Skyliner': someone must have told them I had a new job.

'Is there still someone else?'

'No. Not any more. No one at all.' It was useful to be able to say it.

'Why *not*, then?'

'I just know that it would spoil something.'

'Something for you, or something for me?'

'Both; neither. I don't know that.'

Alison pushed a lock of hair away from her forehead. It was a sudden and endearing gesture. Do you know what you're missing, Charlie?'

'Yes, love,' I told her. 'I believe I do.' No harm in telling someone the truth occasionally.

*

I went to work sometimes. The girls were doing the same goddamned trawlers, and Ronka was teaching the others Polish. They were also beginning to dip into Eastern Zone military traffic as well. Jane was better at being me than I was, and they all still missed Miller. Although nobody said so, they were always glad to see the back of me. Watson poured me a drink whenever I reported to him. I didn't ask him who was doing the flying: maybe they had stopped for a while.

Eventually I sorted through a number of scraps of paper to find a telephone number that Les had given me. I called him one evening, and told him that I was due some demob leave and didn't know what to do with it. I asked him, 'Are you working for the Council the way you told me?'

'Nah. Working for mesself. Cleaning chimneys. You'll never be out of a job, cleaning chimneys. I'm also invited to weddings, and paid to kiss the bride for luck. I've kissed more married women in the last month than in the rest o' my life altogether.' His deep laugh warmed us. Then he said, 'I can get a few days off next week if you like.'

'For what?'

'Drive down to the coast wiv you. Talk about the old days wiv the Major and Maggs. See the kids. You could pick me up on your way . . . I'd like another drive of your car.'

It took me about three seconds. Then I said, 'Yes. OK.'

I knew a sniper in Germany once. I remember asking him what he felt when he shot someone. His one-word reply was 'recoil'. He also told me that snipers develop a sixth sense that tells them whenever another sniper has them in their sights. I could have done with that the day little Dieter put one through my heart: my old man used to talk about the bullet that had your name on it.

Bosham: we hadn't told the Major or Maggs that we were coming down. I got cold feet at the last minute, and went for a beer in a harbour bar, leaving Les to go in to them alone. He didn't come back for me. After a couple of drinks I walked out and round the muddy, sandy bar of the inlet. This was the beach where Canute had ordered the tide to turn, which seemed appropriate.

The air was soft. I was looking at my feet, and not where I was going so I didn't see the running boy until he was alongside me, shouting 'Mein papa! Mein papa!' at me. Like I told you: the kid should have been a sniper, because I was dead meat from the moment he saw me and opened his mouth.

I scooped him up, and we hugged each other so hard that I thought I would die. There was a leather bootlace around his neck. I fished it out and found my old fibre ID tag still on it: the one I had given him in Germany. He buried his face in my shoulder. I said, 'You must say *Dad*, or *Daddy*. You're in England now,' although I thought that reversion to his first language in the heat of the moment was OK. He burrowed in deeper, and asked in careful English, 'You won't go away again? Promise me?'

'Sometimes I'll have to, but I've a new job not far from here. I'll come back here every time I'm not working. You'll see me a lot.'

'Carlo will be so *pleased*.'

I carried him on my back as we walked and talked. Six months of a boy's life can be for ever. So he told me he missed me, and I told him I'd missed him. I cried a bit, but I don't think he noticed. Eventually he pointed me towards a stout old house a few hundred years old, and a few hundred yards away. It had a small restaurant and a bar on the ground floor. White and blue: like the writing and the star on the wall of the room in London. But this was different: it looked a bit like home.

Epilogue

It's too easy for an old man to fall into fixed habits, which is why each autumn always seems to bring an end to my writing these days. It's a season I enjoy: it suits my age.

Today was cold: too cold to sit outside to write. The first of the heavy frosts had turned the garden and the meadow beyond it to glinting crystal. The sky was deceptively high, clear and beautiful; ready to ice-up the wings of an unwary flyer, and drop him into the sea. I sat in the study and let the last few words drift through my mind. Piers and Les circled the driveway together, deep in discussion. Neither had met when they were still alive, as far as I know . . . but they're out there talking now, and although I know that they died I can hear the frozen gravel crunch beneath their feet. Occasionally they glance at me through the window, and smile as if they know something I don't.

The old lady brought me a living visitor with my afternoon dram. Elaine is a young woman from Rogart, a hamlet not far north of here. She seems to have adopted us, and sometimes sits me down with a tape recorder to tell her about flying over Germany in 1944. There aren't that many of us left, you see.

She has a calming presence which helps us through the bad days when my leg is hurting, or there are burning aircraft inside my head. Today she and the old lady were content to sit in the room behind me, sip their drinks, gossip and watch me write. I don't think that Elaine sees my other visitors, but the old lady sometimes does. Last week she told me that she had seen Piers inside the house, standing in the corridor by our bedroom door. He'd never been that close before. He wears a grubby bandage around his neck, and is probably still angry with me.

I left them talking about me over their drinks, to walk around the garden myself. The scarf I wrapped around my neck has been knitted by my granddaughter. I also took my rattan cane, which is my admission of age. Looking out towards the old Tain Airfield on the shoreline, I caught a flash of light against the sea, and then heard the eerie whine of Merlin engines at full chat. A Mosquito aircraft preserved from the Forties flew over at about a hundred feet. If you're one of those new folk who think in metres just divide by three, and you'll be more or less there. If you're one of the *new* new folk who can't even divide by three, because it's no longer taught in schools – then complain about it, and find someone who can. I waved my old rattan at the pilot. He came round again and waggled his plane's wings at me, before flying east.

For a moment it was like falling in love again.

From the corner of my eye I glimpsed Les and Piers: still there. They weren't looking at me; they were looking up at the Mosquito. It won't be that long before they're explaining to me how all this works. I don't mind: sometimes I tire of waiting.

When the walls came tumbling down . . . just a little history and a couple of anecdotes

Charlie's picture of 1947 is coloured by three historical elements: the organized squatter movement of London's homeless that was at its height the year before, the commencement of spy flights into Soviet-controlled territories and, peripherally, the establishment of the State of Israel.

The Communist Party-led squatter movement folded quite quickly, although pale imitations still surfaced from time to time, notably in the early 1970s. That first one was eventually almost entirely killed off by the spread of the ubiquitous prefab. What a fate: death by architecture! I smile as I remember those small estates of prefabricated houses – there must still be one or two left somewhere. What interested me about the squatters was a throwaway remark credited to Clement Attlee. He once said that during his time as Prime Minister it was the only event that came close to bringing his government down. I wonder if the hungry, cold and homeless families – huddling in disused Tube stations, or semi-derelict empty offices and houses – ever saw themselves as a threat to the fabric of society? I salute them, anyway. In fact, the big houses in the Bishops Avenue weren't properly squatted until the 1960s and 1970s. That's where I met a fire-eating stripper, who slept with an open cut-throat razor beneath her mattress – and I sometimes wonder if she's still around. But that's another story.

The only aircraft of theirs that the RAF will ever admit was shot down deliberately by the Russians was one of a pair of Avro Lincoln bombers, *on exercise*, that strayed beyond internationally agreed air corridors in 1951. Forgive the emphasis, and my scepticism, but the fact is that the RAF and military institutions all over the world necessarily describe activities as *exercises* which are anything but.

As it happens, Lincoln losses were about average for its type in the theatres to which it was deployed. The likelihood is that territorial radar mapping of routes to Soviet targets (and targets that were likely to be Soviet by the time that NATO forces pulled their collective fingers out) commenced long before the 1951 incident and now we know that such operations were rightly designated Top Secret. Would aircraft losses in the course of them be admitted, or disguised? You decide. In 1947 the RAF complaining that one of their spy aircraft had been fired upon in Soviet airspace would be like a burglar complaining that a farmer had shot at him in the course of a housebreaking – and until recently we didn't have to put up with nonsense like that.

If you want to see a Lincoln, the RAF Museum reserve collection at Cosford in Shropshire has a fine example. They're not far off the M54, and they'd love you to visit. Their Lincoln has, incidentally, the reputation of being the most haunted aircraft in the world: the alleged incidents in and around it are too numerous to document here. Suffice it to say that folk are reluctant to spend any time with her after dark.

I won't say much about the State of Israel – or more specifically the *state* of the State of Israel – or Palestine: both of them are neighbours from hell, and they probably deserve each other.

My mother loathed the sound of falling bricks for the whole of her life after the Second World War. Fifty years ago it was easy to find women who would have agreed with her. The experience that generated it was digging my two elder brothers out of a buried air-raid shelter with her bare hands, after the house next door had received an unexpected Christmas gift from Germany. After recovering her sons, in her own words, '*I turned round and realized we were homeless*': the neighbours' house, and an entire wall of her own, had disappeared. I don't know what happened to the neighbours, but I can clearly remember walking down a street with Mum in the 1950s, and seeing her check and grow pale as a hundred yards away a wall was demolished in a rumble of falling bricks, and a cloud of pink brick dust lifted to the sky.

Mother gave me a few other elements for this volume of Charlie's life. The ring I described belonged to her, and she adored it. She gave it to my wife on the day I was married, but it was stolen from our house by a sneak thief some ten years ago. I hope that he catches a perfectly vile disease connected to his thieving ways, and dies from a dose of adulterated heroin. I've often wondered whether the ring was destroyed for its scrap value, or whether it's making someone else happy.

And before you ask, yes, I *was* the little boy practising his reading skills on a 157 bus, who read a notice aloud, and asked his mother to refrain from spitting. In the days when we were still wrestling with TB and diphtheria, she was horrified to be fingered publicly as a potential disease-carrier. When she was older she loved to tell the story, and it passed into family lore. Her mother, my grandmother, lived with my family for the last thirty years of her life: it was how we did things then. She was a Coughlin, and full of brooding Irish blood. She could cure anything with a potato; principally warts and bruising, but I don't think that there was a medical condition known to man that she wouldn't have attacked with a potato if we'd given her the chance. The establishment of an efficient National Health Service must have been a great disappointment to her.

Red Rip of Ripon was our Airedale dog. He was an Australian Airedale, and that breed has a curious and relatively short history which might amuse you. It was the result of a deliberate experimental cross, between the Airedale Terrier and the Border Collie. The purpose of the cross was to provide Australian sheep farmers – we still imagined that we ran Australia then – with a dog that had the instinctive herding abilities of the Collie, and the woolly Airedale's ability to cope with high daytime and freezing night time temperatures. The stabilized cross *did* end up with the Collie's instincts, and the Airedale's physical resistance to temperature change, it was just a pity that it couldn't run as fast as a sheep. It wasn't until the first batch reached Australia that someone identified that as a potential problem.

So the failures were returned to the UK, to live out their lives as family dogs. Strange but true. It must have been colonial stupidity on that sort of scale that eventually convinced the Aussies that they'd be better off going it alone, and who could blame them?

I lived and worked in London for fifteen years – more than forty years ago. I love and loathe the place in equal measures. One of my favourite watering holes was the Fountains Abbey in Paddington. There, in the back saloon two stunningly beautiful, and undeservedly notorious women kept court among the medical students. One evening in November 1963 I arrived, anticipating an hour's flirtation and dirty stories, to find the crowded room as quiet as a mausoleum and to be told about the assassination of President John Kennedy. For readers who weren't alive then, I can only explain that the effect of the news of his murder was our 9/11: the world simply stopped . . . and the Mannlicher Carcano rifle, of which Les rather approved, is the weapon that Lee Oswald is alleged to have used on him.

The wonderfully cool (in every sense) wine bar in Camden High Street is long gone, I think, but the Parr's Head is still there – one large bar now, sadly, instead of the three I knew – but it still serves a damned good pint, and is tolerant with strangers.

If you want to learn anything of the men who wear the forget-me-not emblem in their lapels you'll have to find one, and ask him – because I'm not going to tell you.

I was bewitched by the duelling patch in the grounds of Lord Mansfield's Kenwood House the first time I set foot on it – it was inevitable that one day it would provide the backdrop for one of my stories. If it is still there, and you live nearby, pay it a visit one Sunday. You will find a hidden oval clearing in which the original owner expected to kill or be killed – there's something special in the air there. Yes: go yourself, and tell me what you think. Kenwood is one of the best places in my memory; we went to chamber concerts and poetry readings in the orangery in the 1960s and picnicked in drizzle at open-air concerts, on the lawns that you can see in the film *Notting Hill*.

The first and most perfect pistol I owned was a small Colt Navy Sheriff, or Pocket pistol. The first time one was put into my hand it was love at first shot, and my pistol is still with the shooting club who taught me how to use it safely: although that might be a contradiction in terms, if you think about it. I have sometimes wondered if there is a connection between the pleasure I have had shooting antique firearms and the excitement I felt the first time I stepped up to the mark on the Kenwood duelling ground.

I will finish with the jazz. Every chapter heading, bar one, is the title of a number recorded by a jazz band, and I wrote this novel with their music around me in the room. Let me know if you can spot the odd man out. I love jazz – always have, and always will. It's the soundtrack I go back to when the world closes in on me. I can provide a play list for anyone who's interested. Those in the know might recognize the model for the demobbed Guardsman with a horn, blowing up a storm at a (fictional) Cheltenham jazz club in 1947. I won't name him, but he knows who he is – and this is my opportunity to say thank you. Thank you for the music.

Will Charlie fly again? I don't really know, but to a certain extent that depends on you who are reading these words right now. I hadn't originally expected him to fly far enough even for a trilogy, but if, in sufficient numbers, you've enjoyed his memories and want to find out what happened next, my guess is that he will have to pull on his old flying jacket once more. He might have started working for a private outfit, but the Berlin Airlift is just around the corner, and Suez, the last British colonial adventure, is not that far down the road. I have a sinking feeling that Charlie managed to avoid neither: *what goes around, comes around* – he says it all the time.

Finally, my five-year-old granddaughter asked me if she could write something in one of my novels, so these next three words are hers: *Orla, Ciara* and *Katie*. They are simply girls' names: hers and her sisters' – the next generation.

David Fiddimore
Edinburgh: 20 10 2006